"Getting hitched solves all your problems."

Yep, she was JoBeth McCoy, problem solver to the world.

Garrett circled the room and sank onto a chair before his empty dinner plate. "No. This is crazy." Elbows on the table, he cradled his head. "I'm sorry. I don't know what I was thinking. I'm not myself lately."

He was hiding something, she was certain. She had a feeling she knew the source of his reluctance.

No matter the personal cost, she'd pry the truth from him. "Would you say yes if someone else asked?" She fought the rough edge in her voice. "Because there are plenty of other ladies in town."

Marshal Cain bolted upright. "This is the rest of my life. You're the only one I'd even consider."

"Ooo…kay."

That was a decent response, right? He hadn't exactly explained why he'd choose her over someone else, but Jo guessed that was about as good an answer as she was going to get. While she might have hoped for something more revealing, at least he was still considering her suggestion. He hadn't outright refused her yet.

Sherri Shackelford
and
Angel Moore

The Marshal's Ready-Made Family
&
Conveniently Wed

LOVE INSPIRED
INSPIRATIONAL ROMANCE

LOVE INSPIRED®
INSPIRATIONAL ROMANCE

Recycling programs for this product may not exist in your area.

ISBN-13: 978-1-335-50825-6

The Marshal's Ready-Made Family & Conveniently Wed

Copyright © 2020 by Harlequin Books S.A.

The Marshal's Ready-Made Family
First published in 2014. This edition published in 2020.
Copyright © 2014 by Sherri Shackelford

Conveniently Wed
First published in 2014. This edition published in 2020.
Copyright © 2014 by Angelissa J. Moore

This edition published by arrangement with Harlequin Books S.A.

For questions and comments about the quality of this book, please contact us at CustomerService@Harlequin.com.

Love Inspired
22 Adelaide St. West, 40th Floor
Toronto, Ontario M5H 4E3, Canada
www.Harlequin.com

Printed in U.S.A.

CONTENTS

Sherri Shackelford is an award-winning author of inspirational books featuring ordinary people discovering extraordinary love. A reformed pessimist, Sherri has a passion for storytelling. Her books are fast-paced and heartfelt with a generous dose of humor. She loves to hear from readers at sherri@sherrishackelford.com. Visit her website at sherrishackelford.com.

Visit the Author Profile page
at Harlequin.com for more titles.

THE MARSHAL'S
READY-MADE FAMILY

Sherri Shackelford

And above all things have fervent charity
among yourselves: for charity
shall cover the multitude of sins.
—*1 Peter* 4:8

To Barb, Jenn, Deb, Donna, *lizzie and Cheryl—
otherwise known as the Friday Night Critique Ladies.
Thank you for the friendship, the knowledge,
the occasional argument, the food and the laughter.
We always come back to laughter, don't we?

I'm a better writer for the group.

I'm a better person for knowing each of you.

Chapter One

❧

Cimarron Springs, Kansas
1881

JoBeth McCoy knew Marshal Garrett Cain's life was about to change forever—and all she could do was sit with his young niece until he heard the tragic news about his sister.

The towering double doors behind Jo and five-year-old Cora creaked open, and Reverend Miller cleared his throat. "You can send in the child now." He held out his hand for Cora. "Marshal Cain has been informed of his sister's passing."

Her heart heavy, Jo stood, then hesitated in the dappled sunlight. A soft breeze sent pear blossoms from the trees on either side of the shallow church steps fluttering over them like fragrant snow petals.

Cora rose and snatched Jo's hand. "Will you go with me?"

A riot of flaxen curls tumbled merrily around the little girl's face, but her Cupid's-bow mouth was solemn beneath her enormous, cornflower-blue eyes. Cora clutched a paper funnel filled with lemon drops in her left hand. Her battered rag doll remained anchored to her right side.

Jo met the reverend's sympathetic gaze, grateful for his almost imperceptible nod of agreement. He was a squat, sturdy man in his middle fifties with thinning gray hair and a kind smile.

The three of them stepped into the church vestibule, and Reverend Miller directed them toward his tiny, cluttered office. Jo paused as her eyes adjusted in the dim light.

Marshal Cain sat on a sturdy wooden chair before the desk, his expression grim. Her heart skittered, but she swallowed back her nerves and forced her steps closer.

His eyes were red, and the tail end of a hastily stowed handkerchief peeked out from his breast pocket. As though embarrassed by his tears, he didn't meet her gaze. Instead, he focused his attention on the petite fingers clutching Jo's waist. He didn't stand or approach them, and for that Jo was grateful, especially since Cora cowered behind her.

He caught sight of his niece's frightened gaze and blinked rapidly. "Hello, Cora. I know we've never met, but your mother and I were brother and sister."

Jo had only seen the marshal a handful of times, but he was an imposing sight sitting down, let alone standing. Well over six feet tall, he wore his dark hair neatly trimmed. Though he didn't sport a beard, a five-o'clock shadow perpetually darkened his jaw.

His face was all hard lines and tough angles, with a deep cleft dividing his chin. An inch-long scar slashed at an angle from his forehead through one thick, dark eyebrow. Other women might prefer a gentler face, but

Jo found his distinctive features fascinating. *Not that she looked.* A woman simply couldn't help but notice things once in a while.

Cora took a hesitant step from behind Jo. "Mama is dead."

"Yes."

"Papa, too."

The marshal's knuckles whitened on the arms of his chair. "I know," he replied, his voice gruff.

Jo glanced between the two, her chest aching for their shared grief. From what little information she'd gathered, the girl's parents had died in a fire three weeks ago. As Cora's closest living relative, Marshal Cain had been assigned guardianship. Reverend Miller had just broken the news, and the poor man was obviously devastated by the loss.

Realizing the reverend had deserted them, Jo craned her neck and searched the empty vestibule. Everyone in town knew she had all the sensitivity of a goat at a tea party, and this situation definitely required a delicate touch.

She caught sight of Cora's dismayed expression and decided she'd best keep the two talking until the reverend returned. "Why don't you show Mr. Cain what you bought at the store this morning."

The marshal's gaze flicked up at Jo, then quickly returned to Cora as she dutifully extended her arm, revealing her precious stash of candy.

"Want one?"

"Uh, well, sure." He stretched out one hand and plucked a lemon drop from atop the mound. "Your mother liked peppermints," he added.

Cora nodded eagerly. "Me, too!"

Relieved by the girl's easy acceptance of Marshal Cain, Jo spurred the conversation. "Cora rode a train all the way from St. Louis, didn't you?"

"Mrs. Smith wouldn't let me sit by the window." Cora fingered a dangling edge of pink ribbon circling the frilly waistband of her dress. "She was grumpy."

A shadow crossed the marshal's eyes. "Sorry 'bout that. I didn't know you were coming. I'd have fetched you myself."

"Would you let me sit by the window?"

"I guess. If you wanted."

The tension in Jo's shoulders eased a bit. They'd been frantically searching for the marshal since the day nearly two weeks past when Jo had transcribed the telegram announcing his niece's imminent arrival. He'd been escorting a prisoner to Wichita and had run into trouble along the way.

By the time they'd discovered his location and informed him that he was needed back in town posthaste, the poor little girl had already arrived with her grim-faced escort. Mrs. Smith had been terrified of Indians, and certain she'd never make it back to St. Louis with her scalp intact.

Since the skittish escort was obviously frightening Cora with her hysterics, Jo had cheerfully assumed responsibility for the little girl and hustled Mrs. Smith onto an eastbound train. Three days had gone by since then.

"When are we going back home?" Cora asked.

Jo's heart wrenched at the innocent question.

"Well, that's the thing." Marshal Cain cleared his throat. "I thought you could stay out here and live with me." The raw vulnerability in his expression touched Jo's soul. "We're the only family either of us has left."

Cora's solemn blue eyes blinked with understanding. "Don't you have a mama and papa, either?"

"Nope. Your mom and I lost our parents when I was fifteen and your mother was eighteen."

Though his expression remained neutral, Jo sensed a wagonload of sorrow behind the simple words.

Cora clasped her hands at her waist. "Did they die in a fire like my mama and papa?"

Stark anguish exploded in the marshal's gaze, and Jo took an involuntary step backward. His reaction felt too bleak, too powerful for an event that must be almost twenty years past.

Covering his revealing lapse, he absently rubbed his cheek. "Smallpox."

"What's that?" Cora asked.

"It's a sickness." The marshal angled his face toward the light. "It leaves scars."

Jo and Cora leaned closer, both squinting. Sure enough, the rough stubble on his chin covered a scattering of shallow pockmarks. Jo had never been this close to the marshal before and she caught the barest hint of his scent—masculine and clean. Her stomach fluttered. Once again she couldn't help but wonder how all his imperfection added up to down-right handsome.

Cora shrugged. "Your face doesn't look bad."

Jo glanced down at her own rough, homespun skirts and serviceable shirtwaist. Men's flaws made them look tough. But a woman who dressed and acted like a tomboy, well, that was another story. A woman without corkscrew curls and lace collars wasn't worth the time of day. She'd learned that lesson well enough when

Tom Walby, the only boy she'd ever had a crush on, had mocked her for being a hoyden before the entire eighth-grade class.

Turned out men fell in love with their eyes first and their hearts second. Which was too bad, really. Nettles were far more useful in life than roses.

"Did you ride a train after your parents died?" Cora asked.

"I don't remember," the marshal replied. "That was a long time ago for me."

Cora nodded her agreement, her flaxen curls bobbing. "You're old, so that musta been a really, *really* long time ago."

Ducking her head, Jo muffled a laugh. Marshal Cain blinked as though her presence had only now fully registered through the haze of his grief. He hastily stood, knocking his hat to the floor. They both reached for it at the same time, nearly butting heads. Jo touched the brim first. As he accepted his hat, the marshal's rough, callused fingers brushed over hers, sending a scattering of gooseflesh dancing up her arm.

Jo met his dark eyes, astonished by the intensity of his gaze.

"My apologies for not greeting you," he said, sounding more formal than she'd ever heard him. "We met in church once, didn't we?"

"Don't be sorry, Mr. Cain." For some reason, she seemed to have a difficult time catching her breath when he was near. "You've been busier than a termite in a sawmill. I'm JoBeth McCoy."

The admission earned her a dry chuckle. "Seems like you can't turn a corner in this town without running into a McCoy."

Jo grinned. She had five younger brothers, and they never expected her to be anyone but herself. In fact, they'd probably clobber her if she started acting like a regular girl. "They're a handful, yes, sir."

"Reverend Miller says you and Cora have been inseparable."

Jo had taken a proprietary interest in Cora's plight from the beginning. The messages concerning her care had been clipped and chillingly professional. A child thrust into such turmoil needed more than a hired guardian like Mrs. Smith. She needed love and understanding.

Jo squeezed Cora's hand. "I work in the telegraph office. Part of my job is keeping track of unclaimed packages after the trains depart." She winked at Cora. "'Course this was a special case. Everyone needs a friend sometimes, right, Cora?"

The little girl returned the comforting pressure. "Jo-Beth sent twenty-six different messages trying to find you. I counted. JoBeth has five brothers. I counted them, too. I don't have any brothers. Do you have any brothers?"

"Nope."

The marshal and the little girl sized each other up like a couple of nervous spring foals. They were wary, yet curious, too. Suddenly, Jo realized how terribly unnecessary her presence had become. Cora didn't need her anymore—she had Marshal Cain.

Though he'd only been in town a few months, Jo sensed his unwavering resolve. He'd spent his time quietly and methodically cleaning up Cimarron Springs, a Herculean task. Their previous sheriff had been lazy and corrupt, and every outlaw west of the Mississippi had exploited his lax law enforcement. The marshal still had loads of work ahead of him, but he didn't show any signs of slowing.

And now that he and little Cora had each other, they didn't need her.

A band of emotion tightened around Jo's chest. Though she and Cora had known each other a short time, she felt a kinship.

A small hand tugged on her skirts. "How come you don't know Marshal Cain? You said you know everyone in town."

Jo glanced at the marshal and found him studying Reverend Miller's book collection as though it was the most fascinating thing on earth. She wondered if he was thinking about the deluge of invitations he'd received during his first few months in Cimarron Springs. Introducing a new man in town was like tossing raw meat into a pack of wolves. A pack of female wolves.

Warmth crept up Jo's neck. Of course, no one had considered her as a possible love interest. Not even her own parents had invited the marshal for dinner. Not that she cared, since she never planned on marrying. She'd pinched her cheeks and fluttered her eyelashes for Tom Walby and look what that had gotten her. He'd told her he'd rather court his grandfather's mule.

She wasn't about to make the same mistake twice.

Covering her unease, she fanned the tip of her thick, dark braid. "Marshal Cain has only been in town a few months. I guess he's never had call to arrest me. If I was a cattle rustler, we'd be on a first-name basis by now, I'm sure."

Cora giggled. The marshal sputtered, then coughed, and Jo immediately regretted her joke. A little ribbing always worked on her brothers when they were tense, but the marshal seemed embarrassed by her teasing. As the silence stretched out, the walls of Reverend Miller's office closed in around her, and the air grew thick.

Oblivious to the tension gripping the adults, Cora plucked a lemon drop from her paper funnel and popped it into her mouth. "Can I have a puppy?" she spoke, her voice muffled around her candy. "Mama said we couldn't have a puppy in the city. But you live in the country, don't you, Mr. Cain?"

Jo caught the marshal's helpless expression before he quickly masked his thoughts. He'd lost his sister and brother-in-law and discovered he was guardian of his five-year-old niece in the course of a few tragic moments.

He didn't live in the country. He lived in a set of rooms above the jail.

Cora spit the candy into her cupped palm. "The bears won't eat my puppy, will they? Mrs. Smith said Kansas was full of giant man-eating bears."

"Mrs. Smith was mistaken," Marshal Cain replied, his voice no more than a whisper.

Jo instinctively reached out a hand, but the marshal flinched. Flustered, she clenched her teeth and let a flash of anger douse the pain. "I was just being nice. It's not like I was gonna hit you, fool man."

For years after she'd socked Tom in the eye for humiliating her in public, the boys in town had made a point of shrinking away from her in mock terror.

The marshal gingerly touched his side. "It's not that, I bruised a couple ribs in a scuffle up north."

Jo mentally slapped her forehead. Of course he wasn't mocking her, he didn't even know about her humiliation. Why was anger always her first line of defense?

"I'm sorry," she spoke quickly. "Can I get you...a... a pillow or something?"

"No need. I've suffered worse."

Every time she tried to say the right thing with a man, the feminine thing, it always fell flat. And how had Reverend Miller gotten lost in a two-room church?

She whirled and collided with the object of her ire.

The reverend steadied her with a hand on her elbow. "I see the marshal and his niece have gotten acquainted."

"No thanks to—"

A commotion outside interrupted her words. The reverend clasped his hands, his face pinched. "I believe you're needed outside, Marshal Cain." He glanced meaningfully in Cora's direction. "Tom Walby is in one of his moods."

Jo and Marshal Cain groaned in unison. Tom had grown from an adolescent annoyance into an adult bully with a nasty temper and a penchant for drinking. Every few weeks he got into a fight with his wife and took out his frustration on the local saloon. Jo flipped her braid over her shoulder.

Tom's wife never resisted the opportunity to smirk at her, still lording over her victory all these years later. Considering the prize had been Tom, Jo figured it was a loss she could endure.

"Can you look after Cora?" Marshal Cain directed his question toward Jo, and she eagerly smiled her agreement. "I'll take care of Tom as quick as I can."

The marshal knelt before Cora and enveloped her

hand in his grasp. "Don't worry. We have each other now, and everything is going to be all right."

Jo's throat burned with rare emotion. They *did* have each other. They were a family. Not in the regular way, but a family nonetheless. If God had blessed her with a little girl as precious as Cora, she'd never let her go. Except she'd most likely never have a family of her own. Men didn't court girls who wore trousers beneath their skirts.

Jo shook off the gloomy thoughts. She had five brothers, after all. More family than one girl needed. With the boys already courting, she'd have her own nieces and nephews soon. She'd be the favorite aunt.

Just as long as she didn't end up like Aunt Vicky. The woman had fifteen goats and was known to dress them up for special occasions.

Marshal Cain slapped his hat back on his head. "Much obliged for your help."

He strode out the door, taking with him the crackling energy that surrounded Jo whenever he was near. While she didn't envy the marshal's task, she was grateful for the reprieve.

Surely by the time they met again, this strange, winded feeling would be gone. Besides, she liked him, liked the way he smiled at her, and she didn't want to ruin their camaraderie.

Cora tugged on her skirts. "You have something in your hair."

Ducking, Jo checked her disheveled reflection in the reflective glass of Reverend Miller's bookcase doors. She smoothed her fingers over her braided hair and released a scattering of pear blossoms, then threw up her arms with a groan.

She'd spent the entire conversation with white petals strewn over her dark hair.

Jo slapped her faded bowler back on her head. Even if she wanted to attract the attention of someone like Garrett Cain, she didn't stand a chance.

Garrett Cain closed the jail doors with a metallic clang. His prisoner, Tom Walby, paced the narrow space, a purple-and-green bruise darkening beneath his left eye.

Tom kicked the bars. "You don't understand, Marshal, it wasn't my fault."

"Not today, Tom."

Something in Garrett's voice must have penetrated the inebriated fog of Tom's brain. The lanky man groaned and braced his arms on the spindly table in his cell but kept blessedly silent. Dirty-blond hair covered Tom's head, and blood crusted on his chin. His blue-plaid shirt was torn, and his brown canvas pants rumpled. He'd given as good as he'd gotten in the saloon fight, but the whiskey in his belly had finally caught up with him.

Garrett spun the chamber of his revolver. Tom and his wife had two temperatures—hot and cold, love and hate. There was no in-between for those two, and their intensity terrified Garrett. He feared that sort of hard love because he'd seen the destructive force devour its prey with cruel finality.

He absently rubbed his chest. A hard knot had formed where his heart used to be after his parents' deaths. They'd been a fiery lot, too, and he and his sister had huddled together during the outbursts. The senseless deaths of his mother and father had wounded him—not mortally, but gravely.

No one in town knew the truth. That his father had killed his mother and then turned the gun on himself. The shame of his father's actions had shaped the course of Garrett's life.

Everything had muddled together in his brain…guilt, anger, fear. He'd wished more than once in childish prayers that he'd been born into a different family. Then God had taken his away. Garrett had corralled his emotions until the pain had passed, and when he'd finally emerged, he'd discovered his temporary fortress had become permanent. Nothing touched him too deeply anymore—not pain, not joy.

He was content. Good at keeping his emotions contained.

Until now.

The loss of Cora's mother, his only sister and last living relative, buffeted the walls around his heart like ocean waves. Horrors he'd spent a lifetime forgetting rushed back.

Tom paced his cell. "I saw that McCoy girl was taking care of your niece. You better be careful of that one. She'll have your little girl wearing pants and shooting guns."

Grateful for the distraction, Garrett considered his prisoner. "What's wrong with that?"

"Well, because…because it ain't feminine, that's why. I'd never settle with a girl who could outshoot me."

"Probably a good move on your part," Garrett retorted.

He didn't know why everyone in this town was blind to JoBeth McCoy's beauty. Her skin was flawless, her eyes large and exotic, and tipped up the corners. Her lips were full and pink, just made for kissing.

Now, where had that thought come from?

"The man should be the strong one," Tom slurred. "It ain't right when a girl can outscrap and outgun you."

"I don't think you give women enough merit. I've known women to endure things you and I couldn't even imagine."

Tom scoffed and spit into the corner.

Garrett shook his head. There was no use having a sensible conversation with someone who'd drunk away all his good sense. "You're making bad choices, Tom, and it's gonna catch up with you. One of these days you'll make a bad choice you can't sleep off or take back. What's gonna happen to your wife and your son when you're locked up for good?"

"What do you know about it?" Tom said sulkily.

"I know plenty."

Garrett stuffed his hands into his pockets and retrieved Cora's lemon drop. Pinching the candy between his thumb and forefinger, he let sunlight from the jail's narrow window bounce off the opaque coating.

His whole body ached from grief, as if he'd been thrown from a wild mustang. Why had God given him such a precious gift, a beautiful little girl to love and care for? He'd let his sister, Deirdre, down and now it was too late. He hadn't seen her once after she'd married, not even when Cora was born. Her husband was a good man, but visiting Deirdre brought back too many memories. Too many unsettling feelings from his youth.

Not that he'd purposefully stayed away. He kept meaning to visit St. Louis, but something would always come up. One year had passed, then two, then six—all in the blink of an eye. And now his sister was gone.

"Hey," Tom Walby said, gripping the bars with both

hands and sticking his whiskered chin between the narrow opening. "Give me that candy."

"Nope." Garrett slipped Cora's gift back into his pocket. "Tom, do you ever pay attention in church?"

"Nah. I only go on Sunday when the missus forces me."

"Too bad. The reverend was preaching to you last week. He said, *Blessed are the poor in spirit, for theirs is the kingdom of Heaven.*"

"Ah, c'mon, Marshal," Tom garbled, squeaking his sweaty hands down the bars. "You don't believe in that Bible stuff, do you?"

Garrett considered the question. *Did he?* Sometimes yes and sometimes no. At times like this, he wished he found comfort from God; instead, he felt only a deep and abiding sense of betrayal. "Why don't you sleep it off."

"If only it were that easy," Tom declared, stumbling toward the narrow cot lining the jailhouse wall.

He collapsed onto his back and threw one arm over his eyes. Surprised by the man's articulate response, Garrett paused for a moment. He leaned closer, but Tom was already sound asleep and snoring.

"Yep," Garrett muttered. "If only it were that easy."

Confident he had time before Tom awoke and recalled his earlier rage, Garrett walked the short distance to the boardinghouse where JoBeth McCoy stayed. He knew where she lived. Watching her take the shortcut to the telegraph office each morning while he fixed his coffee was the highlight of his day. Even from a distance her forest-green eyes flashed with mischief as she scaled the corral fence, a pair of trousers concealed beneath her modest skirts.

He caught sight of Jo and Cora and his heart thumped uncomfortably against his ribs. They sat crouched over a red-and-black set of checkers, their heads together. Jo's hair was dark and long and stick straight, while Cora's hair was a short blond mass of wild curls. Jo's eyes were vivid green, with dark lashes, and Cora's eyes were crystal blue with pale lashes.

They reminded him of an Oriental symbol he'd once seen in San Francisco—a black teardrop and a white teardrop nestled in a circle. They were opposite, yet somehow they complemented each other perfectly.

JoBeth McCoy was different from other women, and her uniqueness fascinated him. Not that he was interested in courting—a man with his past definitely wasn't husband material—but something in Jo sparked his interest. She didn't simper or flutter her eyelashes, and he was drawn to her unabashed practicality. Too many people created unnecessary complications for themselves, like his drunken prisoner.

Garrett paused on the boardwalk, grateful they hadn't seen him yet. His eyes still burned, and emotion clogged his throat. He pinched the bridge of his nose, not wanting Jo to see him like this—vulnerable and aching to cry like a baby.

After inhaling a fortifying breath, he clapped his hands, startling the two. "Who's winning?"

"I am," Cora declared proudly.

Jo winked at him in shared confidence, and his heart swelled.

"Reverend Miller has invited you two for supper," she said.

Her obvious compassion soothed him, and for a moment the pain subsided. The townspeople were all desperately trying to ease Cora through the transition, and he appreciated the effort. "What time?"

"Five o'clock."

"Five it is, then. Speaking of food, have you two had any lunch?"

"Nope."

"Not yet."

"Why don't we mosey over to the hotel and eat."

Jo rubbed her hands against her brown skirts. "You two don't need me anymore—"

"No!" Cora exclaimed.

Her face pinched in fear, and Jo placed her hand comfortingly over the little girl's. The simple purity of the gesture humbled Garrett.

Pale blue eyes pleaded with him. "Can I stay with Jo until dinner?"

His stomach dipped. Of course Cora was terrified. Her whole world had turned upside down. She'd lost her parents, her home—everything that was familiar. Then she'd been placed on a train with a stranger and shuttled across the country into the care of yet another stranger.

Jo wrapped a blond curl around her index finger and smiled, her face radiant. "I suppose I could stay a tiny little while longer."

Garrett fought back the sting behind his eyes. Who wouldn't be terrified by all that upheaval? The little girl had been adrift and alone until Jo had sheltered her. Now they were connected. He'd seen that sort of devotion before over the years. He'd even been the recipient once or twice of a victim's misplaced allegiance. Those false attachments had quickly faded when people were reunited with their families.

Except Cora didn't have anyone familiar.

"I need you, Jo," Cora stated simply.

Garrett's gaze locked with Jo's. He couldn't mask his churning emotions, and he knew right then she saw him for what he was—exposed, terrified. Yet no censure entered her expression, only compassion and understanding. For a moment it seemed as if everything *would* be okay—as though she'd be strong enough for all of them.

I need you, Jo.

The truth hit Garrett like a mule kick. He needed guidance and Cora had taken a shine to Jo. He'd do everything in his power to foster the budding relationship—even if it risked his brittle emotions.

If only his life had been different.

He and Cora both needed Jo desperately. Yet only one of them was worthy of her.

Chapter Two

The weathered boardwalk planks beneath Jo's feet rumbled. With Cora between them, Jo and the marshal paused beneath the hand-painted sign for the Palace Café. A group of young boys, blessedly minus any of her brothers, dashed around them, laughing and calling to each other. Visibly alarmed by the group's roughhousing, Cora latched on to Jo's leg.

"Don't worry." Jo ruffled her curls. "They're just full of energy. They have the week off while their schoolteacher is visiting her sister during her confinement."

Another baby, and the birth had been particularly difficult. Jo stifled a shudder. Her ma served as midwife around town, and Jo often assisted. Each birth she attended crystallized her fears and renewed her vow to stay single.

While there was joy, too often there was pain. She'd swaddled the tiny bodies of stillborn infants. She'd led distraught husbands from the room and sat with them while they wept. She'd felt the hand of a laboring mother go limp as the woman's exhausted body gave up the battle for life.

After all she'd seen, she'd never experience the innocent hope and wonder most expectant mothers felt.

Not that she had any prospects in the matter, but she didn't like this strange push and pull tugging on her emotions lately. More and more often she found herself lingering over the newborns, inhaling their sweet scent and wondering what it would be like to have one of her own.

Jo mentally shook off the disquieting thoughts. It was no use pining for things that could never be. She'd been rejected before and, while she knew she could survive heartbreak, she dreaded a repeat of the humiliating experience.

Cora peeked out from beneath her pale eyelashes. "When will I go to school?"

The marshal blanched. "I don't know. I'm not sure. Should she be in school now? What should I do?"

"There's no need for panic." Jo chucked him on the shoulder. "We'll talk with the teacher when she comes back next week."

"You're right." He mopped his forehead with a blue-patterned bandanna. "Of course you're right. There's no need for alarm. I'm just new to all this."

The marshal's dedication melted Jo's insides. Seeing a tough, hardened lawman reduced to a bundle of nerves over a tiny little girl was the most precious sight she'd ever seen. She didn't know whether to laugh or cry, hug him or chuck him on the shoulder once more. But she felt better about Cora's new living arrangements than she had all week.

She'd known the marshal was fair and levelheaded, but seeing him this vulnerable lit a warm glow in her chest. Anybody could be a tough lawman, but it took a real man to show his vulnerability.

Cora tipped her rag doll side to side, sending its yellow-yarn braids flopping. "I know some of my letters. But I can't read yet."

The marshal squinted thoughtfully. "I'll talk with the schoolteacher when she returns. Are you ready for lunch?"

"Nope." Cora glanced around. "I dropped Miss Lily's coat."

She dashed back a few paces, leaving Jo and Marshal Cain alone on the boardwalk beneath a cloudless, brilliant blue spring sky. Jo had been thinking about his rattled composure when she'd teased him earlier, and she wondered if he was embarrassed by female attention. She'd noticed the odd affliction with her brothers. They were as tough as buffalo jerky with their friends, but as fluffy as milkweed when it came to a pretty girl.

Testing her theory, Jo smiled coyly, her lips stretching with muscles she rarely used. The marshal returned the smile, his face turning pink.

To her shock, she felt her own cheeks warm.

She'd done it—she'd almost flirted with a man and he'd sort of responded. It was no wonder Mary Louise held court to all those besotted suitors in the mercantile like the queen of England.

"Hey, runt," a familiar voice sneered.

Jo's smile faded. Bert Walby sauntered up the boardwalk, his fingers hitched into his striped vest pocket. Tom Walby's brother never missed an opportunity to bait her. She stood up straighter, bracing for his verbal attack. Tom and Bert looked alike with their gangly frames and straw-colored hair.

Gritting her teeth, Jo faced her tormentor. "You're looking awfully fancy, Bert. You going before the judge?"

He scowled. "That's funny, runt, cuz you look the same as always. You get dressed in a barn this morning?"

Chuckling, he snatched the hat from her head, then reared back and cocked his arm in order to toss it onto the dirt-packed street. The next instant, Bert staggered into the marshal. Unsure what had knocked him sideways, Jo leaped back. The two men slammed into the jailhouse wall. Bert yelped and collapsed onto his knees. Marshal Cain bent, hooking his right hand beneath the man's shoulder, and hauled him upright. The marshal whispered something in Bert's ear before shoving him forward.

With a grumble, Bert circled his right shoulder and rubbed his biceps with his left hand.

The marshal crossed his arms and cleared his throat.

Leaning down, Bert plucked her hat from the boardwalk and dusted the brim against his thigh before returning it. "I was just checking on Tom. Heard you locked him up again."

The marshal braced his legs apart. "Tom's responsible for his own actions. You can pick him up before supper. He should be sober by then."

"It's nobody's business what a man does on his own time."

"Tom makes it my business when he goes smashing up property."

Bert tossed a glare over his shoulder as he beat a hasty exit.

Jo replaced her hat and frowned at Bert's retreating back. "That was odd. He usually doesn't back down that quick."

Marshal Cain shrugged, his expression deceptively neutral. "Seems like Bert's got a grudge against both of us."

"We've been feuding since the eighth grade." Jo snorted. "Since I gave Tom a shiner. The Walbys are too afraid of my brothers to settle the score outright, but whenever Tom or Bert sees me alone… You get the idea."

"I do." A muscle ticked along the marshal's jaw.

Cora skipped between them with her doll. Miss Lily sported a red coat trimmed in navy blue rickrack.

Garrett yanked open the café door, clanging the bell suspended above them, his attention focused on the street. His gaze settled on the spot where Bert had taken up vigil near the jailhouse. Garrett looked between the two of them, and his eyes narrowed. Jo's shoulders sagged. So much for flirting with the marshal. Now he'd see her like everyone else in town did—a rebel who scrapped with the boys.

She set her jaw. It was best not to pine for something she'd never have. Over the years she'd grown wiser, more protective of her emotions. Loosening her resolve was a road paved with disaster.

It was best if Garrett thought of her as a buddy, because a friend couldn't break her heart.

The café bustled with activity. Plates clanked together and the low hum of voices surrounded them. The succulent aroma of fried chicken filled the air. Garrett pulled out a chair for Cora and Jo in turn, then caught the curious glance of a middle-aged woman in a burgundy bustled dress.

He touched his forehead in greeting and leaned

nearer Jo's ear. "Is it all right? You and I eating together. I don't want any gossip."

Jo rolled her eyes. "Don't worry about it. We're fine."

For an instant he thought he saw a flash of disappointment. The moment passed so quickly, he shook off the odd feeling. Why would Jo *want* people gossiping about them?

Starched white cloths draped the wooden tables, and mismatched china covered the surface. The decor was a curious blend of faded elegance and homespun crafts. In the center of the table, a pint-size milk jug tinted a clear shade of blue-green held a posy of coneflowers.

Garrett kicked back in his chair and studied his surroundings. Most of the people in town were familiar by now, and they'd moved passed their initial wariness. A few gentlemen nodded in his direction, and Mrs. Schlautman flashed him a smile.

Jo rested her menu on the table. "How'd you end up here, anyway?"

He couldn't hold back a grin. "You sure are direct."

"Is that bad?"

"No, no. I like it." *Too much.*

Garrett planted his elbows on the table and fisted his hands. "I was bored. I needed a challenge. When I heard what I was up against, what the previous sheriff had let go on around here, I knew this was the perfect job for me."

"Will you stay? After you're done cleaning up the town and all?"

"Hadn't planned on it." His gaze slid toward Cora. "But things have changed."

Their waitress bustled past and took their orders, momentarily interrupting his troubled thoughts. Jo and the woman exchanged a few pleasantries, their friendship obvious by their banter. The woman returned a moment later with a pencil and paper, and Cora happily accepted the distracting items.

Garrett scratched his head. "I never even thought of that."

"You're new to all this. You'll learn." Jo pressed her thumb against the tines of her fork. "Do you have any other family? Someone who could help out for a bit?"

"Just a cousin and his wife." Garrett glanced away. "They won't be much help."

"I thought you said you didn't have any family."

"None that claim me." He ducked his head. "I guess that's different than no kin at all."

There was no love lost between him and Edward. For a time after his parents' deaths, Garrett had stayed with Edward's family. They'd been mortified by the scandal, and resentful of the added burden of two extra children. Especially Garrett, who bore a striking resemblance to his father.

He shook his head. "It must seem strange to you."

"I've never wanted for brothers, that's for certain." Jo drummed her fingers on the table. "Is your cousin a lawman, too?"

"Nope. He owns a sawmill back East. My father was a doctor. I'm the only one who went West."

"I guess that explains your parents' deaths."

His heart stuttered and stalled. "Explains what?"

"You know, the smallpox. Doctors get exposed to all that kind of stuff all the time."

His blood gradually resumed pumping again, moving sluggishly through his frozen veins.

"Of course," he replied.

These people respected him, gave him their trust. What would they do if they knew of his past? A lawman, the son of a murderer. They'd run him out of town on a rail. If he and Cora settled here, he'd have to guard the secret with even greater care. He wasn't alone anymore.

Garrett braced his left palm on the table and his right one against his chest.

Jo leaned forward, a crease between her delicately arched brows. "Are you all right? You don't look so good."

"Fine."

Avoiding her penetrating gaze, he glanced instead at her fingers. They were long and tapered, the nails blunt and neatly rounded. A smudge of ink darkened the tip of her index finger.

He turned from the distraction. Cora scribbled away, her head bent in concentration. Noting his interest, she lifted her paper and proudly displayed her picture. Even with her rudimentary skills, Garrett recognized his sister and her husband on either side of Cora, their hands linked together.

Cora's lower lip trembled. "Look. I made my family."

His throat tight, Garrett knelt before her and pulled her into his embrace. She wrapped her arms around his neck and a single sob shook her delicate body.

"Oh, dear," the woman in burgundy exclaimed, half rising.

Jo gently waved the concerned woman aside. "She'll be all right. She's right where she needs to be."

Grateful for Jo's assistance, Garrett closed his eyes.

After Cora had calmed, he took his seat once more. Jo resumed the conversation as if there'd been no break, and her light chatter was a grateful distraction. As he watched her and Cora laugh, he let his mind wander. What would it be like, courting Jo? Actually courting her like a proper gentleman?

Garrett spread his work-roughened fingers over the stark white tablecloth. No use thinking the impossible. She deserved better. What if the evil that had snapped his father's soul lived within Garrett? He couldn't take the risk.

Jo rested her hand over his. "You don't have to be alone in this. I hope we can be friends."

"I'd like that."

Sour guilt swelled in his throat for even thinking about Jo romantically. She deserved someone who could love her with his whole heart, without reservations. Garrett wasn't that man.

That evening, Jo returned to her solitary room at the boardinghouse. She lit a single candle and perched on the edge of the bed. Without Cora for company, the room seemed unnaturally quiet.

Lately she'd begun to realize what a lonely place she'd carved out for herself. Rising at dawn each day, spending her shift at the telegraph office, home each evening. Every other weekend she helped her family on the farm. She kept herself busy, sure, but even that felt false.

Like at the mercantile, when Mr. Stuart ran low on supplies and spread out the remaining stock to make it look as if there were more goods available. That's how Jo felt lately, like she was spreading herself thin to make it appear there was more to her life. Covering up the empty places in her heart with bits of nonsense.

Except she wasn't hiding them from other people, she was hiding from herself.

Always before, she'd known what she'd wanted, and she'd sought her goal with single-minded determination. Except she didn't know what she wanted anymore.

Jo stood and crossed the room, then pressed her forehead against the cool windowpane. She did know one thing—being with Cora and Garrett felt right.

Blowing out a warm breath, Jo fogged a circle on the glass. Garrett had accepted her offer of friendship. Together they'd look after Cora, ease her through the transition of losing her parents.

Simple as that.

The fog on the glass quickly dissipated. He hadn't shown signs of interest toward any of the single ladies in town earlier, now that he had Cora to look after... Her stomach pitched. A single man around these parts who needed a wife didn't stay single for long. There'd be no setting her cap for Marshal Cain. She'd never set herself up for that kind of demoralizing rejection again.

Jo glanced at the tips of her battered work boots. She knew what she wanted, all right: she wanted something that could never be.

Chapter Three

A week after the marshal's return, Jo shaded her eyes with one hand and searched the horizon. A kick of dust indicated his timely arrival. Her ma had finally invited the marshal and Cora for dinner. By coincidence, this was Jo's weekend home.

A soft object thumped against the back of her head. She bent and retrieved a faded leather glove from the ground.

"Hey!" Frowning at her brother, Abraham, she waved the glove. "Did you throw this at me?"

"You weren't paying any attention." He tugged off his second glove. "Why all the daydreaming?"

"I wasn't daydreaming."

No matter what happened during the week, when Jo rounded the bend and caught sight of her childhood home on the horizon, her mood lightened. Lately, she needed the comforting sight more than ever. That strange yearning hadn't abated, and a restless need for something more in her life itched beneath her collar.

Abraham lifted an eyebrow. "It's like working with Caleb. Are you in love with Mary Louise Stuart, too?"

Jo winged the glove in Abraham's direction. He ducked and easily avoided her revenge. At seventeen, he wasn't interested in courting just yet.

"I don't see what all the fuss is about Mary Louise," Jo grumbled. "What does anybody know about her other than she's pretty?"

"What else do you have to know?" Abraham shrugged.

"Be serious." Jo knelt before a hay bale and clipped the wire. "God gave her those looks. It's not like she had to work for anything."

"How do you think Mary Louise feels? She can't hardly step from behind the counter without causing a stampede."

"It's strange, you know, when you really think about it. Some people are rewarded for how they look, not who they are." Jo sat back on her heels. "While other people are paying the price for how they look, when none of it is their fault. And nobody's happy about it."

"You know what your problem is, Jo? You think too much." Abraham kicked the loose hay over the uneven ground of the muddy corral. "Looks like the marshal and his niece are here."

Her brother had a point. She *had* been thinking too much lately. Only the day before she'd offered to hold Mrs. Patterson's baby while the new mother shopped in the mercantile. When Jo had caught herself wondering how the marshal's coffee-colored eyes would look on a chubby little toddler, she'd promptly returned the baby and fled the store. That sort of behavior had to stop.

In desperation, she'd arrived at the farm earlier than normal and donned her comfortable trousers. She'd tackled her chores with vigor, hoping the physical exertion would ease her mental turmoil.

Her face damp with perspiration, Jo spread another bale of hay while the wagon lumbered up the driveway, stopping only when her visitors halted before the barn.

She pinched off her gloves and met them on the drive.

"JoBeth!" Cora called.

The little girl leaned out of the wagon and wrapped her arms around Jo's neck. Marshal Cain met Jo's gaze over the girl's shoulder, and her breath strangled for a split second. There was something heady about having those dark eyes focused on her. She'd seen him every day this week, and his effect on her had grown rather than blunted. Each time she saw his face, her heart pounded, and her head spun as though she'd been twirling in a circle.

Attempting to break the mysterious spell, she squeezed Cora tight and pulled her from her perch, then set her gently on the ground.

Six-year-old Maxwell, Jo's youngest brother, bounded down the driveway, his knees pumping. "JoBeth, JoBeth!" he called. "Are they here yet?"

"Peas and carrots, Maxwell. Look with your own eyes. Can't you see? Slow down before you run us over."

Her brother skidded to a halt before them. He wore his usual uniform of a tan shirt and brown trousers with a pair of red suspenders. A crumpled hat covered his dark hair. "Who are you?" he demanded of Cora.

The little girl clutched her rag doll close. "I'm Cora."

"How old are you?" Maxwell asked.

"Five."

The front door swung open and Mrs. McCoy stepped onto the porch. "Who do we have here?" She descended the stairs, her fingers busy unknotting the apron wrapped around her waist. "Gracious, you must be the prettiest little girl this side of the Mississippi!"

"Our guests have arrived, Ma." Jo tucked Cora against her side. The McCoy clan could be overwhelming, and Jo didn't want the girl spooked.

Maxwell dashed up the stairs and tugged on his mother's skirts as she approached them. "That's Cora. She said she's five years old."

Edith McCoy smiled, her expression full of unspoken sympathy. "We're pleased to have you. Why don't you come on inside."

Edith labored up the walk, her gait stiff, and Jo sighed. Her ma's left hip sometimes acted up, but Edith McCoy never complained. Complaining wasn't ladylike. When Jo was younger, her ma had dressed her in frills and lace, but that hadn't lasted. Despite being a paragon of feminine qualities in an untamed land, Edith had never swayed her daughter into fripperies.

Her ma waved them toward the house. "Welcome to our home, Marshal Cain. I hope you like pot roast."

The marshal flashed a wry grin. "Just as long it's not fried chicken."

"I see you've taken the fried-chicken tour of all the single ladies in Cimarron Springs." Edith chuckled. "I figured I'd wait until the spring and let you enjoy a pot roast for a change."

Maxwell danced around them, his scuffed boots kicking up a whirl of dust. "Cora! Cora! The barn cat just had kittens. You wanna see them? Their eyes are open and everything."

The little girl tugged on Jo's hand. "Can I?"

Jo waited for Marshal Cain's nod of approval. "Of course you can."

Maxwell spun around, and Jo caught him by the cuff of his shirt. "Cora isn't from the country, so you be nice. No spiders, no frogs, no beetles..."

"Yeah, yeah, yeah." Maxwell rolled his eyes. "I know guest rules."

"Not just any guest. Cora is a special guest. I want you on your Sunday best."

"I'll be good."

Jo released Maxwell and planted her hands on her hips. "I bet Reverend Miller would have a thing or two to say about your Sunday best."

Her youngest brother scowled. "He boxed my ears last week."

"That's because he got to you before I did." Jo pointed a finger. "Now don't get Cora's pretty pink dress all dirty."

"I won't," Maxwell grumbled.

Edith McCoy sighed and shook her head. "I hope that's not her best dress, because dirt multiplies on this farm. And it doesn't wash out easy."

"Don't worry, Mrs. McCoy," the marshal replied, dusting his hands together. "She's got plenty more dresses where that one came from."

Jo and Marshal Cain followed Edith into the cozy farmhouse. The aromas of fresh-baked bread and pot roast drifted from the kitchen, sending Jo's mouth watering. Since the spring temperatures cooled after dark, a fire danced in the hearth.

"You two have a seat," Edith ordered. "I'm putting the finishing touches on dinner."

Marshal Cain pulled out a chair and paused. Jo glanced behind her. He waved his hand over the seat. "Ladies first."

A spoon clattered against the floor.

Her ma bent and retrieved the utensil. "Clumsy of me. I'll just rinse this off in the sink. If you don't mind my being forward, how are you getting along, Marshal?"

Jo snorted and flopped onto the proffered chair.

The marshal sat down across from her. "No need to apologize, Mrs. McCoy. I'm sure Jo has told you all about Cora."

"Not Jo, no. But gossip travels with the speed of boredom around here."

The marshal glanced around the tidy room, and Jo knew exactly what he was noticing. All of the spices above the stove were arranged alphabetically, the pots were hung by size, and even the glasses were arranged by height. When she was younger, her ma's habits had annoyed her, but as she grew older she realized that order made even the most cramped spaces cozy and welcoming.

Marshal Cain shook his head. "How do you manage to keep everything in place with children running underfoot?"

Mrs. McCoy wiped the spoon on a towel draped over the sink. "More help, I guess. I've got more people to make the mess, but I've also got more people to help with the chores."

"I don't think more children will solve my problems." The marshal rubbed a weary hand over his eyes. "I can't keep up. I feel like my whole jailhouse was hit with a pink bomb. That little girl must have come with a magic trunk, because when I opened it, the contents tripled in size."

Jo hid a grin. The marshal *did* look a bit disheveled.

And she'd never heard him so talkative. As she pondered his uncharacteristic admissions, another thought darkened her mood. They'd seen each other in passing each day this week, and yet he'd never once confided his concerns with her.

The marshal pressed his thumb into the soft wax of the candle burning in the center of the table. "I hope nobody gets arrested, because Cora set up a tea party in the jail cell. I can't put a fugitive in there with a couple of rag dolls having tea. There's even a pink blanket on the cot."

Jo clapped her hands over her mouth.

Her ma lifted a lid from the roaster, sending a plume of steam drifting toward the ceiling. "I can see where that would be a problem," Edith replied, her voice ripe with amusement. "Sometimes I wish we had *more* pink in this house. We're full up on boys since Jo left, and she was never one for tea parties anyway."

Jo scowled, her amusement waning. Just because she didn't throw tea parties didn't mean she wasn't a girl. She was different, that's all. Why did everyone insist on bringing it up all the time?

"And it's not just her stuff." The marshal picked off a chunk of wax and rolled it into a ball between his thumb and forefinger. "Cora doesn't eat much in the morning. Should I be worried about that? And she never stops asking questions. Sometimes I don't know the answers. But if I tell her that I don't know the answer, she just asks the same question in another way. Is that normal?"

"That's a five-year-old child for you, all right. As curious as a kitten and just as precious." Edith placed a Mason jar filled with lemonade before the marshal. "You better drink something or you'll get parched."

A flush of color crept up the marshal's neck. "I guess I've been around Cora too much. I can't stop talking all of a sudden."

"Children don't come with instructions, that's for certain." Her ma set out a loaf of bread and a pat of butter on wooden slab.

"I know." The marshal slathered his bread with the softened butter. "Like, how often should you wash them? What kind of soap should you use? I only have lye soap. Is that bad for girls?" A note of desperation crept into his voice. "I don't know what to do. What if I do the wrong thing?"

"The fact that you're worried makes you a better parent than most others." Edith dried her hands on the towel and crossed the room. "The bad folks aren't worried about what's right and wrong, you know?" She perched on a chair beside him and patted his hand. "You're doing fine."

The marshal raked his free hand through his hair. He paused for a moment, his Adam's apple working. "She cries at night."

"Of course she does," Jo exclaimed, her heart twisting at his words. "She's lost both of her parents. She's lost her home. That's enough to make anybody cry."

Something flickered in his eyes, but it passed quickly. Jo ached to reach out and comfort him, but she knew better. She never had words for times like these—soothing, comforting words. He'd said it himself over lunch last week. She was direct.

With grudging admiration, Jo studied her mother. While the rest of the McCoys were dark-haired with green eyes, Mrs. McCoy stood out with her pale blue eyes and dark blond hair. Even the streak of gray at her temple lent her an air of elegance.

Jo had never really valued cosseting before. Blunt truths were faster and more efficient. Now she realized there was a time and a place for coddling.

Marshal Cain pinched the bridge of his nose. "I don't know what to do," he repeated.

"Love her," Jo replied. "Just like you're doing."

"Jo is right." Edith smiled and patted his shoulder. "Love goes a long way."

The door swung open, and her brother Caleb stepped into the room surrounded by a noxious aroma. Jo waved a hand before her nose. "Gracious, did you take a swim in Pa's cologne?"

The tips of her brother's ears reddened. "Mind your own business, runt." He strutted across the room in his crisp blue shirt and navy trousers.

Caleb was the oldest of the boys at twenty-two, tall and slender with the distinctive McCoy coloring of dark brown hair and bright green eyes. They all took after their pa's looks in that regard, though Ely McCoy was short and stout. Jo was the only child who'd inherited his lack of height. Much to her chagrin, she was embarrassingly petite.

Being small with five younger—and much taller— brothers had taught her a thing or two about strategy. "I think someone is going into town. This must be your third trip to the mercantile this week."

"What's it to you?"

"Nothing." Jo studied the jagged tips of her blunt fingernails. "It's just that you're not the only one visiting the mercantile on a regular basis."

The owner's daughter was a pretty blonde with blue

eyes and a ready smile, and since Mary Louise had turned eighteen and started working behind the counter, the store's revenue had leaped tenfold.

Caleb fisted his hands. "Who else have you been noticing?"

"There're too many to count. You better screw up your courage for courting or she's gonna slip away."

Her brother glanced around the room, caught sight of Marshal Cain and stopped short. "Evening, sir." Caleb straightened and tucked his shirttail into his pants before glaring at Jo. "It doesn't matter because I don't care. I'm going into town because Ma is out of sugar. Isn't that right?"

Edith smiled indulgently. "Of course."

"See?"

Caleb stomped out of the room, and her ma shot Jo a quelling glance. "Don't be too hard on the boy."

"What?" Jo drawled. "I'm just trying to help."

The marshal grinned. "Mary Louise better make up her mind soon or I'll be breaking up fights. There's nothing like a pretty girl to get a young man's blood boiling."

An uncharacteristic spark of jealousy pricked Jo. Apparently, Marshal Cain had noticed the pretty little blonde, too. She crossed her arms over her chest. "I bet her pa hopes she never decides on one suitor. He makes sure all those boys buy something while they're panting after Mary Louise. I heard he even ordered a new wagon from Wichita."

"No more gossiping, JoBeth," her ma scolded from her place by the stove. "And let up on that boy. Being in love is harder than it looks."

A huff of anger settled at the back of Jo's throat. They

all acted as if she had no emotions. She couldn't recall one time when her ma had told the boys to let up on her.

Jo braced her arms against the table and locked her elbows. "How come you never tell them to go easy on me?"

"Because you're tougher than they are." Her mother waved her wooden spoon for emphasis. "And smarter, too."

Jo caught the marshal studying her with those dark, intuitive eyes and decided it was time to change the subject. "How are the Elders?"

Her ma's face lit up. "I just got a letter. Watch the gravy while I fetch it."

Marshal Cain rested his hat on his knee, his enormous palm dwarfing the crown. "I think I've heard that name before."

"Probably." Jo stood and crossed to the stove. "The Elders used to live over the rise. They moved to Paris, Texas, going on ten years ago."

"Wasn't there something about an outlaw?"

"Mrs. Elder's first husband was a bank robber. He hid the loot in a cave by Hackberry Creek. The boys sell tours for a penny every summer."

"They do *what?*" The marshal set down the lemonade he'd raised to his lips. "Don't the new owners mind all those kids tramping across their property?"

"No one lives there." Jo shrugged. "The place has been empty for years"

Her pa stepped into the room. A great bear of a man, Ely McCoy vibrated the floorboards with his heavy steps. Jo dropped the gravy spoon and dashed toward him. "Pa!"

He enveloped her in a bone-crushing hug, lifting her

feet from the floor. "There's my little girl. I heard you brought company."

Jo's heart soared. Her pa was the only person who treated her like a girl without making her feel weak. He was a stout man with a thick salt-and-pepper beard and a mop of unruly mahogany hair hanging over his twinkling green eyes.

"This is my pa, Ely McCoy."

Marshal Cain rose from his seat and held out his hand. "Nice to see you again, Mr. McCoy."

"Call me Ely."

Her pa slapped the marshal on the back, nearly launching him into the hearth. "Glad you're here, son. I need help balancing the pasture gate."

Jo grimaced. She loved her pa, but he was always putting the guests to work. "Why don't you get the boys to help you?"

"Because Caleb's cologne turns my stomach, and David has gone to Wichita to buy a horse."

"Glad to help," Marshal Cain replied easily.

Jo appreciated his calm acceptance of the request. She also liked how his chambray shirt stretched across his broad shoulders. He was quiet and thoughtful, never missing a detail. She liked watching as he sized up a room. He looked *at* people, not *through* them.

What did he think of her?

Did he see her as everyone else in town did—as an oddity? Somehow or other she didn't think so. He regarded her with the same deference he showed Cora and her ma. Maybe that's why he appealed to her—he treated everyone he encountered as though they were important, as though they were worthy of his time.

The marshal tossed a resigned grin over his shoulder and followed her pa out the door.

As the two men left together, Jo considered how different they were. Not just in size and shape, but in temperament. Her parents were opposites, too. Ely McCoy was a loud bear of a man whose bark was worse than his bite. Her ma was more refined, more reserved than her pa. Yet they worked well together, and no one expected either of them to change.

Jo had learned early on that boys expected *her* to change. At thirteen years old, a boy had told her flat out that if she wanted him to stop teasing her, she'd best let him win at marbles.

Jo had decided then and there that she'd rather win.

A scant few minutes later, a knock startled Jo from her vigil at the stove. She crossed the room and opened the door. The reverend stood on the doorstep, a dark shadow against the orange glow from the setting sun.

"Reverend Miller. What brings you here this time of the evening?"

He doffed his cap and smoothed his thinning hair. "A telegram arrived for the marshal. The clerk said the marshal should see it right away."

Chapter Four

Garrett strained beneath the weight of the gate, a fine sheen of perspiration forming on his brow. The evening air was cool and a stiff breeze whipped the hair over his perspiring brow. The incessant, relentless gales dried up the earth and left every surface dusty and gritty. When a changing weather front blew in, Garrett stuffed rags around the windows and still awoke with grit on his tongue. He sometimes wondered why the whole prairie hadn't been swept away already.

Thankfully, as the evening stretched on, the breeze gentled, and the sun sank low on the horizon. Hills rolled toward Hackberry Creek, and a smattering of trees softened the view. Garrett didn't consider himself a sentimental man, but he appreciated the quiet beauty of nature settling into nightfall.

Ely broke the silence first, saying, "That little Cora sure is a cute one."

"That she is."

"Heard she's taken a shine to Jo."

"Word travels fast around these parts."

"That it does." Ely ratcheted the hinges tighter. "What are you planning on doing?"

Garrett gritted his teeth against the strain of the heavy metal gate. "Doing?"

"You gonna raise that little girl all on your own?"

"Not much other choice," Garrett bit out over his exertion.

At Ely's signal, Garrett released his hold and leaped back, scooting his boots free from a possible collapse. To his relief, the hinges held firm. He flexed his sore fingers. Ely must be twenty years his senior, but the older man didn't show any signs of strain. Mr. McCoy was a tough, portly man with a fierce scowl and a ready smile. Garrett recalled how Jo had launched herself at her pa earlier. Though Ely could snap a sturdy tree limb with one hand, his children didn't seem afraid of him.

The idea gave Garrett pause. What was it like for the McCoy children, not being afraid all the time?

Ely swung the bars back and forth, examining the smooth action with a satisfied expression. "When I look at your little girl, I wish I could go back in time."

Garrett glanced up in surprise. "Why?"

"Jo never had time to be a baby. To be a girl. By the time she was walking, we already had Caleb. Then David came along and Abraham and Michael. We had a little bit of time, but then Maxwell surprised us. With all those boys, well…let's just say she had to be tough."

Garrett couldn't help but wonder how Jo had survived with all those rough-and-tumble boys. She wasn't as tough as she pretended. He'd seen her vulnerability. Despite her confidence and bravado, she really was a tiny little thing. Those boys should be sheltering and protecting her, not the other way around. A half grin stretched across his face. Garrett had a feeling Jo would never stand for coddling.

Ely considered his dirt-stained hands. "The missus used to dress her up. Jo wouldn't stand for it. It's funny, you know? The missus thinks they butt heads because they're too different. I think they're too much alike. You ever noticed that? It's the parts of ourselves we see in others that frustrate us most."

Ely's insight surprised Garrett. With all those children running underfoot, who had time for speculation?

The older man paused. "Probably why David and I argue like a couple of old-timers." He nodded. "We're too much alike."

A sense of helplessness chased away Garrett's earlier serenity. Ely's observations hit too close to the heart of the matter. That's what Garrett feared—being like his father. The blood of a murderer flowed through his veins like an unlit fuse.

The McCoys were unencumbered by the past. They didn't know the secret he bore like an albatross around his neck. They'd never been burdened with a scandal that had destroyed an entire family.

"Pa!" a voice called.

Garrett glanced up and saw the youngest McCoy dashing toward them.

Maxwell skidded to a halt and grasped his side, leaning over as he heaved in a noisy breath. "The reverend is here. He's got a telegram for Garrett. Says it's about Cora. And it's important. And it's bad news."

Even without the power of Ely's unexpected insight, Garrett had a sinking feeling this evening wasn't going to end well.

* * *

Jo watched as Marshal Cain paced before the fireplace, his hands on his hips, a fierce scowl darkening his handsome face. "I'll go back to St. Louis myself and fight this if I have to."

"No!" Jo exclaimed.

Her ma placed a gentle hand on her arm. "Let him be."

Reverend Miller worried the shallow brim of his black felt hat in his hands. "Perhaps it's better if the marshal's cousin and his wife raise the child. You're a single man with a dangerous job..."

"They don't want Cora," Garrett announced. "They want the money from my sister's estate. It says so right here. They want custody of Cora." He jabbed a finger at the telegram. "And the proceeds of the estate for her care and comfort." He crumpled the paper in his fist. "Care and comfort my foot. My sister's husband was an architect. Did well for himself."

The reverend hung his head, revealing the bald patch at his crown. "Still, we must consider what's best for the child."

The marshal braced his hands against the mantel and stared into the blazing fire. "That's not all. I heard a rumor that Edward's sawmill is failing. He doesn't want Cora, he wants an influx of cash for his business."

Mrs. McCoy stood and faced the group, her hands thrust out in a placating gesture. "I don't like this any better than the rest of you, but we don't know your cousin's motivations for certain. Right now it's only blind speculation."

Marshal Cain turned and shook his head. "Whatever his motivations, he's already got a judge on his side."

Ely fisted his hands beneath his biceps and propped his shoulder against the wall. "Let me get this straight. He told the judge that the little girl is in jeopardy because she has a marshal as a guardian?"

"Because I'm a single man. A single lawman. They think I can't care for her properly."

"Can you?" Edith bluntly demanded.

Four pairs of eyes turned in shock.

Jo glared at her ma, who returned the sharp glance and pursed her lips. "I don't mean because you're a man. But you voiced your own concerns rather eloquently earlier this evening. You can't have a little girl in the jailhouse with murderers and rapists."

"Edith!" Ely exclaimed. "Language."

Jo's ma directed an exasperated look at her husband. "It's the truth, whether we want to face it or not. You've got a sweet little girl living above a jail cell."

Marshal Cain adjusted the gun belt strapped around his narrow hips. "She's barely been here a week. I haven't sorted out all the details. If living in the jail is the problem, then we'll move." He faced the reverend. "What about the Elder place? The one just over the rise? I'll buy that."

"You can't," Reverend Miller declared. "Someone already owns it."

The room erupted into noisy chaos.

"Who?" Jo demanded.

"Why, Jack Elder's brother," the reverend declared. "I heard he was driving a herd of cattle from Texas."

Ely planted an elbow on the mantel. "When did this happen?"

"Last month or so. Haven't heard anything in a while."

"Longhorns, I suppose?" Ely ran a thumb and forefinger along his silver-streaked beard. "Huh. I guess there's good grazing land on the other side of the creek. He better move quick. There's talk of closing the borders farther east. Those longhorns bring Texas Fever."

"Does he have any kids?" Maxwell asked from the doorway.

The adults fell instantly silent at his sudden announcement. Not a one of them had noticed his arrival.

"Back outside." Edith broke the impasse and shooed the youngest McCoy toward the porch. "The adults are talking."

"Sounds like you're arguing."

"It's a heated discussion. You and Cora play with the kittens until I call you."

"I still say you're arguing," Max grumbled, but dutifully latched the door behind him.

Edith straightened the doormat with her heel. "It'll be nice having an Elder on the land again. We should check the roof before he gets here."

Ely grunted. "Enough. It doesn't matter right now who owns the old Elder farm. What matters is what's going to happen to Cora."

Visibly shaking off the distraction, Edith straightened her collar. "I don't think Marshal Cain has much of a choice. Keeping law in this town is unpredictable. If a judge looks at a husband and wife, also relatives, compared to a single man. A single *lawman*." She paused. "How can he think Marshal Cain is the best choice?"

"I am the best choice." The marshal punctuated each word with emotion. "I love her. I don't want her because she comes with a pile of money. I've been raising her for a week. We're struggling, sure. But I'm trying. I'll try harder."

Jo groaned as her ma set out the plates for supper. Heaven forbid Edith McCoy let a simple little thing like the ruin of a man's life disrupt a meal.

"What if you're called away?" Edith slid a plate across the table. "It took us almost a week to find you when we received the telegram about Cora."

The marshal made a sound of disgust.

Panic welled in Jo's throat. Didn't they see how much Marshal Cain and his niece needed each other? Her ma was more concerned with propriety than love.

Jo clenched her hands on the table. "I can help out if he's called away. Cora knows me."

"That's only one of his problems." Edith added flatware next to the plates with infuriating precision. "His job is dangerous. What if something happens? If he's wounded or worse. Who will take care of Cora then?"

Marshal Cain slapped his hat on his head. "I'm not giving up my girl." He gestured dismissively toward Reverend Miller. "If some judge in Missouri…." He glanced pointedly around the room. "Or anyone else tries to take my child, they'll have a fight on their hands."

His expression scornful, Marshal Cain strode toward the door.

The room erupted into noisy chatter once more as everyone began talking and gesturing in overlapping conversations.

"There's a perfectly obvious solution—" Edith began.

"Obvious to whom?" the reverend interrupted.

"You talk to him."

Ely touched his chest. "Me?"

Jo stomped her boot. "This is getting us nowhere."

Her pa's head swung between the competing conversations. The reverend flailed his arms at Ely while Edith pointed a finger at her husband.

Jo brushed past them and blocked the marshal's exit. "Let's get hitched."

"What?"

"You heard me." Jo declared. "Let's get married."

Chapter Five

Shocked by her own words, Jo froze. Immediate silence descended on the room. Marshal Cain's jaw dropped. For several long moments nothing stirred the air except the steady *tick, tick, tick* of the clock on the mantel.

Jo felt her face flame. "That's the problem, isn't it? He doesn't have a wife. As Cora's uncle, he's a closer relative to her than a second cousin. What can the judge say if he's married?"

"Well, uh," the reverend sputtered. "You make a compelling argument."

Marshal Cain hadn't moved. He hadn't even blinked an eyelash. The more time stretched out without a response, the more frustrated Jo became. Why didn't he say something? *Yes, no, maybe, I'll think about it...*

If Mary Louise from the mercantile had asked, he probably would've jumped at the chance.

"Never mind," she declared.

"No." The marshal held up his hand. "Jo is right. If I have a wife, they've lost the balance of their case against me."

"JoBeth—" her ma placed a hand on her shoulder

"—think about what you're saying. This isn't a decision to take lightly."

Ely clutched his head. "You've lost me, Edith. Why were you dropping all those hints if you didn't want them to get married? Why put the idea in her head if you were just gonna talk her out of it?"

"I wasn't talking about Jo," Mrs. McCoy hissed through clenched teeth, her emphatic gaze encompassing their rapt audience. "I was talking about one of the ladies on the fried-chicken tour."

Jo whipped out of her mother's hold. "I might not have been featured on the *tour,* but I know what I'm doing."

She also knew she was acting like a child, but she didn't care right then.

"This is a disaster," Edith snapped.

Affronted, Jo challenged her ma. "How on earth does this qualify as a disaster?"

"Everybody out!" her pa shouted with a clap, startling both women into silence.

No one moved.

"I said everyone outside."

Spurred by the force of his booming command, Jo and Marshal Cain automatically turned toward the door.

"Not you two." Ely rolled his eyes. "The rest of us will leave."

He waved his wife and the reverend toward the door. Reverend Miller scooted out of the tense room as if his heels were on fire. Edith scowled and stubbornly bustled around the stove. "Let me turn down the fire on the gravy."

Ely grasped her elbow and coaxed her toward the door. "Come along, dear."

"But the table," her ma protested, dragging her feet. "The dinner…"

"The potatoes will be here in ten minutes. Those two need time alone more than they need a pot roast right now."

Her ma sputtered and resisted his gentle, persistent guidance. Ely McCoy remained adamant. The door closed resolutely on her muttered protest.

Jo gaped. It was a rare day indeed when her pa over-rode her ma's wishes.

The scrape of boots as Garrett restlessly roamed about the cramped space yanked her attention back to the problem at hand. Alone with the marshal, Jo's courage faltered. She'd acted impulsively, backing herself into a corner once again.

He paced before the hearth, his expression intense. "This could work. Cora likes you."

What about you? The question balanced on the tip of her tongue.

"And you're not the romantic sort, are you?"

Jo studied her hands, the nicks and scars, the half-moon of dirt beneath her blunt fingernails. "Of course not."

His pacing halted. "There's no one else, is there? No one else you've set your cap for?"

Jo shook her head.

"You said it yourself. We're friends." The pacing re-sumed. "We get along okay, don't we?"

"Sure."

"And this wouldn't be a real marriage. More of a partnership."

Her legs trembled and Jo locked her knees. "A part-nership."

"For Cora."

"For Cora," Jo repeated.

She set her jaw. What had she expected? That he'd fall to his knees with joy? She'd offered a solution, and he was, at the very least, considering her offer. This was a good idea. She'd have Cora. She'd have a family. Not a normal family like everybody else, but then again, when had she ever done anything the normal way? She'd have a child without childbirth. Perfect. Fabulous. Just what she'd always wanted.

And if no man ever looked at her the way her pa looked at her ma—as if she was the only candle in a world of darkness—then so be it.

Jo straightened her spine. She didn't need that sort of nonsense. She liked the marshal, and maybe someday he'd even come to like her, too. She might not be pretty like the other girls, but certainly he'd come to appreciate her other qualities.

Thus far, he hadn't laughed in her face or mocked her, and a friendship didn't risk her heart. She'd devised the perfect solution for both of them.

Marshal Cain rubbed the stubble on his chin, drawing Jo's eyes to his lips. He'd have to kiss her when they got married, wouldn't he? Tom had once bussed her with a slobbery peck on the cheek behind the livery and she hadn't been keen on repeating the experience. Marshal Cain was different, though, and she wouldn't mind trying again.

Jo pressed a hand against her quaking stomach.

Garrett stretched his arms nearer the dwindling fire and rubbed his hands together. "We've done great together this week, taking Cora back and forth. With the judge coming through town next week, we don't even need a ceremony. We could just sign the papers and call it good."

No ceremony. No kiss. Jo flipped a length of hair off her forehead. "Nope. No ceremony."

"I mean, we're both solitary people. Independent. And people have gotten married for worse reasons."

The marshal was only repeating her thoughts. Yet her heart wrenched at his words. She had a feeling she'd discovered the source of her strange yearnings. Lately the idea of having babies didn't seem so bad. Caroline from school had five children and she'd once fainted when Tom Walby broke his nose during a game of kick ball. If Caroline kept having children, there was hope for all of them.

But the marshal didn't want a real marriage.

No matter what happened, Jo wouldn't let the marshal see that occasionally, in her weaker moments, she wanted more. "Getting hitched solves all your problems."

Yep, she was JoBeth McCoy, problem solver to the world.

He circled the room and sank onto a chair before his empty dinner plate. "No. This is crazy." Elbows on the table, he cradled his head. "I'm sorry. I don't know what I was thinking. I'm not myself lately."

He was hiding something, she was certain. Jo rubbed the back of her neck. She had a feeling she knew the source of his reluctance.

No matter the personal cost, she'd pry the truth from him. "Would you say yes if someone else asked?" She fought the rough edge in her voice. "Because there are plenty of other ladies in town."

Marshal Cain bolted upright. "This is the rest of my life. You're the only one I'd even consider."

"Ooo...kay."

That was a decent response, right? He hadn't exactly explained why he'd choose her over someone else, but Jo guessed that was about as good an answer as she was going to get. While she might have hoped for something more revealing, at least he was still considering her suggestion. He hadn't outright refused her yet.

Garrett unfurled a pink ribbon from his pocket and stretched it between his hands. "Cora loves you. You're all she talks about these days."

Jo's shoulders sagged. *Cora.* Of course, that's what he'd meant. He was thinking of his niece, not her.

She'd capitalize on his reluctant admission. Carefully formulating her response, Jo skirted the table. When she'd gathered her thoughts, she knelt before him and gently tugged the pink ribbon free. "We have to think of what's best for all of us."

A half smile lifted the corner of his lips, and her mouth went dry. She definitely wanted to try kissing again—just as a comparison. Gathering her wayward thoughts once more, she studied his hands, tanned and dwarfing her own. She didn't feel weak when he was near. She felt buoyant and powerful, as though his strength melded with hers. Despite her own certainty, she sensed his persistent doubt. If this marriage was going to happen, they both needed faith.

Jo swallowed around the lump in her throat. One thing she'd learned over time was never to predict the future. This might not be the ideal solution for Jo—she had an uneasy sense one of them had more at stake in the marriage than the other—but this was the best solution for Cora.

The marshal and his niece had been through so much, had lost so much. If Jo could hold their family together, she'd pay the personal price.

Perhaps in bringing peace to Cora and Garrett, she'd find a measure for herself. "It's just like you said earlier. Neither of us is the romantic sort. We're not bothered by love. We'd be doing this for Cora. She needs a family, and, well, things are changing for me."

The marshal raised his head and met her steady gaze. "How do you mean?"

Stalling, Jo let her attention drift around the familiar room. "The boys will be marrying soon."

"How does that change things for you?"

"Caleb is a farmer, like Pa. He'll stay here and work the land. The house is already crowded as it is, and with another woman around...well, they won't need my help anymore."

Garrett flashed a wry grin. "Looks like Caleb will be spending a lot of time at the mercantile."

"I suppose." Jo resisted a smug rejoinder. Caleb definitely had it bad for Mary Louise. "And once he's married, David won't be far behind. Those boys have always followed each other."

"Even if your parents won't need as much of your help, you'll still have your job in town. At the telegraph office."

"I know. But I want more."

"What more could you possibly want?"

What do you want? His blunt question threw her off guard. No one else had thought to ask her what she wanted. She'd thought about what was best for her parents, for her brothers, for Cora and even for the marshal. But she'd never considered what was best for her.

Her ma had certainly given up on Jo ever marrying. While she loved her family, she wanted more. When her friends got married, it was as if they were automatically considered adults, but since Jo hadn't gotten hitched, they still treated her like a child. All a man had to do was turn eighteen and he was considered grown, but a woman wasn't given that luxury.

It was odd, really, since as far as she could tell, getting married didn't automatically endow you with more wisdom than anyone else. But everyone around her seemed to think so. Her married school friends would smile and give her a patronizing nod, as though they'd somehow been granted admission into a secret club and Jo wasn't invited.

Marrying the marshal bypassed all that courting and foolishness. And at least the marshal hadn't said he'd rather court his grandfather's mule.

Jo glanced away. "I love Cora. I can't explain how it happened, but when she stepped off that train, I felt a kinship. Mrs. Smith was pacing the platform and wailing about Indians, but Cora just stood there with those big, solemn eyes. She was lost and alone, but now she has us. We can make a family."

"I know what you mean about Cora." The marshal ran his hand along his chin. "When I saw her that day at church, peeking out from behind your skirts, I felt the same way."

Jo's heart soared at his reluctant admission. He was softening toward her idea, she could tell.

"This is a lifetime decision, Jo." His dark gaze ran the length of her and Jo suddenly realized she was still wearing trousers. "You're young. Someday you'll fall in love."

She pulled out the chair beside him and hitched her pant legs over her knees, then she sat facing him. If Garrett was disappointed in what he saw, that was his loss.

No matter what happened, she wouldn't change who she was—not on the inside, and certainly not on the outside. "Maybe this is God's way of bringing two people together who wouldn't normally marry otherwise."

"But what if you want children of your own someday?" he spoke, not quite meeting her eyes.

The memories of all the births she'd attended rippled through her. All the fragile bodies she and her ma had swaddled in christening blankets for untimely burials. Not every mother survived the process, and not every baby. Garrett might be a marshal, yet Jo was certain she'd seen more death than he had.

She pushed back a wash of sadness. "We'll cross that bridge when we get there. No one knows what the future will bring. But we do know what needs to be done right now."

She leaned forward and cradled his hands. They looked at each other for a long moment, and her breath grew shallow. His shoulders were broad, strong and capable. Sitting this close, the room bathed in lamplight, she noticed how his eyes were rimmed by a darker circle, making the color appear even deeper.

Could she do this? Could she spend the rest of her life as his friend without wanting more?

He rubbed the pad of his thumb over the back of her hand and her whole body pulsed with his touch.

Jo tightened her grip. What choice did she have? She could marry him and risk her heart, or risk never seeing him again. As much as she adored Cora, they were a package deal. She couldn't have one without the other.

He dragged his hands away, stood and turned his back. A sudden sense of emptiness overwhelmed Jo. In that moment, the room appeared lifeless, abandoned. Unfinished place settings covered the table, unfilled waterglasses sat near the sink, empty chairs remained strewn haphazardly around the room.

When he faced her again, his face had smoothed into an unreadable mask. "We can't rush into this."

A heavy weight settled on Jo's chest. She felt him moving away, physically and mentally, regretting his hasty words already. Her last, best chance for a family of her own was slipping away. Was she selfish for wanting him to agree?

Her stomach churned. "Please don't make any decisions without telling me first."

"I couldn't keep something from you even if I tried." He tossed her a knowing look. "Not with Cora around."

"You can't keep secrets with a child underfoot."

He chuckled, the sound more grim than amused. A flash of lightning sparked in the distance, brightening the room for an instant and illuminating his somber expression.

Garrett squinted out the window. "Looks like we might get some rain. That's bad timing with the creek rising fast from the melting up north."

"Not much use in worrying about something you can't control. My pa likes to say, 'Keep your faith in God, and one eye on the river.'"

"I like the sound of that."

The image of the raging creek resonated in Jo's head. It felt as though her beliefs about herself were slipping away, eroding beneath a deluge of new possibilities. Somehow, she'd always imagined things going on just the way they had. The boys growing and marrying. Her little room at the boardinghouse. Coming home for dinner on Sundays.

Then she'd found herself picturing her own family, having her own Sunday dinners.

Marshal Cain approached her and grasped her shoulders, his touch light. "You have to know something about me. I'm not good husband material. If you're looking for love, if you think this might grow into love someday, you'll be disappointed." He interrupted her murmured protest. "It's not that I don't like you, admire you, but I just can't."

Can't or won't? Once again the words balanced on the tip of her tongue, but her courage deserted her when she needed it most. Besides, what did it matter?

She must remain focused on the true problem. "We'll be friends. We'll both love Cora, and that will be enough love for all of us."

"I still need to think." He rubbed his forehead. "I'm not saying no, but I need to think this through. We can't make a rash decision. There are things about me you don't know."

He said the last words so quietly, she barely registered them.

"You said it yourself," Jo urged. "People have married for worse reasons. At least you and I have good intentions. How can things go wrong if we're making a decision based on what's best for Cora?"

"Things can go wrong." He tipped back on his heels, his voice somber. "Believe me, things can always go wrong."

Jo glanced at her scuffed boots. Once again she wondered if he'd make a rash decision if she looked like Mary Louise at the mercantile. Probably so. Men made rash decisions about pretty women every day. With tomboys, they made rational, thoughtful decisions based on logic.

Jo plucked at a loose thread on her trousers. Was she willing to change? For Marshal Cain? For a man?

Never.

But what about Cora?

Jo yanked the thread loose, exposing a tear in the fabric. Even if she could change, she didn't want to. She liked the person she was—*inside and out*. Marshal Cain either accepted her the way she was or not at all. As simple as that.

"Maybe," Marshal Cain spoke, his voice hesitant. "The answer is maybe. Let's leave it there for now."

Tears threatened, and Jo hastily blinked them away. This was no time for going soft. In life, *maybe* meant *no*. "Promise me you'll think about it."

"I promise."

"Can I still take Cora to the telegraph office with me tomorrow?" she added hopefully.

"Of course. This doesn't change anything."

"Of course."

With fisted hands, Jo rubbed her eyes in tight circles. Her hasty words had changed *everything*. Yet she didn't regret them, not for an instant. "Either way, we should think about finding you and Cora a new place to live. Outlaws and tea parties make strange bedfellows."

The marshal threw back his head and laughed, a rich hearty sound that vibrated in her chest and sent her blood thrumming through her veins.

"I can't argue with you in that regard." He swiped at his eyes. "Thank you. I needed a good laugh."

Feeling brazen, Jo grinned. "Can you imagine if word reached Wichita there was a pink afghan in the jailhouse?"

"Maybe crime would go down. It's hard to be a tough guy when there's a doll in your cell."

"This could be the best thing that happened to Cimarron Springs in a long while."

Garrett stared down at her, and Jo tipped back her head. Their gazes collided and they stood frozen for a long moment.

He reached out and tucked a stray lock of hair behind her ear, his finger coasting along the sensitive skin of her neck. "I had a job in Colorado Springs before this. My deputy told me I was a fool for coming to Kansas. He was wrong. Coming here was the best decision I ever made."

"Even with all that's happening?"

"Especially now. You've been heaven-sent for Cora."

His admission awakened a sliver of hope. "I have next Monday off from work. Cora and I are picking mulberries down by the creek."

Garrett grasped her hand, caressing her blunt nails. "Come Monday afternoon, you'll have purple fingers."

"And purple lips."

His eyes widened and he made a strangled sound in his throat. "Uh, well," he muttered as he dropped her hand and stumbled back a step. "I'd best get Cora home. I don't want her out in the rain." He jerked one thumb over his shoulder. "The wagon and the rain and all."

Frowning, Jo touched her cheek as he made a hasty

retreat. Why did he run off every time she thought they were making progress?

She crossed her arms over her chest. The fool man was running hot and cold and his indecision was driving her mad. Either way, he had to make up his mind on his own. She wasn't chasing down someone who didn't want her, no matter how stupid he was for rejecting her.

Even if she wasn't pretty on the outside like Mary Louise, she was worthy on the inside.

How did she convince Garrett of that truth?

Chapter Six

Garrett plucked a stuffed bunny from his favorite chair and collapsed onto the seat. In five short days, Cora had stamped herself indelibly on the few rooms he occupied above the jailhouse. Before the little girl's arrival, he'd thought the space more than adequate. Now there simply wasn't enough room for all the fripperies that accompanied a little girl.

As he dug a pink ribbon from beneath the cushions, a soft whimper caught his attention. Garrett cocked his head and realized the gentle noise was coming from Cora's room. Worried, he heeled off his boots in a jack and crossed the distance in his stocking feet, then peered behind the partition. Cora rested on her side facing him, her rag doll clutched against her chest.

Tears streamed down her face.

A nauseating wave of sadness buckled Garrett's knees. He knelt beside Cora's bed and brushed the damp curls from her forehead. Her eyes remained closed, and Garrett realized she was crying in her sleep. Hesitant and uncertain, he murmured soothing nonsense words and gently rubbed her back until her sobs eased.

Surrounded again by silence, long-buried memories leaped into his head. He'd been strong for Deirdre after their parents had died, and he'd be strong for Cora, too. He gently tucked the blankets over Cora's thin shoulders.

Doubt chipped away at his resolve. Cora was younger, more innocent and vulnerable than Deirdre had ever been. He and his only sister had been old before their time. Their lives had been torn asunder by their father's frequent rages. A devastating back injury during the war had driven him into constant pain, and the alcohol he'd used to dull the agony turned him mean.

Garrett's father had been a physician, and his inability to heal himself had driven him mad. Garrett used to believe the whiskey bottle held madness, because with each drink, the bottle drained and the rage in his father grew.

When the alcohol had ceased working, he'd turned to laudanum. That's when the hallucinations had started. He'd see things. Hear things. He'd relive the war, shouting commands and calling for his dead comrades. His paranoia ruled the family. Then one day he'd mistaken his wife for an enemy soldier.

He'd shot her.

When he'd sobered and realized what he'd done, he couldn't live with the pain.

Garrett and Deidre had set out on their own for a short time before staying with his uncle. There had been no love lost on the siblings when they'd been thrust upon his aunt and uncle all those years ago. In desperation Garrett had fled, joining the army scouts at seventeen. He'd hoped they'd treat Deirdre more kindly without him around as a constant reminder of their father.

His sacrifice had been unnecessary—Deirdre had soon married a fine man, an architect with good standing in the community.

No matter what happened, Garrett wouldn't let Edward raise Cora. His cousin had a pinch-faced wife with a perpetual expression of sour disappointment. They also had four more children on whom they doted. Garrett might as well send Cora to an orphanage.

Fifteen years had passed and the wound still ached. And now Garrett had another soul to protect. Cora was innocent of all the tragedy in the past. She deserved better than a set of rooms above the jailhouse.

Jo's solution tugged at his conscience.

His legs stiff from the awkward position, Garrett pushed himself upright. The town had been mercifully quiet, but what would happen if he was called out late at night? What happened if a prisoner had to stay downstairs in the jail overnight or longer? A jailhouse was no place for a little girl and he couldn't count on Jo every time he needed someone to watch Cora. He was already too beholden to her already.

Not to mention his other problem. Truth be told, he liked spending time with Jo and he didn't know what to make of his new affliction. Garrett absently rubbed his chest. She deserved someone without a past. She was too honorable for her own good. She'd sacrifice herself to make Cora happy. He couldn't let her.

What did Garrett know about making a woman happy? The only thing he'd ever seen in his life had been pain. Jo needed more. She deserved what she'd had growing up—love and warmth. The only love Garrett had known was hard love, and he was a hard man for it.

He paired up Cora's discarded boots and glanced at

the farm-filthy dress hanging in the corner of the room. Mrs. McCoy hadn't lied—dirt sure had a way of finding you on the McCoy farm. When he'd arrived, even Jo had had a charming smudge on her check.

Jo.

He wasn't a fool. He recognized the signs of fear—heart pounding, palm sweating. But what was he afraid of?

He was terrified Jo was someone he could love.

The more time he spent around her the more time with her he craved. He wanted to protect her from bullies like Tom and Bert Walby. He wanted to hear her laugh. He wondered if she ever thought of him, too.

Only this morning the shaving lather had dried on his face while he pondered whether or not he looked better with a beard. He'd bought two new shirts and he didn't even really need new shirts. His old ones were fine except for a little wear around the seams. He couldn't recall when another person's opinion of him had carried such weight.

Garrett didn't know if he believed in a higher power, but he knew right then he was lost. Always before there had been a clear path in his head, a clear way out of trouble. Not anymore.

"Dear Lord," he pleaded. "Guide me. I've never asked for anything for myself, but Cora deserves better."

He'd done the right thing by Deirdre. He'd given his sister a fresh start by taking with him the reminders of their father. The reminders he carried with him every day—in his looks, in his mannerisms, in his very voice. Things he couldn't change or alter.

Since he hadn't refused Jo's proposal outright, he'd

left her a sliver of hope. His weakness didn't serve either of them.

Garrett had thought leaving Deirdre behind was the greatest sacrifice he'd ever made. Little did he know, one day he'd meet an even greater challenge. Turned out facing a difficult choice was a whole lot more agonizing than running away.

Chapter Seven

❧

The following morning, Jo crossed the distance to the jailhouse fifteen minutes before her shift at the telegraph office began. This was her favorite time of day, watching and listening as the town sputtered awake. In the distance, the steady clang of the blacksmith's hammer beat out a comforting rhythm. The mercantile owner flipped his window sign reading Open and propped up a slate board declaring the daily specials meticulously spelled out in chalk.

A harnessed set of horses stomped and snorted between the buildings. Jo scooted into the street, giving them a wide birth. The cranky old swayback mare on the left nipped if you strayed too close. As Jo passed the butcher, the mouthwatering aroma of smoking bacon filled the air. She inhaled a deep breath.

Sometimes she loathed Cimarron Springs, feeling frustrated and trapped by the hackneyed town. But at times like this, the familiar sights and sounds soothed her like an old pair of boots—battered and worn, but comfortable for having been broken in.

Jo paused and took another deep breath before facing the marshal again. When she encountered him this morning, she'd act nonchalant. They'd go on as they had before, as though nothing had changed.

Jostled along with the bustling morning activity, she nodded greetings to familiar faces. A hesitant figure standing in the alcove between the saloon and mercantile caught her attention.

"Beatrice?" Jo stepped closer, and the figure emerged from the shadows.

The auburn-haired woman lived above the saloon and danced with the cowboys for a nickel a song. She was older than Jo in years and decades older in experience. Beatrice had traveled around the country and seen things Jo couldn't even imagine. Most of the townspeople spurned the saloon workers, but Jo understood a thing or two about being different, and she always made a point of exchanging conversation when they met. She and Beatrice had even become friends over the past year.

"Jo." Beatrice's cautious gaze darted over the crowd, searching for any sign of censure. "Are we still meeting tonight?"

"Same as always. I'll work up some examples this afternoon."

Beatrice wanted a job as a telegraph operator, but feared her boss would fire her if he discovered her plan. Since she still needed her place next to the saloon, Jo met with her after dinner three days a week. Beatrice's work didn't begin until after dark, which gave them plenty of time for their informal lessons.

"I just wondered." The auburn-haired woman's gaze turned mischievous. "Since things have changed and all."

"Nothing has changed," Jo assured her. "You'll be a

full-fledged operator in no time. Why would you think something was different?"

Beatrice winked. "I heard the marshal was having dinner at the McCoy place last night."

Jo hustled Beatrice deeper into the darkened passageway. "What else did you hear?"

"I didn't hear anything. It's just that's he's all any of the girls talk about these days." The older woman patted her auburn hair. "I might just want that handsome marshal to rescue me from outlaws."

She giggled like a schoolgirl, and Jo's eyes widened.

"Beatrice. You sly thing. You've got a crush on Marshal Cain."

"I may be older than you, but my eyes work just fine." Beatrice wiggled her index finger. "If I were five years younger, that man wouldn't know what hit him."

"There are other men more handsome," Jo teased. "He's a bit rough around the edges."

"He's got honest eyes."

Jo pictured the marshal's rugged face and warmth flooded through her. He *did* have honest eyes—compassionate and earnest. She'd only known two other men with eyes like that—Jack Elder and her pa. Mr. Elder had married Elizabeth, the woman whose late husband had robbed banks. Jack was a good man and a good father. As far as she could tell, he was a good husband, too. His wife, Elizabeth, certainly adored him.

Unbidden and unwelcome, elusive longings tugged at Jo's heart again. Everything had seemed so simple a few years ago, but Marshal Cain's presence had muddied the waters. It was easy staying single when there was no one who caught her fancy.

Glancing behind her, Jo searched the street. Satisfied

no one was paying attention, she faced Beatrice once more. "I asked the marshal to marry me."

"You did not!" Beatrice's eyes widened into twin saucers. "What did he say?"

"He said maybe." Jo huffed. "That's how people say no when they don't want to hurt your feelings."

The amusement on Beatrice's face instantly faded. "Well, it's his loss. That's what I say. Did he tell you why not?"

"Not really. Just some nonsense about things in his past that I wouldn't understand."

"That doesn't seem so bad." Beatrice tugged her lower lip between her teeth and studied Jo. "Maybe we just need to butter the biscuit a little."

"What on earth are you talking about?"

"You know." Beatrice touched Jo's sensible bowler hat. "Put a little sauce on the pudding. A little gravy over the turkey. Sweeten the pot a little."

Certain her friend had lost her senses, Jo stared blankly.

Beatrice rolled her eyes. "Fix yourself up. Buy a new dress and let me cut your hair. We'll have a wedding in no time."

"No." Jo huffed with dawning understanding. "Absolutely not. He likes me the way I am or not at all. I didn't let Percy win at marbles so he'd like me better, and I'm not changing for Marshal Garrett Cain. He likes me the way I am or not at all."

"I'm not saying you need to change. Just spruce up the package a bit."

"The package is just fine the way it is." Jo tapped her foot. "Now, I'd best go. I don't want to be late."

The older woman shook her head. "Suit yourself."

"My mind is made up." Jo adjusted her hat. "Besides, he's the one who needs me. Not the other way around."

Beatrice lifted an eyebrow. "Whatever you say."

Jo kept her silence.

"Ah, don't be sore," Beatrice pleaded. "I'm just trying to help."

"I'm not sore. I'm just—" Jo heaved a sigh "—confused."

"Men will do that." Beatrice yanked Jo into a quick embrace. "And thank you. For the lessons. A lot of people wouldn't go to the trouble for someone like me."

"And that's *their* loss. I'll see you at six," Jo replied with no hard feelings. "There should even be some apple cobbler left."

Beatrice flashed a relieved grin and set off in the opposite direction.

Jo caught sight of the marshal and Cora on the boardwalk outside the sheriff's office.

The cool morning air was burning off with the rising sun. The marshal had whitewashed the front of the sheriff's office, and the building appeared too cheerful for prisoners. They'd even etched the oval front window with his name. The marshal kept an open-door policy, and the shades were always raised.

"Good morning," Jo called, her voice a touch too loud.

"Mornin'."

His gaze didn't quite meet hers. He studied the tips of his boots. "Nice weather we're having."

"Seasonal."

"Could be worse."

"Yep."

The knotted muscles in Jo's neck tightened. This wasn't going quite as smoothly as she'd hoped.

He cleared his throat and focused his attention on his niece. The marshal hovered behind Cora, and Jo's pulse trembled. His dark hair hung low over his forehead, and his coffee-colored eyes flashed with worry. "Are you sure you're gonna be all right?"

The little girl leaped up and launched herself at Jo, gripping her around the waist. "You're here!"

Jo mocked an exaggerated stumble. "Easy there."

"I guess that answers my question," the marshal declared.

Cora glanced over her shoulder. "Jo is teaching me how to be a telegram operator today."

"Tele*graph* operator," Jo corrected.

Garrett crouched and handed her a pail. "This is Cora's lunch. If you need anything, I'll be at the lawyer's office. He's got some information from Missouri."

"We'll be fine."

"And after that I'll be in my office going over some paperwork. The judge is coming through town next week."

"Okay."

"I might have lunch at the hotel. If you can't find me at my office or with the lawyer, check over at the hotel."

Jo rolled her eyes. The man was circling like a mother hen. "Relax. I'm taking her to the telegraph office, not a wolf den. Cora and I have developed our own routine. Don't forget, we've already been doing this for a couple of days."

Remorse flitted across his bold features, and once again her conscience pricked. How come she never said the right thing?

Hooking his thumbs into his belt loops, Marshal Cain glanced down the street. "I reckon you're right. This business with my cousin, Edward, has me shook up. I'd best let you two get to work."

"Don't worry, I'll keep her safe."

"I know you will."

"I promise."

"Okay, then."

The marshal tipped his hat with a murmured "Ladies," and set off.

Jo and Cora watched his receding steps before strolling along the boardwalk. So much for all her previous resolutions. She'd blown it on their very first conversation after her staunch resolution only moments before. Her feet slowed.

Cora stared at her expectantly, and Jo plastered a smile on her face. "Ready?"

"Ready!" Cora declared.

Tapping her foot, Jo paused a moment. "I give him an hour before he comes and checks on you."

Cora giggled, and together they crossed the short distance, passing the depot and the platform.

Because telegraph lines followed train tracks, Jo's office sat near the station. Upon arriving, she unlocked the door and flipped over the sign reading Open. The office was little more than a lean-to jutting from the depot. The government had provided a single desk, swivel chair, a brass lamp with a bottle-green shade and a small table. A storeroom had been portioned off along the back. If someone left a package unclaimed at the station, Jo locked it up or delivered the parcel herself when she found time.

The space was cozy, but two windows on opposite sides gave her a cross breeze in the summer. A squat, potbellied stove provided heat in the winter.

She'd put Marshal Cain out of her mind and concentrate on her job. Work was the best balm and the ultimate distraction.

Despite Jo's resolve, her thoughts wandered as she spun around on her chair and arranged her supplies. Outside, a train whistle blew.

She met Cora's frightened gaze. "That's the eight-thirty from Wichita. She's half an hour early."

As was her routine, the little girl scooted beneath the desk and stuck her fingers in her ears. The train rumbled past, rattling the windowpanes and vibrating the floorboards.

When silence descended once more, Jo ducked her head beneath the desk. "That was a coal train. Those trains are the longest, but they usually travel the fastest."

"They're loud."

"You get used to it. When I first moved to town, I woke up with the five-fifteen every morning. Now I don't even notice."

"Really?"

"Really."

Cora had arrived in Cimarron Springs ready for adventures—as long as that adventure didn't involve the teeth-jarring clatter of a passing train.

A moment later Cora emerged from her hiding place and returned to the makeshift play area Jo had set up for the little girl. There was a square of slate board and chalk, several rag dolls and a set of marbles.

An hour later, her busywork finished, Jo tipped back in her chair and considered the child. Cora drew flowers, trees and stick figures on her slate board, but never words. "You said you know your letters, didn't you?"

"Some."

Jo remembered being a child and how much she loathed being forced into learning. Perhaps if she couched the lesson in another way, Cora would show interest. "You want to see what I do?"

Cora danced on the balls of her feet. "Yes, yes, yes!"

Jo laughed. "Okay, pull your chair over here and I'll show you."

They settled side by side, and Jo dug out a sheet of paper.

The bell above the door jingled. Marshal Cain stuck his head in. "I just happened to be in the neighborhood."

Jo suppressed a grin. He'd gone a whole hour without checking on them, and it had obviously taxed him. "Of course you were."

"What are you ladies up to?"

Frowning, Jo studied his expression. That was the second time today he'd used the formal term. No one had ever referred to her as a "lady" and she wasn't sure if she was being mocked.

Then again, he'd never shown any other signs of mockery, and he'd had plenty of opportunity. Especially when she'd bluntly asked him to marry her.

Her cheeks heated at the memory.

"I was about to show Cora how Morse code works. What are you doing, other than checking up on us?"

The marshal glanced around, his gaze innocent of mischief. "Mr. Stuart at the mercantile said he's having problems with a group of boys. I have a bad feeling it's that bunch we saw the other day. One of them is Tom Walby's son. Thought they might have come this way."

Jo quirked a questioning eyebrow.

Marshal Cain set his hat back on his head and revealed an abashed grin. "Okay. I was checking on Cora.

But as long as I'm here, I might as well brush up on my skills. It's been years since I've used Morse code. I used to know my letters. Can I look at your cipher sheet?"

Not many people in town understood her work, and Jo appreciated having someone she could talk with other than Beatrice. "You're a man of many talents."

He shrugged. "It's a good tool if you're in a pinch. I've heard of men signaling each other at night."

"How do they do that?" Cora asked.

"They use a lamp."

Jo tapped her pencil. "I've heard of blasting crews sending signals down the mountain with mirrors reflecting the sunlight. Doesn't seem too efficient to me."

"I guess you learn 'take cover' pretty well."

Jo giggled. She pinched the worn and ink-stained edges and slid her alphabet cipher sheet across the table. Cora and Marshal Cain flanked her, and Jo's heart did a curious ripple. She cleared her throat and scooted her chair tighter toward the desk, then pointed at the sheet, surprised by the tremble in her finger.

She fisted her hand a few times and pointed again. "Each letter has a corresponding set of dots and dashes. You put the dots and dashes together to form letters. For example, the letter *s* is three dots." Jo quickly tapped her finger three times on the desk. "And for an *o,* it's three dashes." She tapped her finger slower.

The telegraph machine whirred, and the twitter of an incoming message filled the room. "Here comes one now."

"Yeah!" Cora leaped off her chair and dashed across the room.

Using her heels, Jo twisted her chair and scooted across the floor. She needed distance between her and

Marshal Cain. Talking with him left her as breathless as though she'd run the length of a field.

After setting out a pencil and paper, Jo acknowledged her station by typing in her call numbers. The telegraph operator on the other end of the line began transferring his message. Jo quickly jotted down the letters, transcribing a rapid-fire series of dots and dashes into words on a neat square of paper.

Cora danced around the table. "What does it say? What does it say?"

"I have a strict rule against gossip." Jo folded the paper with the words facing inside. "Luckily, I have a terrible memory. I couldn't tell you most of what came through yesterday, let alone last week."

Marshal Cain and Cora tipped their heads, their expressions twin mirrors of confusion.

"It's hard to explain... ah ..." Jo stalled. "But I try to write things down without paying much attention. It's easier that way."

After only a short time on the job, Jo had trained herself until the Morse code she translated into words bypassed the part of her brain that remembered details. If she didn't, the tales rumbled through her memory and interrupted her sleep with dots and dashes clicking in her dreams. People sometimes forgot their words were read by others, and they wrote of deeply personal tribulations. Deaths and births, marriages and broken hearts, a deluge of human emotions filtered down into an economy of words.

Marshal Cain rubbed his chin. "That's amazing. I know a little bit of Morse code, but I only translated about three of those words. You're really good. And you just do that automatically?"

"Yep. I hear the dots and dashes like they're words. I remember when the rail line came through town, listening to the Chinese workers talking together, then switching back to English with the foremen. It's like that. It's like learning a foreign language."

"Except not many people have the gumption to learn another language," the marshal said, his voice flush with admiration.

Jo's chest expanded. Most folks took her skill for granted. Certainly no one had ever once asked if learning the process had been difficult.

The marshal glanced around the sparse office. "How did you learn?"

"I left the farm a couple of years ago."

Jo twisted her lips. Her ma had wanted her to take over the midwife duties, and Jo's refusal had driven a wedge between them.

Her ma saw every birth as a marvel of life while all Jo could think about were the potential dangers. The calls they made on laboring mothers filled her ma with anticipation, but Jo felt only dread.

Moving to town had been easier than arguing. "That was around the time the Western Union office arrived. They posted an ad on the building and I applied."

Western Union had specifically requested *female* operators. The men in town had scoffed, saying they wanted women so they could pay less. The company's motivation hadn't mattered. The job was perfect for Jo. Her boss only came through town every few weeks, and the telegrams kept her busy, but not too busy. If the office walls sometimes felt confining, she volunteered for delivery duty or helped out with the ticket counter.

And the job gave her independence. She wasn't beholden on a man to take care of her. She had freedom and security, two things most women could only dream about. Her life was perfect, *wasn't it?*

Cora touched the telegraph machine. "Is it hard to learn?"

"At first." Jo grimaced at the recollections. "For a while, I was so frustrated I felt like screaming. All those dots and dashes sounded like a bunch of gobbledygook. Eventually, though, things started making sense. At first I could pick out a few words, then sentences, then everything just made sense all of a sudden. It's almost like listening to people talk now."

Marshal Cain absently picked up an envelope. "But you don't pay attention to what they say?"

"Everyone has secrets, and keeping them is a powerful responsibility. I don't dwell on the messages. It doesn't seem right, you know?"

Marshal Cain kept his gaze focused on her, his brows knit in a frown. Once again she had that same feeling he was sizing her up, gauging her answers as though he was cataloging her responses for future reference.

Had she passed the test? She couldn't tell by his expression. The longer he stared, the more self-conscious she became. As the moments ticked by, Jo itched to reach up and smooth her braid. Did she have pear blossoms in her hair again? Was he noticing the blueberry stain on her lapel? A scuffle sounded from the train platform, and she broke his gaze.

Marshal Cain straightened and peered out the window. "I sure do hate being right sometimes. It's the boys again from the other day, stirring up trouble. They're chasing something. Probably an animal. I better see to it."

He set his hat on his head and tipped the brim. "Ladies."

Jo inclined her head as he turned and strode out the door. Relieved his attention was no longer focused on her, she released her pent-up breath. She'd never actually seen him at work, and she wondered how he'd deal with the boys. You learned a lot about a person from how they handled conflict, and for some reason, she wanted to know everything she could about the marshal.

She faced Cora and planted her hands on her hips. "You want to follow him?"

With a mischievous grin, the little girl nodded.

Jo threw back her shoulders. She'd survived one conversation without sticking her boot in her mouth. She was on a roll. What could possibly go wrong now?

Chapter Eight

Marshal Cain rounded the edge of the building, and Jo and Cora angled closer until they could peer around. When he glanced over his shoulder, they scurried into the shadows, stifling nervous laughter.

The noonday sun had dried the rain from the previous days, and the streets were mud free for the first time in weeks. Cora appeared lighter, her face less shadowed with their silly antics. Seeing her happy was worth a little skulking around in the afternoon sunlight. They joined hands and followed the marshal from a safe distance.

Jo glanced up and down the deserted street, relieved there were no customers approaching. Observing the marshal sounded a lot more fun than typing out Mrs. Babcock's travel itinerary with the fewest possible letters while the frugal woman huffed and criticized Jo's every choice of word.

A crowd of boys greeted their curious stares. Jeering and jostling each other, the four young mischief makers flocked together. Two of the boys held sticks and poked at something from a jumpy distance. They kicked up dust motes with their boots, obscuring Jo's view of their target. Marshal Cain blew out a piercing whistle. The raucous horseplay ceased in a rolling wave as each boy in line caught sight of the marshal in turn and elbowed the next boy into attention.

From the corner of her eye, Jo caught one of the boys slinking along the wall, his gaze darting between the marshal and freedom. Not fooled for a minute, the marshal cleared his throat, halting the sly escape. Effectively snared, the boy innocently shrugged his shoulders and attempted another step away. The marshal crooked his finger, his expression brooking no refusal. Resigned, the boy dragged his feet into line with the others.

Adjusting his gun belt for emphasis, the marshal sauntered before the cowed group. "What's all the excitement?"

"We're not doing anything bad, sir," the youngest boy, a towheaded cherub with apple cheeks, replied.

Jo recognized the stout troublemaker as Phillip Ryan. Twin dimples appeared on those rosy cheeks as Phillip conjured up his most persuasive smile.

Jo grunted. *That figured.* His mother had practically gotten away with murder in school just by flashing her dimples and flipping her blond curls. Looked as if the apple cheeks hadn't fallen far from the tree.

Keeping hidden, Jo studied the marshal's reaction, relieved at his unbending stance. It was nice to find at least one person who wasn't fooled by a winsome smile and curly golden hair.

When the boy realized his feigned innocence and appealing grin weren't working on the marshal, his dimples retreated and an ugly scowl took their place. "It's just a snake."

The marshal's hands dropped to his sides, and he took a step back. "How big is it?"

"It's big, but we're gonna kill it good."

Jo clenched her jaw. She loathed unnecessary cruelty of any kind. Sure, she'd killed plenty of snakes, but only when necessary, and always humanely. Torturing a creature didn't sit well with her.

"It's huge," Phillip declared, his eyes wide. "And dangerous. We're doing the town a service by killin' it."

Bristling with annoyance, Jo jostled through the crowd until she reached the center.

Sure enough, a three-foot-long red, black and yellow snake lay coiled in the corner of the building. Jo glared at the boys. Hardly a giant at all. And certainly not dangerous. "There's no call for cruelty. A snake is one of God's creatures, too."

The Ryan boy scuffed the ground with his booted toe. "Not the good kind."

"I see." Jo crouched until she was eye to eye with the boy. "You can tell if something is good or bad just by looking at it?"

He shrugged.

Jo huffed as she turned her attention on the snake's brilliant red body, the color broken by bands of yellow flanked with narrow circles of black. She knelt before the terrified creature and murmured softly. Reaching out, she gently grasped the creature around the neck. The snake's tail coiled around her arm.

Jo stood and faced her stunned audience. "See. It's just scared."

Marshal Cain gaped at her, then his face paled.

Her heart thumped at his hard stare. "Did I do something wrong?"

Maybe he didn't like her interfering with his lawman's work.

"Put that down." Marshal Cain held out his hands in a defensive gesture, his voice ominously low. "That's a venomous coral snake."

Relief flooded through her veins. He wasn't mad, he was just scared. "Nah. You can't tell from where you're standing. This here is just a milk snake. It's not poisonous. Come closer and you'll see." She extended her arm.

The marshal stumbled back another step.

Jo thoughtfully angled her hand. "It kinda looks like a coral snake from a distance, but you gotta check the color bands. Like my pa taught us, red to black is a friend to Jack. Red to yellow will kill a fellow. Or you can just remember that yellow next to red will kill you dead. Both kinds of snakes live in the same places, too, which confuses most folks. Except, you know, one'll kill you and the other won't."

"'Course, it's a milk snake," the marshal spoke, his voice husky. "I couldn't see it that well from over here. I musta had some dust in my face."

He poked one finger in his eye, and Jo lifted her face heavenward. "Don't rub 'em like that. You'll only make it worse."

She searched the gathering and found Cora frozen near the edge, her face as pale as the marshal's. Jo sidled closer. "Why do you suppose fur makes everything cuter? Have you ever noticed that? Take a rat—disgusting. Add some brown fur to its body and slap on a fluffy tail. You've got yourself a cute little squirrel. People would probably keep these critters as house pets if they were furry."

Cora giggled.

"I think snakes are misunderstood," Jo continued,

her words low and soothing. "They keep mice and rats out of the grain bin. They help out with the grasshoppers, too. I'd rather have a snake in the barn than a furry raccoon anyday. And snakes are really quite beautiful if you take the time to look close."

"I think they're icky," Cora replied.

"I like the way they move. Like they're going sideways and forward at the same time."

The marshal grunted. Jo never understood why people liked pretty things even if they were useless, and shunned ugly things even if they served a valued purpose. "You want to touch him?"

Cora grimaced and clasped her palms together, twisting her hands back and forth. "Is it slimy?"

Despite her protest, Jo felt the little girl softening. "Nah. He's not slimy. He's actually pretty smooth."

As Jo crossed through the boys, the crowd stumbled out of her way, giving her a wide berth. She knelt before Cora and smiled. "It's okay. He won't hurt you."

Cora's seeking hand tentatively reached out. The snake tightened on Jo's arm and she kept her grip loose and friendly.

Cora stroked the brightly colored scales and sucked her lower lip between her teeth. As the seconds ticked away, her whisper-light touch gradually grew bolder. When the snake hissed, its tongue flicking the air, Cora yelped and jumped back.

The little girl skipped toward her uncle and tugged on his pant leg. "It's not slimy at all."

Marshal Cain patted her hair. "You sure are brave."

"And I'm dirty, too. Look at my boots! Jo says it's okay because if dirt makes flowers grow, it must make little children grow, too."

Jo grinned. Cora's hem revealed a fine layer of dust and her boots were scuffed. The prim and proper city girl was relaxing her rigid stance and learning to enjoy the country. She still had a long way to go, but she grew bolder every day.

"What about you boys?" Jo faced her rapt audience. "Would you like to touch the snake?"

Two of the boys shook their heads and took off running, their shirttails flapping in the breeze.

"Look at that, Cora." Jo chuckled. "You're tougher than a couple of boys."

The little girl puffed up. "I touched a snake and I didn't even scream or cry."

"What about the rest of you?" Jo continued. "Who's feeling brave today?"

One of the two remaining boys, Tom Walby's son, sneered. "My dad says you're a freak. You're just a stupid, ugly snake-lover!" He turned tail and dashed through alley.

Jo glared at the boy. Just like his father. When he felt threatened, he lashed out. The snake squirmed, and Jo realized she'd instinctively tightened her grip. Tom and his son were both just like the snake. Attacking when they were scared. She didn't think the Walbys would appreciate the comparison, but it was true.

"Hey!" Marshal Cain shouted after the boy.

Jo held up a restraining hand. "Don't mind him. He learned it from his pa. Tom Walby still hasn't forgiven me for making a fool of him when we were kids." She turned away and discreetly reached down her bodice, fishing out the snake's tail. "I tell you, if that man had half the fortitude for working as he does for holding grudges, his life would be a whole lot easier."

"Can't argue with that."

Marshal Cain rubbed his chin, and she noticed his gaze resting on the last remaining boy, a pale, sandy-haired six-year-old too scared to run. Again, Jo couldn't help but note the child's resemblance to his parents. Josh's dad had always gotten caught when they were growing up because he froze like a raccoon caught in a lamplight.

The marshal pulled a paper-wrapped peppermint from his pocket and knelt before the frightened boy. "You catch up with your friends and tell 'em to stay out of trouble for the rest of the day. Got it?"

The plump-cheeked boy snatched the candy, nodded and took off running.

Jo tsked. "That's the Smith boy. He's too good for hanging around with that bunch. I better have a talk with his ma." She faced Cora and gestured with her snake-wrapped arm. "You remember that. The people you run with can raise you up or bring you down. Isn't that right, Marshal?"

He gave a distracted nod. Come to think of it, seemed as if he hadn't looked at her direct since she picked up the snake.

Jo scratched her ear with her free hand. "You still look a little pale, Marshal. You okay?"

"Fine." He shook his head as though clearing his thoughts. "I better get back. To, uh. To work."

The marshal pivoted on one heel and strode away.

Jo tapped her boot, pondering his uncharacteristic behavior. The snake's tail wriggled up her sleeve and she considered another explanation for his abrupt departure. Could the marshal be afraid of snakes? When her pa found a snake in the feed bin, he'd fetch the barn cat and let nature take its course. For some reason, she found a lot of men were afraid of snakes.

Jo released the snake and watched it slither off, then stuck out her hand for Cora. "Are you ready to get back to work?"

"Yep."

"Jo," Cora began, her voice hesitant. "Are you afraid of anything?"

"Well, let's see. I used to think I was afraid of always staying the same, but now I'm not so certain."

A woman's life was fixed as train tracks. First stop marriage, second stop babies. Jo had jumped the tracks when she'd taken the position at the telegraph office. For a while the job had kept her distracted, and her restless spirit had bloomed with the challenge.

But lately things had gone stagnant.

Cora wrapped a blond curl around her finger. "I'm not afraid of snakes anymore. But I think Uncle Garrett is still afraid."

Jo glanced down the street and groaned. So much for all her good intentions. In a few short days Garrett had discovered how she'd socked Tom Walby in the eye and now he'd seen her with a snake wrapped around her arm.

No wonder he didn't see her as marriage material.

Jo sighed. "The trouble with change is figuring out which path is the correct path."

She glanced at the dusty, rickrack tracks the snake had left in the dust.

Even if there'd been a slim chance of the marshal seeing her as good material for a wife and mother, she'd gone and blown it.

Chapter Nine

That evening Garrett dreamed he and his sister, Deirdre, were children again. They were living in Illinois, and he and Deirdre were sitting on the back of their pa's wagon, their legs swinging as they bumped along the deep rivets in the muddy road. Deirdre held her stuffed bunny over the street, then yanked it back against her chest. They played the game and giggled while their parents argued. Garrett sensed the tension even though neither of them raised their voices.

As the trip lengthened, and their mother's voice grew shrill, the game became more manic. Garrett snatched the bunny and held it over the road, pretending to drop it. Deirdre squealed in delight. Emboldened by her response, Garrett repeated the teasing bluff, only this time the wagon hit a deep rut and the heavy jolt knocked him sideways. He grasped the sideboard and steadied himself.

"My bunny!" Deirdre shouted.

Garrett glanced down in horror. One floppy ear and a single paw showed stark white against the boggy street.

"Stop!" he'd called. "We have to go back."

There was still time. If they stopped, Ma could clean up the bunny and make it new again.

His father whipped around, a black look twisting his face. "Serves you right. Maybe now you'll give me some peace and quiet."

Garrett caught Deirdre's stricken gaze. Her eyes welled with tears and she stuck her thumb in her mouth.

"Don't be a bab—" He stopped the words.

She was ten years old and too big for such a childish activity, but he sensed it made her feel better. He couldn't scold her.

He reached out a hand, and she pulled away. His heartbeat turned uneven and his blood grew thick like slow-moving molasses. He hadn't meant to lose her toy, it had been an accident—a bit of tomfoolery gone wrong. They'd both lost something that day, something they could never regain. *He'd lost her trust.*

"I'm sorry."

"It's not your fault," she'd replied solemnly.

But she blamed him, he knew she did. He saw the betrayal in her sorrowful eyes.

"I'm sorry," he called again, but the moment was lost in time. "I'm sorry."

Garrett shot upright in bed, his body soaked in sweat. Disoriented, he glanced around the room. A fierce pounding from the second-floor door had awakened him. Fearful of disturbing Cora, he shot out of bed, quickly tossing on a shirt as he padded barefoot across the room.

Without breaking stride, he snagged his holster from its hiding place atop the wardrobe and strapped his gun around one thigh, then angled himself near the exit. Keeping his body protected from the flimsy door, he yanked out his pistol and cocked the next round into the chamber. "Who is it?"

"It's me. JoBeth McCoy."

Sensing the urgency in her voice, Garrett quickly holstered his weapon. The stubborn dead bolt caught. After a sharp twist to the left, he forced open the lock. "What's wrong?"

Backlit by the moonlight, she huddled on the top stair, the alley a dark shadow below. A gust of wind sent tendrils of her hair sweeping across her forehead. She impatiently shoved it aside. "Trouble at the saloon."

"What kind of trouble?"

"I don't know. But it's keeping us awake at the boardinghouse."

Garrett waved her inside, hastily fastened his shirt and took a surreptitious look at Jo. She'd obviously dressed in haste, the buttons on her shirtwaist were mismatched with the third button skipped altogether. Her hair hung in one thick braid down her back as usual, but it was tousled and loose. Her eyes drooped, still heavy with sleep, and she flashed him a wan half smile.

His protective instincts roared to life. He wanted to wrap her in a blanket and keep her safe. Garrett steeled his focus.

He had other priorities right then. "Can you stay with Cora? I'll take a gander. Probably just the boys tying one on."

"I'll wait."

"The railroad workers got their paychecks today and they're spending it at the saloon. This shouldn't take long."

She hovered near the door while he donned his socks and boots, then snatched his hat. Drawn by something he didn't understand, he cast a last reassuring look over his shoulder before stepping outside. Once the cool evening air hit his face, he paused. He was still off kilter from his dream, his thoughts scattered back through the years. Cora's arrival had shaken his peaceful existence. He'd locked away Deirdre's memory, but Cora was too much like her mother. She wouldn't let him forget.

Garrett loped down the stairs. He'd been marking time in his life, keeping the past at bay, but he no longer had that luxury.

A shot rang out, halting his wayward thoughts.

Even a drunk could get off a lucky round, and he needed his mind clear.

Seconds later he crept along the boardwalk, his hearing focused on the raucous sounds. As he reached the double bat-wing doors, a drunken cowboy with a bedraggled beard stumbled outside and collapsed into a heap on the street.

Garrett knelt down and felt the man's neck, relieved at the strong pulse. Judging from the noxious whiskey fumes, Garrett assumed he'd passed out. The drunken man would keep until order was restored.

Drawing his gun, Garrett edged along the side of the building, when another shot rang out. He straightened his back and burst into the room. A deafening melee greeted his arrival.

At least two dozen men had paired up in fisticuffs throughout the room. Fists flew and splattered drinks covered the floor in a slick mess. Two of the enormous round tables had been tipped on their sides, scattering playing cards and betting chips over the sawdust-strewn floor.

An industrious cowboy scooted on his hands and

knees between the overturned tables and scooped up discarded coins, shoving them into his bulging pockets. Garrett blew out a shrill whistle. Several startled heads turned in his direction.

"That's enough. Everybody outside."

A groan erupted from several of the fighting pairs as they realized the brawl was over. From the corner of his eye, Garrett caught a man cocking back his arm over another gambler.

Garrett spun around and pointed his gun. "I said, that's enough."

The aggressor dropped his arm with a grumble. Garrett plucked a cowboy from the floor and tossed him out the bat-wing doors. His arrival had dampened the crowd's enthusiasm, and he felt the mood of the room calm. The weary railroad workers reluctantly dispersed. He stalked between the tables, yanking people upright and setting them on chairs. A group of painted ladies huddled near the piano, their wilted feathers a sad sight against their elaborately coiffed hair.

Garrett didn't feel any censure toward the women, only sorrow. The West was hard, especially on women and children. "Why don't you ladies wait next door."

The neighboring space was taken with the rooms. This half, the part Tom liked to shoot at, featured a cavernous room with a crude two-story stage at the east end.

One of the women, a buxom brunette with rouged lips, stuck out a hip and giggled. "You're in the wrong place for ladies, Marshal."

"I'll be the judge of that." He felt his ears heat up beneath her amused regard. "I can't get my job done if I'm worrying about you."

"Well, ain't he just the cutest thing," one of them trilled.

With a bawdy look she sauntered away.

As they retreated through the side door, Garrett pivoted on one heel, surprised to find David McCoy stalking toward him.

Garrett crunched over broken glass toward the McCoy boy. "Did you see who started all this?"

"Mr. Stuart and Mr. Hodges were fighting about the new store."

"That figures."

Garrett wasn't surprised the two men had been arguing. Mr. Stuart had been running the only mercantile in town for over a decade until Mr. Hodges had arrived from St. Louis and bought up a storefront right across the street. Garrett figured the town had grown large enough for two thriving stores, but Mr. Stuart saw money slipping between his fingers.

David glanced around the demolished room. "A couple of cowboys took advantage of the commotion and that's when the bullets started flying."

"Where'd they go?"

The third-oldest McCoy was tall and dark-haired like his brothers, probably going on eighteen or nineteen, twenty at most.

David scanned the room. "Don't know."

Garrett adjusted his hat. He sometimes deputized the mercantile owner, Mr. Stuart, when he needed extra help. But since his occasional deputy had been knee deep in the brawl, he'd lost his backup.

Garrett studied David's sheepish expression. "We'll talk about what you're doing here later."

An uneasy silence descended around them. The

room had mostly cleared upon his arrival, though one or two men remained, too drunk to flee. An overturned glass of beer dripped steadily onto a scattering of playing cards like sour rain. The mingled odors of alcohol and cigar smoke turned Garrett's stomach. He picked his way through the glass and approached the auburn-haired woman hovering near the door. She looked as if she wanted to say something, and he never turned away a witness.

Tipping his hat, Garrett offered a friendly greeting. "You're Beatrice, right? Did you see the men who started this? Or the shooter?"

"Probably Tom." She shook her head and the drooping purple feather in her hair fluttered. "The whole place went mad at once. There was a new group this evening. They came in from Wichita earlier in the day."

"How many?"

"Four, maybe five. I didn't pay much attention. They didn't seem interested in dancing."

A tingle of apprehension darted along Garrett's spine. "You notice anything else unusual?"

"I noticed one of the McCoy boys in here. That's unusual. He better hope his pa never finds out. Or his sister, for that matter."

Garrett flashed a wry grin. "I'll take care of David."

The woman winked at him and he started, then fixed his attention on the sawdust-strewn floor. He sure was getting winked at a lot these days. "Thank you, Miss Beatrice. You think of anything else, let me know."

"Oh, I'll let you know," she murmured suggestively.

"Don't you get sassy on me, Miss Beatrice."

"You're real cute when you blush." She twisted her waist from side to side, sending her fringed skirt fluttering. "She's cute, too, your niece." Beatrice fiddled with an auburn corkscrew curl resting on her shoulder. "Tell you what, because you called us ladies, I'll help you keep an eye on that David McCoy. I didn't see him drink or gamble, and he wasn't hanging around the girls. He seemed more interested in Mr. Stuart than anything else. Except Mr. Stuart was busy fighting with Mr. Hodges. Besides…"

She studied her tapered fingernails. "I owe JoBeth." Beatrice met his curious gaze. "She's been teaching me Morse code. I'm getting a job in Denver as a telegraph operator. A real job. Not dancing with cowboys for nickels."

"That's a fine goal," Garrett replied.

Another mark in Jo's favor. He'd been raised around people who wouldn't lift a finger for someone below their class, and that had never sat well with him. Seemed like the Bible was pretty clear on ministering to the poor as well as the poor in spirit.

Garrett touched his forehead in a brief salute. "When you and Jo finish your studies, you let me know if you need a reference."

This time Beatrice blushed, making her appear younger, almost girlish. "You're too soft for a marshal."

"And you're too smart for this place."

With that parting comment, Garrett turned. Behind him, the steady clip-clip of heels echoed through the open building as Beatrice walked through the adjoining door.

Garrett sighted David stationed near the door and motioned him over. "Let's straighten up."

Together with Schmitty the bartender, they set about clearing the room. Garrett righted a chair and reached for an overturned table. A pair of boots caught his attention. Another casualty of the brawl, no doubt.

Garrett nudged one of the boots. "Wake up, mister. Time to take it home."

The body remained ominously still. Garrett heaved the table upright, revealing Mr. Hodges. His blank eyes stared at the ceiling, glassy and unmoving. A darkening patch of red covered his white shirt and bled into his faded gray coat. Garrett flipped him onto one side, already knowing what he'd find. A bullet had passed clean through the man's body.

The bartender, a diminutive man with unnaturally dark, slicked-back hair, leaned over Garrett's shoulder. "He's dead. Someone musta shot him."

"I figured that much, Schmitty."

To Garrett's frustration, all of his witnesses had scattered. He'd recognized most of the faces, but there were still the cowboys passing through town he didn't know—the kind of men accustomed to the previous sheriff's corruption. Garrett pinched the bridge of his nose. Despite the lawless atmosphere of the town, there hadn't been a murder in Cimarron Springs for years.

"David." Garrett caught the younger man's stunned expression. "Let the doc know we've got a casualty here."

His Adam's apple working, David jerked his head in a nod and turned away from the gruesome sight. Garrett ticked off another point in the young man's favor. Though shaken, he hadn't shirked from his duties. Cimarron Springs might have a new deputy soon.

Garrett had a feeling he was going to need all the help he could get. He drummed his fingers on his bent knee. By morning, everyone in town would assume Mr.

Stuart had shot Mr. Hodges over the new mercantile store. And for all Garrett knew, he might have.

Money and business had a way of forcing men into desperate measures. Yet Mr. Stuart struck him as the sort of man who was all talk and no action. The mercantile owner rarely ventured from his uneasy vigil behind the counter, and he doted on his daughter. Garrett couldn't see him risking a lynching.

Hushed whispers fell around him and he could almost feel the budding rumors flying through the air. If Mr. Stuart was innocent he'd have an uphill battle saving his reputation. Trying to squash gossip was like trying to put out a brushfire with a cup of tea.

The saloon doors slammed open and David burst into the room. "Come quick, Marshal. The jailhouse is on fire!"

Chapter Ten

Jo settled her head against the back of the chair and lazily fanned herself with a paper. The space atop the jailhouse was long, narrow and airless. A bedroom had been cordoned off by a tall screen, but the only windows were in the kitchen area, where the hazy panes faced the darkened alley. After attempting to pry them open, Jo had discovered they were painted shut. Not that it mattered much since the front of the building was boarded over with a false facade, effectively blocking any chance of a crosswind.

An industrious tenant had cut holes into the floor and fitted the openings with iron grates to vent air from the first level. That meager improvement barely stirred a stale breeze. Jo figured the place must heat up something fierce in the summertime.

She unbuttoned her cuffs and rolled back her sleeves. A faint hint of Garrett's masculine scent lingered in the seat cushions and teased her senses. Cora remained asleep, wrapped in a pink blanket, her rag doll clutched against her chest. The heat lulled Jo, and she let her eyes drift shut.

Glass shattered and Jo bolted upright from her half slumber. The sound had come from the first floor. She wobbled to her feet and glanced around. Two sets of stairs accessed the upper level, an outside set descending into the alley, and the inside set, which spilled into the open space below. She took a few steps and paused. Probably it was nothing, she might have dreamed up the whole thing, but she'd best check anyway.

As Jo descended the stairs, her raspy breathing stirred the eerily quiet building.

Growing uneasy at the unnatural quiet, she sidled nearer the wall. "Marshal Cain? Garrett?"

She cautiously made her way through Garrett's office, her eyes gradually adjusted to the dim light. Glass crunched beneath her feet and she realized one of the panes from the large double-hung windows had been shattered.

Lifting a shard, she angled the glass toward the light. Letters from the marshal's etched name remained partially visible. All that meticulous work, wasted. Kneeling down, she closed her fingers around a weighty brick. Voices called to each other from the street. She crouched and scooted forward until her fingers gripped the sill. When another moment passed without incident, she raised up on her knees and peered through the jagged hole created from the shattered glass.

Four riders galloped by, whooping and hollering. Jo groaned. Looked as if the marshal hadn't succeeded in busting up the fight. It also looked as if neither of them would get a wink of sleep tonight. She stifled a yawn. If those drunken cowboys kept this up much longer, she'd pay for her late evening during her double shift at the telegraph office the following day.

Glass burst above her head. Jarred from her sleepy contemplations, Jo dropped back into a crouch. Pointed shards rained overhead. A piercing sting slashed across her cheek. She threw one arm over her eyes and ducked her head. She cowered in a ball as a warm stream of blood slid beneath her chin.

Light arced through the window at her right. A bottle with a flaming rag stuffed in the neck hit the floor and clumsily rolled along the ridges in the rag rug. Her breath strangled in her throat.

They were lighting the jail on fire. Spurred by a fierce urgency, Jo crawled along the floor toward the flame, wincing as pain seared her palm. Before her horrified gaze, the rag-stuffed bottle ignited the braided rug. She snatched the trailing edge of a pink blanket draped over a chair and beat at the flames. Heat singed her face. The blaze chewed up the fire at an alarming rate. With growing alarm Jo realized her efforts were fruitless against the dry kindling.

Dismayed by the rapidly growing cloud of smoke, she stood and backed her way toward the stairs. Keeping her arms splayed for balance, her eyes on the merciless inferno, she stumbled over broken debris. The pungent scent of whiskey and smoke filled her nostrils. Before she reached the first riser, flickering embers were already lapping against the sheriff's desk.

From the second floor, Cora screamed. Wrenching her transfixed gaze from the growing fire, Jo dashed up the stairs and shoved the partition aside. The little girl sat up in the center of the bed, her hair in beribboned pigtails, her rag doll clutched against her eyelet night rail. Jo scooped her into her arms. The little girl wrapped her legs around Jo's waist and clung to her neck.

"What's happening?" Cora sobbed into her shoulder. "Where is Uncle Garrett?"

"He isn't here. There's a fire downstairs." Jo skirted through the hazy room. "We'll take the back stairs. He'll probably be waiting for us in the alley."

Jo wrapped her fingers around the knob and turned. The latch held firm. She twisted the lock. The brass knob refused to budge. Her arms full, she reared back and kicked. The frame opened an inch then smacked against the stubborn dead bolt. She stumbled back, braced herself and kicked at the base again. Searing pain shot up her leg and into her hip, but the door didn't budged.

After setting down Cora, Jo twisted the knob. As pungent fumes stung her nostrils and sent her eyes watering, her stomach clenched.

Cora hovered beside her, worrying her lower lip between her teeth. "Why won't the door open?"

"It's stuck." Jo gave the little girl a comforting squeeze. "We're going to have an adventure. How does that sound?"

Voices shouted in the distance. The townspeople had discovered the fire. With no windows facing the street and their exit blocked by flames, there was little chance of attracting attention. Jo chewed a thumbnail and glanced around. Would anyone think to circle around back and check on them? Only Marshal Cain knew they were up here and he had his hands full in the saloon.

Certainly he'd hear the commotion and check on them. Then again, what if they waited and no one came?

Jo glanced at the terrified little girl and realized she couldn't risk Cora's safety.

She gently set Cora away from her and met her fearful gaze. "Don't worry, everything will be fine. I think we can get out the back door if we go downstairs. That's where the fire started, but it's mostly in the front. We'll get some fresh air first and hold our breaths for as long as we can."

She gave the frightened girl an encouraging smile. "It might get dark, but we'll stay low, below the smoke and everything will be fine."

"Okay," Cora replied, a tremble in her small voice.

"You're braver than all those boys, remember?"

"I remember."

Relieved she'd donned her trousers before fetching Marshal Cain, Jo slipped out of her skirts.

More muffled shouts and calls sounded outside and she hoped the local townsfolk were setting up a bucket brigade. If the building next door caught fire, the whole town would follow.

How long would it take before the marshal realized they were still trapped inside?

What if he was injured?

Sickening dread pounded in her head. She and Cora would have to assume they were on their own for now.

Centering her thoughts, Jo sucked in a deep breath. "Remember, I won't let go of you."

"Promise?"

"Promise."

With no time to waste, Jo crawled along the floor and felt for the legs of the washbasin. She grasped a dangling rag and wetted it in the bowl, then held it over her face. Encouraged by the improvement in the quality of the air, she snagged a second rag. There'd been a fire on the Elder farm years ago, and she'd seen Jack Elder block the smoke the same way.

She held out her rag for Cora. "Hold that over your nose and mouth and it will help keep the smoke out."

Tears pooled in the little girl's cornflower-blue eyes. "Are we going to die like my mommy and daddy?"

"We'll be fine," Jo lied, a cold knot of dread in her stomach.

She considered shouting for help again, but her throat was sore from smoke and her previous calls. With the crackle of the fire and the commotion out front, no one would hear her anyway.

"I'll keep you safe. I gave you my word and I never break a promise."

Jo clutched the back of Cora's head and pressed her face against her shoulder. They made it down half the flight before billowing smoke blackened the way. The suffocating cloud quickly enveloped them, and Jo worried they'd be hopelessly lost in moments if they moved forward. Her eyes and nose watered profusely, blurring the risers into a hazy obstacle.

Cora gasped and coughed, keeping a death grip on Jo's hand. "I can't breathe."

The racket of splitting wood sounded from outside as the bucket brigade worked to douse the flames. How could help be so close, yet so far away? If Jo couldn't even make it down the stairs, there was little chance of navigating the jail to reach the alley. While she knew the layout of the marshal's office, she'd never been in the lockup.

If only she *had* been a cattle thief, Jo thought wryly.

By the time she reached the last step, her lungs

burned and her eyes watered. Smoke frothed near the ceiling, forcing her to kneel and feel her way along the wall. The flames had definitely abated, but the embers burned like black tar. Time slowed as she coughed and sputtered. Heat stung her cheeks and lapped at her heels.

With renewed purpose, Jo kept low. Freeing one arm, she inched along and felt...a sturdy chair leg. She pried open her eyes and saw nothing but gray smoke. Somehow, she'd gotten them turned around.

Panic welled in her throat and she reached out a hand, searching for anything familiar. Only a few feet separated her from help—a few feet and a wall of smoke and flames.

"Help!" she called fruitlessly.

She reached out her fingers and collided with a wall of hard muscle. A strong hand looped under her arm. Desperate for an escape, Jo clutched the lifeline, then recalled the drunken cowboys who'd started this whole mess. "Who's there?"

"It's me, Marshal Cain," a husky voice reassured her.

He plucked Cora from her weak arms and Jo sagged against his side. For a moment she gave up on being strong and let someone else guide her.

He wrapped his arm around her waist and half dragged, half carried her toward safety. "Stay low and I'll lead you out."

She stilled, instinctively responding to the gentle command in his voice. Her head swam, and she couldn't get enough air into her lungs. She felt as if she was suffocating, drowning in a black sea of smoke. Her legs gave way and she was floating. Heat crushed against her.

Wood splintered and suddenly cool air swept over

her cheeks. She coughed and sputtered, her lungs burning. Tears streamed down her face, and her stomach lurched.

In stark contrast to the empty alley behind the building, Main Street bustled with activity. Three separate bucket brigades had formed—two lines protecting the buildings on either side of the jailhouse, and one, the largest, concentrating on the main fire.

Voices shouted and horses scuffled along the street as more people responded to the urgent clang of the church bell. Unsteady and desperate for oxygen, Jo paused in wonder.

Her thoughts cleared a notch and she frantically searched the growing crowd. "Cora?" she shouted over the din.

Garrett had been holding her and now his arms were empty.

"She's fine. You blacked out for a minute. The doc's checking her over. You're both fine."

"Here's water for her," a voice spoke.

A cup was pressed against her lips, and Jo greedily sucked down the soothing liquid.

"Not too fast," Marshal Cain cautioned. "Cora is fine, but you seem to have taken the worst of the smoke."

Her stomach churned, and she weakly shoved the water aside. "Enough," she croaked, her throat raw. Despite all the commotion surrounding her, she needed the marshal's attention. "I couldn't open the door."

Garrett muttered something beneath his breath. "It's the lock. It sticks sometimes. You twist it to the left. I never thought to tell you..."

"I'm sorry. I panicked."

"There's nothing to be sorry about. We'll talk about

this later," Garrett replied, his voice soothing. "Did you see what started the fire?"

"Someone tossed a full whiskey bottle with a lit rag stuffed in the neck through the window."

"Who?" he asked sharply.

"I don't know. Some cowboys. They lobbed a brick first. I went downstairs to check on the noise."

"You should have stayed safe," he chastised, though his kind eyes blunted the rebuke.

The dirt-packed street waved like a mirage on a sultry summer day. Jo didn't know if it was the heat from the fire or her swimming head. "There were men and horses. Three of them. They ran down the street shouting and calling, then one of them threw the bottle."

"Three you say?"

The world kicked and bucked and Jo swallowed hard. "I think so. Maybe four. I don't remember."

Regret flickered in his gaze. "I shouldn't have left you alone."

"What else could you have done?" Jo questioned quietly.

He wearily rubbed his face. "I should have been there for you two."

"Don't blame yourself. It could have been anybody..." Her voice trailed off. Her thoughts scattered and her tongue grew thick and uncooperative.

She stared at the night sky, her gaze focused on the jagged edge of the half moon.

A gentle hand brushed the hair from her forehead. "Close your eyes. We can talk later. After you've rested."

"No." Jo struggled, unable to sit upright. "We should help."

The bucket brigade kept a steady stream of water traveling from the well, and the smoke had abated. The two lines keeping watch over the building on either side had broken apart and people milled around.

The mood of the crowd shifted, and Jo's ears buzzed. The townsfolk stared at her and the marshal. Hands cupped ears and Jo felt as if she was watching a game of secrets on the playground. One person whispering a phrase to another until the words ended up jumbled and unrecognizable from misquotes. A loud whisper caught her attention. *He pulled her and Cora from the jailhouse. Saw him rush in with my own eyes, then not a minute later, out they came.*

Jo moaned and clutched her head. What must people be thinking? What speculation was running rampant in the crowd? Tight knots of townspeople formed as the work of putting out the fire lessened. How in the name of little green apples was she going to talk her way out of this one? When her pa found out she'd been caught in the jailhouse after midnight, there'd be a reckoning. She might not live at home, but she was still a McCoy.

And her brothers.

"Jo—" Marshal Cain began.

He'd caught the crowd's droning. She could see it in his resigned gaze.

She held her hand over his mouth and silenced his denial. "I know what you're going to say, but you don't have to." The last thing she wanted was his sympathy. "We can explain this. I'll say I saw the fire and went in to help with Cora."

"Sure."

He didn't protest further, but she saw the emotions

flashing in his eyes. By dawn, everyone in town would know she'd been in Marshal Cain's rooms.

Alone.

After midnight.

Her presence put the marshal in an impossible situation. If word got out that he'd left his niece alone, and Cora had nearly died in a fire, he'd be vilified. If he admitted Jo had been there, her reputation was ruined.

She'd fight her own battles, but she couldn't let the marshal take the blame for something over which he had no control. He'd do the honorable thing, she had no doubt of that. Too bad she already knew how he felt about marriage to her.

"Don't worry about the talk," she spoke over her tender throat, wishing the night would end soon. "No one sees me as a girl anyway," she added. "What they say won't matter."

He glanced around the crowded street. "I don't count myself a prideful man, but I do have my honor."

Her gut twisted. She feared he'd say that.

Then again, what did it matter about his reputation? If she refused his impending offer of marriage, the censure would remain with her. People were hypocritical that way. According to society, succumbing to temptation was a man's prerogative and a woman's shame.

For the first time in a very long time, she was stumped. Was Marshal Cain better off if they married, or better off if she spurned his proposal? If only her thoughts weren't as thick as day-old gravy.

He'd lost so much. Jo had her whole family. Marshal Cain was a solitary man who'd suffered more than his fair share of tragedy. All he had left was little Cora, his pride and the respect of his community. Garrett was too honorable for his own good, even though she admired him for his chivalrous ways.

"They'll blame me, not you." She grasped for an argument even as her strength sapped away. "You can go on as though nothing happened."

"Do I have any say in the matter?" he asked gently.

Jo knew where this was leading, and she desperately needed more time. "We don't have to make any decisions tonight."

"Not tonight, no," he replied, his voice low and his face turned away from the curious bystanders. "But morning will come soon, and if I'm not mistaken, so will your pa."

Jo's head throbbed. Her pa wasn't likely to listen to reason. "I'm a grown woman."

"Trust me, you'll always be his little girl."

Confusion swirled in her brain. She had asked him to marry her for practical reasons, and he'd balked. Now they were stuck in an absurd misunderstanding and she didn't trust her own motivations. Her pride still smarted from his rejection, and she couldn't let him see her weakness.

She'd give him an opening and gauge his reaction. If he wanted the marriage, she'd know by his answers. "I'm a strong woman, Garrett Cain, stronger than words and gossip."

She wanted to say more, had more reasons and arguments, but her stomach pitched. The events of the evening were catching up with her stamina, and she desperately wanted to close her eyes and rest.

They stared at each other for a long moment, cocooned in their own world. The townspeople bustled around them. She remained detached from the commotion. Their voices faded, as though she had cotton in her ears. Jo studied his somber expression, searching for answers.

"Believe me," she continued, keeping her voice as bright as her chafed throat permitted. "People's memories are short. They'll forget about tonight soon enough. We'll act as though nothing happened and eventually there'll be something else fit for gossip."

"I won't forget." Garrett jerked his chin over one shoulder. "And I will face your pa an honorable man."

"I hope he doesn't bring any of my brothers," she joked weakly.

They both smiled, though neither mustered a laugh. Even the slightest movement jarred her aching head, sending jolts of pain exploding through her skull.

Marshal Cain doffed and his hat and stared at her, his expression intense. "We suit each other. Circumstances have brought us together, and I think we could get along fine. You said it yourself—we both love Cora."

Weakly lifting her arm, Jo placed two fingers over his lips. If only she weren't so sluggish, she'd argue him out of his hasty decision. "Think about what you're doing."

He clasped her fingers and cradled her hand in his own against his chest. "JoBeth McCoy, will you marry me?"

She took a breath, and her vision blurred. Offering up a quick prayer for a reprieve, she worked her throat. She just had to hold on for another few seconds. "Maybe."

Chapter Eleven

"Ouch." Jo yanked her hand away and shook her wrist.

Garrett tossed her a withering stare. "I have to change the dressing or this will get infected. Now stop fussing or you'll wake Cora."

They sat across from each other in the cozy boardinghouse parlor. Jo's mother, Edith, was upstairs sitting with Cora, and the sounds of breakfast clattered from the kitchen. They weren't quite alone but at least they had a modicum of privacy.

"I'm not fussing," Jo said, dutifully lowering her voice. "Where's the doc, anyway?"

"Busy." Garrett cradled her palm in his hands. "Now sit still."

Exhausted and grumpy, Jo slouched in her chair. Garrett bent over her hand, and she stared at the top of his head. An unexpected urge to run her fingers through his shiny hair gripped her, and she bolted upright. The color reminded her of a buttery-soft bolt of brown corduroy she'd seen in the mercantile.

"Sit still," Garrett gently scolded. "Or this will hurt even more."

Their gazes tangled, and Jo offered a hesitant nod.

He ducked his head. "Don't make me feel any worse than I already do."

"It wasn't your fault."

"I knew about the lock. I should have said something."

A pall fell over his expression, and her chest ached in sympathy. Today his hair curled around his ears, and she realized he needed a haircut. The stubble covering his chin had darkened from the previous evening and there were shadows beneath his eyes. He needed a shave.

He'd also take the blame for her injuries no matter what she said.

Jo stifled a grimace as he ministered to her hand. "Did you sleep at all last night?"

"Some."

His gaze flicked away.

"You're lying."

"Don't distract me," he ordered gruffly.

"If I sit still, will you have a rest this afternoon?"

"I'm an adult. I don't take naps."

Jo rolled her eyes.

Garrett cleared his throat. "You never answered my question."

"Which question?" She teased, knowing full well what he meant.

"Jo," he said in a tone indicating his patience was thin.

"Maybe nobody noticed me last night." She avoided answering directly. She wasn't sure which answer he'd prefer.

Her comment earned a dry chuckle. "Even you don't believe that."

"The answer is yes," Jo whispered.

His shoulder sagged and if Jo didn't know better, she'd say he was relieved. She reached out and tentatively touched the scar along his eyebrow.

She'd buy them some time and think of a way out later. "How did you get this?"

He touched his forehead, and their fingers brushed together. Something fierce and insistent vibrated in the air between them. Mesmerized by his coffee-colored eyes, the painful throbbing in her hand faded.

Garrett captured her wrist and turned her hand palm up. "That scar is from the time I fought a grizzly with nothing but a peashooter and my wits."

"You did not." Jo laughed. He peeled off the last layer of bandage and she squealed. "That hurt!"

"And now it's over."

He had secrets. Those secrets had carved lines of worry into his weathered face. "Tell me the real way you got that scar."

A cynical smile twisted his lips. "I got it because I was too young and too stupid to know better."

"I won't let you bandage this until you tell me the truth." Jo fisted her hand. "And I'm very stubborn."

"That's one of my favorite things about you."

He stared into the distance, as though gathering himself. A chill raised the hair on the nape of her neck.

She'd gone and done it again. Hammered him with the blunt end of her curiosity.

Before she could retract her demand, he spoke. "My parents died and there wasn't much money left after we paid off the mortgages he'd taken against the house. He was a physician, a decorated veteran of the War Between the States."

Garrett paused, collecting himself. "I found work on the docks. They always needed strong backs to unload cargo and they didn't care how old you were. One day I was hooking up a shipping crate and the chain snapped. It barely grazed me. Still split my face clean open."

Using her free hand, Jo rubbed the pad of her thumb over the scar. "That must have hurt."

"Like the dickens." He held still beneath her ministrations. "The foreman stitched me up right on the dock and I went back to work."

"I'm sorry," she said.

Garrett blinked. "For what?"

"All of my life I've had family around. If the boys at school teased me, my brothers rallied around. If I got hurt, my ma held my hand." Jo paused, fighting a rush of emotion. "I'm sorry you didn't have someone to take care of you."

His expression faltered for a moment before his easy grin returned. "I don't need taking care of. And we had some family. My uncle took us in after that. Deirdre stayed on after I went West."

"That's all?"

"That's all."

He'd effectively closed the subject, but she'd seen a glimpse of the real man and she hungered for more. "What were your parents like?"

"Just parents."

He lifted a shoulder and drew in a deep breath. She sensed he was gathering his courage, as though he wanted to say more. She let the silence stretch out, waiting. After a moment, her patience won out.

Garrett exhaled. "I look at Tom's boy and I hurt for

him. I wish Tom knew how hard it was on his boy with all that arguing in the house."

Jo might not be as intuitive as her ma, but even she realized he'd revealed something very personal about himself.

Her throat burned. "Tom's parents were the same way when he was growing up. That's all he knows." Jo winced as Garrett rubbed salve onto her cut. "Why do you suppose some people change and others don't?"

"Maybe they don't change. Maybe they just cover up who they really are."

"You don't think people can overcome their faults?"

"Doesn't seem likely."

Jo considered all the people in her life. How many bad habits were passed down from generation to generation without pause? Did she really know anyone who'd changed for good? She couldn't think of a single soul, yet she desperately wanted an example for Garrett.

She sensed the gravity of his statement, and the weight of her next words. "People can change if they want to. I think that's the difference. Tom doesn't see anything wrong with what he's doing, which means he's not likely to do anything different."

"Name one person you know who actually succeeded in changing."

Jo searched her memory and snapped her fingers. "Jack Elder."

"That the fellow who married the widow?"

"Yep. Jack changed. He didn't want a family, he didn't want to settle down. But once he met Elizabeth and her baby, he changed. He fell in love."

She expected Garrett to laugh, or at least make a joke at her example. Her brothers certainly would have mocked her. Instead, he remained silent as he unraveled a length of bandage and knotted the fabric around her hand.

He tucked his knuckles beneath her chin and angled her face toward the light, studying the wound on her cheek. "The doc says you shouldn't have a scar."

To her disappointment, he didn't appear swayed by her example. "Would you mind very much if I had a scar?" Jo dredged up a smile, attempting to lighten the somber mood. "Would you be upset if I was ugly?"

Garrett lifted a dark eyebrow. "You could never be ugly."

"I could never be pretty."

"That's because pretty is for debutantes and silly girls. You're beautiful."

Resentment welled in her chest. "I'm not. And I'll sock you for teasing me."

"Don't you call me a liar, Miss JoBeth McCoy." Garrett cupped the side of her face with his warm hand and studied her bandaged cheek. "Do you know why Tom is so mean to you?"

"Because I made him look like a fool in front of his friends."

"Nope." Garrett removed the comfort of his touch. "Because you broke his heart."

"I think you musta hit your head last night."

"Don't forget, I was a young man once, too. I know the signs."

"I sure wasn't Tom's first anything."

"Did he ever try and kiss you?" Garrett asked with a knowing grin.

"Once. I stomped on his toe."

"That's your proof. A man will forgive being made a fool of, but he never forgets his first love."

Jo scoffed. "If he had a crush on me, wouldn't he be nice?"

"Boys aren't always good at knowing what to do with their feelings."

Her head spun with his words and she latched on to his earlier comment. "Who was your first love?"

"I never had one."

"Then you don't really know for certain. And you're wrong about Tom. He's told me I'm ugly a thousand times."

"I'm right," Garrett declared. "And someday I'll prove it to you. Just like I'll finally make you realize how beautiful you are."

"Quit foolin' with me."

"For a smart woman, you're awfully dumb about some things." Garrett coasted the backs of his knuckles along her bruised cheek. "The doc stitched this up nicely. Does it hurt very much?"

"Nope."

Her gaze dipped to his lips, and Jo tilted her head. The last time she'd been kissed had left her singularly unimpressed, and she wanted a comparison.

Before she could talk herself out of the impulsive gesture, she leaned forward and pressed her lips against Garrett's. Aching for more, but fearful of being rejected, she pulled away. A gentle touch on her shoulder stilled her retreat. Garrett angled his head, deepening the kiss, and Jo gasped softly.

She threaded her fingers through his hair, astonished at the soft texture. Her heart fluttered in anticipation, and a curious longing surged through her veins. Jo slid her hands behind his head and tugged him closer.

He cradled the back of her neck and he stroked her jaw with his thumb. The sweet awareness growing inside her heightened. His gentle touch felt good and right and she didn't want the wondrous feelings to end.

With a soft sound of regret, he pulled away. Jo pressed two fingers against her swollen lips, mourning the loss of her startling discovery.

Garrett hastily stood. "You're healing really well. I don't think you'll have any problems."

The shadows were back in his eyes. He strode out of the room, and Jo stomped her foot. The one time she'd finally decided she liked kissing, and her partner had fled.

She crossed her arms over her chest and narrowed her gaze. He felt something for her, but she sensed he was frightened and she didn't know why.

No matter what the personal cost, she was going to pry his secrets loose.

Chapter Twelve

This was going to hurt.

Garrett sat on a low stool in the livery while Mr. McCoy paced before him. The sky was clear and cloudless, a faded indigo bleached by the sun. After taking one look at Ely's face, Mr. Lynch, the livery owner, had fled. Garrett wished he could have followed.

The red-faced man crossed back and forth and back and forth again, muttering all the while. This odd ritual had been repeated for fifteen minutes, and Garrett was growing restless. He had an appointment with the lawyer that afternoon. When Mr. McCoy reached the far end of the enclosure, Garrett discreetly fished out his pocketwatch.

"I'm sorry," Mr. McCoy boomed. "Am I taking up your precious time?"

Garrett hastily stowed the watch. "Well, no, but…"

"I had other plans for this morning," the incensed man continued. "And they didn't include that busybody, Mrs. Fletcher, stopping me on the street at first light."

"I'm—"

"I'd like to know how my daughter ended up in your rooms in the middle of the night."

"She—"

"I know she was sitting with Cora while you broke up the fight at the saloon, but that doesn't explain how the two of you wound up lying on the street together."

"We—"

"You rescued her from the fire. Sure." Mr. McCoy raked his fingers through his thick mop of hair. "Jo has always been headstrong, but you're a lawman. You should know better." He paused and glared. "I blame you."

"I blame myself, sir."

"That's, well…" Mr. McCoy sputtered. "Good."

Garrett opened his mouth for a response. Mr. McCoy's fierce scowl silenced his defense.

"I don't know what you two were thinking," Ely continued. "But the missus isn't happy. She's not happy at all. And if she's not happy, I'm not happy. You get my point?"

Not really. "Uh…"

"Jo is special. Not a lot of people realize that, but I think you do. That's why I'm not going to kill you."

"I apprec—"

"You're gonna do the right thing, ain't ya?" Ely glared.

"I already have. Looks like she'll have me after all."

"Oh, she'll have you. Her ma will see to that. But if I hear one bad thing, if you hurt her in any way, I'm gonna, well, I'm gonna… I'm gonna pin your ears back."

Garrett had a feeling Mr. McCoy wanted to expand on his threat or at the very least increase the stakes, but the older man suddenly seemed at a loss for words.

Keeping his head down, Garrett replied, "Yes, sir."

Mr. McCoy stuck out his hand. Garrett jerked back, then flailed as the stool tipped.

The older man grabbed his hand, hauled him forward and slapped him on the back. "Call me Ely."

"Pa," a youthful voice called.

The two men faced the youngest McCoy, Maxwell, who'd been patiently waiting during the past twenty minutes of pacing and muttering. The boy had braced his toes on the lowest railing of the corral fence and draped his body over the top railing. His hands dangled and his hat rested brim up beneath his bent head.

Max raised his eyes. "Pa, does this mean you're not gonna shoot Marshal Cain like you said earlier?"

"Of course not, son. We're family after the wedding. I can't very well shoot my own son-in-law."

The boy screwed up his face as he weighed the answer. A flash of disappointment crossed his expression before he lifted his shoulders in an upside-down, resigned shrug. "Can I drive the wagon?"

"Maybe next year."

Max scrambled over the fence and retrieved his hat, then scuffed at the dirt with his toe. "I thought this day was gonna be fun. But you're not gonna shoot anyone and I can't even drive the wagon."

As Garrett absently rubbed his chest, he pondered the boy's answer. Which part was more disappointing? Not being able to drive the wagon or missing the opportunity to see a man shot? He decided not to ask.

Ely fisted his hands beneath his biceps and Garrett thanked his lucky stars once more that he hadn't had to fight the man.

The McCoy patriarch thoughtfully scratched his

chin. "This town hasn't had a wedding in a month of Sundays. This'll be quite a shindig."

"About that." Garrett shifted on his feet. "I think we'll go before the judge when he comes through town in a few weeks. There's no need for anything fancy."

Ely threw back his head and guffawed. "You got a lot to learn about women, son. A lot to learn." The older man chaffed his hands together. "This is going to be fun."

"Jo and I agreed on this." Garrett bristled beneath Ely's amused regard.

"It ain't Jo you gotta worry about." Ely motioned for his son. "Come along, Max. I need a salt lick for the south pasture and a word with Caleb. I believe we'll find both things at the mercantile."

Abandoning Garrett in confused silence, Ely pivoted on his heel, his merry whistle floating behind him on the breeze.

Garrett scratched the back of his neck. Who would protest if he and Jo went before the judge?

Max threw one last disappointed look over his shoulder, then shrugged in resignation. "You bringing Jo for dinner next Sunday?"

"Maybe."

"Can I shoot your gun?"

"No."

"Peas and carrots. I never get to do anything fun."

The boy flapped his arm in a dismissive gesture and Garrett sketched a hesitant wave in return. That hadn't gone so badly, had it? He'd been dreading the encounter with Ely all morning, but it seemed like Jo's pa wasn't opposed to the marriage. The conversation had been disjointed, but not overly violent. Except for that last cryptic remark.

He had a lot to learn. Garrett slapped his hat against his pant leg before replacing it. He couldn't argue with that.

Either way, Jo wasn't the sort of woman who wanted a big fancy wedding. Thank heaven. The thought of standing before a congregation of people in his Sunday best sent shivers down his spine. Outside of his job, he loathed being the center of attention. Nothing attracted more attention than standing at the altar. That wasn't even the worst part. Afterward, he'd have to sip punch and make small talk.

Memories of his youth drifted through his exhausted brain. A long-dormant sadness suffocated his emotions. In better days, his family had been part of the St. Louis social elite, and his parents had thrown parties nearly every weekend during the summer. He hadn't realized it as a child, but his mother had been putting on a show. Dressing them up and making the world believe they were one big, happy family. Good thing no one had seen behind closed doors.

Garrett didn't want to repeat the same pattern. Plastering on fake smiles and pretending things were one way, when in reality, they were living an entirely different truth.

He shrugged and faced his horse, a bay gelding with a white strip down its nose. "Don't worry, old Blue." Garrett patted the horse's muzzle. "I've only known JoBeth a few months, but I know enough. We've got nothing to worry about."

"JoBeth McCoy," her ma admonished. "You'll have a church wedding and that's the last I'll say on the matter."

"I agreed to the marriage." Jo sulked. "Isn't that enough?"

Edith's pacing stilled in a huff.

Jo drummed her fingers on the arm of her chintz armrest.

Her ma perched on the edge of a wingback chair. Jo had expected her parents to voice an opinion, but not this soon.

Her ma carefully arranged her blue calico skirts over her bent knees. "I was against this marriage in the beginning, but my thoughts on the matter have changed. Marshal Cain has proved himself to be an honorable man, and I respect that."

Jo bit off a groan. Her ma was correct. She'd seen it in Garrett's eyes. He'd do the honorable thing even if it meant shackling himself to her for the rest of his life.

The traits she admired about him were the very things that would make this marriage such a disaster. Would his honor hold up through the years, or would he grow to resent her? She feared the outcome of their hasty union if the marshal felt as if he'd been coerced into the marriage.

Jo dug her heels into the carpet and lifted her toes. "Garrett and I are getting married, but we're going before the judge. Not some fancy church wedding."

"And that's how you want to begin your married life together?" Her ma lifted an eyebrow at the familiar use of the marshal's name. "Alone. Before a judge?"

"I'm agreeing with you and you're still criticizing me?" Jo stalled with a throat-soothing gulp of cool water. "I agreed to the marriage. What else matters?" she repeated.

"You're my only girl, JoBeth." Her ma fiddled with

the crocheted lace at her collar. "When the boys get married, their wives will arrange the wedding."

Jo shrugged. It didn't matter who planned the wedding. "I'm making things easier on you this way."

"Don't you start with me, JoBeth. Nothing about this is easy. In fact, the whole thing is a disaster. Everyone in town already thinks the worst." Edith stood and crossed before the cold hearth once more. "If you and the marshal sneak off before a judge, you'll only give the gossips more fodder."

"There's going to be talk anyway," Jo pointed out helpfully. "The last exciting thing that happened in town occurred when the sheriff got himself arrested and replaced by a county marshal. This will blow over as soon as Tom Walby goes on another bender or Mrs. Fletcher's goat gets into another garden. I'll simply stay low until the next gossip-worthy event. Once someone else slips up, the marshal and I will be old news."

Agnes, her landlady, appeared in the arched doorway from the kitchen. She held a tray with a red-rose-enameled teapot and two cups. A lace napkin fluttered over the edges. Agnes took one look at Edith's stiff back, spun around and retreated.

Her ma cut her hands through the air. "It matters because people's impressions are difficult to change. You're not a goat or a drunk. This sort of gossip sticks. Elizabeth and Jack have been gone for ten years, and their courtship is still legendary around these parts."

"I'll give you that one." For some reason, gossip about a romance had more staying power than other news. "People should have better things to do than talk."

"Of course they should, but that's not the point. You

and Marshal Cain have made a real mess of this. Don't make it any worse."

Jo felt herself losing ground. "Don't you see? Having a church wedding would be a disaster. I'm not like Mary Louise. I'll look like a fool all decked out like a sugar cake, and everyone will laugh at me." Jo slapped her glass onto the table, sloshing water over her sleeve. "I'd rather be known as a fallen woman than a laughingstock."

A fine sheen of tears appeared in Ma's eyes, and her mouth crumpled along the edges. "I've never asked you to be anything but who you are, JoBeth. I never forced you into skirts or made you put up your hair. Maybe I should have, but even when I was tempted, your pa wouldn't let me." Edith swiped at her eyes. "But I'm asking you for this. Let your pa and I give you a nice wedding."

Jo sopped up the spilled water with her sleeve. Sheer desperation kept her arguing. "You have five other children. Why are you picking on me?"

Her ma gasped. "How on earth is planning a lovely wedding, even though I don't agree with the circumstances, picking on you?"

"We don't need a ceremony." Jo sagged in her chair and threw her arms over the sides. "How many times do I have to tell you that? The judge is coming through town in a few weeks, and we'll sign the papers."

"You are making a covenant before God." Her ma planted her hands on her hips and loomed over Jo. "And even if the two of you don't take that seriously, I do."

Rising, Jo imitated her mother's implacable stance. "It's not your wedding. I'm an adult and I can make my own decisions."

"As an adult, you have responsibilities."

"I already have plenty of responsibilities. I take care of myself. I have my own place and my own job."

"You're being selfish."

Jo's jaw dropped. "I'm not selfish."

"Your actions reflect on the people around you."

Her mother's voice caught on the last word, and Jo's chest tightened. Guilt finally won out over the thought of being ostracized in front of the entire town. Though she dreaded the idea of Mary Louise and the others snickering over her, she couldn't refuse her ma's plea.

Edith McCoy had never made a demand on Jo. Even when they'd argued over Jo's midwife duties, her ma had backed down. Obviously, this meant more to her than Jo understood. "If it means that much to you, then fine."

"Fine."

"Fine."

Her ma's face lit up at Jo's grudging reply and she felt like a first-rate heel for putting up such a fuss in the first place. Who cared what Tom Walby or Mary Louise thought of her? No one mattered but her family—and Garrett. She wouldn't embarrass him.

Her ma pulled her into a hug. "You've always been so independent. Let this be our gift to you."

How could Jo refuse? Her ma may have wanted her in frilly dresses with crimped hair, but she'd never forced the issue. When Jo wore trousers around the farm, her ma rolled her eyes but never insisted she wear skirts.

There was someone else they must take into consideration. "I'm not sure how Garrett will feel about all this. We kinda agreed on going before a judge."

"If he knows what's best for him, he'll agree in a lick."

"I suppose."

Jo didn't know much about men, but if she explained about her ma, surely Garrett would agree. She sure hoped so, otherwise she had another tangle to unravel.

"JoBeth, you're taking on an awful lot. I hope you know what you're doing."

For a brief moment Jo considered confiding in her ma, then changed her mind just as quickly.

How did she explain that somewhere along the line she'd gotten lost? That she'd felt a yearning for something she couldn't name, and marrying Marshal Cain felt like a step in the right direction. How could she explain that she was terrified of childbirth, and lately her fear had warred with her loneliness? That she was tired of being treated like a second-class citizen because she wasn't married and raising a family, and she was annoyed with herself for the vulnerability?

How could she explain that she liked how she felt when she was with Marshal Cain.

She and her ma were vastly different people, and sometimes Jo felt as if they were talking to each other in a foreign language. Each of them going through the motions, saying the right things, saying the wrong things, but never really hearing each other. Jo was different from other people, and she'd reveled in her uniqueness. She'd never wanted to be like anybody else. Lately, though, those differences had left her feeling isolated and alone. More and more she wondered if she'd merely been pushing people away.

She and Garrett were solitary people. But they had

each other, and that would be enough. They were making their own future.

Edith straightened Jo's collar and flicked a disapproving glare at the hole in the fabric Jo had never bothered darning. "Bring this by when you come for dinner and I'll mend the tear."

"It's fine." Jo wriggled away. "No one cares but you."

"When you marry the marshal, your appearance will reflect on him. He has a certain standing in the community. As does his family."

Jo considered how her mother always looked impeccable. How she pressed her clothes and put up her hair, even if she wasn't going into town that day. "How come you always look just as nice at home as you do when you're going into town?"

"Because my family is the most important thing in the world to me," Edith replied easily. "Why wouldn't I want to look nice for them?"

Jo pondered the unexpected answer. Somehow, she'd always associated her mother's quirk with vanity. She'd assumed people primped because they liked showing off their looks, but her ma's reply had shattered that assumption.

Humbled, Jo hung her head. "Thank you for helping me with the wedding."

Edith cupped her cheek. "Someday you'll thank me for this."

Jo lifted her eyes heavenward. Getting married meant dressing up like a girl, something she knew nothing about.

How many times had the Walby brothers teased her about her clothes and hair? She touched her serviceable brown skirts. She didn't look as if she dressed in a barn, did she? Cold fear pitted in her stomach.

Jo crossed her arms. "A church wedding and dress. But that's all."

Maybe then her ma would finally understand that she couldn't change Jo into the daughter she wanted. By the time all this wedding nonsense had run its course, she hoped Edith McCoy finally accepted the daughter God had given her.

Chapter Thirteen

Garrett plunged his face into the rain barrel and shook off the excess water. He'd passed the first test, talking with Jo's pa. He wasn't quite sure he'd passed the second test. Kissing Jo had been a revelation and a wonder. Because of his past, he'd learned to shut out physical needs and ignore loneliness. He'd thought he could bury his attraction to Jo, as well. He hadn't counted on the emotional connection. The more time they spent together, the more familiarity developed.

He didn't regret asking her to marry him, but he was terrified of the feeling stirring in his chest. Emotions leaked through the barriers he'd erected, spilling into his heart. How could a lifetime of steeling himself against affection crumble in one fell landslide?

He liked Jo, he admired her, but he couldn't love her. He couldn't let the madness take hold of him as it had his father. He owed that much to Jo.

To Jo *and* Cora, he reminded himself.

Garrett combed his fingers through his damp hair. He could do this. He was an honorable man.

Drawing in a steadying breath, he replaced his hat

and straightened the brim. There'd been a murder, and he couldn't let his personal troubles distract him from his job.

He had one witness in particular he needed to question, and he let the short walk along the boardwalk focus his scattered thoughts. As he swung open the mercantile door, the room stilled.

His head bent, David McCoy lounged against a display of leather belts while the mercantile owner's pretty daughter, Mary Louise, held up a supple mahogany length for his approval. Garrett narrowed his gaze. A certain hitch in the boy's posture indicated he was interested in more than belts.

Garrett sensed trouble brewing like a spring squall. Caleb had already made it clear he was interested in Mary Louise. If both brothers courted the same girl, a heap of trouble followed. Garrett didn't need a blood feud on top of everything else—*especially* between Jo's brothers.

The bell above the door chimed, and David smiled a greeting at someone hidden from Garrett's view. "Hey, runt."

Garrett followed the boy's gaze and his pulse quickened. "JoBeth! What are you doing here? You're supposed to be resting."

She limped into the room looking like an old-timer returning from war with the bandage over her cheek and another knotted over her hand. Why on earth was she up and about? The doctor had declared her fit, but she needed quiet.

His new fiancée tossed him a withering glare. "I can't stay cooped up all day. I need supplies."

Guilt gnawed at his chest. If he hadn't asked her to

stay with Cora, she'd be fine. Had the assault on the jail been an attempt to distract attention from the murder? Or were the two incidents separate? He couldn't discount any possibilities just yet.

"Jo." Garrett kept his voice low, conscious of the tightening crowd. "The doctor said you should be resting."

"Then he should have brought me coffee," she snapped.

Garrett hovered uncertainly near her elbow. Why hadn't he thought to ask her if she needed anything that morning?

Because her enchanting kiss, a sweet combination of boldness and innocence, had distracted him. "Sit. I'll get your supplies."

"I'm perfectly capable of fetching a tin of coffee."

"But…" Garrett started, then thought better. This didn't seem like the best time to point out her surly behavior.

No doubt her wounds pained her. Garrett spied a sturdy wooden chair near the door and scraped the legs across the floor. He set it out of the path to the counter so she wouldn't be bumped or jostled.

"Cora is with Ma." Jo answered his unspoken question and took a hesitant step. "She woke and ate breakfast, but she went right back to sleep."

"She's bound to be tired. That was quite a ruckus last night."

Garrett touched Jo's elbow and guided her toward the waiting chair. Despite her exasperation, she leaned heavily on his arm. He threaded their fingers together, and she rested her cheek against his shoulder. He tilted his head a notch and caught the scent of her hair—

feminine and fresh. Not flowery, but more like a field of cypress trees.

Garrett guided her around a pickle barrel and maneuvered her between two waist-high stacks of twenty-pound flour bags. They closed the distance to the chair entirely too quickly for his liking. With harnessed regret he released her hand and assisted her as she lowered herself onto the seat.

Rubbing the spot where her cheek had rested against his shoulder, he spoke. "You should be relaxing, not running around town. Tell me what you need, and I'll get it."

"Hey." David blocked his path. "You're getting awfully friendly with my sister."

"My *fiancée.*" Garrett emphasized the word for the growing crowd hanging on every nuance of their exchange.

"She is not." David appeared horrified by the suggestion. "Jo's never getting married."

The source of their argument crossed her arms and huffed. "He's telling the truth."

She'd bit out the words like gristle.

"I might remind you," Garrett began, a ball of anxiety knotting in his belly, "you asked me first."

Their curious gawkers tittered. There had been a handful of people in the store when Garrett had arrived. Now that Jo had joined them, the whole town would have their faces pressed against the glass before long.

Twin spots of color appeared on Jo's cheeks. "I didn't come here to debate the facts."

David swung his gaze between them, his expression incredulous. "When did you two start liking each other? When did you get engaged?"

Garrett cut a sidelong glance at Jo's disgruntled expression. "Last night."

"You're his fiancée?" David threw back his head and chortled. "That's the funniest thing I ever heard."

His sister socked him in the gut. "Who's laughing now, huh?"

"That hurt." Scowling, David rubbed his belly. "You're awful cranky for a bride."

"And don't you forget it."

Garrett stepped between them before their good-natured ribbing escalated. "We can celebrate later. Right now we need to get Jo back home."

David sputtered. "I'll be keeping my eye on you two from now on. No funny business before you're married."

Heat crept up Garrett's neck. They'd kissed that morning, nothing more. And David wasn't a mind reader—he didn't know. "Show some respect for your sister, boy." He faced Jo. "Do you have a list?"

"No, I don't have a list. And I don't need your help, either. I'm perfectly capable—" A fit of coughing silenced her outraged reply.

Garrett immediately dropped on one knee beside her chair. He rubbed her back until the coughing stilled, then felt her forehead with the back of his hand, relieved she didn't have a fever. "You inhaled a lot of smoke last night. The doc said you'll probably have a cough for a week or two." He shook his head. "The least you can do is let me help."

"Let *us* help," David chimed in.

"Fine." JoBeth huffed. "I need three candles, a tin of matches, a sliver of soap and a pound of coffee."

In a flurry of arms and legs accompanied by the

scuffle of boots, Garrett and David scrambled in op-posite directions. Garrett scanned the shelves for soap and came up empty. David scooted past him, arrogantly displaying his haul of soap and candles.

The younger man had the advantage. He'd lived near the town his whole life and obviously knew the store like the back of his hand. By the time they both ap-proached the counter, out of breath and huffing in uni-son, all Garrett had acquired was the pound of coffee.

They set their supplies on the counter, and Garrett reached in his pocket. He might not have found the items, but he was sure as shooting going to pay for them. David slapped a handful of coins onto the counter first. Garrett shoved them aside. David shoved them back. The mercantile owner cleared his throat.

The two competitors glared at each other.

Garrett set his jaw. "I'll pay the bill. She's my fi-ancée."

"I'll pay the bill. She's my sister."

The bell above the door chimed, and Garrett lifted his eyes heavenward. That's just what they needed, more witnesses. They already had a rapt crowd fol-lowing their every move. Good thing the town didn't have a regular newspaper, or they'd be front-page news tomorrow. As Garrett surveyed the entrance, he realized Jo's chair sat empty in the middle of the room.

David frowned. "Did she leave?"

"I think she left."

"Why'd she do that?"

"I dunno." Garrett shot the younger man a disgrun-tled glare. "It was probably something *you* said."

While they'd argued, Jo had limped home alone. Garrett dashed for the door and searched the boardwalk, but she'd already disappeared. David joined him outside while a press of noses jostled against the windows behind them.

Great.

They might not be front-page news, but they'd definitely dominate the dinner conversation around Cimarron Springs tonight.

"Something I said?" David innocently rested his hand over his heart. "I was just trying to help. You're the one acting like a bull in spring."

The barb struck home. Garrett tightened his lips as the door behind them swung open once more. Covering his embarrassment, he faced Mr. Stuart. "How much do I owe you?"

"Miss McCoy already paid. She has an account."

The three men stepped back inside, and the dozen or so people who'd crowded the store during the unexpected entertainment slowly dispersed. Still annoyed with the younger man's interference, Garrett pointed a finger at David. "This is your fault. I'm her fiancé. I should pay."

"I'm her brother." David threw back his shoulders. "I should pay."

Mr. Stuart tugged on his black-elastic arm garters. "If you fellows don't mind me saying so, looks like the lady is doing fine taking care of herself."

Garrett and David exchanged a guilty look. Feeling sheepish, Garrett nodded. "Has she always been so stubborn?"

David flashed an abashed grin. "That's JoBeth for you."

"Say, is there anything else your sister likes? You know, if you were buying her a gift?"

David grinned from ear to ear and bobbed his head. "Rosewater. She loves rosewater. Practically bathes in the stuff at home."

"That's odd," Garrett replied slowly. "I've never noticed that particular scent around her before."

David avoided his gaze and hung his head forlornly. "Probably can't afford it since she lives in town. Too bad really."

The younger man glanced up, his eyes wide and deceptively innocent.

Barely covering his grin, David fisted one hand near his mouth and cleared his throat. "We'd best get over to the jailhouse. Check out the damage from the fire."

Their curious onlookers had dispersed, leaving them isolated. Garrett studied a display of tinned peaches. "Does Caleb know about you and Mary Louise?"

David gaped at the blunt question. "No."

"Don't let a woman come between you. If she's playing the two of you against each other, she's not worth it."

The tips of the younger man's ears reddened, and his hands curled at his sides, but he kept his expression neutral. "She knows who she wants."

"That's why you were at the saloon, isn't it? You were approaching her pa?"

"She gave me permission to court her, but I needed her pa's, too."

Garrett stared through the front window at the row of shops across the way. They were all connected, each sharing a wall, supporting the other. He sure hoped Mary Louise didn't drive a wedge between the brothers, but he was afraid it was already too late. "Fair enough. Why don't you go on ahead of me. I'll catch up to you at the jailhouse in a minute."

Garrett had felt the mercantile owner's glare boring into his back during their talk, and decided he'd better give the man another chance to speak. After the door closed behind David, Garrett crossed the room and braced his hands on either side of the spot Mr. Stuart had been rubbing for the past ten minutes.

"You're gonna wear a hole in the marble. Must be quite a stain you keep cleaning."

A telling muscle ticked along Mr. Stuart's jaw. He stuffed the rag into the belted tie of his apron. "I didn't shoot Mr. Hodges. I didn't like him. But I didn't kill him."

"You threatened to kill him. On more than one occasion, as I recall."

"He threatened me enough plenty of times, too, you know. I've also threatened to shoot that McCoy boy, Caleb, if he doesn't stop sniffing around my daughter. And he ain't dead yet."

"Let's keep it that way," Garrett drawled. "Or things won't look too good for you, will they? Besides, the McCoys are a good family."

"Mary Louise has better choices."

"Like who?"

"Like someone from St. Louis, or Omaha or Chicago. She's deserves better than the fellows around here."

"She'll make a fine choice, I'm sure," Garrett replied evasively.

No matter what happened, the courting of Mary Louise Stuart was going to end badly, that much he knew for certain.

Mr. Stuart rested his knuckles on the counter and tilted his head. "You really gonna marry that McCoy girl?"

Garrett's hackles rose at the obvious disbelief in the man's voice. "Why do you ask?"

"Just wondering. She didn't seem like the sort who'd marry."

"Guess I changed her mind." Garrett raised an eyebrow, challenging the man to dispute his answer. Clearly realizing he'd overstepped his boundaries, Mr. Stuart wisely remained silent.

Garrett tamped down his fuming anger. He didn't like the folks around town and their malicious gossip. And he especially didn't like people questioning Jo's suitability for marriage. He sometimes felt that her very strength was an affront to some weaker folks. She put up a good wall, pretending she didn't have any feelings on the matter, but Garrett suspected otherwise.

Mr. Stuart leaned in with a whisper, "Say, don't listen to David when it comes to his sister. He's pulling your leg. If you really want to buy her a present, she's had her eye on this."

He reached beneath the counter and retrieved a boy's leather hat.

Garrett accepted the offering and circled the sturdy brim in his hands. The brown leather was supple enough for comfort yet sturdy enough for practicality. The stitching was close and even and thick for long wear. A perfect gift for his new fiancée.

"I'll take it." Garrett glanced around the shop and spied the pretty yellow bonnet he'd noticed earlier. "And that one, too."

Cora would like the flashy piece. She seemed drawn to brightly colored things with an abundance of frills and lace. Once again he was struck by the difference between the two females and their obvious connection. "If you think of anything else, you let me know."

Mr. Stuart nodded but kept his gaze averted. Garrett took one last look around the mercantile and caught Mary Louise staring at him. She hastily ducked behind a tower of tinned beans when he caught her gaze. Garrett ran his hands down his face. This town was full of undercurrents, and if he wasn't careful, one of those undercurrents was bound to pull him under.

Chapter Fourteen

Two days following the fire, Jo paced before the jail-house in anxious vigil. They'd boarded up the front window, and she missed the etched glass. When Garrett appeared, she gingerly waved her arm to catch his attention. "Marshal Cain," she called. "Garrett."

He faced her, and for a brief moment her resolve wavered. As the marshal approached, she surreptitiously pleated her new moss-green calico skirts. Today he wore his hat low over his forehead and his dark hair touched his collar. He really did need a haircut, but she hoped he put it off. His shaggy locks lent him an enigmatic air of danger that sent her heartbeat racing.

His work and the separate living arrangements from Cora during the repairs on the jailhouse meant they'd only seen each other in passing. While he'd visited his niece twice, Cora had been sleeping both times. He hadn't lingered. They were both painfully aware of the watchful eyes of others. Neither wanted to stir up any-more gossip.

Jo touched the bandage on her cheek. Gracious, the man just kept getting better looking. Each time he was near, she found herself wanting to touch him, brush her hand against his. When they were apart, her thoughts strayed to the dimple in his left cheek that appeared when he smiled. He was a part of her day now, a part of her worries.

And now the two of them had a problem.

Garrett paused before her, his gaze intense. "What's wrong?"

Jo tilted back her head but couldn't get a clear look at his eyes since they were shaded by the brim of his hat. "It's Cora. I'm worried." She glanced around the boardwalk. There weren't many people stirring yet, but it only took one person to spread a rumor.

They'd caused enough talk already. "Let's go back to the boardinghouse."

Jo led him into the familiar boardinghouse parlor, gestured toward the pink-chintz chairs before the hearth and sat down across from him. Her ma had volunteered to sit with Cora while she and Garrett discussed her recovery. Jo's memory drifted to the last time they'd sat across from each other here. When they'd kissed.

The marshal doffed his hat. "Cora has been awfully quiet, but the doc says she's not hurt."

"Not physically, no." Jo paused and carefully measured her next words. "At first I thought she was just tired and I let her sleep as much as she wanted. My ma came by, and well, a lot has happened."

At her words, Garrett shifted in his chair and tugged on his collar as though it was strangling him. "I forgot to tell you, I talked with your pa."

"Oh, dear." Jo almost wished she'd witnessed the encounter. "You don't appear any the worse for wear. I guess that's a good sign."

The marshal chuckled. "He was looking out for his daughter. I'd expect no less."

"That's Pa for you." She braced the heels of her hands against her knees and locked her elbows. "I don't exactly know how to say this, but Cora has barely spoken since the fire."

Garrett narrowed his gaze. "Are you certain? Maybe her throat hurts from the smoke."

"I'm certain."

"She's seen a lot for one so young."

"I know. And this probably brought back all sorts of memories from the night her folks died. What happened, anyway?"

Garrett rested his elbows on his knees and clutched the brim of his hat with both hands. "I sent for the newspapers, but there wasn't much information available. The fire started in the kitchen and spread fast. Looked like a faulty stovepipe. Cora's pa got her outside and went back for Deirdre. They didn't make it."

"I can't imagine what it must have been like for her."

His expression closed, Garrett pinched the bridge of his nose. "I should have been there for her."

"We can't change the past. You did the best you could..." Jo let her voice trail off. She doubted he wanted her comfort. "I guess I shouldn't lecture you on not feeling guilty. I'm blaming myself, too." She curled her hands into fists. "When the fire started and the door was stuck, I didn't think fast enough. I panicked."

The marshal tipped forward out his chair and knelt before her, then grasped her clenched hands. "It's not your fault. Don't ever think that."

Drawn toward his comfort, Jo wrapped her arms around his strong shoulders and buried her face in his neck. "I didn't know what to do," she spoke, her voice muffled against his starched shirt.

Garrett kneaded her tense muscles, rubbing his thumb in circles. "It's not your fault. We'll talk with the doc about Cora. He might have an idea."

He hadn't shaved, and the day's growth of beard along his jaw abraded her cheek. His warm breath caressed her ear with each word.

Her thoughts scattered. "I didn't even think of the doc. I don't know what's wrong with me lately."

"There's nothing wrong with you. It's been an exhausting forty-eight hours. Your body needs time to heal."

Jo relaxed into the luxury of his comforting embrace. The marshal was solid and sure, and it felt good to rest her head on his capable shoulder. Her tightly cinched emotions eased for a moment. Despite her various aches and pains and a throat raw from smoke, a curious serenity possessed her. She angled her head to one side and rested her chin deeper in the hollow of Garrett's neck.

The floor creaked. Jo glanced up and caught sight of Agnes in the arched doorway. The landlady held her tea tray with its red-rose enameled pot and cups. Her gaze slid over their embrace and she puffed a breath, fluttering the gray corkscrew curls resting on her forehead. With a mutter, she spun around and retreated.

Jo and Garrett sprang apart. Jo pressed one hand against her cheek, capturing the comfort of Garrett's touch. Gathering her wits about her, she turned and found her ma descending the stairs.

Edith twisted a lace handkerchief in her hands. "It's no use. She's awake, but she hasn't said a word."

Jo and Garrett exchanged a worried glance.

Edith paused on the landing, one hand holding the

banister. "Maybe you two should talk with her, together. Show her that she's safe now."

Garrett stood and held out his hand for Jo. "Your ma is right. I think it's best if we go as a pair."

Numb with worry, Jo pushed off from her chair and stood.

Garrett touched her sleeve. "No sad faces. This isn't a funeral, after all."

Jo mustered a weak smile.

"That will have to do."

Together they ascended the stairs, and Garrett pressed open the door. Cora perched on the edge of the bed clutching her rag doll, her blond curls a shiny halo around her solemn face. They eased into the room, and Garrett and Jo settled on either side. Jo took in her surroundings. What must Garrett think of her small room? There were no samplers or chintz pillows.

Just the necessities.

"Cora," Jo began, "I hear you don't feel like talking."

The little girl's enormous cornflower-blue eyes blinked slowly as she shook her head from side to side.

"That's okay. You can talk when you feel like it." Jo offered a hesitant smile. "Uncle Garrett and I have a surprise for you. We're getting married. To each other."

Garrett made a strangled sound at her odd declaration.

A wide grin spread across Cora's face.

Encouraged, Jo continued, "Would you like that?"

The little girl nodded.

"Do you want a new dress for the wedding?"

Another hesitant nod.

"I understand you're scared, but don't forget how much we love you. When you're ready to talk, your uncle and I will be here, okay? Just remember, you're safe with us."

A small hand reached out and touched Jo's knee.

Garrett covered the tiny fingers and Jo felt his gentle pressure.

"I'll tell you a secret," he spoke in a conspiratorial whisper. "I'm afraid of snakes. When I saw Jo holding that ten-foot-long monster, I nearly fainted. Why, it was as big around as my leg."

Cora giggled.

"And the fangs." Garrett crooked two fingers like a hook in front of his upper lip. "They could put out a man's eye. But while all the boys were shaking in their boots, you braved that monster like it was a tiny little worm."

Jo couldn't tear her gaze away from the marshal's face. His voice wrapped around her like an afghan. The security of his hand felt comforting and right. They might have gone about it the wrong way, but marrying Garrett was the right thing to do. The three of them together supported each other, giving each other strength.

As long as they were focused on their family, only good could come from their union. Garrett had an affinity for children that surprised her. Cora's expression had lightened beneath his genuine confession.

While Cora still hadn't spoken, Jo was encouraged. "Tomorrow we'll spend the day together. Just the three of us."

Garrett snapped his fingers. "I almost forgot. I bought you something."

He reached into his coat pocket and retrieved a wrapped package.

Cora's eyes lit up. "For me?"

"Of course for you."

She ripped open the package and pulled out a yellow lace bonnet. "It's just like the one at the store!"

Jo smiled at his thoughtfulness.

Cora rubbed the lace edge of the bonnet between her fingers. "Will we still have to live over the jail?"

Jo and Garrett exchanged a glance over her head. Jo grasped for an answer. "I don't know where we'll live. I guess we haven't thought much about that yet, have we?"

Garrett considered each of them in turn. "There's the Miller place on the edge of town. It's big. Too big for the three of us, really. But it'll do in a pinch. We haven't much other choice."

A tinge of apprehension skipped down her spine. Her impending marriage had been at the forefront of her mind, but she hadn't considered their living arrangements. Of course, they'd need a new place. Garrett couldn't stay at the boardinghouse, and the jail was no place for a family. Despite the obvious conclusion, she'd imagined them all staying put.

Living with Garrett.

Jo mentally shrugged. It would be like living at the farm again, tripping over her brothers' discarded shoes and fighting over whose turn it was to fetch the water.

Garrett flashed an encouraging smile, and her skin tingled with nerves. This was what her ma had tried to warn her about. She wasn't just becoming a mother to Cora, she was becoming Garrett's wife.

Only her living arrangements would change. Her life needn't change with their marriage.

Three days later, Garrett walked Jo and Cora to the telegraph office. He would have preferred they rest another few days, but both of them were chafing at the confinement. Jo craved a return to her regular routine, and Cora's boundless energy had returned tenfold.

They'd promised him a shortened workday and he'd accepted the compromise. An overwhelming list of tasks loomed ahead of him.

He tightened his grip on the package he held, the leather hat he'd bought for Jo. He'd thought of giving it to her a dozen times, but the moment had never been quite right. What if she didn't like the gift? Garrett blew out a hard breath. Maybe he'd find the courage tomorrow.

Upon reaching the jailhouse, he paused. The door hung open. Cautiously stepping inside, his eyebrows lifted at the sight of six McCoys lined up before the wall by height—Caleb, David, Abraham, Michael and Maxwell, with Ely rounding out the group.

He couldn't tell from their impassive expressions whether or not this was a friendly visit.

Garrett widened his stance and propped his hands on his hips. "What brings you folks around this early?"

Perhaps Mr. McCoy hadn't been as accepting of the situation as Garrett had supposed.

Ely stepped forward. "This place isn't livable. David gave us a list of the repairs. The office will need to be taken down to the studs and rebuilt before it's fit for work. We'll get your stuff out and finish boarding up the windows this afternoon. You know where you're staying in the meantime?"

"I thought I'd take a look at the old Miller place."

"Good choice. The boys and I will get started on the jail."

"I appreciate the help, but I can manage on my own."

"We're family now," Ely replied matter-of-factly, as though that explained everything.

Garrett wasn't adept at family life, and the McCoys would find that out soon enough. He swiped a hand across his forehead. "I'd be much obliged for the assistance."

"You're coming to dinner on Sunday, right?" Ely inquired in a voice that indicated an order rather than a question.

Usually Garrett spent his day off alone, but it sounded as if the McCoys had a ritual, and he didn't want Jo disappointed. "I'll be there."

"Good."

Uncomfortable with all the attention, Garrett glanced around. "I'll box up what's left upstairs, then I'll visit the lawyer's office about the deed."

David braced a hand against the soot-darkened wall. "I'd rather be busting down walls than sitting in a lawyer's office anyday."

Garrett grunted. "You and me both."

He'd been spending the majority of time in the law offices these days. Unsure what else to say, Garrett stood in silence while the McCoys filed past him. As each of them crossed his path, they chucked him on the arm. By the time it was Maxwell's turn, Garrett figured his arm was black and blue. The McCoys didn't seem to know their own strength.

The littlest McCoy stared up at him. "Are you going to be my new brother?"

"Um, yes."

Garrett hadn't considered the full significance of his decision. He wasn't just marrying Jo, he was marrying into her family. The feeling was odd, but not entirely unpleasant. The McCoys had seemingly accepted him without question.

Maxwell tugged a slingshot from his back pocket and extended his hand. "I made this. For you."

Garrett accepted the gift and made a point of studying the rudimentary craftsmanship. "This is a fine piece. I'm proud to have it."

"Jo is the best shot, but I've been practicing."

"That's good."

"I have a target range behind the barn."

"Um, that's nice."

"You can practice with me."

Garrett figured shooting *with* Max was better than being shot at *by* Max. "It's a deal."

The boy trailed behind his family and sketched a wave over his shoulder. Pondering the unexpected encounter, Garrett replaced his hat and adjusted the brim. He tested the stairs and gripped the banister, his hand coming away darkened with soot. He unfurled his bandanna and rubbed the black from his palm before continuing upstairs.

A fine layer of powdery gray dust had settled on every surface, and the pungent smell of burnt wood stung his nostrils. Even after a good cleaning and repainting, Garrett figured they'd be fighting a lingering stench.

They'd removed Cora's belongings first, washing and airing everything. The lingering scent of fire brought back too many disturbing memories. With the McCoys' help, he'd erase the evidence of the fire in no time.

They'd put their trust in him. Would they be as welcoming if they knew his past? Garrett shook his head. He'd kept his secrets this long—there was no reason he couldn't keep them forever.

Chapter Fifteen

Two weeks later, Jo stood on a dais in the backroom of the mercantile wearing a perfectly ridiculous concoction of heavy ivory satin. The lace collar choked her throat and stretched so it tickled her earlobes.

"Stand still!" Mrs. Hankins ordered, the seamstress's words muffled around a mouthful of pins. "I can't properly measure the hem if you don't stop wiggling." The aggravated woman sat back on her heels. "Are these the shoes you'll wear?"

"Yes," Jo replied curtly.

Her ma clutched her chest. "While I'm afraid of the answer, I have to ask. What are you wearing?"

Jo hiked her skirts. "The usual."

"Oh, good gracious." Edith slapped one hand over her mouth. "You're wearing a drover's boot."

"Nope." Jo bent at the waist. "It's called a cowboy boot. Mr. Stuart says they're all the rage in Texas. Check out the stitching on the side." She tipped her stacked heel and admired the elaborate craftsmanship.

"I don't care what you call it. That shoe is positively hideous. You cannot wear those."

"No one will see them."

"*I'll* know you're wearing work boots during the ceremony. That is absolutely unacceptable."

"If no one can see them, why does it matter?"

"It matters."

Jo glowered. "That doesn't make any sense!"

Cora shifted in her perch on a chair in the corner and Jo immediately regretted her outburst. *Good heavens,* she was behaving like a child and frightening Cora in the process. Jo straightened and turned toward the little girl.

"It's all right," she called with a reassuring smile. "We're just agreeing on a dress." Pressing down a mountain of itchy ruffles with one hand, Jo grimaced. "What do you think of this one?"

Cora wrinkled her nose and shook her head.

Jo tossed a withering glare over one shoulder. "See, Ma? I told you I looked ridiculous."

"That's not the only dress in town." Edith raised her eyebrows. "If this wasn't such a rush, if we had more time, I could sew something nice for you."

"You're the one who insisted on setting a date for the wedding."

"And you're the one who's been avoiding me."

"I don't like to dress shop."

"Hiding from the task isn't going to change anything."

"Either way, I need a break from all this girl stuff." Jo scurried behind the screen. As she yanked the suffocating yards of satin and lace over her head, the bell above the mercantile door chimed.

Footsteps sounded and Mary Louise called out,

"Marshal Cain is here. He wants to know if he can talk with you."

Jo's heart lodged in her throat. She hadn't seen him in days, and it felt like an eternity. "Be right out."

At least his timely arrival offered her a much-needed reprieve from wedding shopping. After licking her palms, she smoothed her hair and pinched her cheeks.

When Jo emerged from behind the screen, her mother stood before her, her arms crossed over her chest.

"Almost a reprieve," Jo muttered beneath her breath.

"I'd like a word with you."

Uh-oh.

"I can see you don't want my help." Edith ducked her head and tugged on the lapels of her jacket. "You wear whatever you think is appropriate for the occasion. Just promise you won't embarrass me in front of the whole town."

The comment prickled. Jo opened and closed her mouth. Anything she said was bound to drive the conversation in circles.

She glanced around the room and realized Cora was studying a rainbow display of ribbons. The little girl needed all the love and attention they could provide. "Maybe you could see about a dress for my most special attendant?"

Cora smiled and played with the other children in town, but she'd still suffered a trauma, and they were all hypervigilant to signs of difficulty.

"Would you like that?" Jo directed her question toward Cora. "Since Garrett and I are getting married, this is your grandma."

Her ma gasped and covered her heart with one hand. "A granddaughter. Why, I didn't even think... Well, what do you know…everything happened so quickly. What a perfectly wonderful thing." She cupped her hands over her mouth and stood for a moment in stunned silence.

When the realization finally registered, Edith grasped Cora's hand. "We'll buy you a new dress and some ribbons. You've got the most wonderful curls. We won't even have to put your hair up in rags. Would you like that?"

Cora stared up at the older woman in awe, but didn't seem to mind being hustled deeper into the store. Jo's heart warmed at their easy chatter. Why hadn't she thought of encouraging their relationship earlier? Cora was the perfect distraction against her mother's meddling. Not to mention the little girl could use a bit of fussing over.

Jo was still smiling when Garrett stepped into the room, his hat in his hands. Her smile faltered as she took in the serious look on his face. "What's wrong?"

"Nothing is wrong."

"You look like someone peppered your porridge this morning."

He attempted a halfhearted grin and pulled a folded square of paper from his breast pocket. "I bought the Miller place for us. I hope you don't mind."

Jo lifted one shoulder. "Why would I mind?"

"Because I realized that you haven't even seen the inside yet. It's been empty for almost a year. It needs a fresh coat of paint and some repairs, but I think it's worth the elbow grease."

"Whatever you think."

"You're sure you don't mind?" he asked, his voice

rising in a question. "We'll have a lot of work ahead of us. What if you don't like the house?"

"It's a roof over our heads." Jo snorted. "Don't forget. I'm not like other ladies. I'm not afraid of getting dirty and it sure doesn't take much to make me happy."

Garrett flashed another half grin, then he tucked his chin to his chest and circled the brim of his hat in a now-familiar gesture. "That's one of my favorite things about you."

A giddy sense of joy filled her heart. For once she believed him. She truly believed he appreciated the qualities that made her different.

A perfectly brilliant idea sprang into her head. She couldn't believe she hadn't thought of it before.

Her old neighbor, Elizabeth Elder, had given Jo a dress for courting when she'd left for Texas. Jo had taken out the dress once before, but it was too fancy for Cimarron Springs. Maybe if she removed some of the trim and a yard or two of material from the skirts it might suit. She loathed sewing, but there was someone in town who owed her a favor—Beatrice.

Jo snapped her fingers. She'd stumbled upon the perfect solution. She'd have Beatrice fix her dress and arrange her hair, and keep her ma distracted with her new grandchild.

Garrett tilted his head. "What are you thinking about?"

Filled with a renewed sense of purpose, Jo pivoted on her heel. "I realized I own a dress I can wear for the ceremony. A dress that will even meet my ma's approval."

She made it to the door before realizing Garrett remained frozen where she'd left him.

He backed into a display of creamware and the whole

shelf clattered ominously. "You're sure you're not upset about any of this?"

"Nah." She hesitated. "Actually, you've saved me a lot of trouble. Why are you so worried?"

"I'm used to doing things on my own. I keep forgetting I need to think of someone else."

"I guess it depends on the kind of things you're doing, right?" Jo nibbled on her jagged thumbnail. "You don't think it's bad, do you? That I don't care."

Garrett shook his head from side to side. "Nope. I don't think it's bad at all."

"There's something else I should warn you about. I know my ma said the wedding will be small, but I have a feeling the whole town is going to be there."

"Okay."

"Are you sure you don't mind? I know you wanted to go before the judge. Just the two of us."

"I don't mind." He cleared his throat. "Actually, I I'm glad we're having a church wedding."

They stood in awkward silence for a moment before Jo finally broke the impasse. "It never bothered me what other people thought when I was younger. But as I got older, something changed. I started worrying about what I *should* be doing and what I *should* be saying. Which only made things worse. I'll make you a deal. We'll both forget about everyone else and do what feels right instead."

"That's a deal."

Garrett studied an array of brightly colored sewing thread. Framed examples of samplers decorated the wall above the display. Cross-stitched alphabets as well as Bible verses and flowers.

He touched the edge of a wooden frame. "My mother

once asked me to memorize a Bible verse. 'For we are his workmanship, created in Christ Jesus unto good works, which God hath before ordained that we should walk in them.'" He straightened a row of blue-speckled enamelware coffeepots. "I memorized the words but I never thought about why they were important to her."

"I suppose she wanted you to remember that we are created in God's image to do good things." Jo joined him before the display. "I believe in His word."

Clearing his throat, Garrett glanced away. "I don't know what I believe anymore. Seems like there's an awful lot of pain out there considering He has plans for us to grow and prosper and all that."

Once again Jo sensed a deep sorrow behind his words. Garrett had lost his parents and his sister. He had a right to be bitter, to question his faith. Other people had been shaken by lesser tragedies. Yet there was a profound agony behind his troubled spirit. Jo had a suspicion there was a dark place hidden in his soul. Despite her fears, her instincts urged her not to push him. He'd reveal his secrets when the time was right for him, and not a moment before.

The impulsive side of her nature chafed against the restraint. What if her instincts were wrong? Would his shadowed past prevent them from having a future together?

She offered the only wisdom she had. "You know how the rocks on the bank of a stream are jagged and sharp, but the rocks in the water are smooth and almost soft? I think that's how God sees our hardships, like water rushing over us and smoothing the hard edges, polishing us up for Heaven."

"Well, I must shine like a new penny." Garrett

laughed humorlessly as he replaced his hat. "How about tomorrow we stop by the Miller place after we visit with the reverend?"

Jo nodded. "Let's bring Cora along, too."

"If we keep on agreeing all the time, we'll have the quietest marriage in history."

"Sure."

Jo shivered despite the heat. If they didn't have strong feelings now, would they ever? She considered Tom Walby and some of the other fellows she'd known over the years. Garrett wasn't likely to shoot up a saloon because of her, but did she really want that?

The marshal touched her shoulder, halting her exit. "I almost forgot, I need you to send a telegram."

Jo tilted her head to one side. "Mrs. Schlautman is working today. She'd be happy to help."

Garrett's expression grew somber. "It's about Cora. About the marriage. I'd like you to send it. I'm tired of people gossiping about us."

Jo nodded.

His trust with the correspondence was minor, but it was a start. Maybe someday he'd trust her with the secret corroding his soul.

They exited the shop and walked the length of the boardwalk beneath the curious stares and knowing smiles of several townspeople. They'd definitely become a source of entertainment for the townsfolk.

After arriving at the telegraph office, Jo sent out a missive addressed to a solicitor named Flynn O'Neills concerning an accounting of the estate of Cora's parents. Garrett directed the solicitor to put the little girl's inheritance into trust.

Jo printed out the final words and pulled her lower

lip between her teeth. "You're a good man. She'll have a secure future."

"I'm not."

The despair in his voice startled her. "There's nothing you can say that will change my mind about you."

"You don't know that." He held her fingers, his grip bordering on painful. "You don't know that."

"Tell me then," she declared boldly. "Tell me one thing that will change my mind about you."

He held her gaze, his coffee-colored eyes dark with pain and indecision. She kept her eyes steadfast, unyielding, willing him to trust her with his pain.

They stayed like that for what seemed an eternity while an odd battle of wills played out between them.

Garrett released his hold first. "It's not too late—"

"I'm not calling off this marriage unless you give me a good reason."

She felt the indecision raging within him, a palpable thing. At last he spoke, "Thank you for helping with the telegram."

Jo sighed. "You're welcome."

He folded the notes she'd taken for his telegram and slid the paper into his breast pocket.

A lawman always had secrets. It was part of the job. She'd have to trust that he'd eventually confide his worries to her, because she had a feeling Marshal Garrett Cain knew a lot more about keeping secrets than most men.

Chapter Sixteen

Almost three weeks after Garrett had purchased the Miller house, he squinted his left eye and leveled his hands.

"Shoot already," Maxwell ordered.

Tossing a quelling glare over one shoulder, Garrett aimed the slingshot once more. He released the elastic and the rock sprang free. A split second later, his tin-can target ricocheted off its perch.

"Peas and carrots." Maxwell stomped. "You beat me again."

"I haven't beaten you yet. If you make the next shot, it's a tie."

The young boy snatched another pebble from the mound at his feet. He bit his lip and took aim, his single front tooth showing white against his lower lip. He'd lost the other front tooth the previous evening and the story of how he'd wiggled it loose had been repeated with epic drama.

Maxwell squinted and released his fingers. His shot glanced off the edge of the second can and for an agonizing moment his target teetered before tumbling triumphantly off the stump. Maxwell waved his fists in the air, giddy at having matched an adult shot for shot.

Garrett swiped the back of his hand across his damp brow. "That's a tie."

He had a feeling they'd be here all night if Max had lost the round.

Jo smiled indulgently from her seat atop the corral fence. The sun flamed behind her, and he couldn't tear his gaze from the sharp relief of her profile. As was her custom, she wore her trousers for chores around her parents' farm. Today she'd donned a striped vest over a crisp white shirt. The combination should have been masculine. He'd never seen a more feminine sight in his life.

The buttoned vest accentuated the curve of her tiny waist. The collar of her shirt revealed the delicate hollow of her neck. She'd tucked her pants into the tops of her knee boots, and he couldn't help but notice her delightfully proportioned legs.

In town she carried an edge about her. In the country she relaxed. Steady, easy chatter rang between her and her brothers. They teased and taunted each other, always with underlying respect and restraint. She was akin to the hills rolling into the distance—quietly beautiful and deceptively fierce.

Not for the first time it struck him how constrained a woman's life must be. They toiled from sundown till sunset. They bore children and cared for elderly parents while their husbands worked the fields. The only weakness he'd ever observed amongst their fiery lot was men. Look at his mother. She'd remained married to a madman. A man who cared more about drink than his own family.

A man who'd murdered her and left his children orphans.

A hearty gust of balmy June wind whipped a lock of Jo's hair across her forehead, and she hastily shoved it aside. He'd never seen a more curious mix of temperaments in one person. She had a spine of forged steel and a heart of pure light. Even as he watched, she turned toward the house with a smile of dazzling joy. Distanced from the event, he felt his heart open as she threw back her head and laughed. He couldn't see the source of her amusement. He didn't care.

He clung to the moment. Time crystallized as she caught his transfixed gaze.

Her green eyes flashed with amusement, and they shared a brief moment of united thought. Though no words were spoken, he imagined they were connected, linked in a mutual appreciation of the beauty and joy surrounding them.

His feet drew him inexorably forward. He needed to touch her, ensure she was real. How, in such a short time, had she stitched her way into the very fabric of his existence? When they were apart, she remained at the forefront of his thoughts. When they were together, his senses remained attuned to her unique scent, that curious mixture of sunlight and evergreens. He felt her emotions as though they were his own. Her joy resonated in his chest and her sorrow wrapped around his heart like a vise. He didn't understand what was happening to him, and for once he didn't care.

He held out his hand to assist her down from her perch. "I think your brothers are warming to me."

"They must be. You're still alive, aren't you?"

Garrett laughed, and she clasped his fingers. As she

leaped off the top rung, her vest caught on a splinter. She stumbled into him.

He lassoed her around the waist. "Be careful. You're still healing."

"I'm fine. The fire was ages ago."

His heart thumped against his ribs as he gently touched the fading pink wound on her cheek. She captured his wrist and turned her face into his palm. His whole body quivered with awareness.

Jo lifted her head, her alluring eyes flashing with mischief. "Sometimes I think you're afraid of me. Like right now, you're trembling."

He glanced behind him and realized they were alone. A rare thing around the McCoy farm. "I'm terrified of you, JoBeth McCoy. You can outgun me, outscrap me and outsmart me. You're so beautiful you take my breath away."

"I've never seen you like this." Her voice caressed his palm. "I don't know whether you're teasing me or not."

"Funny, I was just thinking the same thing about you. Except I'd never tease a woman who can shoot a tin can from a hundred yards."

"Be serious." Her expression grew somber. "You really don't mind that I'm not like Mary Louise Stuart?"

Garrett held her at arm's length and made a point of studying her features as a delicate flush crept up her neck.

This was a side of Jo she kept hidden, her insecurities and worries. Yet she'd confided in him, trusted him. Her faith renewed his tattered soul. "The world is full of girls like Mary Louise, but there's only one JoBeth McCoy."

If anything good came of their marriage other than

creating a family for Cora, he'd make Jo see that she was beautiful and desirable. "You have enough confidence for ten men in everything but your own appeal."

He felt as though he'd been given a precious gift. God had saved one perfect bloom. A treasure hidden in plain sight for him and no one else. She didn't know about his past, and there was no reason she'd ever discover his secrets. Maybe it was possible for people to change. The more time he spent with Jo, the stronger he felt. As though he could move mountains with his bare hands. He'd take on a grizzly with Maxwell's slingshot.

She ran the tip of her tongue along her full lower lip, and he couldn't resist the invitation. He leaned in, and she tilted her chin. The moment their lips touched, a sense of peace overwhelmed him. For the first time since the tragedy, he felt whole again, like his soul had finally begun to heal.

The dinner bell rang, startling them apart. Maxwell rounded the corner, his face flush with excitement. "Someone has come to call!"

Chafing at the interruption, Garrett glanced around the clearing. He'd been so distracted, an army of soldiers could have marched by and he wouldn't have noticed. Jo appeared dazed, her face adorably flushed and her lips parted.

Maxwell yanked on her vest. "Jo, did you hear me? There's a fancy gentleman here come for dinner."

Garrett threaded his fingers with Jo's, exchanging an indulgent grin before following the boy. They rounded the corner and Garrett froze.

"Garrett Cane!" Flynn O'Neills shouted. "As I live and breathe. I heard you were sheriff of some Podunk town, and here you are."

His father's solicitor, a man Garrett hadn't seen in over fifteen years, crossed the distance between them before Garrett could catch his breath. As Flynn embraced him, Garrett stiffened. He kept his hand firmly anchored in Jo's comforting grasp. The McCoys gathered around.

The whole family was home for Sunday dinner. Caleb and David stood together, Abraham hung back, Michael and Maxwell appeared in the door of the barn. Visitors were rare, and unexpected visitors even more so.

Flynn spread his arms in an encompassing gesture to the curious family. "I haven't seen Garrett here since he was a strapping lad full of fight like his old da."

Mr. and Mrs. McCoy, alerted by the commotion, emerged from the house.

The solicitor's hair was grayer and his face and chest softer, but other than that, he hadn't changed much over the years. Flynn was just as Garrett remembered him— larger than life and as slick as a moss-covered rock. He was stout and well groomed, his jowls and nose pink from years of drink. And he still had that same air of easy charm about him.

If he noticed Garrett's odd response, nothing showed on his face. His gray hair was greased back against his head, and his suit was impeccably cut. A heavy gold chain ran between his watch pockets.

The group exchanged a noisy round of greetings, and Flynn made a great show of repeating back the names of each McCoy in turn.

The past came rushing back, and Garrett struggled for breath.

Jo squeezed his hand. "Are you all right? You're whiter than a sheet on bluing day."

"Fine, I'm just surprised. That's all." Garrett shook his head, clearing the memories. "Flynn, what are you doing here? I didn't think Cimarron Springs was your sort of town."

The solicitor lifted his gold-tipped cane. "I got your telegram, of course."

Sensing the underlying current of tension, Edith McCoy gathered her family. "Let's set the table for dinner and give these gentlemen a chance to catch up."

While Flynn offered a few charming words, Mrs. McCoy blushed coyly, Jo loosened her grip.

She smiled at their unexpected guest. "I hope you'll join us for dinner, Mr. O'Neills. Especially after you've traveled all this way."

"Much obliged."

Garrett clung to her fingers for another long moment. He caught her gaze and saw the confusion in her eyes.

The solicitor sauntered over, his watch chain flashing in the brilliant sunlight, and made a point of sizing up Jo. "And who is this lovely young lady?"

His gaze dipped pointedly at their linked fingers.

Garrett released his hold. His feelings were too raw and new for sharing. "This is my fiancée, JoBeth McCoy. Flynn was my father's solicitor."

"More than that, surely," Flynn boomed. "I've been a close friend of the family for many, many years."

Jo and Flynn linked hands in a greeting, and apprehension snaked down Garrett's spine. What would Flynn say? Would he let something slip?

Garrett's hackles rose and he instinctively felt the need to protect her. "I'll meet you inside, Jo."

She hesitated, her curious gaze shifting between the two men, then dutifully retreated into the house.

Flynn slapped him on the back as the door closed behind her. "You always could pick a winner. That's a diamond in the rough you've discovered. I wouldn't have thought it possible in this wilderness."

Garrett clenched his jaw. "You're a long way from home."

"I'm on my way to Denver." Flynn tugged his leather gloves over his unnaturally pale wrists. "I couldn't pass up the opportunity to see an old friend of the family. Especially after you'd contacted me personally."

"Did you discover anything?"

"It's just as you suspected. Edward hasn't turned a profit since your uncle died. He isn't the businessman his dad was. Your sister, on the other hand, left a tidy sum."

"You think Edward is after Cora for the money?"

"It's a fair guess. He's been making a lot of noise around town. Bringing up the past."

Garrett felt the blood drain from his face. "Do you think that will hold sway with the judge?"

"Not if you're married. They can't hold your father's actions against you. And you've proven yourself an honorable man over the years."

Garrett's uneasiness grew with each word. He'd kept his life sequestered. He'd left St. Louis behind and started over. For fifteen years he'd kept his secrets hidden, safely tucked away in another time. With Flynn here, his past and future collided.

"Don't worry," Flynn spoke. "Edward hasn't the stamina for a fight. He'll drop the case once he realizes you won't give up Cora. He's a coward at heart."

Staring sightlessly into the distance, Garrett struggled with his growing dread. "My dad was a decorated hero during the war. Look what that got him."

Flynn braced both hands on his walking stick. "They don't know about your parents, do they?"

"They don't."

"You can't hide forever."

"I have to." Garrett paused. "For Cora's sake, don't say anything."

"I won't, but you should. A foundation of lies is a poor way to build a life. They're good people. Give them a chance."

"I'm a lawman, too. I have a family to support now. It's not just me, it's Cora's future I'm risking."

Garrett had already set the wheels in motion, and there was no halting the marriage. He'd compromised Jo in the eyes of the town, and he'd do the right thing by her. This time he'd stick to the original plan. He'd pull away and put some distance between them—physically and mentally.

A voice called and Garrett turned.

Jo motioned from the porch. "Supper is ready."

As for the kisses they'd shared, Garrett would lock away the precious memories. They'd go back to being friends, back to the way things were before the fire.

Jo rested her forehead on the door. "I don't want to interrupt, but if we don't sit down quick, the boys are going to gnaw into the wooden table."

Despair tightened in his chest. How could a person gain and lose everything in a single day?

The wagon tipped along a deep rut, throwing Jo into Garrett. She savored the contact until he steadied her with one hand, keeping his other fisted around the leather reins.

"Tell me about Flynn?" she asked.

He glanced at her, his face inscrutable in the twilight. "There isn't much to say."

"I thought you'd be happy seeing someone from your past."

"A lot of years have gone by," he replied, his tone clipped.

Jo recalled the inquiry she'd sent to the solicitor. "Did he have the information you were searching for?"

"Yep."

His curt tone raised her hackles. There'd been a ridge of tension around Garrett since his old friend's arrival. The camaraderie they'd shared was gone.

A dozing Cora stirred against Jo's side as Garrett halted the team and wrestled the brake into position.

He slanted a glance at his slumbering niece. "My cousin is in financial trouble, just as I suspected. Edward doesn't want custody to protect Cora from me. He needs her inheritance to save his business."

Jo titled her head. "Is something else wrong?"

"I wanted a minute to talk with you." Shadows played across his face. "While Cora is sleeping."

"Okay."

"I'm sorry. About earlier today. At the corral."

Jo grasped his arm. "I'm not."

"We agreed to get married for Cora's sake, to give her a family. I forgot myself, and I apologize for that. We agreed this was a partnership, a friendship, and I didn't hold up my end of the bargain."

"Does this have something to do with Flynn's visit?"

Her voice cracked. "You've been different since he came along."

"I've just been thinking, that's all. Do you really want to get married?"

He was doing it again, running hot and cold. She should be used to his changing attitude by now, but she wasn't. "Are you sore at me?"

"No, of course not." He swiveled on the bench seat and grasped her shoulders. "I care about you, Jo. And I want what's best for you. We've been treating this whole thing like we don't have any other choice. But there's always a choice. If I leave, the gossip will die down soon enough."

His sudden change of heart wasn't about the two of them—this was about Flynn. The solicitor had said something that spooked him. "Did Flynn threaten you?"

"Of course not. This has…this has nothing to do with him. Maybe we were taking the easy way out. We can say we fought. I can say you called off the marriage. I'll take the blame."

He had secrets, but he was a good man. Jo knew it in her heart. Whatever Flynn held over him, she didn't care. Nothing could change her mind about the man she'd agreed to marry. "What do *you* want?"

The agonizing question stretched out between them while crickets chirped in an early-summer chorus. Jo clutched her hands together and waited. She'd thought they were growing closer. They talked together, they laughed together, he'd held her close and kissed her until she was breathless.

Another thought brought her up short. Unless he hadn't enjoyed their time together. Perhaps his indecision had nothing to do with Flynn's arrival, and everything to do with the kisses they'd shared.

Garrett shifted. "I want to do the right thing, but I don't know which choice is right."

"What's the best choice for Cora?"

"You are," he answered immediately, "You're the best thing for her. She loves you, and I don't want her to lose any more than she already has."

Jo's ma had accused her of being selfish. Was she? After all, she'd moved into town rather than take over the midwife's duties.

She wasn't the kind of girl men courted—she'd known that from the beginning. He'd wanted a partnership; she was the one who'd wanted more. If he wanted a friend, she'd be a friend. They'd go back to the way things were.

Jo studied the purple-tinted twilight sky and gathered her nerve.

She touched his leather-clad hand, heartened by the almost imperceptible tremble she felt in his fingers. "Then let's do what's right for Cora, and never mind about anything else."

"Okay." Garrett spoke so quietly she wasn't even certain she'd heard him correctly.

Each tentative step she'd taken forward had been met with resistance. He'd called her beautiful, and then he'd pulled away. She feared this power he held over her. His embrace left her feeling exuberant and capable, his rejection shook her faith.

Jo squared her shoulders. She'd pull away, too, just as Garrett had. She refused to let him hurt her anymore.

Chapter Seventeen

The house stood a half mile from the edge of town, a two-story white clapboard with a gabled roof and whitewashed picket fence. According to local gossip, the home had been empty for over a year since the Millers had moved to Denver.

Garrett yanked at the overgrown weeds until he found the gate hook. The fence had collapsed in two places and several of the boards were rotted through. He surveyed the sparse lawn and unlocked the front door with the rusted key he'd acquired from the lawyer, then pried open the stiff hinges. The dank, moldy smell of disuse triggered an unexpected jolt of melancholy.

How quickly abandonment turned to disrepair. Houses were meant to be lived in. A spindly chair rested on its side, and Garrett lifted it upright. Lulled by the quiet, he meandered around the sprawling floor plan, weaving his way through the sitting room, parlor, dining room and finally the kitchen.

He took the back steps to the second floor and discovered three good-size bedrooms devoid of furniture. The floorboards creaked as he crossed the spacious hallway and glanced out the window toward the rolling hills. Someone had planted a brace of poplar trees, and they'd grown as high as the second-floor eaves. An excellent windbreak.

Garrett rested his hands on the dusty sill. He wanted to ensure the house was sound before Jo arrived. Despite his good intentions, he'd hurt her last evening. She didn't understand and he couldn't offer an explanation without dredging up the past.

A train whistle sounded, and Garrett caught sight of the 3:15 from Wichita on the horizon. Everything was going according to plan, yet he couldn't shake his unease. *Nothing good ever lasted long.*

Garrett shook off the odd feeling. The train posed no danger. It was just another passenger train, just another group of weary travelers stopping for lunch on the way to someplace else. Families seeking a better life, soldiers transferring West, adventurers itching for their next exploit. Flynn's arrival had shaken him, that's all. And for good reason.

The country was shrinking. Each new set of rail tracks brought the coasts closer together. Once the Union and the Central Pacific rail lines had joined, there was no going back. The moment two merging railroads had driven in the golden stake at Promontory Summit, they'd forged the destiny of a nation.

A man couldn't hide anymore.

Garrett turned away from the window, but the sense of unease followed him. He'd run out of places to hide. How long before his past caught up with him?

* * *

Jo rested her chin on the rounded tip of the broom handle. She'd steeled herself against her attraction, and so far it had worked.

She and Garrett were getting along well, pretending nothing had sparked between them. "This isn't so bad."

Garrett sat back on his heels and wiped the perspiration from his forehead with the back of his hand. "Could be worse."

They'd been working since dawn, scrubbing floors and walls and trim. Beneath a year and a half of neglect they'd uncovered a relatively sound house. "If we paint tomorrow, I can oil the floors on Thursday."

"I'll help." Garrett ran the back of his hand over his forehead.

"Can you take that much time away from the town?"

He rose and dusted his hands together. "About that. What do you think of David as a permanent deputy?"

Scratching beneath the red bandanna she'd knotted over her hair, Jo considered his announcement. "I never thought about it. I figured he'd move to Wichita. He spends enough time there."

"He needs work. He's not a farmer like Caleb."

Jo lifted the broom and dusted the cobwebs hanging in the corner of the spacious dining room. "I still think he'll opt for Wichita."

"He'll stay."

"How can you be so certain?"

Garrett cleared his throat.

Stifling a sneeze, Jo dropped the broom and caught his guilty expression before he quickly turned away. "You're keeping a secret. What are you hiding?"

"Nothing."

"You're lying. I can tell." Brandishing her broom, she pointed the bristles at his chest. "Tell me or I'll cover you in cobwebs."

Garrett held up his hands. "He's been spending more time at the mercantile than Caleb."

Her hands went slack and the bristles hit the floor, stirring a plume of dust. "No."

"Yes."

"Well, what are you going to do?"

"Nothing." Garrett dropped his arms. "What am I supposed to do?"

"I don't know, talk to them. Mary Louise isn't worth fighting over."

"It's none of our business. But I suspect she's got a shine for David."

Jo groaned. "Then someone should talk with Mary Louise."

"Leave it alone. Anything you or I say will only make things worse. This has to play out on its own."

"Fine. But don't you think he's awfully young for all that responsibility?"

"You lost me." Garrett frowned. "Did we change subjects?"

"Don't avoid the question."

"David is young, but he'll learn. I was an army scout at seventeen."

She tried to imagine Garrett as a young man. Wide-eyed and innocent. The picture didn't form. "What was that like?"

"Hot in the summer, cold in the winter and hungry year-round."

"A dockworker at fifteen, an army scout at seventeen. You've led a full life, Garrett Cain."

A call from the second floor interrupted her next question. Jo dashed toward the stairs. "Cora?"

The little girl appeared at the head of the stairs. "I found another mice nest."

Propping her broom against the wall, Jo grimaced. "I'll come and take a look. That'll be the fourth one we've found so far."

She took the stairs two at a time and followed Cora into the smallest of the upstairs rooms. The house was a basic foursquare, with a master suite, two good-size bedrooms and a utility space all grouped around an open landing.

Cora knelt before a cupboard and pointed. Sure enough, a soft nest of wool, leaves and a bright length of orange yarn nestled in the corner.

Garrett's footsteps sounded behind her. "More mice?"

Glancing over her shoulder, Jo nodded. "I think we should consider taking one of Maxwell's kittens."

"I don't like animals in the house." Garrett knelt beside her. "But I guess I'd rather have a cat than mice."

"The cat can stay in the house while we finish cleaning up. She can stay in the barn after that."

As he leaned in for a closer look, their shoulders brushed together. Garrett reached around her, and Jo leaned into his arm. He scooted back and she leaned the opposite direction, crowding him, forcing the contact. He wasn't immune to her, she knew it, felt it in her bones. Yet each time she initiated even the lightest touch, he pulled away.

It was wrong, it was dangerous, and she couldn't help herself.

Her reluctant fiancé sat back on his heels. "Sounds like a good compromise to me."

Though they didn't touch, he remained only a breath away. Warmth rushed through her veins, and her pulse quickened. The memory of their last kiss sent a shiver down her spine. She recalled the feel of his shoulders, the corded muscles against her fingertips.

Cora danced on the balls of her feet. "Can I pick the kitten? Please?"

Garrett rubbed his chin. "I suppose."

The little girl glanced around the tiny space with its single bank of whitewashed cupboards. "What's this room?"

"A nursery," Garrett replied.

Jo's legs quaked. If this were a real marriage, she'd have added curtains, and her mother would have passed on the hand-carved bassinet from her grandmother.

The realization sank through her body like a stone, dragging down her spirits. Emotions flickered across Garrett's face, and she wondered if he felt the same loss, the same disappointment.

Suddenly chilled, she wrapped her arms around her body. "This would make a better playroom for you than a nursery."

Garrett flinched and turned away.

Cora stepped between them, jerking Jo's thoughts back to the present.

"Which room is mine?" the little girl asked.

"You can pick," Garrett replied, his voice hoarse. "I guess Jo gets the biggest room."

"It doesn't matter." Jo ran her finger along the window sash. There'd be no need for curtains at all, not for a playroom. "You can have the larger room."

"I couldn't."

"Fine then." She turned, but couldn't bring herself

to look him in the face. "I'll take the room at the head of the stairs."

Anything to end this painful conversation.

"How come you're not sharing?" Cora asked. "My mommy and daddy shared a room."

Jo sputtered, and Garrett coughed.

"Well." She cringed. "There are so many rooms, there's no need for any of us to share."

Jo snatched the bandanna from her head and rubbed the perspiration from the back of her neck. "You can pick the kitten. We can go next weekend."

"Today." Garrett spoke a notch too loudly. "We could leave right now."

Jo giggled at the absurdity of it all. The tension in the room eased at her outburst, and she and Garrett backed away from each other, putting space between them. Separating them from the swirl of emotions permeating the cramped room.

Garrett caught her amused expression, and a smile spread across his face. "Maybe it's time for a break."

"That's a good idea."

Jo remained in the room long after they'd both returned downstairs. There was no going back now. Even if she refused the marriage, where did that leave her? Back to her room at the boardinghouse, back to her job each morning, back to Sunday dinners at home.

The boys would bring home their new brides, and soon the babies would follow.

A baby.

It was like a revelation, this sudden driving need. Worse yet, it had appeared out of the thin blue sky with no warning. She'd long ago given up the thought of a family of her own. Standing with Garrett, imagining the nursery decorated as it was intended, she'd been rocked with a need stronger than anything she'd ever known.

Alone, her future was certain. Married, there was always a glimmer of hope. Perhaps through the years he'd come to see her as more than a tomboy. More than a companion.

She'd thought marrying someone out of friendship was the easy solution.

Turned out there were no shortcuts in life.

Chapter Eighteen

Stunned, Jo focused on her image in the looking glass. "Is that really me?"

Beatrice fluffed her veil and let the lace settle around her shoulders like a gossamer mantle. "You're lovely."

A gasp sounded from the far side of the room and Jo turned. Her mother stood in the doorway, one hand clutching Cora's and the other covering her mouth.

"Oh, my goodness," Edith said, her voice watery with emotion. "How? When?"

Jo pleated her ivory skirts with two fingers. "This is the dress Elizabeth left for me. Beatrice took the lace off the collar and we left the pin tucks."

"But what about the dress from the mercantile?" Her ma took a hesitant step forward, her arm outstretched. "And your hair."

"Beatrice arranged it for me this morning." Jo touched the elaborate knot at the base of her neck. "How do I look?"

"Lovely. Absolutely lovely."

For once, Edith McCoy didn't look pressed and polished. Her ma had obviously dressed quickly that morning and a loose end of her shirttail hung limply beneath the bodice of her best Sunday dress. Her hair had been whipped into a serviceable braid and wrapped around her head, but one loose end trailed down her shoulder. She appeared more frazzled than Jo could ever recall seeing her.

"Ma, why don't you have a seat." Jo hooked her arm beneath the dazed woman's elbow. "You were up all night with Mrs. Hendrick's newborn. Didn't the doc's wife come by? She said she was going to help when the time came."

"She was dear," Edith replied with a distracted nod. "She trained as a nurse back East, you know."

"Pa said everything went all right."

"I couldn't leave the poor thing alone. Her husband had his hands full with the two little ones and she was frightened something would happen to the new baby. She's still terrified since the last one was stillborn."

"That's why we let you sleep." Jo pressed her finger against a poking hairpin near her ear.

Beatrice slapped away her hand. "You've got ten more minutes. Stop wiggling."

"But it hurts."

With an air of long suffering, Beatrice adjusted the pin. "That better?"

"Yes." Jo scratched at the sore spot. "Beauty is painful."

"And your veil," her ma added breathlessly. "Is that your grandmother's veil?"

"Don't you remember? You sent it over yesterday."

"I know, but I thought… I thought *I'd* help you get ready." A fine sheen of tears formed in her ma's eyes.

Unsure of the cause of Edith's distress, Jo awkwardly patted her hand. "I did just fine on my own."

Her ma choked out a sob.

"Uh…" Jo hesitated. Everything she said made the situation worse.

Beatrice clucked and steered the distressed woman before the looking glass. "You look a bit windblown from the ride. Why don't I fix your braid and give those cheeks a pinch of color."

"My cake didn't turn out," her ma moaned as Beatrice fussed around her, smoothing her hair and brushing the dust from her jacket. "It's too hot and the frosting melted. It looks like one of Maxwell's mud pies."

"I'm sure it tastes fine," Jo chimed in helpfully.

"And I didn't fix the lemonade," Edith continued without pause. "Now we'll be stuck with Mrs. Stuart's lemonade and she never puts in enough sugar."

"I'll have the boys sneak in an extra cup."

Edith remained limp beneath Beatrice's ministrations. "I wanted today to be special for you."

"It is special." Jo stood behind her ma and met her gaze in the mirror. "Now, stop worrying."

Her ma whirled and squeezed Jo until the tiny pearl buttons bit into her back. "I love you."

"I love you, too."

Jo groaned, and her ma loosened her hold and held her at a distance. "You look beautiful. You look just like your grandmother."

Jo grimaced at the dim memory she held of her paternal grandmother, a squat woman with dark, bushy eyebrows. "I guess I didn't know Grandma McCoy when she was young."

"Not her!" Edith lightly swatted Jo's shoulder. "*My*

mother. She was quite a beauty in her time. Gracious, the stories they used to tell about her. Your grandfather followed her from England. He said he would have followed her around the world and back again."

A pang of emotion fluttered in Jo's chest. She resolutely tamped it down. This wasn't a dime novel, this was her life, and she was facing the truth of her situation head-on. They were doing this for Cora, and the sacrifice was well worth any personal doubts. Cora was opening up, smiling and talking. She still didn't speak of her parents or her loss. They took each good day as a blessing and each painful day as a cobblestone on the path toward healing.

A gentle knock sounded, and Mary Louise peered in. "Are you ready? Looks like the whole town turned out. They're getting restless."

"I'm ready." Jo glanced down as Cora lifted a basket for her inspection. "They look like pear blossoms, don't they?"

Cora nodded.

"I love you." Jo grinned, then knelt and embraced the little girl in a warm hug. "Do you know you get the seat of honor during the wedding? Right between Grandma and Grandpa."

The little girl's cornflower-blue eyes widened, and Edith sniffled. "Come along. We'd best claim our seats."

As Beatrice, Cora and her ma hustled from the room, Ely McCoy appeared in the doorway. He wore his finest navy suit, pressed and cleaned for the occasion. He'd even trimmed his mustache and shaved his beard for the occasion. When she'd seen him early that morning, he'd been as bristly as a bear.

Jo gaped. "You look so...so young! Did you go to the barber?"

Ely rubbed his hand down his face, dislodging a bit of cloth covering a nick from his close shave. "Couldn't walk my little girl down the aisle looking like a fur trapper."

Tears prickled in Jo's eyes as her pa pulled her into his comforting embrace.

He stepped back and held her at arm's length. "I don't want to muss you up now. You look as pretty as a princess."

"Thank you."

"You're sure this is what you want?"

"I'm sure," Jo lied with newly practiced ease. "More certain than I've ever been about anything in my life."

Her reply wasn't the whole truth—there were parts of her future she feared. No one need know of her unease.

"Because I've got the wagon hitched outside." He jerked his thumb over one shoulder. "We could high-tail it outta here."

"Pa," Jo warned. "Garrett Cain is a good man."

"I know. But I'm losing my little girl. Give your old man a chance to hang on a little longer."

"You'll never lose me, Pa."

"I will lose a part of you, but that's how it's meant to be. You grow and go your own way. It doesn't mean it's easy, though. I remember the first time I held you in my arms. You fit right in my hand." He held out his arm, palm up, as though reliving the memory. "I still you see you that way."

Jo pressed a hand against her quivering stomach. "I'm all grown up now."

"I want you to know what a blessing you've been in

my life. You're the spring in my step each morning. I know you and Garrett will make a fine family together. Despite my teasing, I have a good feeling about you two. A real good feeling."

"I don't think Ma is too happy. She hasn't said anything outright, but whenever the subject comes up, she pinches her lips together and inhales through her nose."

"It's never good for any of us when your mother gets to looking like she ate a lemon. I do know one thing—your ma wants what's best for you."

"*This* is what's best for me."

"Then you'll have to show her, won't you? She'll come around."

They linked elbows, and her pa covered her hand with his and gave her fingers a squeeze. "You know in your heart if what you're doing is right."

"I know, Pa." If she said the words enough, maybe they'd come true. "I know for certain."

Cora needed her, and Garrett needed them both.

Ely searched her face. Appearing satisfied with what he saw, he asked, "Did you get the present I left you?"

Jo lifted the hem of her skirts, revealing her brand-new cowboy boots of butterscotch-colored leather with cream floral stitching. "They're perfect."

"I had 'em sent down on the train from Wichita special."

"Aren't you afraid of what Ma's going to do when she finds out?"

"Why should I be?" Her pa toed open the door. "She picked them out herself."

Garrett paced a tight circle in the tiny church vestibule, fidgeting with the red rose in his lapel. Had it only been a few short weeks since he'd sat before the reverend, absorbing the news of Deirdre's death?

Little Maxwell tugged on his pant leg. "Do you know why bees buzz?"

"Uh, no."

"Because they can't whistle."

Garrett chuckled. "That's a good one."

The little guy had attached himself to Garrett earlier in the day and didn't show any signs of disappearing. "Shouldn't you be with your family?"

"Nah. I'm okay with you. Caleb said if you were nervous I should tell you jokes. Are you nervous?"

"A little bit."

"How come?"

"Because I want to do the right thing, and I'm not certain what that is anymore."

Garrett considered Flynn's advice. He should have told Jo the truth. He'd started telling her a thousand times and then stopped himself short. He craved her respect. She liked him, even trusted him. Exposing his past risked their untried friendship. Was he betraying Jo for his own peace of mind?

"I have another joke," Maxwell announced.

Garrett nodded. "I'm listening."

"How do you get a rooster to stop crowing on Sunday?"

"I dunno, how?"

"Eat him on Saturday."

Garrett chuckled again. "That's a good one, too."

"My ma says that she hopes Jo knows what's she's doing, or you two are going to be miserable."

"Your ma's right." Garrett thought of the one thing that had given him courage over the past weeks. "Have you ever known a time when Jo didn't know her own mind?"

The littlest McCoy screwed up his face in concentration. "Nope."

"Me neither."

"Can I come play with Cora when you and Jo are married?"

"Certainly."

A knot of townsfolk filed through the vestibule. Ely McCoy approached the opposite door, and Garrett spun around. He didn't want to see JoBeth before the ceremony. Not that he counted himself a superstitious man, but he wanted to wait.

"Do you have a ring?" Maxwell asked.

"Yep." Garrett fished in his vest pocket and revealed a circlet of flat ruby stones set in gold. "What do you think? It's been in my family for generations."

Deirdre had insisted he keep the ring, and he was glad for once he'd listened.

"Wow." The young boy's eyes widened. "That's fancy."

Garrett ruffled Maxwell's dark hair, then turned at the press of a hand against his shoulder.

Reverend Miller motioned. "It's time."

Sucking in a deep breath, Garrett nodded. "Max, I reckon we're the two best-looking fellows in Cimarron Springs."

"I reckon we are."

The two joined hands and set off down the aisle. Garrett kept his attention focused on the altar. The church was packed with townspeople, and he felt their curious gazes following his progress. Voices rippled like waves with each of his steps.

Doubts crowded his thoughts. If his past was a lie, did he deserve a better future? As his steps slowed, he caught sight of the back of Cora's head, her coronet of flowers and the yellow ribbons trailing down her back. He shook his head, clearing the cobwebs. Cora deserved the best he could offer. Jo was a gift to each of them. He'd do right by her.

Sunlight streamed through the stained-glass window and cast angled rainbow patterns over the wooden floor. He'd pretend his past was the blank slate he'd created in his mind. The doubts would return; they'd worm their way into his heart and soul once more, but for now he held them at bay.

For today, he'd pretend nothing chained his soul.

He caught sight of Jo at the end of the aisle, and his heart tripped. She glided toward him, hand in hand with her father, an aged lace veil draped over her thick, dark hair. From beneath the fluttering edge, he caught the elegant curve of her neck. She wore an ivory gown— simple, elegant. His heart ached at the missing braid she usually wore tossed over one shoulder.

The barest glimpse of the nape of her neck warmed his blood. His gaze swept down the length of her, taking in the graceful sweep of her dress. The bodice had a modest V neck lined with delicate pin tucking, nipped in at an impossibly slim waist. She clutched a posy of wild red roses in her hand.

Her father flipped her veil over her hair, then kissed the bloom of each cheek. Garrett's palms dampened, and his mouth went dry.

She paused before him, and he found himself mesmerized by her rose-colored lips. The sound of someone clearing his throat sent the congregation tittering, and Garrett jerked his gaze away from Jo. Ely McCoy stared at him, one bushy eyebrow raised in censure.

Garrett flashed an abashed grin. "Sir."

Grasping his hand, Ely leaned in and whispered, "You take care of her or you'll answer to me."

Garrett nodded. The older man pumped his hand in a bone-crushing grip and took his seat in the first pew with Cora and his wife. The little girl remained solemn, but she appeared brighter than she had since the fire, and Garrett took that as a sign of encouragement.

The rest of the ceremony passed in a blur. The resonant words of the cleric echoed off the timber ceiling in solemn declaration. Garrett repeated his lines on cue and slipped the ring on Jo's finger when the moment arrived. She glanced at the rubies and back up at him. Garrett held his breath and waited for her reaction. When she smiled her approval, the tension drained from his shoulders. He hadn't even realized he was nervous until she'd flashed her assent.

The relief remained when Reverend Miller closed his Bible and cleared his throat. "You may now kiss the bride."

Garrett blinked.

Jo tipped back her head.

The church and all the congregants faded into the background. In that moment, only he and Jo existed. He slipped one hand around her waist, his callused fingers catching on the satin-wrapped buttons at her back. The arm clutching her bouquet lifted, and the scent of wild roses drifted through the air. For the rest of his life, he knew he'd always associate the scent with this moment.

The moment their lips touched, Jo sighed. Her hands crept up his neck, lifting her bouquet as a floral shield against their rapt audience. She clung to him with a fervor that matched his own before they broke apart and stared at each other in breathless silence.

The room erupted into noisy applause, and he and Jo faced the congregation. They trusted him, and he was more determined than ever to keep that trust.

Chapter Nineteen

The next few hours passed in a blur for Jo. Seemed like everyone within a fifty-mile radius of Cimarron Springs had come. Her ma's cozy wedding had turned into a bustling crowd, and Jo's feet ached in her new boots. The party had been too large for the confines of the church and spilled into the sunny afternoon.

Checkered cloths covered the tables and children crowded hip to hip along the benches. They eagerly jostled forward, loading their plates with cakes and pies. Abraham emerged from around the corner of the church, a pitcher of lemonade in his hands, the contents sloshing from side to side.

He winked at her. "Sweet enough even for Ma."

Edith McCoy stood in a clutch of women holding their ribboned bonnets against the afternoon breeze. Once the ceremony had passed, her ma had finally relaxed.

Jo snagged a glass of lemonade and ducked behind the shed. Her solitude was short lived. Tom and his wife circled around the opposite side, their voices raised in harsh, arguing whispers. Jo gulped her lemonade and slipped around the other side. She didn't want Tom ruining her day with any of his rude comments.

Unaccustomed to being the center of attention, she plastered a stiff smile upon her face and called cheerful greetings in response to the many well-wishers.

Catching sight of her sagging against a doorjamb, Garrett grasped her hand and pulled her away from the crowd.

Jo groaned and patted her face. "My cheeks are going to crack if I smile anymore."

"Mine, too."

"Do you think we can sneak out of here?" she muttered. "Cora is staying with my family tonight, remember? Maxwell promised her a slingshot lesson in the morning."

Garrett rubbed his forehead. "I'll have two women who can outshoot me in the family now."

"Then you'd better behave yourself."

"Come along." Garrett clasped her hand. "If we cut behind the buildings, we can make it home in no time."

"It's a half mile down the road from town."

"A good stretch of the legs."

Jo groaned. Her feet ached, but she wanted an escape more than she wanted to rest.

They'd spent the past week painting and cleaning the house, and Jo had delivered her belongings that morning. Working beside Garrett had finally made their impending marriage real. After spending days scrubbing every dusty corner of the house, she'd grown no more accustomed to the idea of living with Garrett.

Together they tiptoed behind the livery, giggling and shushing each other. As they slunk around the corner, Garrett flung his arm around her waist and pressed a finger against his lips. Jo stilled. He cupped one hand against his ear and Jo leaned forward.

She caught the low hum of her brothers' voices from inside the livery.

She heard David's voice first.

"Are you sure you saw them leave?" he asked.

"They're sneaking back home, I know it," Caleb replied.

"We can throw the marshal in the horse tank."

"Nah," Caleb muttered. "This is better."

"Okay," David agreed. "I've got the lard for the door-knobs and pots and pans."

Jo gasped, and the marshal pressed a hand over her mouth, then scooted her away from the boys' hushed conversation.

"It's a shivaree!" she exclaimed in a harsh whisper.

"What's that?"

"A horrible country custom," Jo declared. "They'll run through the house making noise and causing pranks."

"Then let's not go home."

"What do you mean?" Torn between duty and propriety, Jo hesitated. "Where will we go?"

Garrett flashed a mischievous smile. "Do you trust me?"

"Yes," Jo answered, feeling as addled as when he'd kissed her at the altar.

"Then let's go for a ride."

Garrett grasped her hand and tugged her into a dash. Joy rushed through her, and the pain in her feet faded into the background. They rounded the corner of the livery, and Garrett peered in the door. He held a finger to his lips, compelling her to silence, and disappeared inside. A moment later he returned, grasping the reins of his horse.

Jo glanced behind her, relieved her brothers were distracted by their plotting. Garrett leaped onto the horse and held out his arm. She clambered onto the mounting block and perched sidesaddle before him, one knee looped around the saddle horn.

A voice called, and Jo craned her neck. Beatrice chased after them, waving her arms.

"Wait," she called breathlessly. "Don't ruin your grandmother's lace."

Jo reached up and touched her head. She still wore the heirloom veil. She quickly released the pins and shook off the decoration. "How did you find us?"

Gasping, Beatrice leaned heavily on Jo's leg and pressed a hand against her side. "I came to warn you. Your brothers are planning a shivaree."

"We caught them in the livery. They're getting lard for the doorknobs." Jo scowled. "And after I spent the whole week cleaning."

"Don't you worry. I'll let your pa know they're up to something. He'll keep them in line."

"You'll be saving their hides from me." Jo leaned down and shared an awkward embrace from her high perch. "Thank you for remembering my veil."

Beatrice sketched another wave and backed away from the prancing horse. Jo heaved a sigh of relief. Between her parents and Beatrice, the boys couldn't cause too much mischief.

Garrett fiddled with the saddlebag at her knee and pulled out the hat Jo had been eyeing at the mercantile weeks ago. A leather drover's hat.

"How did you know?" She gaped.

Garrett winked at her. "Can't a groom give his wife a wedding gift?"

She lifted her gift and felt the supple brown leather.

Garrett reached for the hat, and she pulled it away

"You don't have to wear it now," he said. "I didn't think about your hair."

Touching the pins poking her tender skull, Jo grimaced. "I think I can let it down now. I've suffered enough."

She loosened the pins and shook her hair free of all Beatrice's careful ministrations. For a blissful moment she ran her fingers over her sore scalp, groaning with relief. "That's better." Jo caught his pained expression. "Oh, dear, I didn't get you anything. I'm sorry."

"Yes, you did."

Jo searched his expression. "What?"

"I'll tell you later. Now hang on."

She slapped the hat on her head and smiled. It fit perfect. Not too loose and not too snug.

She sneaked a peek at his relaxed expression. He obviously wasn't holding a grudge over her oversight. "Let's go."

Kicking his horse into a gallop, Garrett let out a holler. Unused to the awkward position, Jo clutched the corded muscle of the arm anchored around her waist.

He was strong and solid. He'd never let her fall.

She clutched her hat with one hand and glanced over her shoulder. "Where are we going?"

"It's a surprise."

As the horse galloped, the wind tugged on her hair like a thousand fingers, ripping loose the carefully created curls at the nape of her neck Beatrice had worked on only hours before. With the wedding done, and the ground rushing by, Jo was herself again.

Garrett kept his right hand looped in the reins, his left arm protectively around her waist. "You okay?"

"Yes," Jo shouted over the whistling wind. She was more than okay. "I want to holler," she called.

"Then do it."

Jo whooped, her voice lost on the breeze. She released one hand and raised her palm to the sky.

The horse's gait slowed as they rounded a corner out of town, out of sight of any curious eyes that might have seen their escape.

Jo adjusted her hat and glanced around at the familiar surroundings. "Say, we're going back to the house."

"Not quite."

Garrett reined in the horse and cut across the field toward Hackberry Creek. Tall grass brushed at her knees, and Jo tucked her skirts tighter to her body as they crossed into the tree line.

When the underbrush became too impassable for the horse, Garrett halted. "We'll walk from here."

Growing more curious by the moment, Jo slid down first, and Garrett followed. He looped the reins around a low-hanging tree branch and fished in his saddlebags.

After a moment he turned and shook out a long duster. "Put this over your dress so you don't get too dirty."

He wrapped the enveloping coat around her shoulders, and Jo sank into its warmth. The sun was setting, cooling the evening air. Garrett clasped her hand and led her deeper into the wooded area surrounding the creek. The smell of damp earth teased her nostrils. Her feet sank into the soft earth, and branches tugged at her skirts. It would take a load of elbow grease to remove the stains, but she didn't mind. She was ready for an adventure, and nothing was going to hold her back.

Garrett halted and pointed toward the towering branches. "I found this when I was walking the property line."

Jo tilted back her head and shaded her eyes. "It's a tree house."

A great pin oak towered above the timberline, and someone had built a crude structure in the sheltering cradle of its branches. Jo circled the enormous trunk, her fingers trailing along the rough bark. "I bet if we held our hands together, we couldn't circle that trunk."

"This tree must be fifty years old."

"Can you imagine? Think what this tree has seen. There wasn't even a town around here fifty years ago."

Boards had been nailed into the sturdy trunk and Garrett grasped one. "They're solid. I climbed up myself two days ago. There's a break in the trees, and you can see all the way to the road."

Jo gauged the distance. "Let's climb up."

"Are you certain? You'll ruin your dress."

"I don't care."

His expression remained dubious. "Can you climb in skirts?"

Jo flashed a mischievous grin. "All my life."

She grasped the bottom rung and hoisted herself up. Her boot caught on her hem and Garrett tugged the material loose. She looped her skirts over one arm and easily climbed the rest of the way. The wood was rough with age, but she barely noticed with her work-roughened hands. A trapdoor had been cut into the floor, and she hoisted herself over the edge.

As Jo studied the tiny house, Garrett clambered inside. Someone had built a perfect little structure, complete with a roof and open-air windows. The enormous trunk burst right through the middle of the floor and the branches stuck out through the center of the shingled roof. Every surface was dusty, and Garrett's previous footprints showed in the dirt.

He pushed off with a hand on one knee and stood, his back hunched against the low ceiling, then reached for her. "C'mon, I'll show you the best part."

Curious, she let him guide her to the opposite edge. A window cut in the side offered a view all the way to the road, and the roof of their new house showed in the distance.

Clouds gathered on the horizon, blocking the setting sun. "Looks like we might get a storm."

Garrett shrugged out of his coat and laid it over the floor. He helped her down and sat beside her. "We can wait here for a while until your brothers lose interest."

"Or until the rain comes." Jo glanced up at the spotty ceiling. "There's not much shelter."

Jo shivered, and Garrett wrapped an arm around her shoulders. "Are you too cold? We don't have to stay."

"No," Jo protested quickly. She liked it here. She liked being alone for once. Since Cora's arrival, her life had been full of people and activity. Not that she minded, but having an hour to themselves felt like decadent luxury.

Jo studied her hands. "I saw you talking with Mr. Stuart."

"Yep."

"Are you any closer to finding out who shot Mr. Hodges?"

"Some."

His clipped response soured her jubilant mood. At times she thought she'd gained ground, earned his trust. Then she realized he remained rigid and unyielding, closed off from her behind his monosyllabic answers.

Garrett pressed his cheek against the top of her hair. "I'd rather talk about something more cheerful."

"Fair enough," Jo replied.

They sat in companionable silence as darkness fell. She yawned, and Garrett soon followed with a yawn of his own. "Why don't you close your eyes and rest a moment," he said. "I'll wake you when it's time."

A curious lethargy stole over Jo. She hadn't slept well the evening before, worrying about the wedding. She'd risen earlier than normal to get ready. "You don't mind?"

"Nope."

She closed her eyes and rested her head on his shoulder. Cottonwood leaves rustled overhead and crickets chirped around her, lulling her into sleep. She dozed off and on, comforted by the warmth of Garrett's embrace. At one point she heard voices in the distance, and figured the boys were up to their mischief.

"Garrett," she said around another yawn. "Thank you for a perfect day."

Garrett woke with a start. Disoriented, he glanced around and realized he and Jo had fallen asleep in the tree house. He rubbed his eyes with the heels of his hands and stretched. Dew dampened his hair and face, and he shivered in the purple light of dawn.

He hadn't won any awards for romance, that's for certain. Jo curled against his side for warmth, and he cradled her against his chest, savoring the moment. Rarely did he have the chance to study her, and, suddenly, it seemed important he take this rare opportunity. Her face was serene in repose, innocent. Surrendering his rigid self-control, he remained still until she stirred against his side.

He reluctantly broke the contact, determined to keep the promise he'd made to himself. To Jo.

The sun hadn't yet banked the horizon, and only a faint hint of Jo's ivory dress glowed in the darkness. Lightning sparked in the distance, briefly illuminating the canopy of leaves above his head. As much as he wanted to linger, he feared the gathering storm.

He felt around the floor for the lamp he'd left there earlier. Upon discovering the tree house, he'd made plans to show Jo the charming structure. Not on their wedding night, of course, he thought with a wry chuckle, but he was grateful they'd avoided the shivaree.

Careful not to jostle his sleeping bride, he lit the wick and adjusted the light. Jo grumbled beside him, then stretched and yawned. His heart thumped against his ribs. She'd been breathtakingly lovely in church, but he preferred her this way—wild and untamed. Her hair, shaken free from its pins, hung over her shoulders in loose waves beneath her leather hat.

Even as he watched, her eyes fluttered open. A delicate frown appeared between her brows. She stared at him for a long beat, her pale face sleepy and vulnerable. He'd give every possession he owned to kiss her awake, but he held himself rigidly in check. Since Flynn's arrival he'd kept his distance. Yesterday had been a dream, but it was after midnight and yesterday was gone. Their brief peck in the church had shaken his resolve, but he hadn't faltered.

Another flash of lightning startled her upright, and he immediately felt the loss of her comforting warmth.

Jo hugged his slicker around her shoulders and trembled. "Looks like we'll get more rain this evening."

Reluctant to abandon the precious cocoon of the evening, Garrett nodded. "We'd best get back."

He descended the crude ladder first and reached for the lantern. Jo handed down the light and scaled the ladder, her movements quick and agile.

"Do you know your way in the dark?" she asked.

"Mostly. Let me fetch my horse. Take my hand, there's a lot of underbrush."

Her fingers were cold, and he tucked them into the crook of his elbow. She tightened her grip and leaned into his support. Holding the lantern ahead of them, he lit their way through the darkness. Jo made a soft sound, and he halted. She plowed into his back.

"Is something wrong?" he asked.

"Nope," she replied, but he sensed the strain in her voice. "Actually, it's my feet. I'm breaking in a new pair of boots."

She revealed a pair of pointed-toe butterscotch-colored boots with cream stitching.

Garrett blew out a low whistle. "That's some fancy footwear."

"They're called cowboy boots. A fellow up in Wichita makes them. The stitching helps the leather keep its shape. My folks ordered them special."

"You sure are one of a kind."

Garrett let out another, louder whistle and his horse, Blue, nickered in response. The underbrush crackled as they neared the horse, and trees rustled overhead in the increasing wind.

He reached out one hand. "You can ride and I'll lead the way with the lantern."

Jo gave a weary nod, and Garrett realized she'd reached the end of her endurance. "Not much longer now," he offered by way of reassurance.

He circled her waist and easily lifted her onto the saddle. She rearranged her skirts and they set off once more. As they resumed their weary journey, the indigo horizon lightened enough he extinguished the lamp flame. The air was thick and damp, but no rain fell, and for that he was grateful. The path from the creek led them to the back of the house, and he paused on the freshly cut lawn.

Garrett caught sight of the porch and a trickle of apprehension stilled his progress. The back door stood open.

Jo slid off the horse, and he placed a restraining hand on her arm.

"Wait here," he ordered as he relit the lantern.

Without his gun, Garrett moved cautiously. He pressed open the door with one hand and lifted the lantern. His stomach clenched at the shocking sight. The entire room had been ransacked. Broken crockery littered the floor between piles of flour, sugar and salt. The overturned kitchen table and chairs blocked his path, and he sagged against the doorjamb.

He felt rather than heard Jo close the distance behind him.

"What happened?" she asked, craning her neck. "Oh, gracious," she said, her voice faltering.

Attempting to block her view, he turned and grasped

her shoulders. "Let me check the rooms first. The people who did this might still be here."

"Why?" She stared up at him, her eyes wide and bewildered in the dim lamplight. "Why would the boys do this?"

"The boys didn't do this."

She shoved him aside and stepped into the kitchen, her hands on her hips. "When you find out who did, I get first go at them."

Garrett grunted his response and studied the ravaged room. The damage was malicious and angry, and he didn't for a moment believe the McCoys had been involved. He considered searching the outbuildings, but there was no place to hide except the barn, and the animals would be agitated if they had company.

Besides, if he left Jo long enough for the trip to and from the outbuildings, she'd search the house herself and he didn't want her stumbling into danger.

Though reluctant to leave her, even in the kitchen, Garrett needed the building searched. "Promise me you'll wait here?"

Looking dazed, she absently nodded her head. Garrett quickly toured the house, his rage growing with each room. The mattresses had all been slashed and feathers littered the floor. Even Cora's room had been tossed.

He soon realized the pillagers had fled, and the house was empty. He returned downstairs and found Jo kneeling on the littered floor, a broken plate in her hand, her expression stunned.

Garrett crouched behind her and gently wrapped his arms around her shoulders. "I'm sorry."

"It's not your fault," she spoke, her voice no more

than a whisper. "I don't know anyone who would do this."

Even the Walbys, who'd been cruel with their words and their deeds, had never shown this kind of violence in their actions.

"I don't know, either."

The dish fell from her limp fingers. "I wanted our wedding day to be perfect."

Garrett fished out his pocket watch and checked the time. "It's six in the morning. Our wedding day ended at midnight. It's still perfect."

A sob shook her shoulders, and he couldn't recall a time he'd ever felt more helpless. He cradled her against his chest and brushed the tangled curls from her forehead.

Her body stiffened. "I can't make up my mind if I'm angry or sad."

"I'll find out who did this. I promise."

"I know you will." She sniffled and swiped the back of her hand across the pink tip of her nose. "I don't understand why someone would do this. It's so destructive, so hateful."

She clutched his hand and he realized she was ice-cold. Garrett chaffed her shoulders and nestled her against his warmth. "It's early and we're both exhausted. I'll rustle up some blankets and we can snatch an hour or two of sleep down here. I don't think they'll come back, but I want you close just in case."

After arranging a couple of makeshift beds in the dining room, Jo limped around the room, stepping over broken dishes.

"Sit," Garrett ordered.

"I can't. I can't relax."

"Let me help."

He lowered her onto the blankets and arranged the pillows behind her back, then tugged off her boots. Jo groaned. Encouraged by her response, he massaged the delicate arch of her foot with the pads of his thumbs.

"That's wonderful." She sighed.

He continued the gentle pressure on her other foot. Gradually her shoulders drooped, and her eyes fluttered shut. After tucking the blanket more securely around her shoulders, Garrett started the cleanup in the early dawn light. The lantern burned low and flickered shadows on the walls as he swept up feathers and straightened their scattered clothing.

The damage was targeted and personal. Done by someone who wanted revenge. Garrett had an idea who that person might be, but he couldn't reveal his suspicions without proof. If his hunch was correct, the troublemaker was guilty of more than vandalism.

Garrett was searching for a murderer.

Chapter Twenty

Two days following her marriage, Jo lifted a bolt of fabric from the mercantile display and held the yellow calico before her in the mirror. She tilted her head to one side and made a face.

Mary Louise appeared behind her in the reflection. "We have a ready-made in the blue. I think that color would go much better with your hair."

"There's not enough gravy for this goose." Jo sighed.

The blond-haired girl lifted an eyebrow.

"Never mind," Jo added quickly. "I'll see the blue."

Mary Louise disappeared into the backroom.

With her family watching Cora to give the newlyweds time alone together, she and Garrett had spent the two days following the wedding cleaning up the house. They'd kept the damage a secret from the McCoys, since she didn't want to worry them. Despite her casual demeanor toward the incident, a sense of unease had permeated her days. Garrett had assured her they were safe, and she'd put on a brave face.

For two nights she'd tossed and turned, and she'd finally decided a trip into town was in order. Though school was out for the summer, Cora was studying with the teacher three mornings a week. Garrett avoided Jo at every possible opportunity.

Mary Louise returned holding a deep blue calico dress with blue, yellow and white flowers woven into the pattern.

"Try it on. The seams are only slip-stitched. I can have it finished in a day or two."

Without waiting for an answer, Mary Louise hustled her into the change room, where Jo struggled into the dress. Minutes later, a knock sounded on the door.

"Are you finished yet?" Mary Louise called.

Jo emerged from the room and smoothed the material over her stomach. "It's one piece. I never wear one piece."

"Maybe you should. You look lovely."

She guided Jo before the full-length mirror propped against a shelf of fabric bolts.

The dress was deceptively simple, a scoop neck with three-quarter sleeves and a deep V seaming at the waist. Jo turned from side to side. "It's not so bad."

Mary Louise lifted Jo's braid and draped it over the top of her head. "We could put this up with only a few pins."

Jo touched the side of her face. "What will people say?"

"You never struck me as the sort of person who wasted time on what other people thought."

Despite her quiet demeanor, Mary Louise had pinned Jo's braid around her head before she'd even thought of a suitable protest. Mary Louise fussed for another minute, then stepped back.

"That's better."

Jo glanced at her reflection again. She looked older, more sophisticated. Not foolish or silly at all.

Voices sounded from the store, and Mary Louise stepped before the door. Her face lit up, and Jo followed the direction of her gaze.

David.

Mary Louise fluffed her hair with both hands. "I have to see to a customer."

Jo quickly donned her serviceable shirtwaist and skirt and ventured into the main store. One look at David and Mary Louise together and Jo realized Garrett had been right. The two were sweet on each other.

David caught sight of her and flushed. "Garrett asked me to come by today. Do you know what it's about?"

"I think so. Why don't we have lunch?"

He stood in indecision, and Jo smirked. "Do you have a better offer?"

David cast a lingering glance at Mary Louise and slowly shook his head.

After they'd sat down at the Palace Café and the waitress had taken their orders, Jo frowned. "You'd best tell Caleb how you feel about Mary Louise."

David blanched. "Did your husband tell you?"

Her pulse stuttered at the title. That was the first time someone had referred to her as Garrett's wife. "Anyone can see by the way the two of you look at each other," she replied evasively.

"Nothing is settled yet. I can't marry unless I can support her. She wants to stay in Cimarron Springs, but there's more work for farmhands around Wichita."

"Garrett wants you to be his deputy."

David's face lit up like Christmas morning. "No fooling?"

"No fooling."

He threw back his shoulders and puffed out his chest. "I like the idea of that."

"Garrett is a good man. Don't let him down."

Tilting his head to one side, her brother squinted. "Did you do something different with your hair? You look older or something. Pretty."

Jo swatted his hand. "I hope you do better when you compliment Mary Louise." Her grin disappeared. "It still means you have to settle things with Caleb."

Her brother's face crumpled. "It's not going to be easy."

"The right thing never is." Jo rested her hand over his. "And the longer you wait, the harder it's going to be."

Garrett stood as Jo and David entered the room. He was suddenly conscious of the watermarks covering the battered desk he'd inherited from the previous sheriff. Glancing down, he caught sight of his loosened shirt-tail and surreptitiously tucked the beige material into his waistband.

His gaze lighted on David and lingered on Jo. She'd done something different with her hair. Instead of her usual, single braid, she'd wound the braid at the base of her neck. The difference was subtle, but pleasing.

Garrett circled the desk and scraped another chair into place. "Sit down, you two."

After they'd all gotten settled, he rubbed his face, wishing he'd shaved more carefully that morning. "I suppose Jo has told you what this is all about."

David leaned forward. "You need help."

"There are a lot of rumors floating around town, and business has slowed at the mercantile."

"People think Mr. Stuart shot Mr. Hodges?"

"Yep."

"What do you think?"

Garrett cast an uneasy glance at Jo. He trusted her, but he wasn't ready to speak about his theory just yet. "I have some ideas. But I need help."

As though on cue, Jo stood. "Why don't you two finish your discussion. I'll see if Cora is finished with the schoolteacher."

She swept out of the room and Garrett followed her progress. Since the marriage, he felt more estranged from her. They were testing the waters of this new relationship, carefully feeling for the boundaries. Too carefully. Their encounters were brittle and stilted. He didn't know how to keep his distance without jeopardizing their friendship.

"You were saying," David prodded.

Garrett startled to attention. "I need you to keep an eye on someone."

"Who?"

"Tom Walby."

David's eyes widened, and the younger man let out a low whistle. "You're in a real pickle, aren't you?"

Garrett thought of the evening ahead. Dinner with Jo. Small talk over the chores. His gaze drifting to her ripe, pink lips at every opportunity. "You don't know the half of it."

Chapter Twenty-One

The next few weeks passed in relative peace for Jo. Her routine started at first light as she and Garrett rustled around the kitchen in companionable silence.

A gouge in the floor was the only evidence of the destruction from the night of their wedding, and Jo absently rubbed it with the tip of her boot. "How are you and David getting along?"

"Good. He's a hard worker. Smart."

Garrett had deputized her brother the week after their marriage and David had taken the sheriff's rooms above the jailhouse. Just as she'd suspected, the living arrangement with her new husband was similar to growing up with her brothers.

They treated one another like fellow boarders, each wary of disturbing the other patron. They took great pains to avoid encountering each other on the stairs or in the hall. There were no highs and lows, just the steady, polite talk of weather and the occasional outing with Cora. He'd been leaving earlier and earlier in the morning, and this time Jo wasn't letting him get away without talking to her.

She opened the pantry and searched the shelves. She was certain there was a single jar of peach preserves hiding in the back somewhere. "I bet he's chomping at the bit for some excitement. We haven't had a fire or a shooting in weeks. Even Tom's been awful quiet."

"Yep."

Jo's curiosity peaked at his abrupt answer. "Maybe Tom has finally learned his lesson."

"Hope so."

She struggled with the lid on the jar of peach preserves. Garrett wasn't much of a talker first thing in the morning, but normally he didn't mind her idle chatter. "David said you had an idea who killed Mr. Hodges?"

"Suspicions. That's all."

"What about your cousin, Edward?"

"He landed an army contract from Fort Ryan." He plucked the jar from her stranglehold, easily popped the seal and handed it back. "Now that he's flush with cash again, he figures I'm a suitable guardian."

Jo smiled her thanks and set about making Cora's lunch. Growing up, she'd preferred being outside or in the barn caring for the animals. Lately, though, especially at times like this, she enjoyed the simple pleasure of sharing a quiet moment with Garrett.

Marriage was a lonely business. "Mrs. Fletcher said her husband has a milk cow he'd be willing to sell."

"That's a lot of work. There might be days when I'm gone, and I won't be able to help out."

Reaching for Cora's lunch pail, Jo considered his answer. "I bet Abraham could use some pocket money. Do you want me to ask if he'll come by once in a while for chores? I can pay him from my salary at the telegraph office."

"I have enough money."

While Jo didn't want to jeopardize this rare bout of comfortable chatter, a question had been gnawing at her since the wedding. "Mrs. Fletcher said this was the first two-story house built in Kansas."

Garrett poured twin mugs of coffee from the blue enamel pot on the stove. "And she's wondering how a poor county marshal can afford such a fine house."

"Something like that." Jo felt her cheeks flush beneath his steady regard. "I told her to mind her own business."

"Empty houses sell cheap." Garrett passed her the steaming mug. "A drifter doesn't need much. I've built up some savings over the years."

"I didn't mean to pry. But I'm prepared to pay my fair share. Not enough for the house, of course, but I can help with expenses."

"You spend your money how you please. I've got enough to keep us set for a while." He named a sum that had her eyes widening.

Jo tittered nervously. "I can't believe you didn't starve. You can't have spent anything."

All her life she'd worried about money—the McCoys never had much. It was odd to think she'd changed her financial status simply by marrying. It felt like cheating. Then again, there weren't many chances for a woman to make money. And she definitely held her own with her share of the work and chores.

Jo sliced bread for sandwiches and slathered them with peach preserves. Behind her, Garrett knelt and retrieved his lunch pail from the bottom cupboard.

Their movements turned familiar, almost practiced, yet Jo felt as though she was playacting—like Cora and her dolls serving a make-believe tea party. There were times like this, when she felt as if her new life wasn't real. She could simply walk out the door and go back to her room at the boardinghouse and no one would even know the difference.

Jo shook her head. Cora would notice.

She glanced around the tidy kitchen, and her chest tightened. Freshly whitewashed cupboards and beadboard trim brightened the room, a perfect backdrop for the wedding gifts lining the shelves. Blue creamware pitchers, plates and opaque glasses stood beside the few brightly colored tins of spices she'd bought from the general store. On the walls, Garrett had hung the copper pots in a line by size. Jo figured that's why they got along so well. They both enjoyed order and routine.

He reached for the knife resting on the counter before her, and his arm brushed her shoulder. His hand drifted down and covered her fingers, and the air between them sparked like flint rocks. He reached his other arm around her back and gently crowded her against the counter.

Tucking his chin in the curve of her shoulder, he said, "You're cutting the slices too thin. Let me show you."

He guided her fingers over the handle of the knife and braced his other hand on the crusty loaf, then directed her motions.

"That's as thick as two slices." She laughed at the enormous cut he'd taken.

"You have five brothers. Surely you know a man needs more to eat than two thin slices of bread and a slather of jam."

Jo inhaled his dizzying scent. As large as the house was, living together beneath the same roof had driven them into closer and closer contact. It seemed inevitable they'd eventually be forced to touch each other.

He shifted and positioned the knife over the bread again. His skin was dark against hers and his hands coarse from years of labor. She'd never liked her own hands—they were rough and chapped and her nails never grew beyond the tips of her fingers. But next to Garrett's, they appeared almost delicate.

She wondered if she turned her head, would he kiss her. Her stomach tightened.

"Why are you smiling?" he said, his breath tickling her ear.

Embarrassed by the turn of her thoughts, Jo kept her attention focused on the counter. "What do you think about chickens?"

His chest rumbled against her back as he chuckled. "You're full of surprises, Mrs. Cain."

Blood rushed in her ears and she felt almost dizzy. She forgot sometimes she had a different name, but she liked the way he spoke it with his gravelly morning voice.

He carefully sliced another chunk of bread. "I like chickens. I like eggs in the morning. I like barn cats and watchdogs. Any other animals you'd like for your menagerie? How about a goat?"

"Absolutely not."

"What do you have against goats?"

"It's a long story." Jo smiled.

"What about sheep?"

"Definitely sheep. My pa would be so proud. His family raised sheep for wool back in Ireland."

"We'll knit the whole town sweaters for the winter."

"Even Mr. Stuart?"

"Especially Mr. Stuart. He doesn't have enough meat on his bones to keep him warm in the winter."

Garrett spun her around, pulled her into his embrace, and belted out, *"My wild Irish Rose, the sweetest flower that grows,"* in a low, pleasant baritone.

While she giggled, he whirled her through the kitchen in a clumsy waltz. *"You may search everywhere, but none can compare with my wild Irish Rose."*

Giddy with his infectious joy, Jo followed his lead. She'd never seen him behave with such abandon. They crashed into a chair and sprang apart. Smiling, Jo smoothed her hair. "You're usually so quiet in the morning, and here you are singing and dancing around the kitchen. What's gotten into you, Mr. Cain?" she said, mirroring the use of his name.

Appearing flustered, he reached for the overturned chair. "I don't know what came over me. Must have been all that talk of chickens."

He flushed, avoiding her gaze. Her lips tightened. While she'd enjoyed their spontaneous fun, Garrett appeared almost embarrassed by their shared enjoyment. Before she could voice her confusion, she caught sight of Cora at the top of the stairs.

"Did we wake you with our silliness?" Jo called.

The door closed behind her and Jo glanced over her shoulder. Garrett had fled. From past experience she knew he'd be quiet for the next few days. She clenched her jaw. If he was ashamed of her, he shouldn't have married her.

She recalled his words all those weeks ago—*I'm not capable of love.*

He'd lied to her.

She saw how he behaved with Cora, with his animals. He was more than capable of love. Which begged the question, why couldn't he love *her?* Though she'd vowed to let him keep his secrets, she didn't know how much longer she could take his changeable behavior.

She caught Cora's curious gaze. "It's almost time for your lessons. Why don't you get dressed."

Twenty minutes later Jo knelt before Cora and adjusted her collar. "It was nice of Mrs. Harper to help you with your numbers and letters over the summer. Are you enjoying your lessons?"

Cora clasped her hands. "I like it here. Maxwell is my best friend. I still miss my old room. I miss my mommy and daddy."

"Oh, baby." Tears pooled in Jo's eyes. "I'm so sorry."

"I like you. I like Uncle Garrett."

"I know. You can like us and miss your parents at the same time."

The little girl's brow furrowed. "Grandma said that, too."

"Grandma Edith is smart." Jo held out her hand for their morning walk. "She'd like you to stay overnight tonight." Her voice lowered. "Just between you and me, I think she's lonely. With David gone and the other boys spending so much time in the fields, the house is quiet. And Maxwell wants to show you his new dog."

The little girl grinned and eagerly nodded. Edith McCoy had fallen hopelessly in love with her new grandchild, and the feeling was obviously mutual. The two enjoyed their time together, and Jo encouraged the interaction. It brought them all together as a family. Cora needed plenty of love, and the McCoys had plenty of love to give.

Stepping outside, Jo glanced left and right. The street

from their house curved right toward Cimarron Springs, and she adjusted her leather hat against the sun. While she'd made certain concessions toward a more feminine wardrobe, she wasn't giving up her gifted hat. The days were growing longer and hotter, though not intolerable just yet. Thankfully, a wet spring had turned into a stunningly beautiful early summer. The countryside bloomed with wildflowers and the creek bed swelled.

Garrett had offered to hitch the wagon for her, but she and Cora preferred the walk. By the time they arrived in town, a fine sheen of perspiration covered Jo's forehead.

She squeezed Cora's hand. "Tomorrow let's take the wagon. It's getting hotter than baking day."

Cora nodded with a grimace.

Jo left Cora in the teacher's capable hands, passed the boardinghouse and paused outside the marshal's office. Garrett felt something for her, she knew he did, and she deserved answers for his behavior. Gathering her courage, she lifted her hand, then paused midknock.

Bearding a lion in its den was never a good idea. If she confronted him before David, he'd turn defensive. She'd lived her whole life surrounded by men and had discovered a few things along the way.

She'd let Garrett work. But tonight, with Cora gone, they were going to talk. And this time she'd make certain he couldn't run away.

She'd glue him to the chair if need be.

Chapter Twenty-Two

Mary Louise burst into Garrett's office, her face flushed. "They're fighting." She gasped. "And it's all my fault."

"Where?" he responded immediately.

"Behind the livery."

Garrett strapped on his gun and snatched his hat on the way out the back door. If Mary Louise was involved, it had to be the McCoy brothers. He followed the frantic woman to the corral behind the livery where Caleb and David wrestled in the dirt. Garrett fetched a bucket of water and doused the brawling pair. Coughing and sputtering, they sprang apart.

"What'd you go and do that for?" Caleb demanded.

Garrett tossed the pail aside. "You boys were making a mess. You want to tell me what this is all about?"

He already knew, but the two needed to work things out in the open with words, not fists.

The brothers exchanged a sullen glance. David broke away first, raking his hands through his hair.

Caleb glared at his back. "He stole my girl."

"She isn't a horse, son." Garrett raised an eyebrow. "It's not like he rustled her from the corral one night."

Caleb swiped the wet hair from his eyes. "He stole her just the same. She was sweet on me."

"She was being nice," David said. "That's how she is."

"What do you know? You don't love her."

David's arm shot out and he grasped a fistful of his brother's shirt. "That's not for you to say, is it?"

Garrett latched his hand around David's wrist and shook loose his hold. "Fighting isn't going to solve any of this." He encompassed the two in his question. "Has the lady made her choice known?"

Caleb aimed an accusing glare at his brother. "She's going for a buggy ride with David tomorrow. That don't mean she's sweet on him. She's probably just being *nice*." He bitterly drew out the last word.

David's face hardened. "You asked her for a buggy ride, too. What did she say?"

"She was busy." Caleb's face reddened. "That's all. That's why she couldn't come."

"She didn't want to hurt your feelings."

"You don't know that."

The two leaped for each other again, and Garrett held his arms askew between them. "This isn't going to be solved with a brawl. Why don't you two cool off."

David stalked away, and Garrett studied Caleb. He'd been paying close attention to Mary Louise over the past few weeks, and he was certain she'd chosen David. The two sweethearts were walking on eggshells, afraid of hurting Caleb.

Garrett swiped the back of his hand across his forehead beneath the brim of his hat. "It's time you moved on."

"How do you know? What has David said? Whatever it is, he's lying."

"It's not what your brother has said. It's how Mary Louise looks at him."

Caleb's face caved in defeat. "She just doesn't know me well enough. If he hadn't distracted her, we'd be together."

A sound caught his attention, and Garrett caught sight of David.

His battered deputy stepped forward and hung his head. "She's given me permission to ask her pa if we can court. She's already made her choice."

Garrett caught Caleb's stricken expression and waved David away. "Why don't you call it a day? Your brother needs a moment alone."

David hesitated for a moment, then dutifully turned away.

His heart heavy, Garrett propped his forearms on the top railing of the corral fence and stared at the brown earth stirred up by the brothers' fight.

He gave Caleb a few minutes with his thoughts before speaking. "There are two truths in life. You can't keep people from dying, and you can't make people love you. It's as simple as that."

"But if she spent more time with me, she'd know me better. She could sort out her feelings." The younger man's voice broke and he swallowed hard. "He stole her right from under my nose. My own brother. I trusted him and he—"

Garrett held up his hand. "I'll say it again. She's not a piece of chattel you can steal and steal back again. She's a living breathing person and she can make up her own mind. She *has* made up her own mind."

"Then why didn't she tell me?"

"I suspect she didn't want to hurt you."

"But—"

"Look, I know you're all torn up, but blaming David won't change anything."

A sheen of tears appeared in Caleb's eyes. "It's like someone ripped my heart out, and I'll never be whole again."

Garrett reached out a hand and gripped the younger man's shoulder. "It feels like that now, but it won't always. You're a fine man, and someday you'll find someone who loves you back. Don't settle for anything less. A one-sided love is like a poison. It eats away at you from the inside until you're just a shell."

"What does it matter? I already feel like I'm dying inside."

"You'll heal."

"How do you know?"

"I just do."

Garrett silently questioned his oft-repeated answer. The pain lessened, but did a heart ever truly mend? Or did a person carry around the reminders of the pain like a scar?

At least with one's heart, the scars were hidden.

Garrett caught a glance of the raw pain apparent in Caleb's mournful eyes.

Then again, maybe the scars of the heart were the most obvious of all. He wondered if his showed.

Jo sat in the sheriff's office and held her arm around a sobbing Mary Louise. She awkwardly patted the distraught girl's shoulder. "They've fought before. This isn't even the worst."

"I should have said something sooner." The blonde heaved in a shaky breath. "I just couldn't."

Garrett slipped through the door and he and Jo exchanged a glance. With a slight nod, she motioned him toward his desk. "I was just telling Mary Louise this isn't the end of the world."

The girl hiccuped. "It feels like it. Everything has gone wrong. Nobody is coming to Daddy's business anymore. Everyone whispers behind his back. They're calling him a murderer. Now the boys are fighting over me."

Garrett spread his hands along the table. "I'm doing what I can to find the killer. Hopefully, we'll have this case solved soon."

"I don't know what to do." Mary Louise blew her nose with noisy abandon into her lace-edged handkerchief. "It's even worse now that Daddy tried to buy all of Mr. Hodges's old stock at a discount. Everyone thinks badly of us."

Jo glanced at the sobbing girl. For such a beauty, she certainly didn't cry pretty. Her face had gone all blotchy and her frown disappeared into her chin.

Feeling like a first-rate heel for her uncharitable thoughts, Jo patted Mary Louise's hand. "Garrett will get to the bottom of what happened, won't you? Something will work out. Something always does."

"I hope so. Pa won't even talk about David, and I'll simply die if we can't get married. I love him so much."

Jo rolled her eyes. "You won't die."

The sobbing girl sprang to her feet and glared. "How do you know? You've never been in love. Everyone knows you two only got married because you had to!"

Jo sprang upright. "I know you're upset, but there's no need to be rude."

"You don't know what it's like. You've never even been courted!"

Mary Louise flounced out of the room and slammed the door, leaving them in stunned silence.

Garrett half rose from his seat, and Jo waved him down. "Let her go. She's young and in love."

Garrett fisted his hand on the desk. "That's no excuse for her behavior."

"It's all right." Jo stood and grasped the door handle. Her lungs squeezed and she desperately needed fresh air. "I'll see you at supper."

"Jo," he called.

She ignored him, scurrying along the boardwalk, her eyes burning. What did she know? Maybe Mary Louise *would* die if she and David couldn't be together. If *not* being in love hurt this much, Jo didn't want to know what the true emotion felt like.

A week after Jo's brothers' epic battle in the livery corral, Beatrice passed her deciphered message across the table and chewed on the end of her pencil while Jo reviewed her work.

Carefully checking each letter, Jo circled part of the translation. "You're still mixing up the *c* and the *y*."

Beatrice groaned as she accepted the corrected sheet. "I thought I got it right."

"Everyone gets those two letters mixed up at first. You'll get it. It just takes practice."

"I suppose."

Jo gave her hand an encouraging squeeze. "Don't worry. I was overwhelmed at first, too."

"Speaking of overwhelming." Beatrice perked up at the change of subject. "How is married life?"

"Well..." Jo carefully measured her answer. "Different than I thought."

"Different good or different bad?"

The office door swung open, interrupting her answer.

Mr. Sundberg doffed his hat and ran a hand through his disheveled hair. "It's the missus. She's in labor, *ja*. Mrs. McCoy needs Jo."

The Sundbergs lived on a homestead just north of town. They'd emigrated five years ago, and Mrs. Sundberg pined for a baby. She'd lost three already, and Jo and her ma feared she'd never deliver a healthy child.

Dreading the answer, Jo spoke. "Where's the doc's wife? I thought she was helping out."

"Can't find her, *ja*. Must help. You."

A refusal balanced on the tip of Jo's tongue, but her ma wouldn't have called on her unless it was an emergency. "Bea, can you close up the office?"

"I'll take care of it," the older woman answered immediately.

Jo snatched a few belongings and followed the harried man outside to his wagon. The two-mile trip passed in strained silence. By the time Jo reached Mrs. Sundberg's bedside, the woman's brilliant blond hair hung damp around her face. She moaned and rolled her head from side to side on the pillow. She clutched her distended belly and grimaced.

Sensing the gravity of the situation, Jo snatched a rag from the bowl on the side table and made quick work of washing her hands. Mopping her damp forehead, Jo

caught her ma's gaze. Edith gave an almost imperceptible shake of the head.

Her ma leaned closer and lowered her voice. "There's
a complication with the baby."

Jo's heart sank.

Chapter Twenty-Three

Garrett couldn't clear his thoughts. Caleb had thought Mary Louise the only girl for him, but Garrett was certain he'd find another love. How did a fellow know if he'd found true love? Was it possible to find that love more than once in a lifetime?

He kept picturing the look on Jo's face when Mary Louise had made her angry accusation. She'd appeared...defeated. And he'd done that to her. He'd taken the fire out of her heart with his distant ways. He'd talked himself into the marriage knowing it was wrong because he wanted her near.

He'd wrapped himself in ice as protection and had frozen her out in the process.

"Hey." David rapped on his desk. "Are you listening?"

Garrett bolted upright. "No. Were you talking?"

His new deputy rolled his eyes. "You've been daydreaming all morning. What's wrong with you?"

Everything. "Nothing."

Garrett rubbed the back of his neck. He couldn't get Jo off his mind. She must think him a first-rate loon after his antics the other morning. His feelings definitely felt like madness, but not like the madness of his father. His emotions were strong but not violent. More like forged steel than burning embers.

Not the black darkness he'd grown up with. He and Jo were friends before the marriage. He'd seen couples who acted almost as if they hated each other. Could you have love and romance with your best friend?

He'd never know unless he risked telling her the truth about his past.

David rapped on his desk again.

"What?" Garrett snapped.

"I've been following Tom Walby for days. He hasn't done anything out of the ordinary. Are you certain he's the culprit?"

Garrett checked his watch. "I called Tom in today. We'll put the pressure on him. Give him a chance to do the right thing. If we don't do something, there'll be a mob after Mr. Stuart."

The door swung open and Tom Walby stumbled inside looking as if he'd been dragged behind his horse instead of riding it. He collapsed onto the chair set before the desk and groaned.

Though his visitor was here sooner than expected, Garrett was relieved. He motioned for David. "Can you take notes while Tom talks?"

Understanding dawned on the younger man's face and he quickly retrieved paper and pencil from his desk opposite Garrett's.

Tom rubbed his face. "You know why I'm here?"

"I think so." Garrett tented his hands and kicked back in his chair. "Why don't you tell me what happened in your words."

"I didn't mean to do it." Tom's rough face screwed up in a grimace. "I was drunk."

"Didn't mean to do what? You'll have to say the words outright."

"I think I killed Mr. Hodges."

"You think or you know?"

"I was drunk." Tom repeated.

"Had you been drinking all day?"

"Most of it." Tom squared his shoulders. "There was a good crowd that afternoon and I'd been winning at poker. Those cowboys were full of money and the railroad boys had gotten their paychecks. They were buying us all drinks. Then I started losing." Tom grunted. "I don't remember much after that."

"Do you remember shooting the gun?"

"I don't." Tom swiped at his eyes. "When I woke up the next day, I had a shiner and my gun was short two bullets."

David's pencil frantically scratched across the page.

Garrett gave his deputy a moment to catch up before continuing. "You blacked out?"

"It's happened before."

"Why, Tom?" Garrett asked the question he'd always wanted to ask his own father. "The drink was bound to catch up with you. Why didn't you ever quit?"

The other man hung his head. "I don't know. I say I'm gonna quit. I make promises. To myself, to my wife. I go a day without drinking, sometimes more. Then, I don't know, something happens and I talk myself into coming to town. It's never going to be more than one. Never."

Garrett fought against the pull of time, keeping his

thoughts rigidly in the present. "What about the shiva-ree at my house? That was you, too, wasn't it?"

"Yeah." Tom hung his head. "Mr. Stuart thought one of them cowboys was back in town. He was trying real hard to shift the blame. It was eating at me, you know? Because I knew Stuart didn't do it. I thought if your place was messed up at the same time, you'd blame the cowboys."

A low rumble of anger vibrated in Garrett's chest. "Was that the only reason?"

"Jo, too," Tom added sheepishly.

"You were sweet on her once, weren't you?"

"I didn't think she'd marry anyone. Ever. I guess I was mad when I found out the two of you were getting hitched. I married the missus just to show Jo someone else would have me. Jo was always too good for me anyway. Even in the eighth grade."

Garrett watched as David's eyes widened.

He'd been certain about the shooting, but the shivaree was only a hunch. "You've got a child now. You made a commitment. It's time you made peace with that. No matter what your reasons for marrying, it's your choice how you live your life each day. What you're doing isn't fair to any of you."

The day of the wedding Tom had been skulking around the edges of the festivities. The damage he'd inflicted on the house had been vicious, personal.

Tom cleared his throat and he dabbed at his brow with a dingy red handkerchief. "What's going to happen to me?"

"It's not up to me." Containing his anger, Garrett yanked the keys from his top drawer. "Your punishment is up to the judge. I'll keep you in the jail here. With no witnesses, I'm not certain how it will go for you."

"You'll put in a good word for me, won't you?"

"I gotta be honest, Tom, I'm not feeling all that charitable toward you right now. You killed a man and you can't even remember what happened. You took a life. For all I know, it was self-defense. Mr. Hodges was known to have a temper. But you've lost all your credibility and I can't bring it back for you. Then you damaged my house. And on my wedding day, no less."

Garrett walked Tom back to the jail and locked him inside, then returned to the front office.

David sat in the chair, stunned. "You said the only proof you had was flimsy."

Garrett slid open his top desk drawer and fished out two bullets, then set them side by side on the dark blotter. "They look alike, don't they?"

David studied the bullets, rolling them over the leather surface. "Yes."

"This is the one that killed Mr. Hodges." Garrett brandished the warped metal cylinder. "And the other is from Tom's gun. I keep track of people who shoot first and aim later. Folks around here make their own bullets, and a lot of times you can tell who they belong to. Not always. But Tom's got a distinctive mold."

Garrett indicated three identical deep grooves on the side of each bullet.

David slumped in his chair. "Why did we need a confession?"

"Could have been a coincidence. No one saw anything. Tom doesn't even remember what happened." Garrett shrugged. "I didn't want to leave it up to chance."

"I still can't believe he had a crush on Jo." David frowned.

"You see what you expect to see. You don't appreciate the person she's become."

"Hey," Tom yelled from the rear of the jailhouse. "How about some lunch?"

David and Garrett exchanged a look.

"Next time, eat before you confess," Garrett called back, then leaned forward in his chair. "We'll set up something with the hotel for meals. It'll be double shifts until the trial. They might want him up in Wichita. It's murder, after all."

David scrawled something in his notes. "That solves all the crimes in Cimarron Springs."

"I got a telegram from Guthrie this morning." Except Jo hadn't delivered it. "They found the four cowboys who started the fire in the jailhouse. They've been arrested for cattle rustling." Why had Beatrice delivered the message and not Jo? The question had been eating at him all morning. "Yep. Everything is wrapped up neat as a pin." Garrett tucked the two bullets into his vest pocket.

He pictured Jo's once-lively green eyes, now dull with regret. He'd been a coward, and he'd made a real mess of things. The lies he'd told wouldn't clean up easy.

Jo rinsed her hands in a bowl and wiped them on a towel. After several tense hours, and though the baby had the umbilical cord wrapped around his neck, Mrs. Sundberg had delivered a healthy baby boy. Edith motioned for Jo and they stepped into the kitchen while the doc examined mother and infant. They took turns washing up in the sink.

Edith collapsed onto a chair. "I'm getting too old for this."

Exhausted and inexplicably cranky, Jo snapped, "Then why didn't you ask the doctor's wife, Mrs. Johnsen, for help?"

Ever since Mary Louise had shouted her accusations, Jo had been irritable and out of sorts. The words had echoed hollowly inside her chest. She had naively thought she'd grow closer to her husband with time and nearness. Instead, they'd grown further apart.

She pictured their future together. Two people in the same home, sharing the same name, and yet thousands of miles apart—speaking to each other across a chasm of stilted civility. How long could she live like that? How long before she turned so brittle a strong wind would break her into a thousand pieces?

Her ma huffed. "I didn't ask Mrs. Johnsen for assistance because she wasn't available."

Jo remained stubbornly silent. Garrett cared for her, she knew he did. She caught him looking at her when he didn't think she was aware. He kept his distance, circling further and further away.

"I'm scared," Jo whispered the admission, staring at her hands.

Her ma leaned forward. "Scared of what?"

"Of all this." Jo waved a limp hand in the general direction of Mrs. Sundberg's closed door. "What if that boy had died?" Jo choked back a sob. "Doesn't it ever bother you?"

Edith blanched. She opened and closed her mouth a few times. "Of course it bothers me."

"Then why do you do it?"

"Because it's my Christian duty. Because I feel good

knowing I can help. Because…" Her voice trailed off as Jo's words finally sank in. "You really are afraid, aren't you?"

Jo swallowed around the lump in her throat. She hated this, hated feeling vulnerable. Truth be told, she liked having people believe she wasn't afraid of anything. She didn't want to admit her weakness.

Hiding had only driven a wedge between her and her ma, and she hated the lie. The hiding. "If I'm ever going to have children of my own, I have to stop delivering babies."

Emotions flitted across her ma's face—disbelief, remorse and finally understanding. She knelt before Jo and cradled her face in her hands. "Oh, gracious. I've been blind, haven't I? I never realized you were too young to understand." She studied Jo's defeated expression. "Is this why you never went courting? Is this why you married a man you hardly know?"

"Part of it."

And because she'd never found someone she was interested in spending her life with—until Garrett.

Her ma clutched her hands. "I thought you didn't want to be with me, that you were rejecting me. I've always been a little in awe of you."

"Me?"

"You're not afraid to speak your mind."

"But you always say the right thing."

"I say the correct things," Edith spoke earnestly, "because that's the easy way. You're brave enough to say what you feel even when it pains you. Like now." She stood and held out her hand for Jo. "This is why I do what I do."

Her ma pushed open the door, revealing the new

family. Mr. Sundberg perched on the edge of the bed beside his wife, the swaddled infant cradled between them. They both looked radiant, stunned and overjoyed all at the same time.

Doc Johnsen latched his leather satchel as his wife caught sight of them in the doorway.

Mrs. Sundberg followed her gaze, and her face lit with a smile. "Would you like to hold him?"

Jo accepted the tiny bundle and stared in wonder at the sleepy new life. She'd held plenty of babies in her life, but never with the sense of awe she felt now. Something shifted in her chest. A door opened in her heart, and she felt a burst of light rush into it.

The child was perfect, beautiful and helpless. Each tiny finger was capped with a perfectly formed nail, a shock of dark hair covered the baby's head. That tug of emotion became an incessant pull. She wanted this. She wanted to be a mother.

For years she'd come up with excuses. Hidden herself away behind wide-brimmed leather hats and boys' clothes. She'd been afraid her whole life. Afraid of being weak. Afraid of wanting something she might never have.

The infant mewled, his tiny mouth working, and Jo reluctantly returned the swaddled bundle to Mrs. Sundberg. Her ma ushered out the bystanders and quietly closed the door behind her, giving the new family some privacy.

After exchanging a few words with the doc and his wife, Edith led her outside and held her hand. "I'm sorry, Jo. I should have paid more attention to your feelings and respected your wishes. I shouldn't have called on you today. I've been mule-headed. I realize that now.

I saw things the way I wanted them to be, not the way they really were. Working with you as a midwife kept us close. I thought once you became a woman, my job was over. I was afraid of being useless."

"Like a hand break on a canoe?"

Her ma laughed. "Just like that."

As much as Garrett had been running hot and cold, holding back his feelings, Jo had been just as guilty. She'd been guarding a part of herself because she was afraid of being weak. She was afraid of having more to lose than Garrett. In their relationship, she'd been balancing the scales, only giving as much as she thought she could get in return, terrified of showing weakness, of losing the upper hand.

One of them had to give.

Edith touched her shoulder. "We're all afraid. Sometimes courage is merely the point when our need overcomes our fear."

Jo considered her ma's words. Unless one of them changed, she and Garrett would keep drifting apart. The day was still young enough for gathering some supplies for a picnic. It was time she gave him more than she received in return. No more balancing the scales of affection like a greedy banker.

She had to find her courage. And Jo knew just where to start.

"Ma," Jo said, her voice ragged with emotion. "Your job will never be over. I'll always be your daughter and I will always need your love and help."

Edith pulled her into a sobbing hug, and Jo returned the fierce pressure.

Being vulnerable was tougher than feigning courage, but it sure felt a whole lot better.

Chapter Twenty-Four

Garrett snatched his saddle and tossed it over Blue's back. He tightened the cinch and then led the horse into the clearing. Hoisting one foot into the stirrup, a sound caught his attention. He turned and discovered Jo meandering up the driveway, blissfully unaware of the panic she'd caused.

He tossed the reins over the hitch and stalked toward her. "Where have you been?"

Her eyes widened at his tone. "Mrs. Sundberg had her baby."

"Why didn't you send word?" Garrett planted his hands on his hips. "I've been worried."

Jo halted. "Why didn't you ask Beatrice?"

A flush crept up his neck. "I was just heading back into town. In the future, let me know if you'll be late."

"Okay."

"Okay," he snapped back.

With the sudden release of tension, he fully absorbed her disheveled appearance and the dark smudges beneath her eyes. She appeared fragile, exhausted, and all his worries rushed back. "You scared me," Garrett reluctantly admitted.

"I said I was sorry," Jo grumbled. "What more do you want?"

"I'm sorry, too. Except I get mad when I'm scared."

"You'll fit right in with the McCoys," Jo grunted. "Once, Abraham stepped on a nail and he got so mad, he threw a hammer at the wall."

"And that didn't scare you?"

"He didn't throw it at me."

Garrett's heart continued pounding uncomfortably in his chest as he wrangled his emotions back in check. "Let's start over again."

"Agreed," she replied, her voice thick with exhaustion. "How was your day?"

"Fine. I guess I should ask about the baby," he added sheepishly.

"He's doing well now." Her lips trembled. "I didn't know what would happen. The baby had the cord wrapped around his neck. But Ma managed to save him."

Garrett wrapped his arm around her shoulders, and she sank into his embrace. "I'm glad you were there for her."

An air of melancholy surrounded her. She leaned against him, and he felt a swift, sharp relief at her show of trust.

"Actually, so am I." She linked her arm around his waist. "And Ma and I had a good talk."

Garrett let out a low whistle. "What about?"

"I'll tell you, but not now."

Hesitating, Garrett opened his mouth then changed his mind. "Fair enough."

He didn't understand the complexities of a mother-daughter relationship, and he respected Jo's privacy. Yet she'd always been open and honest with him, more than he'd ever given in return. Emotion shimmered in her expressive emerald eyes, sparking a pang of yearning. He had no right to ask her for her secrets when he'd guarded his own so fiercely.

They broke apart when they reached his tethered horse, and the heat of her touch lingered against his side. "You look exhausted. Why don't you wait inside while I take care of Blue."

"I'd rather hear about your day." She trailed him into the barn and opened the first stall door. She grasped the top slat, then rested her chin on her knuckles. "Word in town has it that Tom Walby's been arrested for Mr. Hodges's murder.

Garrett lifted the saddle off Blue with a grunt. "Word travels fast."

"Did he really kill him?"

Garrett met her sorrowful gaze. "That's how it appears. He doesn't even remember what happened that night. His day in court would have gone easier if Tom had come forward sooner."

Tugging off his gloves, he approached her, nervous at the soft reproach in her gaze. "I had to arrest him, you know that."

"I know." Tears pooled in her eyes. "There's no love lost between us, but I'm worried about his wife. His son."

"Tom can't change the past. He can only move forward."

She tossed him a cryptic smile. "I thought you said people didn't change."

"Can't a man be wrong sometimes?"

"We all get to be wrong sometimes," she answered enigmatically, then straightened her shoulders, throwing off the somber mood. "Say, do you realize we just had our first fight?"

Her announcement threw him off for a moment. "I guess so."

Jo shut the stall bar behind him. "That wasn't bad, was it?"

"You're right." He absorbed her words, hoping he didn't look as addled as he felt. "It wasn't."

Jo tilted her head. "You feeling all right?"

For the first time in a long while, he felt strong in spirit. He was addled, all right. "Great. I'm feeling better than I have in a month of Sundays. I'll finish mucking out the stalls and then I'll help you with dinner. Unless you want to rest first," he added quickly.

She'd perked up during the conversation, but he sensed she'd had an exhausting day.

"Nope," Jo replied. "I think I'm getting my second wind."

She sketched a wave and retreated into the house.

Mulling over the revelation, Garrett set about his chores. As he lifted another pitchfork full of hay into the milk cow's stall, his sense of bewilderment increased.

He'd spent their brief marriage walking like a man crossing grizzly country, tiptoeing around and dreading a confrontation. But they'd actually survived their first argument. Jo hadn't cried, and he hadn't yelled. All in all, the experience was nothing as he'd expected. For the first time since he'd made his hasty proposal, he felt more optimism than fear.

Staying away from her had been a good choice. In

a few more months, when they had a solid foundation, he'd tell her the truth. First, he needed to foster their relationship without the distracting pull of attraction.

A sound caught his attention and he turned. Jo stood in the open double barn doors, her outline silhouetted against the late-afternoon sun. She'd changed into a pretty blue calico dress with lace at the collar.

Garrett couldn't see her features and he shielded his eyes against the sun. She approached him, her steps more hesitant than usual, a basket hooked over her elbow and an unfamiliar red tartan blanket thrown over one shoulder.

"Is it suppertime already?" Garrett asked, brushing his hands together.

Jo held the basket aloft with both hands. "I thought we'd do something different tonight."

She tilted her head, and Garrett glanced behind him, feeling as if he'd missed something. "Like what?"

"A picnic."

"Ah, okay." He glanced down at his dusty clothes and Jo's neat dress. "I'll be right back."

Garrett stepped into the house, dashed upstairs, rinsed his hands and face in the washbasin and slicked back his hair. Cora was staying with the McCoys overnight, and he sensed a difference in Jo this evening.

He slipped into a clean jacket and considered changing the rest of his outfit, then reconsidered. He didn't want to keep her waiting. After a final assessment before the looking glass, he loped down the stairs and across the clearing toward the barn.

Jo lifted her head as he approached. "There's a lovely spot by the stream."

"Sounds perfect. I'll carry the basket."

With a shy smile, Jo handed over the burden. Garrett hooked the handles beneath his arm. On a whim, he stuck out his opposite elbow. To his surprise, Jo looped her hand through the crook. His chest swelled.

Though Jo normally charged ahead on any journey, she kept the pace slow and measured. The summer days had lengthened, and the heat had given the late afternoon a lazy feel. A peaceful lassitude stole over him.

Nature had bloomed over the countryside, brilliant and unrestrained. As they neared the creek, sheltering trees rose before them, their leaves saturated with emerald-green.

Jo touched his sleeve with her free hand. "David caught up with me on my way home from Mrs. Sundberg's. That's how I found out about Tom."

"Your brother should have given you a ride."

"I wanted to walk. I needed to think. And of course I had to ask him about Mary Louise."

Garrett recalled how his deputy had been mooning around the office. "How is the courting progressing?"

"Excellent. He's ready for marriage."

"Her father won't be pleased."

"Nothing short of a fortune will please Mr. Stuart. But if Mary is content, that's all that matters."

"What about you?" Garrett asked, gathering his courage. "Are you content?"

She tilted her head, considering the question. "Cora laughs, and she seems happy and healthy."

Two spots of color appeared on her cheeks. She pointed out the site for the picnic and unfurled the tartan blanket draped over her arm.

The girl who'd boldly demanded his hand in marriage had disappeared, leaving behind this shy, beautiful woman. There was an air about her, a sense of hesitant determination.

Garrett helped arrange the covering. "Is this blanket new?"

The blush on her cheeks intensified, and his mood soared. She'd bought the blanket specifically for this outing. That had to mean something, didn't it?

He set down the picnic basket, and Jo flopped onto the edge of the blanket.

She plucked a black-eyed Susan from a scraggly patch of wildflowers and twirled the stem. "David said Tom was sweet on me growing up."

"I told you so." Garrett raised his eyebrows, daring her to refute him.

Jo playfully chucked him on the arm. "Don't let it go to your head."

The sun hovered low on the horizon, blazing red behind a thin cover of clouds. Jo's hair fluttered in the breeze, pulled loose from its bindings. Instead of wearing her dark hair in a single braid down her back, she'd been twisting several braids in a knot at the base of her neck. He realized she'd been taking more care with her appearance lately and the result was breathtaking.

She'd always been beautiful and now she was stunning. Other people had noticed, too. With pride and not a little jealousy, he'd seen gentlemen tip their hats to her on the boardwalk. As much as he wanted the secret of Jo's allure all to himself, he liked seeing the townspeople react to the radiance he'd always seen, a beauty the folks around her had taken for granted.

He reached for a stray lock and tucked the soft strands behind the gentle curve of her ear. "You've been wearing your hair different. I like it."

"Thank you." She smoothed a stray lock, her movements jerky and self-conscious. "I guess I was afraid of trying something new."

Her announcement stunned him. "I can't imagine you being afraid of anything."

"You're the second person who's said that to me today."

He thought he'd been the only one in town who saw Jo, really saw the person inside, but he'd been just as blind as the rest of them.

She caught his gaze and smiled shyly. "Can I tell you a secret?"

"Of course."

Secrets and lies. How much of his life had been shaped by secrets and lies? He went through all the false motions—smiling when he was sad, laughing when he was angry and never telling anyone of his past. He was exhausted from hiding, exhausted from covering his true feelings.

Jo cleared her throat. "Remember when you asked me what Ma and I talked about?" She plucked at the weeds near the edge of the blanket. "We made our peace. I didn't like helping my ma with midwife duties. We had a big fight about it a couple of years ago. Everyone thinks I'm tough, but I'm not. I'm afraid of childbirth."

"That seems normal to me."

She absently braided several long, green stalks. "None of my friends from school are. They all have babies."

Garrett handed her a black-eyed Susan, and she delicately wove it into her chain.

"That doesn't mean they're not scared," he said.

"What are you afraid of?"

She needed his honesty right then, but he couldn't reveal his shame just yet, not when their budding relationship was this new and fragile. "I'm afraid of not being the man I want to be. Of hurting someone I love."

Jo stilled at the revealing admission. "What do you mean?"

"Nothing. I don't know." His gaze dipped to her lips.

Something happened then that he could not explain later. One moment he was revealing his deepest fear, the next moment she was wrapped in his arms. The evening sun warmed his back, and the air around them smelled deliciously of new leaves and freshly tilled earth.

Stirred by a depth of emotion he hadn't thought himself capable of, he surrendered to the foreign sensations. The embrace was right and good, a culmination of the feelings he'd kept rigidly in check since the moment he'd met JoBeth McCoy. *His wife.*

Nothing in his past had prepared him for the feelings rocking his carefully ordered world.

Realizing the enormity of what he was doing, he abruptly let go. Jo stared at him, her body still, not even breathing for a moment.

A shy smile spread across her face. "When I asked you to marry me last spring, you asked what would happen if I ever wanted children of my own."

"You said we'd cross that bridge when we got there."

"We're there."

His chest constricted. He knew what she was telling him. She wanted children. She wanted a real marriage. Garrett stood and stumbled back a step, putting some distance between them.

He was no better than any other addict. Like Tom

Walby swearing off drink, he'd sworn to keep his distance. He'd broken that promise. "I can't. I'm sorry. But I just can't."

What if he hurt her? He'd promised himself he wouldn't touch her and he hadn't even kept that promise for a day—for an hour. He was a weak man, and weak men did not make good husbands.

"Why?" Jo demanded. "Is it me?"

"No, of course not." He raked his hands through his hair. "You're wonderful. It's me. I'm not the man you think of I am."

"Then who are you?"

Her words shot through him like a bullet. The question was deceptively simple, the answer needlessly complicated. He was a flawed man. No better than Tom. No better than his own father. He made promises to himself he didn't keep. Promises to his family he broke.

"I'm not the man you think I am," he repeated, his voice a jagged whisper. "I can't."

She deserved a whole man. And he wouldn't be whole until he made his peace with God, and with himself. Only then could he be a man worthy of Jo's love.

Love.

"Give me time." He dragged in a ragged breath. "Please just give more time."

As a cloud drifted over the sun, the radiance of the afternoon leached away. The budding confidence in Jo's eyes faded into a dull torpor.

A nauseating wave of self-disgust sent pressure pulsating behind his eyes. He'd done this to her. He'd robbed her of her confidence.

She stood and snatched the blanket, folding it in a disheveled square. "Never mind."

"No." He reached out a hand, and she flinched. He dropped his arm against his side. "There's something I need to do first."

She met his gaze, her chin set at a determined angle. "I know you have secrets. I thought I could live with that, but I was wrong. And it's not because I'm unworthy of your trust, it's because you're a coward."

He reared back as though she'd struck him. "I am a coward, but I can't change overnight."

She hugged the tartan blanket against her chest, her smile sad and tinged with defeat. "Ironic, isn't it? That's all we have together. Time."

Her voice was vulnerable, the small voice of a woman who'd wanted to please him and had been rebuffed.

A hopeless pall fell over him. He'd waited too long. He'd already run out of time with Jo.

Chapter Twenty-Five

The following day, Jo sat at the telegraph office and
seesawed a pencil between her fingers.

Can't or *won't*.

The words had been swirling around her head all
morning. At least she'd learned one thing: rejection
wasn't fatal. She'd faced her worst fears and come out
only slightly worse for wear. She pleated her new navy
blue calico between two fingers.

If anything good had come of her marraige, at least
her ma had stopped ribbing her about her attire. Dressing nice wasn't so bad. And since she'd put up her hair,
the grocer had ceased eyeing her as if she was going to
nip an onion and run.

That definitely made her shopping trips less tense.

The 12:15 from Wichita rumbled into the station
with a shrill whistle and a belch of steam. Jo stood and
stretched. Her ma had said she was expecting a package today.

Edith had been awfully mysterious about the contents. Watching the passengers depart, Jo decided she

needed a breath of fresh air. Or at least as fresh as the station permitted.

A smattering of passengers departed in a flurry of baggage, their feet disappearing in puffs of steam from the train's engines. With a jaundiced eye Jo watched as they sized up the town, holding handkerchiefs to their mouths against the dusty wind. No doubt grateful this was only a stop and not their final destination.

She was turning away when a tall gentleman caught her attention. After a quick double take, she launched herself at the unaware man. "Jack Elder!"

He stumbled back a step and tightened his grip. "How are you, JoBeth?"

Releasing her hold, she backed away. He hadn't changed much over the years. He was still tall and lean, his hair a touch grayer at the temples, and the lines on his forehead deeper.

She glanced around. "Where are Elizabeth and the boys?"

"At home. I had business in Wichita that finished up early. Thought I'd spend the night here."

"I can't believe Ma didn't tell me it was you. She said she was expecting a package."

"Well, I did bring a wedding gift." He tipped his hat. "Let me fetch it."

Jo shaded her eyes against the sun. Garrett had driven the wagon into town. He set the brake and hopped down. "Your ma said I should bring the wagon. Did you find this mysterious package?"

She kept her gaze focused on a point just behind his head. She wasn't going to let him ruin her day. "I did!" Jo exclaimed. "He's coming now."

She turned and discovered Jack leading two men carrying a slated crate. The crate tipped and the contents bleated. After the men set it down, Jo crouched before a stamp reading Live Animals.

She straightened and planted her hands on her hips. "It's a goat."

"I didn't bring the hat and coat, but—"

Jo playfully socked him in the arm and cast a glance over her shoulder. "That's our secret."

"I told you that you wouldn't end up like your aunt Vicky."

With another surreptitious glance over her shoulder at her unyielding husband, she held her index finger before her lips. "Shh."

Garrett cleared his throat. "We haven't been introduced. I'm Garrett Cain."

The two men exchanged a quick, single-pump handshake. "Jack Elder."

"I've heard a lot about you."

"Haven't heard much about you."

The goat in the crate bleated again. Jo grinned. "We'd best get back to the house. I'm sure they're all excited to see you."

The two men easily hoisted the crate into the back of the wagon. Jo lifted her skirts and scrambled onto the platform seat. The wagon dipped as Jack entered on her right, then dipped the opposite direction as Garrett alighted. Off balance, she slid across the seat, and they bumped hips.

"Sorry," Jo mumbled and sat stiffly upright.

She turned away and caught Jack's startled expression. No doubt he was curious about the strained relationship between two newlyweds.

Time, Garrett had said. She'd married a man who could never love her. She had all the time in the world.

Mustering a cheerful smile, she spoke. "I can't wait for you to meet Cora. She's five and the most precious thing."

"She'll be the same age as Maxwell and my littlest one. That's a handful."

"I almost wish she were. I'd know what to do. She's too well behaved for me."

Jack chuckled.

They chatted for the remainder of the trip, catching up on old news. Garrett sat beside her, his expression stiff and unwelcoming. When the wagon pulled before the barn on the McCoy farm, the McCoys swarmed. Jo caught up with her brother Michael and together they pried open the goat's crate.

Michael scratched his head. "What kind of present is that?"

"It's a joke."

Her brother shrugged. "I don't get it."

He wandered off, and Garrett knelt before the animal. "I don't get it, either."

Jo heaved a sigh. "I used to worry that I'd end up like my aunt Vicky. She never had children, but she had a whole herd of goats. Rumor had it she dressed them in flowered hats and coats at Easter."

"Nah. You'd dress them as soldiers."

Jo's smile buckled. She'd pinched her cheeks and bought a new dress, but he'd always see her as a tomboy. Her heart sank along with the last of her hope.

Cora dashed from the house. She enveloped Garrett in a hug, then offered another to Jo. "Michael says we have a goat. Does it have a name?"

"Nope. Why don't you pick one." Garrett grinned.

"Buttercup," Cora declared.

"It's an odd name for a boy goat." Jo considered the animal. "But I think it's perfect."

Cora skipped away, and the goat leaped after her. Together they cavorted around the yard.

Garrett touched Jo's arm. "Looks like Buttercup just might wind up in a coat and hat after all."

The words from the previous day hung between them. Her mood swung between anger and despair. She'd thought they could be friends. The attraction flaring between them prevented such a simple solution.

When she saw Cora, the obvious affection they shared toward one another, despair lanced her heart. They'd married to give the little girl a secure home, a safe future. Cora had blossomed beneath their care. If things hadn't turned out for Jo the way she'd hoped, she had no one to blame but herself for building her hopes on a rocky foundation.

She pulled her new bonnet over her head, shading her face. "I think I'll stay here tonight. You can go home if you want."

Hurt flickered in his eyes. Hurt and something she'd never seen before—doubt.

He swallowed, his Adam's apple bobbing. "I'll fetch you in the morning."

"I'll walk."

His shoulders sagged.

For a moment her resolve wavered. "Garrett."

He turned. Their gazes met and locked, and the tension pulsated between them. A thousand possibilities fluttered through her head, and she shooed them all away.

Jo ducked her head. "Never mind."

She'd given all she was prepared to give. He had to meet her halfway.

After Garrett's hasty departure, the next few hours passed in a distracted blur for Jo. Jack caught them up on news of his family, regaling them with stories of his three children.

Gradually, her family dispersed. Her brothers scattered for evening chores, her ma and pa disappeared out the back. Her parents did that sometimes. Walked by the creek in the evenings. Summer had turned and the days were long and hot. The sky clear and dry. Evenings by the creek were sometimes the only relief from the relentless heat.

Jo turned to her old friend. "When will you bring Elizabeth for a visit?"

His face lit up at the mention of his wife's name. "Soon, I think. You heard my brother is taking over the old Cole farm."

Jo nodded. "Reverend Miller said he's trying the land with cattle."

"It's not a bad notion."

"Why isn't he staying on your family's ranch?"

"Good question." Jack rested his forearms on the porch railing and leaned over, staring into the distance. "It's harder for some men, finding their place in the world. John is the youngest. He's got something to prove."

Jo stood beside him and rested her chin on her knuckles. "Men are odd creatures."

"So are women." Jack barked out a laugh. "I know it's not my business, but..."

He let his unspoken question hang between them.

Jo heaved a sigh. "We married for Cora's sake. He

needed a wife. I was available." She twisted her mouth in a wry smile. "That's all there is."

"Oh, I think there's more. That man has something weighing heavy on his soul. I've been around long enough to see that much."

"I thought if we were together we'd grow closer. But the more I try, the more I feel the distance between us."

"There's something holding that man back. And I'd wager it has nothing to do with you."

"How do I change that? How do I make him see that we have a future together?"

"Be patient with him. It's harder for some people to trust. If that doesn't work, I'll knock some sense into him when I visit next fall."

Jo laughed. "If I thought that would work, I'd have the boys take care of it."

"He might not be able to change." Jack touched her hand, his gaze earnest. "Sometimes the things that happen to people in their childhood, in their past, changes them too much. It warps them and they can never grow straight again."

"You don't think people can change?"

"He has to want to change. You can't force him."

Her eyes burned, and she blinked away the tears. "I wish I'd figured that out sooner."

Jack turned and leaned his hip against the porch railing. "Marriage is hard work. But it's good work. Worthwhile. Put in the effort."

"I can't put in all the effort alone," Jo scoffed. She'd ignored the warnings from those who loved her most— her ma, her friends. She'd trapped herself in a loveless marriage and she had only herself to blame.

Chapter Twenty-Six

Jo sucked in a fortifying breath. She took a step forward, then paused. Garrett had cleared the corral outside the barn and mended the fence. This morning he was working with his horse. He stood in the center of the corral and held the lead rope as the animal circled him.

He called out commands, sometimes with words, sometimes just with whistles and clicks of his tongue. The horse responded with lightning-fast precision.

Garrett wore his blue work shirt, the sleeves turned back. She stared at the corded muscles of his forearms and her pulse quickened.

She loved him.

She loved him and she'd pushed him too hard. That was her way. Full steam ahead with no thought other than victory. All she'd done with her dogged persistence was push him away. If she loved him, she owed him some space. Jack had urged her to be patient, and she'd decided to heed his advice.

She smoothed her skirts and plastered a serene expression on her face before calling his name.

He turned, and her determination wavered. She recalled their first meeting at the church, when she'd had pear blossoms in her hair. Even then she'd known she wasn't the sort of woman to attract a man like Garrett Cain. That knowledge hadn't stopped her from trying.

At her continued silence, he released the lead line from the horse's halter and crossed the corral. "Do you need anything?"

"Cora and I are going to the pond. Would you like to come?"

"Sure."

Jo exhaled a breath she hadn't even known she was holding. He rolled down his sleeves and buttoned the cuffs, then shut and latched the gate behind him.

Turning, she motioned for Cora. "He's coming."

The little girl skipped her way down the road, her blond curls shimmering in the sunlight.

Garrett took her small hand. "I don't know the way."

"Jo does," Cora declared proudly.

They linked hands as they set off for the road.

"Lift me," the little girl demanded with a giggle.

Jo and Garrett exchanged an indulgent grin over her head. On every third step, they hoisted their arms into the air, lifting the giggling little girl from the ground. They repeated the playful activity until Jo's arm ached.

She let go and rubbed her shoulder. "Enough." She laughed. "We should look for some rocks."

Keeping her hands above her waist, she waded through the dense brush toward the creek. She assisted Cora down the bank, and they sloshed through the water, their heads bent.

Garrett paused above them. "Why are we looking for rocks?"

"For skipping."

He joined them in the creek, then plucked a stone from the creek bed and handed it to Jo. "Will this work?"

Squinting, she studied his find. "Nope. It needs to be like this."

She held up a flat, rounded stone.

"Got it," he replied, resuming his search.

Jo crouched next to him. "Haven't you ever skipped stones before?"

"Never."

She pressed off from her knee into a stand again. "It's too bad Abraham isn't here, he once got twelve skips off one rock."

"Is that good?"

"The best I've ever seen."

She forced herself to look away. If they were going to spend their lives together, she must foster the friendship. She'd feared from the beginning one of them had more to lose. Perhaps she'd even find a way for both of them to gain something.

As she struggled back up the hill, he took her hand. She steeled herself against the sudden rush of attraction.

Cora kept her proud stash of stones tight against her chest. "I've never skipped stones, either."

Upon reaching the small pond nestled in a shallow valley, Jo proceeded with her demonstration. She showed them how to flick their wrists, sending the stones skipping across the water. After several tries, Cora managed two skips.

She laughed and clapped hands.

Jo glanced at her husband as he crouched before his niece, pulling her into his embrace.

He'd only ever asked her for one thing. *Time.*

Marriage was work. But it was good work. Worthwhile.

She stood behind him, not quite touching. His request was a small enough thing to ask. She'd give him more time.

Garrett stood before the towering church doors. He felt as though he'd come full circle. This was where it had all begun between him and Jo. When he'd dropped his hat and she'd retrieved it. Their hands had touched, the feeling still lingered.

She deserved the truth, and he was finally prepared for the cost. Cora had grown fond of him, but his niece still preferred Jo. His cousin, Edward, had lost interest in demanding custody of Cora. The reason for their marriage had dissipated, and he needed another, better one. Garrett rolled his tense shoulders.

Everything was wrapped up neat as a pin. All he need do was screw his courage and tell Jo the truth.

Simple as that.

Reverend Miller opened the door, a question in his watery gray eyes.

Garrett cleared his throat. "I need a word."

The older man stepped aside and motioned him into the shaded interior of the cozy space. Without asking why, Reverend Miller led him through the smaller set of double doors into the church. They sat in the front pews facing the altar. Garrett braced his hands on his knees and hung his head.

The reverend touched his shoulder. "You can talk with God alone, or with me here."

"Stay," Garrett implored hoarsely.

He let the words flow. He spoke until his throat went dry. All the fears, all the horrors of his youth. Things he'd forgotten welled up in his heart and spilled over the side. The feelings tumbled loose, raging free as the dam within him burst.

A sob shook his body and he buried his face in his hands, letting go.

Reverend Miller rested his hands on his knees. "That's a heavy burden for one man to carry alone."

"Yes."

"And why must you carry this burden alone?"

"Because…because it's my shame."

"It's your father's shame. You were but a child. Would you blame Cora for her parents' death?"

"Of course not." Garrett shot upright.

"Then you must forgive. Forgive your father and forgive yourself." The older man leaned away and rested his forearms on the back of the pew. "I served in the war myself."

Garrett lifted his head in surprise.

"It does things to a man." Reverend Miller shook his head. "We'll never know what shaped your father. What drove him into such a black place."

"He stole my faith."

Garrett whispered a truth he'd only just realized.

"Forgiveness can restore that faith. Forgiveness and love."

"My mother should have left him sooner." Garrett spoke the words that had rotted his soul for years, eating away at him like a poison. "She should have been stronger for us."

Until that moment he'd never realized the anger sparking in his chest. "She should have been stronger."

"I don't fault your anger, son. As we grow, we come to realize those we love are flawed. My guess is that your mother did the best she could. She couldn't change your father."

"Why did he do it?"

There was so much more in the simple phrase, but he couldn't speak anymore.

"I can't answer that. I can only advise on matters of faith. Forgive them both. For being human. For being weak. Only you can heal the rift in your soul."

"But I can't forget."

"God does not require us to forget. You have a lovely niece who dotes on you. A beautiful wife who loves you. Take those gifts without the taint of hatred."

Garrett's heart stuttered. Jo didn't love him. If he told her the truth, she might never. He clutched his hat, bending the brim. He'd rather know if she could love him than live in a prison of his own making.

He loved her.

A moment of clarity cleared the fog from his brain. He'd driven away the people he loved from his life. He'd run from them, hidden from them, frozen them out—all because he was afraid of losing someone again.

And what had it gotten him? Fifteen wasted years that he could have spent with Deirdre. Five years he could have spent with Cora. He'd asked Jo for time when he'd wasted all of his. Instead of protecting himself, he'd created more hurt. For all of them.

His head throbbing, Garrett held out his hand. "Thank you."

The reverend took his proffered hand in both of his. "Forgive yourself first, son, and the rest will go much easier."

Garrett lifted his eyes toward the stained-glass window. Mary and Joseph held a swaddled Jesus in colorful, angled splendor. God had sacrificed his only son for the sins of mankind.

The reverend followed Garrett's thoughtful gaze. "It is written in Ephesians. 'Be ye kind to one another, tenderhearted, forgiving one another, even as God for Christ's sake hath forgiven you.'"

His thoughts reeling, Garrett walked down the center aisle, leaving Reverend Miller alone. The moment he pushed open the double doors to the vestibule, the stench of cigar smoke hit him like a wall. The doors closed behind him.

Garrett stiffened and reached for his gun. The cold barrel of a pistol jabbed him in the ribs.

Bert Walby's dank breath puffed near his cheek. "Don't do anything stupid, Marshal."

Garrett raised his hands. "This isn't going to work," he said, keeping his voice low. He didn't want the reverend involved.

"Sure it is. If you don't help me, I'm going to tell the whole town that the man they entrusted to keep the peace is the son of a murderer."

Tensing, Garrett lowered his hands. "Then why do you need the gun?"

"Because I don't trust you." Bert fished in Garrett's holster and snatched his revolver. "We're going to the sheriff's office. The 10:15 to Guthrie is leaving in twenty minutes, and me and Tom are going to be on it."

Bert stuffed the extra gun into the front of his pants. Garrett pushed through the outside doors and blinked against the sunlight. A half-dozen people bustled along the boardwalk, too many to start something with Bert.

He'd bide his time and wait until there were fewer by-standers.

Bert kept the gun beneath his jacket as they walked, his shifty gaze darting between Garrett and a couple, their elbows linked, passing them as they crossed before the mercantile. Garrett tipped his hat.

When they reached the sheriff's office, Garrett paused. Bert shoved him forward.

"Wait," Garrett ordered. "My deputy is young and green. If he thinks something is wrong he's just as liable to shoot me by accident. Let me get rid of him."

"You do that. But don't try anything funny. I'll kill you both."

Garrett nodded his understanding and stepped inside. David sat behind his desk. When the younger man saw him, he leaped to his feet, his expression flooded with guilt.

"I was just doing some paperwork."

"My desk is the best place," Garrett soothed. "Bert here wants to talk with his brother. Why don't you go see Jack Elder off."

David checked his watch. "I don't need to. I saw him last night."

"I have things under control here. Tell Jack it's always welcome having the assistance of a fellow lawman around."

David tilted his head to one side, then looked between the two men. Garrett held his breath. After a moment, David shrugged. "Suit yourself."

Garrett didn't exhale until the door closed. "Let's get Tom."

He snatched the circle key ring from the hook on his desk and led Bert into the backroom.

Tom sat up in bed when he caught sight of them. "What are you doing here?"

Bert waved his gun. "I'm busting you out. We're taking the train to Guthrie."

Tom shook his head. "It won't work. Even if we bust out of here, there'll be a posse waiting for us at the next stop."

"I got us some insurance," his brother declared. "I been trailing the marshal here. Figured I owed it to him after he had you and me followed. A man who goes to church on a Tuesday must have some powerful sinning to confess." Bert shoved Garrett forward. "The folks of Cimarron Springs have entrusted their lives to the son of a murderer."

Tom's eyes widened.

His brother cackled. "His pa shot his ma then killed himself. The marshal isn't gonna want anyone knowing that, are you?"

He jabbed Garrett in the ribs again. Garrett grunted.

Tom remained seated. "I'm still not going."

"You are the dumbest son of—"

"Not that dumb." Tom lifted his doleful gaze. "Since I've been here, I sobered up. I've been remembering bits and pieces of what happened that night. I didn't shoot Mr. Hodges. You did."

Bert sneered. "I was doing you a favor. We coulda opened the store across the street. Hodges was sitting on a gold mine of stock. We coulda bought it cheap." He spat at Tom's feet. "Who goes and confesses to something they didn't do?"

"I figured it must have been me. My gun was missing bullets... I'd been losing at poker to Hodges for an hour and then he wound up dead. I didn't know what to think." Tom's expression hardened. "You wanted them to believe I did it, didn't you?"

"Don't get yourself in a lather. I figured if they caught up with you, everyone would think it was an accident. You're always shooting off that gun."

Tom lunged toward the bars. "Get out of here. I got a wife and kid. I'm clearing my name and staying."

"You can't clear your name without ruining mine. Now let's get out of here."

"No." Tom sat back down and gripped the straw mattress. "I'm not like you. It's been eating away at me, thinking I killed someone. I'm not like you at all."

Garrett looked between the two brothers. So similar and yet so different. They'd been raised by the same parents, reared in the same town. Yet Bert had gone bad. Worse even than Tom because there was no going back for him.

Bert cocked the gun and leveled his hand at Tom.

The color drained from his brother's face. "You'd shoot your own kin?"

"You're too stupid for your own good, Tom."

He squeezed the trigger and Garrett lunged. The shot went wide. Garrett tossed the keys into the cell to give Tom a fighting chance and reached for the shooter. The move slowed him down. Bert leveled his gun at Garrett's forehead.

"Wait!" Tom hollered. "Don't kill him. I'll go with you."

He clumsily reached around the bars and jammed the key into the lock from the awkward angle. "You're right, I can't stay. We'll figure it out together."

Bert wiped the perspiration from his brow with the back of his hand. "That's better."

He flipped Garrett around and twisted his arm behind his back. Garrett cringed and arched his back.

Bert kicked him forward. "Get out there ahead of us, Tom. I'll follow."

Garrett was going to die. He knew it in his heart, in his soul. There was no way Bert was going to let him live. He thought of the morning he'd spent with Jo and cursed himself.

He'd lost his one opportunity to tell her he loved her. *Time.*

He'd asked for time, and he'd just run out.

Chapter Twenty-Seven

Jo hugged Jack Elder and stepped back. "Don't wait so long between visits."

"I won't."

"And give Elizabeth my love."

"I will." He glanced at someone behind her. "David?"

Jo spun around as her brother skidded to a halt before them. "It's Garrett."

At the panic in her brother's voice, her heart shot ahead three beats.

"He came into the jail with Bert Walby," David gasped. "The prisoner's brother. He told me to leave, but it was real strange. He told me to tell you that he appreciated the help of a fellow lawman."

Jack dropped his bags and began rummaging through the contents. He pulled out a pistol and spun the chamber, then stuck it into the back waistband of his pants. "You armed?" he asked David.

Her brother nodded.

"Do you think they'll come out the front or the back?"

"Bert came in through the front door. I'm guessing that's the way he'll leave."

Jack squinted toward the street. "All right. You circle around back, just in case. I'll watch the front."

Jo blocked their exit. "Give me the extra gun."

"No." Jack shook his head. "Absolutely not."

"I'm the best shot. He'll be holding Garrett as a hostage. That's the only reason he would have made David leave. I'm the best shot if there's an opening."

The men exchanged a look, and Jack reluctantly nodded. He handed her the gun, keeping his grip on the barrel. "Stay out of sight. If I see an opportunity, I'll give you the signal. When you fire, try to nick him, just for a distraction. I'll make the final shot."

Her mouth dry, Jo nodded.

David circled the row of connected buildings toward the rear of the jailhouse. She and Jack dashed down the street. Jack cleared the boardwalk of people while Jo crouched behind a rain barrel and leveled her gun toward the door. She hadn't told Garrett she loved him because she was afraid of spooking him. What if it was too late?

An eternity passed before Tom stepped out. He glanced left and right, his expression stunned. Garrett came next, his arm twisted behind him at an odd angle. Bert cowered behind him.

Garrett scanned the street and for a moment Jo thought he was looking at her. Then his gaze slipped away. She breathed a sigh of relief.

Bert caught sight of Jack and stopped short. "Out of my way, or I'll shoot the marshal."

"You won't get far without a hostage."

"Far enough."

"You willing to take that risk?"

Jo aimed her gun.

Bert yanked Garrett to the right, searching the deserted street as he calculated his odds.

Jack gave her the signal, a slight shake of his hand.

Jo fired.

Garrett shouted and went to his knees, clutching the wound at his thigh.

Jack fired almost simultaneously.

Bert jerked. He glanced at his chest, astonished by the growing bloom of red covering his white shirt. His knees buckled and he collapsed onto his back, his eyes staring sightlessly at the clear blue sky.

Jo emerged from her hiding spot and crouched before her wounded husband. "Are you all right?"

"I'm fine," he replied, his expression rife with amusement. "You shot me, didn't you?"

"It's only a flesh wound." Jo pressed her hand against the bleeding.

He twisted to the side and unfurled his blue bandanna from his back pocket. She quickly tied it around his thigh.

Jack leaned over her shoulder. "I told you to nick the bad guy, not the hostage."

Jo grimaced. "My way was better. It gave you a clearer shot at Bert."

She glanced over her shoulder and realized Tom was sobbing over his dead brother. Her heart ached at the sight.

Jack stepped before her and blocked her view. "Let's get your husband inside."

He hooked his arm beneath Garrett's shoulder. Doc Johnsen, drawn by the commotion, followed them, his bag in his hands. Jo trailed behind the three.

Since the holding cell was the only place for Garrett to lie down, they shuffled him into the back.

The next fifteen minutes passed in a blur as Doc Johnsen sterilized the wound and added a few stitches.

The handsome, blond-haired doctor smiled at Jo. "Remind me not to get on your bad side. If you'll shoot your own husband…"

Jo scowled and crossed her arms over her chest. "He'll live?"

"He'll live."

Garrett motioned at the doc. "I need a moment with my wife. Alone."

The doc nodded. "Don't walk unless you absolutely have to." He adjusted his hat and closed his satchel. "Don't put any strain on that leg. I'll be back in a week to take out the stitches."

After he left, an unnatural quiet permeated the room.

Suddenly shy, Jo blurted, "Are you sore at me for shooting you?"

"Nope."

She grinned.

Garrett frowned. "I'm furious with you for putting yourself in danger." His soft voice blunted his harsh words. "You're the bravest woman I've ever met."

"No." Jo held his hand to her chest. "I haven't been very brave during our marriage. I didn't want you to reject me. I should have let you marry some pretty girl who would always know the right thing to say, but I was selfish. I wanted you for myself."

"Hey," he spoke sternly. "No one gets to speak badly about JoBeth Cain. Not even you."

She blushed. "Let me finish. When I realized you were in danger, I died a little bit inside. I love—"

"There's something I have to tell you."

He placed two fingers against her lips. "Don't finish that sentence until I've said my peace."

Jo sucked in a breath. Whatever happened, she was prepared to face the truth.

"I lied to you." Garrett drew himself into a seated position as Jo perched on the edge of the bed. He tried not to let the disappointment in her expressive face waylay his confession. "My parents didn't die from smallpox. My father killed my mother and turned the gun on himself."

She clutched his hand tighter against her chest, and her heartbeat quickened beneath his fingers. "He wasn't a well man. He'd served in the war. He'd been wounded. He drank to ease the pain and when that didn't work, he turned to laudanum. He started having hallucinations. He thought my mother was an enemy soldier. He couldn't live with what he'd done."

Her mouth worked. "Did you see—?"

"No," Garrett hastily replied. "My sister and I were at school. A neighbor heard the shot. He found my father babbling like a wild man. He left to fetch help. I guess. I guess it was too much."

"You said you worked on the docks after that?"

"Deirdre was eighteen. We tried to live on our own for a while. It didn't work out. We stayed with my mother's uncle after that. And my cousin."

"Edward? The one who wanted custody of Cora?"

"Yeah. He didn't have much use for me. It was difficult…on my aunt and uncle. I looked too much like my father. My uncle and I fought…" His voice trailed off. "I should never have become a lawman." He laughed humorlessly. "It's not such a big deal if a blacksmith has a murderer for a father, but a lawman is held to higher standards."

"Garrett..."

"I don't know what will happen when the town council hears about my past. I don't know if I can keep my job. We'll go someplace. Maybe I can apprentice as a blacksmith after all."

He smiled encouragingly, but tears welled in her eyes. His heart sank. "You know, never mind. You deserve better. We'll get an annulment. I'll—"

She mirrored his earlier gesture, pressing two fingers against his lips. "I'm sorry you thought your father's actions would change the way I feel about you. What he did makes me ache inside for you. For your family."

Garrett closed his eyes against the memories. "I was terrified of being like him. Then I saw Tom today. His brother wanted him to escape, but he couldn't. They're brothers, but they're different. Tom didn't have it in him. They'd faced the same difficulties and chosen separate paths. I'm different from my father."

"I know you are."

"I knew I loved you, but I couldn't tell you until I made my peace with God. I'd blamed Him all my life. I thought I'd been singled out for punishment. But then I realized I was only punishing myself. I didn't want to lose anyone I loved again, so I drove them all away. You changed that. Once I forgave my father, it was like I forgave myself."

She offered him a watery smile. "I love you, too."

His throat worked. "Are you certain? Because if my past is too much for you, I understand. If we have to start over, it'll be hard."

Jo snatched his coat lapels and fisted the material in

her hands, jerking him upright until their noses were a hairbreadth apart. "If you leave me, I'll shoot you. Again."

Garrett grinned. "I believe you."

He cupped the back of her neck and kissed her. The past melted away, and he felt new, reborn.

She pressed her hands against his chest and frowned. "Your leg must hurt something fierce. You should be home where you can rest."

Garrett brushed the pad of his thumb over the faint scar on her cheek. "Not until I get this right." He sucked in a fortifying breath. "I'm sorry I lied. I've loved you since the moment you wrapped that snake around your arm. You're brave and honest and I can't wait to wake up in the morning just so I can see you." He paused. "You bring light to my world. You helped restore my faith in God. In myself."

She launched herself into his arms and hugged him tight. "That's all I ever wanted to hear."

"Then I'll say it to you every day for the rest of your life. I love you."

Epilogue

He didn't show it, but Jo knew her husband was nervous. She squeezed his hand. "Whatever happens, we'll stay together."

Cora and Maxwell played marbles in the dirt beneath the sun. In light of his past, Garrett had offered to tender his resignation. The town council had met in the empty schoolhouse to discuss the matter.

Jo didn't figure the council had any reason for voting him out, but Garrett felt it was important, and she respected his wishes. They were waiting outside the schoolhouse while the decision was made.

Following the shooting, they'd buried Bert in the small cemetery outside the church. Tom and his wife had left for Oklahoma City soon afterward, with Tom declaring his need to start over.

David stepped out the door, and Garrett stiffened beside her.

Her brother winked at them and sketched a wave. "They're letting me keep my job."

Garrett stood and shook the younger man's hand. "I'm proud of you. Proud to have had you as my deputy."

Before David could reply, Jack Elder emerged. He approached Garrett, and Jo held her breath.

"I don't know whether you'll think this is good news or bad news."

Jo fisted her hands.

"They want you for five more years."

She jumped to her feet. Garrett stood beside her and caught her around the waist.

Keeping his arm around Jo, Garrett shook Jack's hand. "Thank you for everything. I hope to meet your wife and children one day."

"Might be sooner than you think. Elizabeth is beside herself with worry. My brother, John, set off on his cattle drive and we haven't had word in a month. She'll be up here soon to scold him herself when he arrives."

Cora tugged on her skirts. "I beat him. I beat Maxwell at marbles!"

Maxwell stood and dusted his trousers.

Her husband sighed. "You have to be on your toes around these ladies."

"I'll try again next Sunday when you come for supper."

Garrett groaned. "Your pa already asked me to balance the gate again."

"You adore my family," Jo said.

"Almost as much as I adore you." He moved his lips closer to her ear. "I thank God every day for bringing us together."

"Me, too," Jo replied simply.

Despite all the tragedy in his life, the shadows in his eyes had abated as his faith had grown. And she never tired of the way he looked at her.

As though he saw who she really was, even with her faults, and loved her all the more.

"Say." Jo pressed a kiss against his cheek. "You said I gave you a gift on our wedding day, but you never told me what it was."

"Peace. You gave Cora and me peace," he continued, ignoring their rapt audience. "Our family is the greatest gift I've ever received."

Tears pricked behind her eyes. She'd set out to win the marshal's heart, and he'd gone and turned the tables on her.

* * * * *

Angel Moore fell in love with romance in elementary school when she read the story of Robin Hood and Maid Marian. Who doesn't want to escape to a happily-ever-after world? Married to her best friend, she has two wonderful sons, a lovely daughter-in-law and three grandkids. She loves sharing her faith and the hope she knows is real because of God's goodness to her. Find her at www.angelmoorebooks.com.

Books by Angel Moore

Love Inspired Historical

Conveniently Wed
The Marriage Bargain
The Rightful Heir
Husband by Arrangement
A Ready-Made Texas Family

Visit the Author Profile page
at Harlequin.com for more titles.

CONVENIENTLY WED

Angel Moore

But they that wait upon the Lord
shall renew their strength;
they shall mount up with wings as eagles;
they shall run, and not be weary;
and they shall walk, and not faint.
—*Isaiah* 40:31

To Tina James for the time and encouragement
she invested in my first sale.

To the friends and family
who read the drafts along the way.

To Austin for being my champion
on the adventure of entering the writing world.

To Bob for believing in me
and motivating me to write my first manuscript.

And to God for His mercy and constant help.

Chapter One

Pine Haven, Texas
October 1879

Daisy Mosley pulled back both hammers on the shotgun, lowered the barrel onto the windowsill and aimed at the center of the rider's chest. No stranger had been down the lane since her husband, Murdock, had been killed by horse thieves three weeks earlier. Daisy was determined that no harm would come to James and John. She could hear the eight-year-old twins shushing each other as they scurried under her bed in the far corner of the cabin.

Watching carefully, she followed the rider's slow approach with her gun. Very tall and broad with a straight back, a worn Stetson and red hair, he was definitely not a local. His mount was the prettiest pinto she'd ever seen. He was almost close enough for her to shoot when he stopped. He leaned forward in the saddle, his face still shielded by the Stetson.

"Daisy Marie, put that gun down before you hurt somebody."

"Who are you?" Daisy didn't flinch. "And how do you know my name?"

The stranger chuckled. "You know who I am. Have for years. And you know I don't trust you with a gun. Not after what happened when your papa was trying to teach you to shoot."

"Oh, my goodness!" In one swift movement, Daisy lowered the gun, released the hammers and put it in the rack over the mantel. "Boys, come meet Tucker Barlow!" she called to her sons as she unbolted the door and raced across the porch, barely skimming the steps.

Tucker dismounted just in time to brace against the impact of Daisy throwing herself into his arms. She remembered fondly that, even though she carried quite a lot of momentum for such a petite lady, she was no match for his strength. Not many could stand against the power of her exuberance. He lifted her and swung her around in a circle before setting her on the dusty ground. He held her hands, and she leaned back to look up at him.

"Daisy, you are a sight. And what kind of welcome was that for you to think about shooting me before I even met these fine-looking men you've got here?"

James and John stood behind their mother, timid of the big stranger.

Daisy withdrew her hands from Tucker's and turned to the twins. "James, John, meet Mr. Barlow. Mr. Barlow, these are my sons."

"Strong Bible names. Glad to meet you both." He held out a hand for James to shake and then turned to John. "I'm glad you've got that freckle over your lip, John. Otherwise, I might never know who I was talking to."

John ducked his head shyly. "It's a birthmark.

Momma said God put it there so she wouldn't mix us up when we were babies."

James spoke up. "If he didn't have it, we could trick people and trade places and stuff."

Daisy chuckled. "They look alike, but it doesn't take long to find out how different they are." She smiled at Tucker. "Boys, Mr. Barlow works for Papa Warren. He was a good friend to me when I was a girl. I haven't seen him since I moved here when me and your papa got married over ten years ago."

Looking directly at the young boys, Tucker said, "You don't need to call me Mr. Barlow. We're gonna be working side by side as men. You can call me Tucker."

"What are you talking about, Tucker?" Daisy rested her hands on the boys' shoulders as they flanked her and watched the giant stranger.

Tucker removed his hat and lowered his gaze to the ground reverently. "Your father felt it was for the best—given the circumstances and all."

The excitement of having a visitor gave way to sadness as her little family remembered their fresh grief. Daisy appreciated Tucker's respect of Murdock's memory.

"Boys, why don't you go fetch a cool drink of water from the well while me and your momma talk in private?"

Daisy nudged the twins toward the side yard and looked into Tucker's face, shading her eyes against the sun with one hand. She didn't remember him being so tall. "What are you talking about, 'Papa says it's for the best'?"

"Now, Daisy, just hear me out." The tapping of her toe rustled the hem of her skirt. She wasn't in the mood to be patient—not that she ever was.

"I'm waiting…" Her words provoked Tucker to explain.

"Your father came to me the day he got your telegraph about Murdock's murder. He was so concerned about you and the boys. He wanted to know how you were holding up under such a tragic loss. Would the men who killed Murdock come back and harm you or the boys? Would you lose your land? He was beside himself." Tucker paused as if choosing his next words carefully. "We talked for a long time that night." Tucker stopped and drew in a deep breath.

"And…" Daisy's toes still tapped, and now she folded her arms across her chest, anticipating she wouldn't like the next part of the conversation.

Tucker looked at the hat in his hands and smoothed the brim. "And…" His mouth set in a firm line, and his eyes raised to meet her stare. "We think it would be best for you and the boys if you and I get married." His words spilled out in a rush.

Daisy shook her head and turned one ear toward him with her brows wrinkled in confusion. "Who thinks what for who?"

Tucker could hear the disbelief in her voice. Thinking she might take it better when she realized it was her father's idea, he emphasized Mr. Warren's perspective.

"Your father—and I've come to agree with him—thinks it would be best if you and I get married. Today."

"Wait just one minute. I'm not following your train of thought. Why would you think this?" Daisy said, sounding befuddled.

"Not just me," Tucker reiterated. "Me and your father. We both know a lot about what you're facing now.

Your father lost your mother and had to raise you girls alone. He knows the pain you're in. And my father passed away when I was young. I know how the boys are feeling." Tucker maintained a calm demeanor. He knew how quickly Daisy could go from confused to angry or indignant. Many times he'd seen her jump from one emotion to another.

"Just because you think you know what I'm feeling doesn't mean I need to marry you." Daisy's voice rose a bit.

"It's not just about that, Daisy. You've got two sons to raise. You'll need help with that."

Tucker proceeded with caution, trying not to set her off before she understood his motive. "You've got the farm, too. It's too much to do alone. I remember what my mother went through after my father died. She worked herself to death. Those boys need you." He couldn't imagine Daisy suffering as his mother had. He'd been too young to save his mother. But he wouldn't risk this woman—who he'd once hoped would love him—falling to the same fate.

Daisy lowered her arms and clenched her fists at her sides. "I am managing this farm just fine. And my boys are okay, too. They've just been through a lot, that's all." Her words couldn't hide the concern in her voice, which revealed how badly she must want to believe what she was saying. Tucker knew she wasn't convinced. "I don't know who put this fool notion in your head, but marriage is not what I need right now." She stopped and thought for a moment. "And why would you want to marry me in the first place?"

"It's not a fool notion. Your father and I talked and prayed about this before I decided to come. I'd have been here a couple of weeks ago, but it took time to tie up some business in East River." With a grin and imploring gaze he added, "We've always been friends. We get along and understand one another. That's what you need now." He'd given up on love a long time ago. At thirty-one he knew his chance at being anyone's true love was behind him. His youthful efforts to love and be loved had taught him well. This chance at marriage to a good friend would give him comfort from the loneliness he'd known for so long.

Daisy unclenched her fists and reached her hands to his. She went up on her tiptoes and placed a small kiss on his cheek. "Oh, Tucker. Thank you." She spoke sweetly near his ear. "You're such a dear friend." She released his hands and backed away. "But I disagree with you and Papa."

Tucker saw the resigned strength in her eyes. She'd always plowed full steam ahead into whatever she set her mind to do. No doubt she was determined to survive and take care of James and John by herself.

"Daisy, we're concerned about you and the boys. It's too much—"

She cut him off, her tone indignant. "Did you and Papa think you could just come here and tell me what to do like I'm still a child? I'm a grown woman with responsibilities."

"I want to help with those responsibilities." Tucker kept his voice calm with great effort. "Think about it. Who'd ever marry me? I'm too old and set in my ways. You and I are friends. We'll be good for each other. I'll help you with the boys and the farm. You'll keep me from being a lonely old man." He smiled, hoping to break through her resistance. "And you're too fine a

Christian woman to have a man here on the farm who isn't your husband."

Daisy was quiet for a moment. He saw the hesitation in her eyes as she pondered all they'd talked about.

"Tell you what. You just read this. Then we'll talk." He pulled an envelope from the inside pocket of his leather vest and handed it to her. "I'll go keep the boys occupied. You come find us when you're ready." He settled his hat back on his head, took the pinto by the reins and headed to the well, stirring up a path of dust as he went.

Daisy turned the envelope over in her hand. The wax seal was her father's unique design. The curling vines woven together in a heart pattern represented the things her dad loved best—his three daughters, all named after flowers and whom he collectively called "Papa's Garden." She walked to the porch and sat on the wooden rocker Murdock had made when he'd found out they were going to have a baby.

Daisy carefully broke the seal and removed the fragile paper. Unfolding it she braced herself for the first communication she'd received from him since his telegraph of sympathy after Murdock was killed.

Tears spilled over her lashes as she read her father's concern by relating it to her mother's death. They now shared the common thread of the loss of the love of their life. His words about how prayer had helped to heal his grief gave her comfort.

She pondered his main concern about the boys needing a man in their lives. Her eyes lit on the paragraph warning her she could lose her land in spite of the new laws assuring women in Texas could own land outright.

Her heart clenched at the thought of losing everything Murdock had worked so hard to build for the future of their sons.

The letter ended by confirming his wishes that she marry Tucker. He wanted her to do it today, so Tucker's presence on the farm wouldn't reflect poorly on her reputation in town. He'd given Tucker his gift to them of money for a wedding supper to share in town that afternoon. He assured her it was all for her own good.

The sound of boots on the porch caused Daisy to look up as she finished the last line.

Tucker leaned against the porch railing and folded his arms. Pushing his hat back so she could see his face, he asked, "Well, Daisy? What do you say?"

"What do I say?" The chair rocked violently as she practically leaped from it. "What do I say?" Daisy stomped down the steps and across the yard in the direction of the barn. She caught a glimpse of the boys playing behind the corral.

Emotions raced through her mind and heart. She was reacting like the schoolgirl she'd once been. She used to tromp off into the woods to be alone when her feelings were hurt or her father hadn't let her get her way. Oh, to be that girl again and kick against the grass and head to the edge of the stream by her childhood home after being scolded for some prank she'd pulled on her sisters. Her mind took her to the times when she needed to get some emotion or event out of her system. Tucker was a shadow in the background then. Today he followed her in silence.

Without warning Daisy turned on him. "What do I say?" She shook the letter in her hand near his face. "I haven't even had time to process this silly idea of Papa's, and you want to know what I say?" Just as quickly she turned and marched away.

After going only a few feet, she stopped and stared into the sky. Her vision blurred as tears filled her eyes. Sobbing and clutching the letter to her heart, Daisy wailed, "Why, Papa? Why did Murdock have to die? I miss him so badly! And I need you here now."

Daisy felt Tucker's hands settle on her shoulders. "I'm so sorry, Daisy. Your father's health kept him from being here for you. His heart was breaking for you when I left. And no one knows why bad things happen like Murdock dying. Life isn't fair sometimes. You've been through an awful lot. Taking care of the land and raising those boys…you shouldn't have to do it alone."

He gently turned her around to face him. He knelt down on one knee as he held her hands in his. "Daisy, I'm asking you to do me the honor of marrying me. I promise to take care of you and James and John. I'll do my best to be a good husband to you. Your papa asked me to come here, but I'd be obliged if you'd let me stay." Was there an unsettledness in his expression? What would make him want to marry a grieving widow with two young sons?

"Oh, Tucker, I can't let you do that. You've got your own life to live. The boys and I will be fine." She pulled against his grip, but he didn't let go.

She was reeling inside. This morning she awoke with a world of responsibilities on her and God alone. Now someone was offering a lifeline of friendship and help, but she couldn't accept. She still loved Murdock—with every piece of her broken heart.

"Daisy, I'm not doing this because your father asked me. I'm doing it because it's the right thing to do. Think about the future…your boys…this land. Those boys need a man to look up to. I'm not their father, but I promise to be a good example to them. Your father is right about the land and the new laws. You don't want everything you and Murdock worked for to be taken away." He tugged gently on her hands and smiled up at her. "Please say yes. For the boys. For the land. For you. For me? I know we can make it work. We were good friends before. We can be again. But only if you want me here. I won't stay if you don't."

Daisy looked into Tucker's green eyes and saw the sincerity of his offer. Many times in her youth she had found comfort in his friendship. More than once he'd rescued her from some scheme she'd thought up, either by helping her out of the dilemma she caused or by preventing her from doing something in the first place. She knew she could trust him. Four years older than her twenty-seven, she wondered if he was still as resolute as ever. Her papa said he was a great foreman because he was quick to make decisions and to handle situations. Would he try to handle her? Or her sons?

Daisy's mind swam with all the things she faced—twin boys to raise, running a farm, the possibility she couldn't keep the land without a husband. She considered herself to be a strong woman, but the workload was overwhelming. She'd hoped it would ease as she adjusted to doing everything without Murdock. It hadn't.

She also realized the value of the sacrifice Tucker was making to give up his freedom to help her raise another man's sons. How many times as a girl had she longed for a mother? Her father had been good to her and her sisters, but she'd ached for a woman's nurturing touch. She didn't want her sons to grow up without a father. Tucker was a good man. But she wanted her sons to know the value of a loving marriage. Could she grow to love Tucker as she had loved Murdock? Not now. The very idea was unfathomable. Could anyone have two chances at perfection?

"Okay." Daisy heard herself speak without realizing she was going to agree.

"Okay?" Tucker tilted his head to one side, and his brow puckered. "You're sure?"

"Okay." A new resolve at saying it aloud settled in her soul. "Let's do it. Why not? I haven't had control of anything in my life for the last month. Why should today be any different? Let's get married." Daisy pulled her hands free and smoothed her father's crumpled letter. "I'm sure Reverend Dismuke will be happy to accommodate us today. He can perform the ceremony, and his wife can be our witness."

She headed to the house almost at a trot, beckoning to the boys as she went. Then she stopped and looked at him over her shoulder. "Are you just going to kneel there in the dirt, or are you going to go get cleaned up for your wedding? You should find everything you need in the tack room in the barn." In an instant she was off again, picking up her skirt in both hands to keep from tripping.

"Impetuous as ever," Tucker called out behind her. The echo of his whistle caught the breeze and followed her up the porch steps and into the house.

Daisy sat at the foot of the table in the center of the small cabin. At the side of the table, James and John climbed onto the bench they had helped their father build.

"Boys, we need to talk." She wasn't sure exactly what to tell them first. "We've all been through a lot in the last few weeks. You have been such good boys. And you know I'd do anything in the world for you."

"Yes, ma'am," they answered in unison.

She took her father's letter from the pocket of her skirt. "You know how happy your papa was when you did something he asked you to do?" They both nodded, then looked at each other curiously before turning back to her and crossing their arms on the table in front of them. Matching brows drew together to join mirrored frowns.

"This is a letter from Papa Warren." She laid the letter on the table and smoothed it with her palm. A breeze lifted the lace curtain at the window by the door, causing the pages to flutter. The air's freshness helped her draw the breath for her next bit of news.

"He wants me to do something that will help us keep our home and make a way for you boys to still have this land when you're grown up—just like your papa wanted." The lack of understanding in their eyes caused Daisy to move straight to the point.

"I'm going to marry Mr. Barlow."

"Why, Momma?" There was a chorus of disbelief. "You can't! You're already married to Papa. You can't marry somebody else!"

Tears formed in her eyes, to be quickly blinked away. Daisy swallowed and reached out to the twins, inviting them into her embrace. They scrambled to her, and she wrapped them in her arms. "I know you don't understand. I did marry your papa. He and I loved each other very much." She pulled back and cupped one chin in each hand so James and John would see directly into her eyes. "I will always love your papa—just like you will. It hurts me as much as it hurts the two of you that he isn't here anymore. We know he's with Jesus."

Small tear-stained faces waited for her to continue. "Papa worked hard for this land. He wouldn't want us to lose everything because he isn't here anymore. That could happen if I don't marry again. It doesn't mean I don't love your papa. It means I love him so much that I want to make sure his dreams come true for you boys."

James spoke. As the firstborn he usually took the lead, and John rarely objected. "How could we lose our house, Momma?" Clearly the eight-year-old didn't understand.

"The government controls who gets to keep a house. Ladies have problems owning land that men don't have. It's complicated, so you're going to have to trust that Papa Warren knows best."

"Are you sure, Momma?" John's concern reflected in his small face. "Can't we keep it? It's ours now."

Daisy drew the boys back into a hug and kissed both blond heads. "I wish we could, but because of the laws of the state of Texas, this is the best way. I promise." Again she felt the press of helplessness that had threatened to overwhelm her since Murdock had been killed. It went against her stubborn nature to need someone else to rescue her.

"Mr. Barlow is a good man," she assured. "I've known him for many years. He's a godly man, like your papa. He'll take good care of us. He'll teach you things I can't. Like how to plow a field or take care of a broken wagon wheel. There's so much you'll need to know that only a man can teach you."

James and John leaned back and looked at her. "Are you sure, Momma?" James asked.

"I'm sure, son." Daisy smiled at them. "And you'll grow to love him, too. He's a respectable man."

The twins looked at each other in resignation and dropped their heads. Her amazement at their matching mannerisms never dimmed. "Okay, Momma. But it's gonna take a bit for us to get used to having another man around here." John paused. "We just got used to being the only men. Now we've got to train another one. He can show us how to fix wagon wheels and plow, but we'll teach him how to take care of the farm like Papa did."

Laughing, she released them and tussled each head with one hand. "Now I'm going to get ready for our trip to town. I need you boys to get washed up and put on your Sunday best." She rose from the chair and smoothed her skirt. "I certainly can't get married looking like this." She shooed them both outside to the well.

The twins brought water in and then dressed in their room. Satisfied with their appearance, she sent them to wait on the porch.

Daisy freshened up using the washbasin and mirror behind the screen in the corner of the cabin. Murdock had given her the screen as a gift, wanting her to have some privacy in the cabin full of males. She stood back to stare at her reflection. The lost weight from the pain and stress of the past three weeks did nothing to improve her appearance. Dark brown eyes looked hollow and bruised in her slightly freckled face. The gentle wave of her blond hair pulled tendrils loose from the pins she'd pushed in this morning before attempting to do the chores of two people. The weeks without him had worn her down more than she'd realized.

Daisy knew marrying Tucker would be the easiest

solution to her problems, but she wondered if she could muster the strength to go through with the wedding. She still ached for Murdock.

Tucker was a good man and a good friend. Could she be patient while he adjusted to marriage? He'd never answered to anyone except a boss. Would he be willing to work alongside her? Or would his natural tendency to take charge make her more defensive of her boys and the farm?

Lord, I'm trusting You and Papa now. I am starting to think this is Your plan for my life. Help me get it right.

Taking a deep breath, Daisy went to the chest at the foot of the bed she and Murdock had shared and lifted the lid. She pulled out her best dress and, lifting it by the shoulders, let the breeze catch it as it floated onto the bed. Smoothing the soft, sea-green cotton, she thought about the last time she'd worn it. She and Murdock had gone to the spring social at church. They had strolled by the river, arm in arm, laughing and talking, while the boys played ball with their friends in the churchyard. Murdock had bought the dress for her birthday and told her to be happy on the days she wore it.

A tear slid down her cheek as she knew in her heart he'd want her to have a happy future. She would have wanted him to move on with his life if the situation had been reversed. However, knowing she should move forward was easier than actually taking the steps to do it.

Daisy wiped her face with the back of her hand. "I will not cry in the dress bought to make me happy." And then she put it on. Could she take the joy of her past into a future that offered contentment, but not true love?

The heaviness of Tucker's boots sounded on the porch steps as she took a final look in the mirror. Her hand trembled as she reached up to touch the delicate white lace collar at her neck—and then she saw it. Her wedding band.

Daisy's knees buckled, and she collapsed to sit on the side of the bed. She held her hand out to look at the ring. The plain gold band had been there so long it was like a part of her. Murdock had given it to her on their first anniversary. The scratches and worn places testified to the hard work and commitment of their relationship. Spinning it on her finger and rubbing the cool smoothness of it, she blew out a determined breath and pulled the ring from her hand. She went to the chest and found the small velvet bag the ring had come in. She kissed the ring and slid it inside. With the pull of the drawstring she tied her past into a bow and lovingly placed it in the chest before lowering the lid.

Digging deep inside for energy she wasn't sure she had, Daisy pushed against the closed chest to stand. With her shoulders back and head held high, she straightened the ribbons of the bow that held her Sunday hat in place. Numbness froze her countenance in resignation. Her father's letter was tucked inside her small reticule for comfort as she journeyed forward into the day's events.

Sunlight sliced into the cabin when she opened the front door.

James and John sat on the front steps, looking into the fields. Tucker leaned against the porch railing staring at the door. He stood to his full height as Daisy joined them on the porch. Hat in hand he smiled at her.

"Miss Daisy, you look lovely." He took a step closer to her and hesitated, turning the Stetson in his hands.

"I took the liberty of hitching my horse to your wagon for the trip into town."

With a curt nod in his direction, Daisy said, "Thank you, Tucker," before turning to her sons. "Well, boys, let's go. Hop up into the back of the wagon." Daisy set the boys into motion with her no-nonsense tone. Hands in his pockets, James kicked at the dirt as he walked. John scampered ahead of his brother and vaulted into the wagon.

Daisy cautioned her eldest. "James, mind your manners and do as you're told."

His "Yes, ma'am" was muttered so quietly Tucker almost couldn't hear it. Tucker walked down the steps ahead of her and turned to offer his hand as she followed. He didn't meet her gaze. He took her small gloved hand in his calloused one and assisted her down the steps. She immediately withdrew it when her feet touched the ground. He watched her twist the drawstrings on her reticule around her fingers as they slowly walked to the wagon.

Again Tucker offered a hand to steady her as she climbed into the wagon. Again she permitted only the briefest of contact and settled into the seat while he walked in front of his horse to climb up beside her. He was a bit surprised by how quickly she'd agreed to marry him. When it was all said and done, he was a friend from so far in her past she had not recognized him when he rode onto her land a mere hour ago.

Grabbing the reins and sending the horse forward, he said, "I'll see about getting a couple of horses next week. We'll need them for working the farm. Mack here is more for riding than pulling a wagon. He's a ranch horse."

Daisy kept her eyes straight ahead and her voice low so James and John wouldn't hear her above the sounds of the wagon on the narrow lane leading to the main road. "If you don't mind, I'd like to keep to the topic of the day. We can talk about such business later. I don't want to remind the boys of the loss of their papa and our horses."

"Good idea." Tucker matched her volume. "I'm sorry I brought it up."

"It's not a problem," she said between taut lips. "It's just that so much is happening today. I don't want to add to the weight of all that's already on their minds. They've had a rough go of it."

"I understand." He turned the wagon onto the main road and signaled his horse to pick up speed as they headed toward town. They traveled in silence for a few minutes.

"If you don't mind, I'd like to be married in the church, not the parsonage." Daisy began to rattle off details for the afternoon's agenda. "We can have a nice supper at the local hotel. It's a very impressive establishment for a town as small as Pine Haven. The food is very good. I'd also like to stop in at the general store. The boys haven't had a treat in a long time. I think this is just the occasion for it."

"Whoa, Daisy. Seems like you've got this all planned out in your head already. Mind if I interject some thoughts?"

"Interject away." She lifted her arm in a sweeping gesture. "It's not like any of this was my idea in the first place. I was just trying to make the most of it."

"Oh, good. That'll help." Tucker kept his eyes on the road ahead. "Sarcasm will be just the right spice to add to today. Keep it up and James will be back to kicking dirt by the time we get to town." He grinned to let her know he was teasing her the way he had when she was a teenager. He turned and winked at her. He saw the corners of her mouth tug into a smile before he looked back to the road.

"You always had a knack for getting me out of a mood." She settled her hands in her lap again and looked up into the bright sky, appearing to relax for the first time since he'd ridden onto the farm just after lunch. She took in a deep breath and let it out in a whoosh. The boys had curled up on the hay in the back of the wagon and fallen asleep in the sunshine. Their clothes would be wrinkled, but he was glad to see they'd settled down.

"How are you, Daisy? Really?"

"I'm better now. Not over it by any means, but better. Working the farm will take the stress out of you if you let it." The underlying sadness in her voice revealed the true depth of her pain.

"If you ever need to talk about it, I'll listen."

Daisy put one gloved hand on his arm and he felt her gaze on him as he drove. "I remember many times when you did just that. Thank you, Tucker." She cleared her throat. "Not just for being a friend who's willing to listen, but for everything. I know what a sacrifice it is for you to give up your life to help me and the boys."

"Don't you worry about that for one minute. I'm sorry those little fellows lost their papa. I know what it's like to grow up without a father. You might remember mine was gone before I was old enough to know much about him. Tuberculosis took him the winter I turned five. I want to be to your sons what your father has been to me." He tried without success to cover the gravel in his tone. She gave his arm a slight squeeze of comfort, and he continued. "I also hope to be there for you in a way my momma needed when she was trying to raise me alone. It was a hard life. One I hope to spare you from." He cleared his throat and snapped the reins, effectively ending the conversation. "Get up, Mack. We need to get to town."

His mother had done her best but life without a father had been difficult.

Daisy's dad had raised his daughters with the help of a housekeeper who came during the daytime. Mr. Warren had made it seem so simple. Tucker knew that wasn't true. Parenting was a difficult job for two parents. It was more than double the work when one parent was left to do the task alone.

He knew Daisy was strong. She'd managed to care for her boys and the farm since her husband's death. The spiritual comfort of God and those precious boys had probably bolstered her courage. But she couldn't survive on courage alone.

He stole a glance at her. He knew in his heart that she still loved the man in the grave at the top of the hill behind her cabin. Tucker had been her friend all those years ago. He'd come here as her friend. Would she ever see him as more that?

Chapter Two

Tucker pulled the wagon to a stop and set the brake in front of the general store. He called to the boys. "James and John, come with me. How would you like some candy?" Sleepiness evaporated at the promise of the treat, and the boys tumbled from the wagon.

Walking to the side of the wagon, Tucker offered his hand to Daisy. She moved to accept his help, and he could see she was surprised when he grabbed her by the waist and set her on the ground. He wondered if it was because he lifted her. Did he make her skittish? He'd have to be careful not to make her uncomfortable.

Tucker leaned close so the boys wouldn't hear. "Do you want a few minutes to speak to the pastor before I come to the church? I can take the boys into the store and meet you later." He knew she must be overwhelmed with the day's events. He could see the strain on her face ease at his suggestion.

"Thank you." Daisy gave him a slight smile. "I'll go there now and meet you at the parsonage in a half hour. That should give me plenty of time."

"Are you okay with all of this?" Mr. Warren had insisted the wedding take place on the day of his arrival, but Tucker was concerned about Daisy's peace of mind.

She didn't look at him when she answered. "Papa's right. This really is for the best." Was she trying to reassure him or convince herself?

"I think so, too, but I could get a room in town and stay for a few days. If that would make you more comfortable." It would delay his start on the work he needed to do at the farm, but if it helped Daisy, he could make that small sacrifice.

"No. Thank you, but that won't be necessary." She shook her head, and he saw the resignation in her eyes. "There's no need to spend money on a hotel when you'd just be coming to the farm in a few days."

The sadness of her circumstances struck him anew. Thinking of the weight she must be under had been a driving force in his agreement to this arrangement. Her face was thin and pale. She lacked the vitality that was such a part of her personality. The sooner her life was settled, the sooner she could start to heal from her pain.

Tucker knew her sons would help to heal her heart. He hoped he could give her mind rest from the pressure of running the farm alone.

"I'll meet you in a few minutes, then." He nodded and looked over his shoulder to see the boys staring into the large storefront window.

"The boys can show you the way." Daisy turned, and the heels of her shoes clicked a rhythm on the boarded sidewalk as she hurried away.

Tucker watched her go, thanking God for the opportunity to have her in his life. In the years after she'd left her father's ranch, Tucker had kept busy with work.

He'd focused on being a successful rancher and put all thoughts of love out of his mind.

He knew in his heart Daisy would never love him as she'd loved Murdock. And he certainly wasn't interested in being a second-best husband. But he did hope her friendship would fill the aching loneliness he suffered.

"Daisy, what a lovely surprise!" Peggy greeted Daisy and ushered her into the parsonage. "David, come into the parlor. Daisy Mosley is here." Peggy offered Daisy one of the two chairs by the front window. "Sit down and tell me how you're doing." Peggy sat in the other chair.

"I'm doing better. As a matter of fact, that's why I've come to town today. I have news." Daisy was interrupted when Reverend Dismuke entered the room.

"Mrs. Mosley, to what do we owe the honor of your visit?"

"I was just about to tell Peggy. I've received a letter from my father."

"Does he want you to move back home?" Peggy asked anxiously.

"No." Daisy looked from Peggy to Reverend Dismuke. "He sent Tucker Barlow. Tucker came to work for him when I was still in school. He's been a dear friend to me and my sisters."

"That's seems a sound idea," the reverend approved. "You'll be needing a man's help with the farm."

"And the boys," Peggy added.

Daisy bit her lower lip before continuing. "Papa wants me to marry Tucker. He doesn't think it would be proper for a Christian woman to have a man on her property unless they've been wed. He wants to protect the boys and me from gossip."

"Also a wise consideration," Reverend Dismuke agreed. "People can be cruel. Children are especially vulnerable to be hurt."

"What about you? Are you okay with this idea?" Peggy asked.

"I won't lie and tell you it'll be easy. I miss Murdock terribly." Daisy reached and covered Peggy's hand with one of her own. "But I don't think I have a choice. Papa's right about the boys needing a father in their lives. There's also the question of the land."

"You can own the land now. There's a new law," Peggy offered.

"It's not been tested. I can't risk losing everything Murdock worked so hard to give to James and John."

"But what about…love?" Peggy wanted to know. "You can't just marry someone to save the farm. You've got to consider your heart, as well."

"Tucker's a good man. And my father picked him. Besides, there's more to think about than love." Daisy tried to hide the uncertainty in her voice.

"Mrs. Mosley, may I speak frankly?" Reverend Dismuke asked.

"Of course. I trust your counsel." Daisy waited for his next words.

"As the shepherd of this flock I've seen many women go through what you're facing. Their husbands die or are killed suddenly, leaving them as widows with land and children. Many with little or no money. I have yet to see one survive without help. This is not the kind of country a woman alone can conquer safely. What if you find a way to handle everything about the farm and the boys, and then one day those thieves come back?"

"David! Don't frighten her!" Peggy gasped.

"I'm not trying to frighten her," he assured, "but I saw Sheriff Collins yesterday, and he still hasn't had any success in tracking down Murdock's killers."

Peggy clicked her tongue in disapproval. "I'm not sure why we trust that man to protect this county."

"He's a good sheriff, Peggy. He's just not much for decorum," Reverend Dismuke disagreed.

"Well, he always looks as if he's just rolled out of bed," Peggy insisted. "How do we know he's done all that can be done to find those thieves?"

"I've talked with him at length, and I assure you he's doing his job. It's just not an easy one." To Daisy he said, "I'm sorry. I know this is very difficult for you."

"I've wished a thousand times that I'd been home that day. Maybe I could have saved him." Daisy's remorse was palpable.

"Oh, Daisy, you can't torture yourself like that. You and the boys could have been hurt—or worse—if you'd been there," Peggy lamented.

"My wife is right. God was protecting you and your sons that day. I don't pretend to understand all He does or why, but I know He had a purpose for you to be spared." They all sat in silence for a moment.

Daisy couldn't bear the thought of those murderous thieves returning and harming her sons. She hoped each day to hear news of their capture. Would she always have one eye on the lane while she worked? Would she be able to let the boys return to school? She wondered if they'd ever be safe again.

Reverend Dismuke was the first to speak. "I think you should accept Mr. Barlow's offer of marriage."

Daisy nodded her agreement. She hadn't been able to save Murdock, but at least she could protect his sons.

"Are you sure, Daisy?" Peggy leaned over and grasped both of Daisy's hands.

"I've prayed, Peggy, and I feel this is what the Lord would have me do." The resolve in Daisy's voice won her friend's agreement.

"Okay, then." Peggy sat back up straight and smoothed her dress. "Well, when do we meet this Mr. Barlow, and when is the wedding?" Peggy asked.

A knock sounded at the door.

"Now. And now," Daisy sputtered with a laugh.

"What?" Peggy exclaimed.

"I'll answer that. You calm down," Reverend Dismuke teased his wife as he went to the door.

Both ladies stood as Tucker and the twins entered the room. The boys stood on either side of Tucker, making an obvious effort to stand at their full height, so much so that their small necks stretched to achieve full advantage of their stature. Small grins tugged at their matching faces, but she saw the restraint to prevent pride from bursting forth. Then she noticed the reason for this new posture. Tucker stood, hat in hand, and each boy had a smaller, though very similar hat, held in the exact way. John stole a look at Tucker to confirm he had the stance correct.

James could hold his peace no longer. "Momma! How do you like our hats? Mr. Tucker helped us pick 'em out!" He offered her a closer look without moving from Tucker's side. "These are real Stetsons just like Mr. Tucker's! Only they're different 'cause everyone can make his Stetson how he wants. I like mine with the brim down, like Mr. Tucker. John likes his with the top pushed in just so. They're great, aren't they Momma?"

"That's very nice, James." Daisy touched the felt

brim. "What about yours, John?" She moved to stand in front of the youngest twin.

"I like mine just fine, Momma. They were expensive, but Mr. Tucker said we needed them." He didn't meet her gaze. John was always cautious, and a matter was never settled for him as quickly as it was for James.

Daisy turned to Tucker, tilting her head to see into his eyes. She saw the mirth there. He was enjoying the happiness of her sons. She was grateful to see them excited. They hadn't had a treat in a long time, and certainly nothing so grand.

"Need them?" She raised her eyebrows and waited for an explanation from Tucker. Surely he understood they didn't have that kind of money.

Tucker stretched his neck to pronounce his height and tilted his head to one side ever so slightly. "Yes, ma'am. Every working farmer needs a good hat. These young men are no exception. It wouldn't be proper for me to expect them to work without the tools they need." His barely suppressed grin reminded her of the twins forced restraint. They'd only met a few hours ago, and already these males were forming an alliance she was certain she'd have to confront on a regular basis.

Looking from one to the other she addressed all three at once. "Well, I see you had a successful trip to the general store. Now it's time for us to go to the church."

Everyone made their way to the front door and down the steps to walk toward the church. Daisy looped her arm in Tucker's, easing back into the friendship they'd shared for years. In a voice for his ears only, she leaned in and said, "When I said they could have a treat, I meant something like a piece of candy or fruit. I don't know how you thought we could afford something like that."

"Oh, they got candy, too."

Daisy looked ahead to see both boys pulling a handful of candy from their pockets to compare.

"In the future we need to talk about things like this before they happen. And why are they calling you Mr. Tucker?" Daisy almost sounded as if she was scolding Tucker.

Leaning closer to her, without losing his grin, Tucker spoke. "There are a lot of things we'll talk about in the future, but buying those hats was my decision, and I stand by it. And they're calling me Mr. Tucker because I prefer it to Mr. Barlow. We're going to be family in just a few minutes."

"Well…" she interrupted.

He held up his free hand. "Well, nothing. You said you wanted us to stay focused on the events of today. We'll talk about other things later, but right now…" Tucker gestured to the door of the small church that John held open for them. The others had walked ahead and were already inside. "Right now, we're going to a wedding. And I think we both need to concentrate on that." His fingers brushed the length of her jawline, and he smiled.

Daisy drew in a breath to calm herself. "Okay. I'll focus." She lifted her skirt just enough to keep from stepping on it as she climbed the steps. "But we have a lot to talk about, Tucker. And we will talk about it." She dropped her hem and smoothed her skirt as they passed through the doorway.

"I'm sure we will, Daisy." Tucker removed his hat and handed it to John for safekeeping during the ceremony. "I'm sure we will." He offered her his hand, and they proceeded up the aisle.

Daisy stood beside Tucker at the altar of Pine Haven Church. She took advantage of the opportunity to study him in what must be his best shirt and trousers. The red hair had been tamed with a fresh combing. He was every inch a man—and a tall one at that. He stood a good foot taller than she did with strong shoulders and a broad chest. His boots wore a fresh shine.

James and John sat on the first bench, watching as Reverend Dismuke performed the wedding ceremony, their new hats carefully resting beside them, Tucker's much larger hat on John's farside. They giggled a little at first, but Tucker silenced them with a look. Daisy was surprised by how quickly he'd taken command of the boys' behavior. She'd been prone to leniency since their father's death. Truly things were changing today. Daisy would do her best to keep the changes at a manageable pace. The twins would need time to adjust to Tucker's authority.

Reverend Dismuke went through the vows with great reverence, explaining the weight of the commitment of the marriage ceremony in the eyes of God.

"Tucker, wilt thou have this woman to thy wedded wife, to live together after God's ordinance, in the holy estate of matrimony? Wilt thou love her, comfort her, honor, and keep her, in sickness and in health, and, forsaking all others, keep thee only unto her, so long as ye both shall live?"

Tucker looked at her and answered, "I will."

Daisy, in turn, promised herself to him. With each word spoken a heaviness settled on her soul. She knew she had no choice—knew she was doing the right thing.

But could she find the inner strength to build a relationship with an old friend into a marriage? Her first husband had captivated her fancy, and she'd fallen deeply in love with him. Now she stood in her church before God and witnesses and pledged to give Tucker the same commitment she'd shared with Murdock. Tucker had been a dear friend. But her husband? Never had the thought crossed her mind. Daisy was surprised by how quickly the ceremony progressed. Before she realized it the reverend asked if there was a ring. Something she hadn't thought about.

"Oh, we don't—" Daisy shook her head, only to be stunned into silence when Tucker pulled a ring from his shirt pocket and handed it to the preacher.

"Let us pray." Reverend Dismuke bowed his head and spoke. "Loving God, we ask You to bless this union. Help Tucker and Daisy to grow together as husband and wife. Build a strong bond between these two souls." Daisy felt the heat rush to her face and prayed her own prayer that she hadn't blushed as deeply as she felt. "God help these two fine young men, James and John, to bring You honor by the way they respect their momma and their new papa." The boys both opened their eyes at this point. "And most of all, God, we thank You for bringing these folks together as a family. May they live, as this ring represents, an endless circle of love that shines with beauty and strength. Amen."

"Amen." Tucker and Daisy spoke softly in unison. James and John sat in silence. Peggy wiped a tear away with her handkerchief.

Reverend Dismuke returned the ring to Tucker, who reached for Daisy's hand. She stared at him, unbelieving, as he slipped the delicate ring on her finger. Intricately carved leaves and vines wrapped around the gold band. Tucker repeated after the minister, "With this ring I thee wed, with my body I thee worship and with all my worldly goods I thee endow."

Reverend Dismuke finalized their commitment by saying, "I now pronounce you man and wife. You may kiss the bride."

Tucker looked to Daisy, asking permission with his eyes. Feeling it would be unfair to deny Tucker this right after all he was sacrificing for her and her children, Daisy nodded her assent with the slightest tip of her head, lowered her gaze and waited. He gently took her face in his large hands and tenderly brushed a kiss across her cheek. She opened her eyes wide and thanked him from her soul without speaking a word. His smile acknowledged his understanding of her gratitude.

As the small group left the church, Reverend Dismuke pulled Tucker and Daisy aside. "Sheriff Collins has been trying to find the men who killed Murdock. He sent word of the killing to sheriffs in the neighboring counties. I'm sure he'd be glad to meet you, Tucker. He's been concerned for the safety of your wife and the boys."

"Thanks," Tucker said. "I'll stop by his office and introduce myself."

"He's a bit rough around the edges, but I think he's doing all he can."

"I'll see if there's anything I can do to help him." Tucker settled his hat back on his head. "Right now, though, I'm going to take my new family to supper. Thanks, Reverend, for your time today."

Tucker's words rang in her head as she walked with him to the wagon. They were a family on their way to supper. Only they weren't an ordinary family. Nothing about this day had been ordinary.

"Boys, put your hats on the rack here by the door." Daisy noticed Tucker hung his hat up high so the twins could use the lower pegs.

"Are we really gonna eat in the hotel, Momma?" the ever-curious James wanted to know.

"She already said so, James." John was losing patience with his brother today.

"Yes, we're eating here. I want both of you on your best behavior," Daisy admonished as she pulled her gloves off and tucked them into her reticule. "Papa Warren is giving us this wedding supper as a gift. I want everyone to enjoy it. So mind your manners."

The hostess escorted them to a table set with linen and glassware. The smell of freshly baked bread filled the room.

Tucker held a chair for Daisy, signaling the twins to wait until their mother sat. When they were all seated, a young girl wearing a starched white apron over a simple brown dress offered them menus.

Daisy skimmed the choices before looking to Tucker. "Roast beef for everyone? With creamed potatoes and carrots and some of that delicious-smelling bread?"

"Sounds wonderful to me." Tucker closed his menu. "I think this is just the kind of place your papa had in mind for our wedding supper."

"I wish he could be here." Daisy's heart ached for the comfort of her father's love. She sniffed and straightened in her chair, neatly folding her hands in her lap. Her voice went up just a notch in tone, but not volume. "But that's not possible, so we'll make the most of the occasion he's provided for us. I'll write him a letter tonight and tell him how much we appreciate his gift." Her head was still spinning with the knowledge that she was married again. Table conversation was a great effort, but she did want to honor her father by enjoying this meal. It was a great luxury that wouldn't likely come their way again soon.

"I'm sure he would like to know things have worked out like he hoped. Let's send him a telegraph on the way home. Then you can write a letter with all the details, and we can post it the next time we're in town," Tucker suggested.

"That's a fine idea. Then he'll know everything is settled, and the boys and I are safe," Daisy agreed.

The boys grew fidgety at the table, most likely in response to all the candy they'd managed to eat by sneaking pieces whenever they thought no one was looking. Now they both had empty pockets.

"Stop kicking me." John sent James a glare.

"I'm not kicking you." James spoke just a little louder than John.

"That's enough." Tucker's voice was even, but serious. "James, stop swinging your legs under the table. John sit up straight in your chair, and you won't be close enough for James to accidentally kick you." The twins immediately obeyed, looking to Daisy as their eyes worked to conceal their displeasure at his command.

Daisy was again taken aback when Tucker corrected James and John. Murdock had always left the day-to-day manners and attitudes for her to deal with. She wasn't accustomed to someone taking over her responsibilities, and she was certain she didn't like it.

Tucker spoke again before she could decide how to address the matter with him. "I need to take care of some business before we leave town." The young waitress approached and filled his glass with tea. "If you need anything from the general store, I can drop you there, and you can shop. I'll pick you up when I'm finished." The waitress circled the table to serve the boys and Daisy before leaving.

"What kind of business can you possibly have? You just arrived today," Daisy said, picking up her glass. James had inherited his curiosity from his mother. She'd always had a deep-seated desire to know everything that was going on around her at all times. Constant observation and well-placed questions kept her from feeling uninformed. She never liked to be caught unaware.

"Just some business matters I need to handle." Tucker answered vaguely. "I won't be long."

The door to the kitchen swung open as the waitress backed through it carrying a large round tray with their food. James and John sat up eagerly to watch each plate be set on the fancy table. Daisy had instructed them on the flatware, but she knew they'd be hard-pressed to muzzle their excitement over this new experience. The waitress left after placing a large basket of bread in the center of the table next to a silver dish of fresh butter.

Daisy leaned forward and reached across the corners of the square table to take the twins by the hand. They looked at one another and then at her. She raised her eyebrows toward Tucker before they reluctantly reached their other hands to him. This was the kind of reluctance she expected from her sons today. It was a wonder they'd been as agreeable as they had for much of the day. Accepting a new hat from an old friend of hers was one thing. It was another thing entirely to include the same friend in their family traditions—like prayer over a meal.

* * *

Tucker had been leaning back with one leg crossing the opposite knee before the food arrived. He'd pulled his chair closer to the table as the waitress retreated behind the still-swinging door. His hands held the edges of his chair. Looking up, he met Daisy's gaze and saw her intent. Unfamiliar with his new family's mealtime expectations, the cowboy turned to each boy and took the offered hand.

"Will you give thanks, Tucker?" Daisy asked.

"Hmm-hmm." Tucker cleared his throat. He wasn't accustomed to praying aloud. "Dear, Lord. Thank You for this bountiful supper. We thank You for Your protection and guidance. Help us all to follow You in everything we do and to be good examples of Your love. Amen."

"Amen," Daisy said with the boys before they all tucked into the delicious food.

"This is a fine supper. I didn't realize how hungry I was." Tucker put a bite of bread in his mouth.

Daisy agreed with him. "The roast is so tender. I would never have had time to cook something this nice for us tonight. Not starting so late in the day."

He was glad to see her enjoying the meal and kept the conversation away from anything that would spoil it for her.

Careful of Daisy's admonishment to mind their manners, the boys didn't talk because they were too busy eating. Only after John finished the meal and put his fork down, did he speak.

"That was good!"

"I really liked it, too. But I like Momma's best." James joined the conversation.

"That's very sweet of you, James. Thank you. It was a fine supper." Daisy took her napkin from her lap and folded it neatly before laying it on the table. "Now let's go see what we need from the general store before we head back home." She moved to push her chair back.

"We haven't had dessert yet." Tucker had watched her speech and knew she was trying to set the agenda again. He knew she liked to know all the details beforehand, but he wanted to surprise her.

"Dessert?" two boys chimed in unison.

"Cake, actually." Tucker caught the attention of the waitress by lifting one hand.

"Yes, sir? Are you ready now?" she asked as she approached the table.

"I believe we are. Thank you."

The waitress cleared away their plates and disappeared into the kitchen.

Tucker watched Daisy as the door opened again, and the girl turned toward their table.

"It's the most beautiful cake I've ever seen." Smooth white icing with intricate layers of piping created a look of lace. "I've heard of the hotel's reputation for great desserts, but never seen one." Her face glowed with admiration for the unexpected treat.

"Would you like me to serve you, or would you prefer to cut it, ma'am?" the waitress asked while setting dessert plates on the table.

"I think we can manage, thank you." Daisy reached for the knife and hesitated. The waitress left them. The boys were wide-eyed at the cake. Tucker sat leaning back with his arms folded across his chest, smiling.

"You did this," she accused. "How?"

"I confess. I stopped in on my way through town

and asked about a special dessert before I went to your place to propose. I thought it would make a nice ending to the day." He was pleased by their reactions.

"What if I'd said 'no'?" Daisy pointed the knife at him teasingly.

"Oh, I thought you'd come around to your papa's way of seeing things." He couldn't stop the grin that pulled at the corners of his mouth.

"I see," Daisy said before slicing a substantial slab of cake. "We'll just have to see about how well you can predict my thinking in the future." He heard the taunting tone in her statement as she passed a dessert plate to him.

Tucker smiled. "I fully expect to be challenged on a regular basis. And I expect to rise to the occasion." Using the side of his fork, he cut off a large bite of cake and paused before putting it in his mouth. "Don't forget I've known you for a long time. I know a lot about how you can be." His smile almost became a smirk, effectively returning her challenge and making her smile.

"I'll keep that in mind." She cut practically identical pieces of cake for the boys. Tucker imagined equality was the only road to peace between them.

Daisy served herself, and Tucker watched her savor the sweet dessert with all the fervor of the twins. While they ate, he remembered how he'd once hoped for a strong and healthy marriage with this beautiful woman. If she'd been older, he would have told her how he felt. Before she had ever met Murdock. Now he knew that even after she had time to grieve the loss of her first husband, Murdock would always be her one true love.

Falling for Daisy all those years ago was the last time he'd risked trying to find lasting love. As a boy, he'd seen his mother never recover from the loss of his father. He also watched Daisy's father choose to live alone after losing his wife. He wouldn't let himself dwell on how he'd learned firsthand the power of someone's first love. Rejection was hard to live with. It was harder to leave behind. He vowed never to put himself in that position again. He would be Daisy's friend—but nothing more.

Chapter Three

❦

Daisy held the edge of the seat as Tucker pulled the reins and stopped the wagon in front of the general store. James and John leaped to the dirt and assisted their mother from the wagon.

"Good job, boys. I'll be back as soon as I've taken care of a few errands." To Daisy he said, "Get whatever you need. I'll stop in and settle up when I get back." Tucker signaled Mack, and the wagon lurched forward.

James and John each grabbed one of Daisy's hands and tried to pull her into the store. "Come on, Momma. We can help you shop. Mr. Tucker says we're good shoppers. He says we got good taste." James rattled away as usual.

Daisy resisted their pull long enough to see her wagon turn right at the corner. Tucker could be going almost anywhere. Pine Haven consisted of two intersecting streets lined with businesses that served the small, growing community. Pine Haven Church sat at the opposite end of the street Tucker had turned on, and the livery was at the other end. The general store was just shy of the main crossroads.

Standing on the porch of the general store, Daisy wondered what business Tucker could be conducting. He'd turned in the direction of the bank and the lumber mill. There was also a post office and a blacksmith in that area. Or could he be going to the livery? He'd mentioned wanting to purchase horses. They hadn't discussed money yet. Daisy hoped he wasn't going to take on too much without at least talking to her. She'd always known what Murdock was doing with their money. Was Tucker a man who considered their money to be his money? Did he think a woman should leave matters of business to the man? Murdock had taught Daisy how to keep the financial records for their cotton crop. She was well versed in the costs of farming, how to balance the funds to make it from one harvest to the next and how to survive lean times.

Feeling a tug on each hand, Daisy followed James and John into the store, still thinking about Tucker's errands. For all their past friendship, there was a lot Daisy didn't know about the man who was now her husband.

Tucker opened the door of the sheriff's office and stepped into the dank atmosphere. The two small cells on the back wall each had a tiny window lined with bars to prevent escape. Minimal light came through the dirty front window. The smell of gun oil and dust assailed his nostrils. A man sporting a heavy mustache and several days' growth of beard dozed behind the massive wooden desk. The tarnished star on his vest was the only clue the unkempt man was indeed the sheriff. He was of an indiscernible age somewhere between thirty and fifty. The chair creaked under his weight as he shook himself and lowered the front legs to the floor at Tucker's appearance.

"Sheriff Collins?" Tucker extended his hand. "I'm Tucker Barlow."

The sheriff fumbled to his feet and squinted at Tucker from beneath scraggly eyebrows. "What can I do for ya?" His face remained wrinkled as he stirred himself from sleep.

"I'm new in town. Just wanted to stop by and introduce myself. I married Daisy Mosley earlier today. I understand you've been searching for the men who killed her first husband."

"Yep." Sheriff Collins sat back in his chair. "Wanna sit? Sorry you caught me nappin'. I've been up late most nights trying to keep an eye on things in case those thieves head back this way."

Tucker took the offered seat. "Have you had any success?"

"Not much to go on. The sheriffs from the counties around us haven't been able to help me, either. Nobody's seen nothin'. I sent out flyers and telegraphed everybody I figured would know something. Even got the Rangers lookin' into it for us. Only know more horses were taken from a county south of here. Owners weren't home so nobody got hurt."

"What about clues from the Mosley farm? Did they leave any signs of who they were?"

"We know for sure there's two of 'em. Know that from the horseshoe prints they left. Murdock's horses was shoed here in town. Blacksmith here knew which marks was from Murdock's horses and which ones wasn't. Tracked 'em to the creek at the edge of the property, but lost 'em. They knew to get in the water and ride. Smart thieves, too. Murdock had some good horse-flesh. I want you to know we've done all we could. It's hard when nobody saw or heard what happened. The little missus was in town with her boys."

"Will you let us know if you hear anything? I'd like to see these men brought to justice. I hate to think of them hurting other people like they did the Mosley family." Tucker stood and put his hat back on his head.

"I'll sure do it, Mr. Barlow. You take care out there. Don't like them fellas being on the loose myself." Sheriff Collins leaned the chair back and propped his feet on the desk again. "I been especially worried 'bout the missus and those cute little boys. Didn't want no more harm to come to 'em."

"I'll be protecting them now. By the good Lord's help, we'll be fine."

An hour later Tucker returned to the general store. Daisy stood at the porch railing, her toe tapping the boards, impatience growing by the minute. She and the boys had finished their shopping within twenty minutes. The twins' restlessness with waiting caused her to send them across the street to the Ledford Dressmaker Shop. Milly Ledford had a son, Reilly, who was a year younger than her boys. They were playing upstairs in the Ledfords' living quarters.

"Ahh, you're ready. I'm glad. It's going to be dark soon. I didn't want to have to wait long." Tucker pulled the large brake handle and vaulted from the wagon to the ground in front of her, smiling. "What do I need to load up?" He was looking around for her purchases. "And where are James and John?"

"Ready?" The word came out slowly. Daisy took a

deep breath. "Yes, you could say we're ready. We have been for the better part of an hour." She indicated a small package wrapped in brown paper and tied with twine. There was also a crate with a few grocery staples. "The boys could only be still so long. I sent them across the street to play with a friend."

"Will you get them while I go in and settle the bill?" Tucker set the crate over the side of the wagon and brushed his hands together to remove the dust.

"I'll get them now." Daisy descended the two front steps, pretending she didn't see his offered hand. "But the bill is already settled." Daisy kept walking without looking back. She disappeared inside the dress shop for the briefest moment and then returned to the wagon.

Tucker reached out a hand to help her, leaning in closely to speak softly against her golden hair so only she could hear. "I told you I'd settle the bill."

"I already had it covered." Caught off guard by his sudden nearness and not wanting to fall and embarrass herself, she was forced to accept his hand to climb up and take her seat.

"It's my responsibility to provide for the family. I can pay for the things we need." Tucker climbed into his seat and took the reins.

"I have already made provision for the things we will need until next year's harvest. You don't have to spend your money on us." Daisy's stubborn streak refused to allow her to relinquish complete responsibility for her family.

"We're in this together now, Daisy. I know your stubbornness has helped you survive all you've been through. I admire your strength and spirit, but we've got to work together now. We can't build a future if you refuse to let me help. I didn't sign up to be a farmhand. I signed up to be your husband."

Daisy sat with her back straight in stony silence. Part of her knew he was right. She finally looked at him. "I've had to do everything on my own since Murdock died."

"I understand that. I'm only saying you're not alone anymore. I'm here to help."

The boys sprinted out of the dress shop, yelling their goodbyes to Reilly and Mrs. Ledford, before jumping into the back of the wagon.

"Whoa, there, boys. Be careful. Your momma has her packages back there. And there's a crate of mine that I don't want you to get hurt on." Tucker admonished the twins and released the brake. Once again he took the lead in instructing the boys.

"What did you get, Mr. Tucker?" James couldn't resist being nosy.

"Just some things I'll be needing at the house, James, nothing for you to concern yourself about. You boys have a seat. I'm going to press Mack to get us home before dark. Hang on." With a crack of the reins they were soon leaving town in the distance.

The sun was just visible on the horizon when Tucker turned the wagon onto the lane that led to their cabin. The boys had again fallen asleep. This time they'd covered their faces with the new hats. Daisy smiled at their attempts to appear grown as she roused them before Tucker had a chance to speak.

"James and John, we're home. I need you to wake up and help with the wagon."

Sleepy boys in rumpled clothes leaned over the back of the seat to collapse on Daisy's shoulders. "Momma, do we have to help? I'm tired." James buried his head in her sleeve.

"Yes, you do. Mr. Tucker is tired, too. He's been traveling for several days. You can help with the wagon and see to the animals. Then you can go to bed. If you hurry, I'll have milk and another piece of cake waiting for a snack."

Everyone carried something into the house when the wagon came to a stop. The waitress had boxed the remainder of the cake before they left the restaurant, and Tucker had stowed it safely under Daisy's seat.

"Boys, I'll unhitch the wagon while you see to your regular nightly chores. Let's see who can get to the cake the fastest." Tucker challenged the twins, who responded more for the cake than the challenge. He laughed when they stirred up a trail of dust in the evening twilight as they ran to check their animals.

Tucker turned to Daisy as she moved to close the door from inside the cabin. "I'll be a few minutes. I'd like another slice of cake, too. After the boys are in bed, I'd appreciate it if you and I could visit for a bit."

Daisy stood in the doorway framed in the glow of the lamp she'd lit on the table behind her. "Okay. We certainly have a lot of catching up to do." She closed the door softly. Leaning her forehead against the door, she heard him whistling a happy tune as he stepped off the porch.

Icing on the tip of John's nose let Tucker know the boys started eating their cake before he finished his chores. James was putting his empty plate and cup in the dishpan on the cabinet under the front window. Tucker hung his hat on the highest peg inside the front door.

"That's papa's peg," James spouted. "No one hangs their hat there but my papa."

Tucker stood still, assessing the situation. Daisy turned from where she was stoking the fire and put the poker aside.

"James. Be quiet," Daisy cautioned her eldest.

"But it's Papa's peg. Not Mr. Tucker's. He can't take Papa's place." The youngster was working himself into a panic. His breathing was starting to come in short rasps, and his shoulders started to shake.

"James, I'm not trying to take your papa's place." Tucker said, as Daisy put an arm around James's shoulder.

John started to whimper at the table. He put his head down on crossed arms and began to cry in earnest.

"Oh, boys, don't cry. Tucker is here to help us. Not to take your papa's place." Daisy steered James to the table and sat on the bench between them, gently rocking with an arm of comfort around each son.

Tucker sat at the head of the table. "Your momma's right. I'm not here to take anyone's place. Only to help."

"But now you're sitting in Papa's chair," James wailed. "And you whispered in Momma's ear while we were in town. You're doing all the things our papa did!" John continued to weep, but didn't say anything. Daisy looked at Tucker over the tops of their small heads. He saw the pain in her eyes.

"Look at me, boys." Tucker's tone was gentle, but firm. Two blond heads tilted upward. Tears still flowed, but they were silent now. "No one can take your papa's place. He was a fine man." James sniffed loudly and wiped his face with the sleeve of his nightshirt. "I knew your papa. I met him years ago when he started courting your momma." John dried his eyes. Tucker had their complete attention.

"You did?" This quiet question came from John.

"I did." Tucker nodded. "I remember the first day he came to see your papa Warren and ask if he could come calling on your momma. He was tall and lean. A handsome young fellow, about twice your age, I'd say." The twins sat up to listen. Daisy's arms fell to her sides, and her eyes misted over as he continued telling his story.

"He was wiry, but strong. Went right up the front steps, took off his hat and rapped with the knocker. Your momma came to the door, all shy and sweet. Her hair was down and full of curls. She was wearing a blue dress the color of the sky in springtime. Her eyes sparkled, and her face went all pretty and pink when she saw it was your papa on the porch." Daisy's eyes widened in wonder. Tucker knew she'd been unaware he'd stood just inside the barn door watching the events unfold that day. She only had eyes for Murdock then.

"Really? Tell us more!" James was intrigued.

"Well, I couldn't hear what he said, but I saw your momma go inside and come back with your papa Warren. He walked outside, and him and your papa took a walk down by a stream that runs by your momma's old home place. They were only gone a few minutes. I could see your momma peeking through the parlor curtains trying to see what they were doing. She was trying to be all sneaky and hide, but I could see her. She never has been much for waitin' and seein'. She always wants to know what's happening right when it's going on."

Daisy's mouth dropped open as if to refute him, but closed when he met her stare and raised his eyebrows. The twins chuckled. Tucker figured they knew this firsthand, but that no one had ever described her like this.

"What happened next?" John asked quietly.

"Seems like I remember your papa whooping out loud and slapping his hat against his leg. Then he turned and started to trot up the hill back to the house. But he stopped real sudden like and hollered down the bank at your papa Warren. 'Thank you, sir!' he said. Then he broke out in a run and took the porch steps two at a time. You would've thought the knocker was gonna break right off the hinge the way he beat on that door." Everyone laughed at that.

"What did Momma do?" James interrupted, again showing his inherited impatience.

"James, your momma's a lot like you, I think. She'd seen your papa celebrating and must have figured out her papa had permitted their courting. She was at that door swinging it open so fast your papa almost fell in when she opened it. She was grinning from ear to ear. I've never seen her look happier. Except on the day she married your papa." Silence settled over the small group as they each absorbed the sweet memory he'd shared.

"So you see, I know how special your papa was to your momma. And I know what a good man he was, or your papa Warren would never have let him court your momma. I watched them court and saw their relationship grow into a deep love. That's something special. Not everybody gets to love, or be loved, like that. Your papa was always good and kind to your momma. It was obvious to me, and anyone else who took the time to notice, that your momma and papa were meant for each other."

Seeing her true love for Murdock had prevented

Tucker from declaring his own love for Daisy back then. He had loved her so much he wanted her to be happy. Even if that happiness came from her being with Murdock. He remembered the ache in his chest that day. His heart had started to grow a protective shell as his hope of having Daisy for his wife had been extinguished.

"Out of respect for their relationship, I promise I won't try to take your papa's place. But I'm your momma's friend—have been for many long years. I came here because I care about her, and I care about you boys. Do you think you could grow to respect me as your momma's friend and someone who cares about all of you?" Tucker waited while the boys thought. He looked at Daisy. Tears slid down her cheeks.

"Yes, sir. I believe we can." James answered for both twins. John nodded his agreement. "But what about Papa's hat peg and his chair at the table?"

"Well…" Daisy spoke for the first time since Tucker had started his story. "Since Mr. Tucker and your papa were friends, do you think Papa would be okay with letting Mr. Tucker use things that he used, since Papa's in heaven and won't be needing them for himself?"

"It hurts so much that he's never coming back, Momma." John's broken heart seemed to cry out for the papa he could no longer see and touch.

"I know, John." Daisy pulled him close. "Papa didn't leave because he wanted to, but we know he's safe with Jesus. He'd want us to be happy and make new friends and build new relationships. Mr. Tucker has been my friend for a long time. I'm sure your papa's glad he's come to help us. I think it would be okay with your papa for us to share his things with Mr. Tucker."

"If you're sure," James said.

"I'm sure." Daisy hugged both boys close.

"Okay," John added.

Daisy stood up and patted her hair smooth. "I think it's time for the two of you to get to bed. Tell Mr. Tucker good-night."

Watching the three of them go into the boys' room, Tucker almost wished his heart hadn't frozen over when Daisy married Murdock. But experience taught him that Daisy would never love anyone the way she had loved Murdock. His heart was better left cold, rather than warming only to be rejected yet again.

Chapter Four

Daisy joined Tucker in the front room after settling the boys for the night. She sat in her rocking chair near the fire. The night had cooled to a chilly temperature. Tucker sat on the other side of the fireplace in Murdock's chair. The warm glow of a lamp cast the room in shadows.

Her family had happily shared this small space for many years. This morning it had seemed cavernous without Murdock. Tonight it felt suddenly cramped. Tucker was a big man. His presence and person would be impossible to ignore in the confines of the room.

"They are finally asleep. It was quite a day for them." Daisy stared into the fire. She noticed Tucker had added more wood to it and stacked several logs on the hearth to be used during the night, if necessary. His act of kindness made her realize how bone tired she was. Carrying the load alone for almost a month had taken a toll on her body and mind.

"It was quite a day for all of us, Daisy." Tucker leaned forward and placed his elbows on the arms of the rocker. "You've got to be as exhausted as those boys."

"I am tired." Daisy leaned her head back against the chair and closed her eyes while still rocking the chair. Moments later she started slightly. Tucker stood over her with a hand on her shoulder.

"I'm sorry. I must have drifted off." Daisy shook her head. "Please forgive me. I can make us some coffee." She moved to get up from her chair.

"No need." Tucker took his hat from the peg by the door. "I enjoyed the evening with you and the boys. I'll leave you to get some rest."

"Oh, I hadn't thought. Where will you sleep?" Daisy said in a small rush. "I can fix a place for you here between the fireplace and the front door. Or you can take the bed, and I can make a pallet with the boys." She started to chatter nervously, having only now thought about sleeping arrangements and what Tucker might expect.

"Relax, Daisy. I've already fixed a place in the barn. I'll stay there for now. You go to bed."

"You can't sleep there. It's cold, and the animals are there. It's not right."

"I'll be fine. I've slept with animals more times than I can count. They'll help keep the barn warm. It's not too cold out tonight. We'll get something more permanent figured out soon. Now get to bed. Bolt this door after I go. I don't want to take any chances with your safety." Tucker opened the door. The night breeze found the opening and stirred the flame of the lamp on the table.

"Tucker?" Daisy stopped him with a hand on his sleeve as he put his hat on.

He turned and looked down on her with green eyes. "Yes, Daisy?"

"Thank you for what you told the boys about their papa."

"Glad to do it. Their papa was a good man. They need to know I'm not trying to take his place." He patted her hand and lifted it from his sleeve.

"I didn't know you'd seen all that, much less that you'd remember." Daisy spoke quietly.

"I remember a lot of things from back then, Daisy." He touched her cheek with the back of his hand. "Sleep well." Tucker stepped onto the porch and pulled the door closed behind him.

After she slid the bolt in place, Daisy heard his boots descend the steps. The lonely strains of his whistled tune barely reached her ears.

How could she have fallen asleep on her wedding night? Of course, it wasn't a real wedding night, but it was still an important day for both her and Tucker. She knew his life had changed today in ways he could not have imagined. He'd never been married. He didn't know firsthand about the responsibilities of a family. This wasn't like signing on for a cattle drive that ended with a sale and profits. Would he be sorry when he found out that the work never ended and the goals were so long-term, they seemed illusive in the good times and unattainable during the hard times?

"Anybody awake in there?" Tucker called out the next morning and knocked again on the front door of the cabin.

"We're up." He heard Daisy's muffled voice. "John, open the door for Mr. Tucker."

The bolt slid and John pulled the heavy door open. Tucker watched in amusement at the flurry of activity inside.

Daisy set the coffeepot on the stove. "James, run

down to the smokehouse and bring me a slab of bacon. John, you get us some eggs." She was grabbing a bowl from the shelf when James grumbled.

She pointed a wooden spoon at the oldest twin. "We're running late today. Skedaddle."

Tucker entered the cabin and took off his hat. He hesitated before he hung it on the controversial peg. "Morning, James. John." The boys watched and looked at each other and then their mom. Silent agreement passed among them all. The issue of Tucker using their papa's things was settled.

Both boys headed for the door. "Morning, Mr. Tucker!" they shouted in unison as they raced to see who could get to the outhouse first before retrieving the items Daisy needed for breakfast.

Tucker laughed and reached for a mug on the shelf above the stove. He grabbed a towel to protect his hand and poured himself a cup of coffee before going to look out the back window.

"Sorry to wake you by chopping wood so early, but daylight is limited this time of year, and there's a lot of work to be done."

He turned from the window near the foot of her bed, noticing she hadn't taken the time to straighten the quilt. He could see the imprint where her head had rested on the pillow. He stepped around the chest that held her most precious possessions, remembering the day he'd gone to town for her father and picked it up from the general store. Mr. Warren had ordered it for her sixteenth birthday. The same year she'd met Murdock.

How ironic that God had brought him to this place. After giving up hope of ever having Daisy for his wife, he'd resigned himself to live life alone. Now God had put him in a place where he and Daisy were together, but neither of them could love the other. He'd proposed to a young woman long ago. Alice Fields's abrupt dismissal of his heart in favor of a former beau had shown him the depth of a woman's first love. Then he'd allowed himself to grow fond of Daisy, but never told her. Now her heart would always belong to Murdock, and his had long since retreated into the hollow of his soul—never to risk rejection again.

Daisy's voice broke into his thoughts. "I'm sorry things are so behind. I've done the best I could, but it's really more than one person can keep up with. James and John do their best, but they're so young." She opened the oven and put a pan of biscuits inside.

The front door blew open, and James dropped the bacon on the cabinet beside the dishpan. Just as quickly, he trotted back outside.

"Eager, isn't he?" Tucker observed.

"He knows he has to do his chores and lessons before he gets any free time. He likes to get as much done before breakfast as possible. It makes him feel like he's got some say in the latter part of his day." Daisy was slicing the bacon and laying it in the bottom of a hot skillet. The sizzling sound promised to become a delicious smell soon.

"He's a lot like you." Tucker had removed the ashes from the fireplace and put in fresh wood for the evening. He took the ash bucket to the front porch to empty later. John came in with a basket of eggs and left to help his brother in the barn.

"What makes you say that?"

"He's always asking questions, always seems to be taking charge, and just a little impatient." Tucker teased her with his observations about James. "Not that those are bad things."

Daisy turned with one hand on her hip and the butter dish in the other. "If you mean he's constantly aware of what's going on around him, learning by inquiring, has good leadership skills and doesn't like to waste time, then, yes, he is like me." Daisy set the butter down on the table with a thud to punctuate her speech.

"See. My point exactly. He's a lot like you." Tucker opened the door when he heard James coming up the steps with a fresh pail of milk. James set the pail on the cabinet and went to wash his hands behind the screen. John was only steps behind his brother.

Tucker poured milk for both boys and coffee for Daisy. Then he refilled his own mug. The boys sat on their bench, and Daisy put the last of the food on the table and took her place on the end, by James. The twins and Daisy joined hands. John was seated next to Tucker and reached for him. Tucker couldn't resist smiling at the quiet child and took his hand. Daisy and the boys bowed their heads.

Tucker took the opportunity to study her. Tresses of golden hair escaped the bun twisted at the nape of her neck. Her face was hollow from the grief she'd suffered. Her freckles stood out against pale skin. One small hand held the hand of James. The other lay on the table, and his mother's ring caught the shaft of morning sun that peeked through the window. The whole picture painted a stark reminder of the toll a person suffered on losing their true love.

Daisy lifted her head and caught him staring. She indicated that he should pray. Raising her eyebrows higher and leaning her head toward the boys, she let him know she was asking for the sake of the twins. Tucker bowed his head.

"Lord, we thank You for all Your blessings. Thank You for the food, and help us to make the most of this day You've given us. Amen."

Daisy and the boys added, "Amen." She was looking his way when Tucker reached for the biscuits, and she smiled her thanks.

It might take Tucker a while to adjust to the day-to-day workings of family life, but that's what he'd come here to do. Would Daisy be willing to adjust to him? He could see them beginning to rebuild their friendship from the past. He hoped she never expected more than that, because that's all he had left to give.

After breakfast Tucker disappeared into the barn. Between breakfast and lunch during the week, Daisy did lessons with the boys. When Murdock had been killed, the twins were terrified of leaving her alone. She'd agreed to let them school at home until after Christmas. In just over two months they would head to the town school every morning. She hoped the thieves would be found by then.

She cleared away the dishes while James and John brought their books to the table. Watching out the window while she washed the last of the dishes, Daisy caught sight of Tucker riding out the back of the barn in the direction of the creek on the rear of the property.

"Did you boys tell Mr. Tucker where the creek is?" Daisy dried her hands, untied her apron and hung it on a peg to dry. She joined James and John at the table.

"Yes, ma'am. He asked us all kinds of questions yesterday on the porch while you were getting ready for the wedding." James climbed onto the bench and opened his speller. "We told him about the fence line from the ranch next to us, and about the pond where we go swimming in summer and even about how far the cotton fields go out toward the Dixon place."

"James told him lots of stuff. I still don't know how to talk to him much, Momma, but I'm trying real hard to like him because he's your friend." John had opened the Bible to find the place they would pick up their reading today.

Daisy pushed the curling edges of John's hair out of his face. "Thank you for trying, John. Mr. Tucker is a good man. I know you'll both grow to like him. It's okay to answer his questions. He has a lot to learn about our farm." Daisy added quietly to herself, "And us."

Tucker joined them for lunch. They ate the rest of the bacon and biscuits from breakfast. A piece of wedding cake prevented the lunch from being ordinary.

"We're going to miss this cake when it's gone." Daisy covered the remaining cake and put it on the cabinet under the window.

"You can make us something sweet, Momma. You're the best cook ever!" James licked icing from the corners of his mouth and headed for the door. "Can I go finish my chores now? I'm thinking I might want to go fishing later."

"Go ahead. Just don't leave to go fishing without coming to the house and letting me know first." Daisy poured water from a bucket into the dishpan. "John, you go with your brother. You've both studied enough for one day."

John stacked the books and carried them to the shelf

in their bedroom before joining James at the door. They both put on their new hats.

"Why don't you save those new hats for church and trips to town? Special occasions and such?" Daisy didn't want to see the hats come to harm during their everyday activities.

"Mr. Tucker told us these hats were for protecting our heads from the elements while we work. We're supposed to wear 'em every day." James adjusted his brim and looked to Tucker for confirmation. "I don't know what elements are, but I want to be protected."

Tucker chuckled. "I did say that. Elements are the weather. Rain, sun, heat and that sort of thing."

"Oh," the boys responded together.

"You'll need to wear a bandana, too," Tucker added. "Today's work is going to be hot work. You can tie it around your neck, or around your head and wear it under your hat, or you can just use it to wipe your brow when you think you might be getting too sweaty."

"That's a great idea!" James was eager.

"But we don't have any bandanas," John complained.

Tucker's gaze met Daisy's, and without looking away from her, he asked the boys, "Did your papa have any bandanas?" She searched his eyes and saw only tenderness for her sons there.

"He sure did!" from James.

John added, "My favorite was his red one."

"What about it, Momma? Do you think these boys can wear their papa's bandanas while they work?" Daisy saw the twins brighten at the thought and decided it would help keep Murdock's memory alive in their minds.

"That's a fine idea. I'll get them." Daisy went into

the boys' room and came back with two bandanas. She gave the red one to John and offered a blue one to James.

"We don't know how to tie 'em." James wrung the fabric in his hands while John lifted the red one to his nose.

"It still smells like Papa," John said.

Tucker approached the boys saying, "That's the smell of a hardworking man. You'll be smelling just like your papa before you know it." He took James's bandana and tied it around his neck with the knot in the back. "Working hard makes a man smell like a man." He tied John's bandana with the knot in the front. "What do you think?" Tucker backed away and let Daisy look her boys over.

"I think you look just like your papa. Both of you." This drew big smiles from both boys.

"Now head on over to the barn and start putting fresh straw in the stalls. I mucked them out before lunch. We've got to get the barn ready for some new animals." Tucker nudged the twins toward the front door. "I'll be along to help in a minute. I just need to talk to your momma first."

Happy boys bounced off the front porch, admiring each other and their new look. The hats were adjusted and the bandanas tugged until both were satisfied. Then the race for the barn ensued. Daisy smiled at them and turned to thank Tucker.

"Thank you. That was a wonderful idea." Daisy moved to start washing the dishes and watched the boys through the window.

"It's important for them to remember their papa. And to feel like they can be like him. I'm glad to do it. Thanks for agreeing and letting them have the bandanas."

"They were just in the drawer. I didn't know what to do with them." Daisy put both hands on the cabinet and dropped her head to her chest, eyes closed, fighting back tears. Tucker came to stand behind her and put his hands on her shoulders.

"It'll get easier. I promise. I know it's hard right now. But you're doing the right things. You're letting them talk about their papa and reassuring them that he's with the Lord." His strong hands began to gently knead the tightness of her muscles. Daisy pulled her head to one shoulder and then the next trying to relax away her stress. Then suddenly she shrugged both shoulders to her ears and pulled away from Tucker. She went to stand on the other side of the room, putting the table between them. A shiver ran down her spine and she rubbed her arms to stop the tingling.

"I'm sorry. I just can't relax right now. I'm so tense all the time. I feel so much pressure to make sure the farm is a success and the twins are taken care of, and now I'm so obligated to you for all you're doing." She raised a hand to each temple and rubbed her fingers in small circles in an effort to release the pain.

"I'm the one who's sorry. I didn't mean to make you uncomfortable, Daisy. Please forgive me." Tucker made no move toward her. He actually took a step back.

"It's not that. I just hate that my emotions go from such grief and sadness one minute, to joy at seeing something make James or John smile the next." She picked up the remaining plates from the table and moved toward the dishpan. Tucker moved to the door, giving her plenty of space.

"You said you had something we needed to talk about." Daisy put the dishes in the water and began to work without looking at him. She heard him take his hat from the peg and knew he was spinning it in his hands. Daisy had noticed he often did this when he was choosing his words carefully.

"I'm getting the stalls ready for new horses. I know you said we'd have to talk about it later, but I feel we need to get things back on track as soon as possible."

"Okay. If you think that's best." She began stacking the clean dishes on the shelves above the cabinet. "We can go to the bank the next time we're in town and get the money out. I don't keep much money here. Murdock never thought it was a good idea to keep cash around. I finally understood why on the day he was robbed and killed. Those men took a lot of things from us, but most of our money was safe in the bank." A tear ran down her cheek. Turning her back to Tucker, she caught it with the dish towel and sniffed. Raising up to her full height, Daisy pivoted to face him again. It surprised her to see that anger virtually oozed from every fiber of the man. His red hair seemed aflame on his scalp. His nostrils flared, and he took deep breaths. She couldn't ever remember seeing him so mad. Not even the day she shot him when her papa was teaching her to shoot.

"I will pay for the horses." Tucker rammed his hat on his head. "And if those murderous thieves ever come near here again, I'll see that they pay, too." The force of the slamming door caused it to bounce open again as she watched him stomp across the yard. It took a moment for her to realize she was holding her breath.

Daisy hadn't meant to upset him. Her papa was right. Being married to each other was definitely going to be a major adjustment for both of them. She knew he was just being friendly when he touched her, but she wasn't ready to be touched. It was too soon. And she couldn't let him pay for those horses. The farm expenses were her responsibility. And that temper!

Help us, Lord, or this is going to be a rough road.

Chapter Five

Tucker entered the barn and saw the boys had finished two of the stalls. Calming himself with great restraint he said, "Good job, men. I need to ask you something." He stood in the middle of the barn. James and John stilled their pitchforks. "Are you good fishermen?"

"We sure are!" James bragged. "We catch something every time we go!"

"Almost every time, James," John added. "Sometimes the fish don't bite."

"But that's not our fault, so I say we catch something every time. If the fish are biting, we're bringing 'em home." James hesitated and looked at Tucker. "Why? You want us to teach you how to fish, Mr. Tucker? We can. I just thought you might already know since you're so old and all." The boy spoke with youthful sincerity. On any other day Tucker would have laughed, but right now, he just needed some time alone.

"That's a mighty fine offer, James, but not today. I may let you give me some pointers next time. For today, though, I'd like the two of you to go see if you can bring home some supper. Part of a man's job is to put food on the table. Think you're up for the challenge?" He looked from one boy to the other.

"Yes, sir! We can do it." John turned to his brother. "Come on, James, let's get our gear. I'll race you." Pitchforks fell to the ground as eager boys headed to the other side of the barn for poles.

"Whoa, just a minute. There's another important thing a man does. He takes care of his tools. Put these pitchforks away, then get your gear and don't forget to tell your momma where you're going. Make sure she knows I'm sending you to get our supper."

"Yes, sir!" they said in unison. Within seconds Tucker had the barn to himself. He was so angry he knew he needed to be alone. Hoping some hard work would relieve his stress, Tucker rolled up his sleeves and finished spreading straw.

Enough bad things had happened to Daisy lately without him adding to it by showing her his anger. He didn't know why those men came and took her husband from her and the papa from those fine boys. He couldn't bear to see her in pain. He came here because her father asked him to, but the good Lord knew no real man could stand by quietlike while a woman suffered.

Marrying Daisy was supposed to alleviate his loneliness, not confuse him. He gained a sense of accomplishment when he helped her or the twins do something. Just being on the property to protect them brought him peace. More than once last night he'd looked out the barn door and checked to be certain everything was as it should be at the cabin. It was his duty as her friend.

But watching Daisy cry tugged at the edges of his hardened heart. That was not part of his bargain with Daisy or her father. Or God. Tucker was trying to be patient and not make her uncomfortable, but he wasn't accustomed to a woman's tears. It was a hard thing to watch without offering comfort. Yet she rejected his attempt to comfort her when he touched her shoulders. He'd need to remember not to do that again.

And he certainly didn't know how to deal with a woman who wanted to handle the money! His heart broke for her over all her suffering. At the same time he wanted to grab her and kiss her senseless when she wanted to take charge of everything.

Where had that thought come from? If she didn't want him to touch her, she sure wouldn't want him to kiss her. And he wasn't about to open himself up to more rejection. Better to keep a safe distance. Keep things friendly. Just not too friendly.

Lord, give me patience! And I think You better hurry.

Needing to steer clear of Daisy for a while, he tackled the broken boards on the stall in the corner because he felt the need to swing a hammer. Then he moved outside and repaired the chicken coop. He even moved the outhouse.

He worked until he was exhausted, but nothing could erase the memory of a single tear trailing down her face when she turned her back on him and refused his comfort.

Supper was fish, grits and hush puppies. James and John were praised for their success. They celebrated by finishing off the rest of the cake before the boys went to bed.

When Daisy came out of their room Tucker was on his way out the front door. She noticed he had stoked the fire and hauled in more wood.

"Wait, Tucker." Daisy spoke softly.

Hand on the door, Tucker shook his head without looking back, put his hat on and took a step onto the porch.

"Please." That stopped him. She'd hoped it would. "I want to apologize. I didn't mean to be so sensitive this afternoon. Please stay and sit in the warmth for a while. Have a cup of coffee." The last was almost a question.

Tucker turned and stepped back inside, closing the door to keep out the night chill. "You don't owe me an apology, Daisy." His hat once again was spinning in his hands. He stared into the fire instead of looking at her. "I didn't mean to make you uncomfortable. I promise to be more careful." He glanced up then.

Daisy smiled and reached for his arm. "You were being a kind friend, Tucker. I'm truly sorry. Please forgive me."

He patted her hand briefly and withdrew his arm. "If you'll forgive me," he said with a smile.

"Okay." Daisy went to pour the coffee. She added honey to her delicate cup and stirred it gently.

"Okay, then." Tucker hung his hat on the peg and took a seat by the fire. He moved the rocker back from the hearth, then slid low in the seat and stretched his legs. He propped his arms on the sides of the chair, moaning a little. "We sure do seem to be apologizing to each other a lot." She heard the effort he made to keep his tone light.

Daisy put a heavy mug of rich black brew in his hand. "Well, there's one thing for sure—" She untied her apron with one hand, pulled it loose, and took her seat. She draped the apron across the chair arm. "If we keep having these disagreements, you'll have this place in fine order in no time." She grinned and took a sip of the sweet liquid.

Tucker laughed and immediately grabbed at his stomach. "Don't make me laugh so much! It hurts!" This sent her into giggles.

"Are you very sore?" At his nod she added, "That's what you get for being so hot-blooded." She couldn't stop laughing. Catching glimpses of him working that afternoon, she had worried he might be trying to do too much at once. He'd moved from one project to another without so much as a break to rest.

"Me? Hot-blooded? You have no idea." He chuckled, only to stop and grab his side again.

"I've heard about you redheads." She teased him mercilessly, knowing it hurt him but enjoying watching him squirm. "I'm trying to think what I need to do tomorrow to get the smokehouse door fixed. It's awful hard to close. I've been afraid some animal might get in there and get our winter stores. I might have to sleep late or burn the flapjacks or something."

"Is that what you're thinking?" he asked still smiling. "Let's just see if your little plan works. Next time I may ride off just to see the lay of the land."

"You wouldn't!" She tossed her apron at him.

"I heard in town that the neighboring ranch was really nice. Might come up for sale soon. Who knows? I may surprise you and ride over there and buy it." He chuckled, but she immediately sobered.

"The Thornton place?" Daisy stopped rocking and leaned forward, eyes wide.

"I think that's what they said." Tucker's tone was serious now. "Seems her folks are real sick. Want them to come take care of them and their home place. When they pass, the Thorntons will inherit the land."

"Oh, how sad. Judy has been a dear friend for years. I'll surely miss her." Daisy leaned back and set her chair in motion. She stared into the fire, her coffee forgotten on the small table between the chairs. "Nothing stays the same, does it, Tucker?"

"No, Daisy, it doesn't. That's the thing about life. You just have to keep moving forward. Sometimes you walk, sometimes you run and sometimes you soar like the eagles. I've tried to live by that Scripture. It keeps me from giving up."

"'But they that wait upon the Lord shall renew their strength; they shall mount up with wings as eagles; they shall run, and not be weary; and they shall walk, and not faint.'" Daisy quoted the verse from memory, still staring into the fire. "I've been walking for the last little while. I'd be lying if I said I haven't grown weary."

"I understand. I've been through long times when I had to keep walking the path God laid out for me, even though I didn't understand why life couldn't be another way. I've learned He's faithful." Tucker took a drink of his coffee and continued. "I spent most of my childhood growing up in a hotel, watching my sweet momma work herself to death. She taught me that verse to help me when times were hard."

"I never knew you grew up in a hotel, Tucker."

"Momma went to work in a hotel after my father died. Those were hard years, but I learned a lot from her about how faithful God is."

Tucker turned up his mug and drained the rest of the coffee. "I best be getting to bed. I've got a lot of soreness to sleep off tonight." He pushed up on the chair arms and gave an exaggerated groan.

Daisy looked at him and smiled. "You've done it again, my friend."

"What's that?" Tucker stood over her, and she had to tip the chair backward to see his face.

"Made me smile when I feel like crying." She stood and followed him to the door as he set his hat in place. "Thanks for being such a good friend to me."

Tucker tipped his hat to her. "Anytime, ma'am, anytime." With a smile he was gone, into the darkness.

Daisy bolted the door and leaned against it wearily. She wondered why more sad news had come. She would miss her friend Judy. She hoped the Thorntons would be able to help her parents recover. Daisy made a mental note to pray for them. She placed the cups in the dishpan and put out the lamp on the table.

She smiled again at Tucker's exaggerated movements and groaning when he'd got up from the chair. Years before she would laugh at the way he teased her. Many times as a young woman, she'd become frustrated or upset with some situation or another. She could count on Tucker to lighten her mood if he was around. Now it seemed he was able to lighten her heart.

After changing to her gown and climbing beneath the chilly quilt, Daisy suddenly realized what Tucker had said. *I may surprise you and ride over there and buy it.* She sat up in bed. Surely he wouldn't buy the land next to hers! Not without talking to her. After all, the Thorntons had a ranch. Daisy grew cotton. He must have been teasing. No. She refused to believe he would make such a major decision without her knowledge. Daisy thumped her pillow and buried her head in it, determined to get a good night's rest. She had a feeling she was going to need it.

After a few minutes she rolled over to face the wall. Had it really only been two days since Tucker arrived? A month ago she would have been snuggled close to Murdock.

Tonight she lay alone, after telling Tucker good-night and sending him to the barn to sleep with the animals. Tucker was her husband now.

Lord, let him be satisfied with friendship. I just can't love another man. It's too painful.

For years Murdock had been such a presence—the heart and soul of the farm and family. There were reminders of him everywhere. But in just a matter of weeks, his essence was fading away. She tried to hang on to it, but it was evaporating. Daisy pulled Murdock's pillow close and realized even his scent was gone. Silent tears wet the pillow. How long would she cry for Murdock?

Chapter Six

Breakfast was over, and Daisy got the twins set up to study on their own. She hung up her apron and headed out the door in search of Tucker. She needed him to confirm he was only joking about buying the Thornton ranch.

The barn door opened, and he appeared. At that same moment the sound of an approaching wagon reached them. They both turned to look up the lane, and Daisy realized it was two wagons.

"Aha. They made it." Tucker pulled heavy leather gloves from his belt and tugged them on as he headed to meet the wagons. Daisy recognized Will Thomas, owner of the lumber mill, driving the first team of horses. The wagons were loaded with fresh boards, boxes with nails and hardware, and what looked to be two windows wrapped and tied in brown paper. She followed Tucker, trotting a little to keep up with his pace.

"What is this?" Daisy demanded.

Tucker didn't slow his speed, but spoke over his shoulder. "It's lumber, Daisy."

"I can see that." Exasperation began to boil to the

surface. She'd been none too happy coming to see him in the barn, and now here was another surprise. A big surprise. And so far, no explanation. Daisy heard the boys come onto the front porch. They were both wearing the now ever-present Stetsons.

"Can we help?" James eagerly approached Tucker.

"Do you think we can, Momma?" John came more cautiously.

"Sure," Tucker said.

At the same time, "No!" Daisy snapped.

Tucker stopped so abruptly that Daisy bumped into him. Confused boys looked at one another and shrugged their shoulders.

"They are big enough to help unload a lumber wagon, Daisy." Tucker turned to speak to Will Thomas. "Can you pull around to the back of the house and let us unload there?"

"Wherever you want it, Mr. Barlow. What about stowing the windows in the barn till you're ready for them? Might be safer."

"Good idea," Tucker said. "James, show Mr. Thomas the first empty stall, the one with no straw."

Will Thomas urged his horses toward the barn and directed the other driver to the back of the house.

Daisy stopped, put both hands on her hips and patted one foot repeatedly. "Tucker Barlow, what is going on here?" Her voice brooked no argument.

"We're about to unload a wagon. Now if you don't mind, it's mighty hard work. Do you think you could make us a refreshing drink for when we've finished? With five men working, we should be done in about half an hour." Tucker signaled John to follow him. John adjusted his hat and puffed out his chest to rise to the title of "man."

"John, you go ahead. Tucker, I need to speak with you for a minute." At Tucker's raised eyebrows, she added, "Please."

"Go show the driver where we need to stack the wood, John. I'll be right there." John started up the hill, and Tucker walked close to Daisy. James jumped on the back of Mr. Thomas's wagon and rode around the house to join his brother.

"What's the matter, Daisy?" Tucker stifled a grin.

"Is something funny, Tucker? Obviously I'm missing something." She pointed up the hill to the working men. "Everyone seems to know what's going on around here—except me."

"Oh, that." Tucker followed the direction of her finger with his eyes, before turning back to her, his back to the others. Speaking so only she could hear, Tucker asked, "Do you really want me to sleep in the barn all winter?" A teasing grin punctuated the question. "Would you do that to me, Daisy? I thought we agreed to be friends."

"Friends share secrets. They don't keep them from each other." Her foot began to tap again. Her appreciation for his lightheartedness was completely forgotten for the moment. It was being overridden by the feeling she no longer had control over anything in her life.

Tucker quietly explained. "I knew it wouldn't work for me to sleep in the barn when winter hits full force. I anticipate some issues with the boys, too."

"Of course I don't expect you to sleep in the barn in the winter. I'm not heartless. What issues?" Daisy was growing more frustrated by the second. He had yet to answer a single question.

"I don't have time to go into everything right now, but I promise we can talk as soon as Mr. Thomas and his helper leave." Tucker put a hand on each of her shoulders. "Please let me go to work now, before they think you want them to unload everything without me." He released her and walked away, calling over his shoulder. "Do you think you could fix those drinks?"

"Of course, Tucker. Be glad to," Daisy called bittersweetly. "Ooh, the nerve of that man! We will talk before this day is done." Daisy muttered under her breath while going up the steps. "And it won't just be questions. There will be answers."

A full hour later, Will Thomas and his two wagons rode off the property while Daisy watched.

"Boys, go back to your lessons now. I'll be busy for a bit, so don't interrupt me."

"Oh, Momma, can't we help Mr. Tucker?" James was reluctant to end the excitement.

"You heard your momma. Get back to your studies. There'll be plenty of work for everybody." Tucker looked at Daisy. "I'm not going to be getting started right away. Your momma and I have some things to take care of first."

"Yes, sir." A dejected James followed John into the cabin and closed the door.

"Want to walk down to the creek with me?" Tucker offered.

"That will be good. I don't want the boys to hear us." Daisy huffed along ahead of Tucker for a short distance.

"We could probably talk better if you slow down and walk beside me, Daisy." The teasing began anew.

"I'm not in the mood for your joking, Tucker." Daisy stopped and turned in a split second. He had to grab her arms to keep her from falling as he plowed into her.

"You okay?" he asked.

"Yes." Daisy brushed her sleeves to straighten them and turned to walk beside him. "Tucker, you've only been here two days. And I don't know how you've managed to do it, but you've completely turned my world upside down." She pulled at the tall dry grass that bent in the breeze, tearing a stalk loose to peel into layers while she walked.

"I didn't mean to upset you, Daisy."

"There you go apologizing again. Can't we get beyond that and lay some kind of ground rules to help us communicate better?"

"What do you have in mind?" Tucker adjusted his hat as the late-morning sun climbed higher.

"Well, for starters, how about you stop asking questions and start answering some?"

"What questions?" Tucker asked innocently.

"See! That's what I mean!" Daisy walked ahead of him and took several deep breaths. She was beginning to wonder if he just enjoyed teasing her or if he wanted to provoke her outright.

"Tell me what you want to know. I'll answer." He stopped and waited.

She turned to face him. "Several things." Rolling her eyes toward the sky, Daisy thought about the order to proceed. If he suddenly clammed up, she needed the answers to the most pressing questions first. "First, what is the lumber for?"

"I'm going to build another bedroom onto the cabin—a large one with a private dressing area for you. It's my wedding gift to you." Tucker's mouth turned up slightly at the corners. "Surprise." His eyebrows climbed, and his grin grew to full size. He asked, "Do you like it?"

"Oh, Tucker," Daisy spoke breathlessly. "What on earth?"

"After I saw the cabin, well…the boys are small now, but they'll be young men before you know it. You need privacy. Remember, I grew up with my mother. There were times she needed privacy, and it wasn't possible. I couldn't do anything then, but this is something I can do for you. I wanted to surprise you." He paused. "Did it work?"

Daisy was flabbergasted. "You! That's another question." They both laughed. Daisy's face grew serious again. "That's very sweet, Tucker, but you don't have to do that for me. It's too extravagant. We don't have a lot of money. We've got to pay for more horses, and our money has to last until next harvest. I budgeted it all out. There's not a lot of extra."

"This is my wedding gift to you, Daisy. It's not coming out of the money you have in the bank. I used my own money for this." Tucker tilted his head to one side and held out his arms. "Say you like it…please." Green eyes sparkled. She'd forgotten how much he made her laugh.

"Okay. I like it." She gave him a friendly hug and backed away. "But I wish you hadn't done it."

"Really?" He lifted his hat and ran his hand through his hair.

"Stop with the questions. I'm asking them today." She smiled back at him.

"There's more?" he teased.

Daisy blew out a quick breath. "What did you mean about the boys having issues?"

Tucker sobered. "You saw how they reacted when I put my hat on their papa's peg and sat in his chair at the table?"

"Yes. But they're adjusting. They haven't said anything else have they?"

"No. But that doesn't mean they've accepted me. They haven't even seen me sit in their papa's chair by the fire." He paused and spun his hat by the brim several times while he thought. Putting the Stetson back in place he said, "I don't want them to be upset when I move into the cabin. Winter will be here before you know it. I think it will be easier for them if you have your own room. I can sleep in the main room."

"I hadn't thought of that at all." At his lowered gaze she rushed to reassure him. "Thank you for your consideration of their feelings. And for your patience with me. It means more than I can say."

A heavy silence hung between them.

Finally Tucker spoke. "Any more questions?" he chuckled.

She smiled. "No. I think I've asked quite enough questions today. Don't you?" She laughed in earnest. Daring to look at him as he raised his head in her direction, Daisy saw something in Tucker's eyes she'd never seen before. There was a depth she hadn't contemplated, an intensity she wasn't expecting, a pull she found magnetic. She blinked quickly and looked away. "Well," she said, looking over her shoulder at the house. "I better go see what those two are up to." She cleared her throat and took one hesitant step before pausing to look at him again.

"Thank you, Tucker. It's a lovely gift."

"You're welcome, Daisy." Tucker turned and walked to the creek.

She watched him squat and draw handfuls of the cool water to splash his face.

How could she ever repay him for his kindness? He wasn't just protecting her and her sons physically. He was guarding their wounded emotions. Tucker was once again proving himself to be a dear friend. A generous friend at that.

If only she could discern the look she'd seen in his eyes.

Lunch was a lively meal. Tucker listened as everyone gave their opinion on the big surprise.

"You really were surprised, weren't you, Momma?" James had been thrilled to keep such a big secret from her. At her nod, he said, "Mr. Tucker told us in the barn this morning. We knew and didn't say anything! We're good at secrets." He beamed at this accomplishment.

"I didn't want to tell you and ruin the surprise. I'm glad you like it." John was much calmer.

Daisy laughed and told them how pleased she was with the surprise. "I was very impressed with how hard both of you worked this morning unloading those wagons. Weren't you, Tucker?"

He nodded in agreement. "Very impressed, indeed. Not just with the work but also with the ability to keep a confidence. It's important for a man to have a good reputation. Once you give your word about a matter, you have to keep it. No matter how difficult that is. I'm proud of both of you."

"Does that mean you'll trust us again, Mr. Tucker?" John wanted to know.

"It does, John. You've both proved yourselves to be trustworthy men." His praise brought big smiles to the two young faces. He hoped to win their confidence and respect, too. Losing his dad at such a young age and never having siblings had caused an emptiness in Tucker.

He'd often been jealous of the families he'd seen come and go at the hotel where he and his mother had lived. The closest he'd come to being part of a family after his father died was when Daisy and her sisters were young and had looked to him for advice and friendship. He'd longed for a real family most of his life. One complete with a father, a mother and several children. Now he had all the pieces. Could God help them grow the love that would make them become a true family?

"It's time to get after the chores now." Daisy started clearing the table. "There's still plenty to be done before dark."

"Your mother's right. The two of you get the chores done, and I'll go get the drawing for how we're going to build this room." Tucker's chair scraped across the floor as he pushed it back and stood.

"We?" James didn't miss a lick.

"We," Tucker confirmed. "I bought some extra tools so you can work side by side with me. So let's get to it."

Hats came off pegs, and whoops of excitement echoed in the afternoon air as the boys jumped from the porch, skipping the steps entirely.

Daisy expressed concern. "Tucker, I'm not sure they're old enough for tools of their own."

"I think they're ready. Boys grow up faster than you'd think," he assured.

"I just don't want them to get hurt."

"I promise to teach them to be careful." Tucker continued cautiously. "But getting hurt is part of growing up."

"They already know more about pain than any boy their age should!" Daisy was visibly upset now.

"I know." Tucker kept his tone gentle. "Remember I was in the same place at an even younger age."

Daisy's anger deflated. "I guess you're right." Was that apprehension in her gaze? "But do be careful."

He smiled his promise. "We will."

Daisy turned to wipe the table with a cloth. "Thank you for teaching them lessons about character and such. A lot of men overlook that in an effort to make boys tough."

"A man is more than a strong back and provider. He needs to be reliable in spirit and heart, as well." Tucker put his hat on. "I'll see you after a while. Thanks for the meal."

He left the cabin and headed to retrieve his tools from the barn. Daisy's reluctant acceptance of his wedding gift affirmed his need to guard his heart. She'd been so determined to persevere on her own that she greeted any effort he made at easing her load with suspicion. She'd agreed to let him stay, but he knew she hadn't abandoned her refusal to need him.

It might be easier for both of them if he gave her wide berth. If only the sight of her didn't threaten to ignite something inside of him—like an ember in a long extinguished fire searching for a rekindling spark.

While Daisy washed clothes later that day, she pondered Tucker's words about a man having a strong back and being a provider. For years at her father's home, she'd seen him work as hard as a man could. When she turned to hang clothes on the line, she had an unobstructed view of Tucker across the yard moving lumber and sawing boards to provide shelter for her. His dependability was never in question.

But she was just beginning to realize the value of his spirit and heart. His faithful character was a good example to her sons. She was grateful to God and her father for sending Tucker to her family.

Daisy stretched up to hang one of his shirts on the line. Tucker looked up at the same time and caught her gaze. She couldn't deny she was drawn to the sight of him as he worked in the afternoon sun. He was different from Murdock in so many ways. She had never imagined herself with anyone other than Murdock. Until now. Guilt flooded her at the thought.

Daisy turned her full attention to the washtub and continued scrubbing the barn dirt from his shirts, only to catch a glimpse of him watching her again as he wiped his brow with his forearm. He set his hat back on his head and acknowledged her with a nod. When she blushed, he chuckled and went back to work. She watched him take his time instructing the twins.

She hung the next shirt to block the line of sight between them. Could she really move forward with her life? Tucker had sacrificed a lot to move here and marry her. Now he was building a room for her—for them.

But he was attaching it to the house Murdock had built. Was it possible to make the home that was hers with Murdock into a home and family for her and Tucker?

Chapter Seven

The next day saw a new pattern emerge. Chores were eagerly done before breakfast. Schoolwork was exchanged for life skill lessons as James and John learned basic carpentry. By supper all the menfolk were exhausted. No argument over going to bed occurred. Tucker only stayed long enough to bring in firewood and stoke the fire before heading to the barn.

On Saturday the rooster crowed, but it was too late to wake Tucker's new family. Both boys were already dressed and doing their chores. Watching Daisy slice bread for their breakfast, Tucker decided they probably woke the rooster. Ham sizzled on the stove. John brought in a basket of eggs, and Daisy prepared to scramble them.

"Boy, it smells good in here." Tucker closed the door against the morning chill and went to stand with his face to the fire. He extended his hands and rubbed them together before turning to warm the other side of himself. "We may have an early winter. We're going to have to keep a steady pace to get everything done before the cold weather comes in earnest."

"How much longer will you be staying in the barn?" Daisy kept her back to him as she cooked. When he didn't answer she turned around. Her brown eyes met his as if searching for something. Neither of them moved nor spoke. Her cheeks flushed, and she turned to the stove. Was she as confounded as he was by their new relationship? Friends? Yes. Husband and wife? Yes. And no.

Daisy asked again, "Do you know how much longer?" She set the plate of ham on the table.

"What?" Tucker cleared his throat and pulled his attention to the day at hand.

"How long will it take to finish the room? When will you be able to stay in the cabin and not in the barn?" She placed the eggs and bread beside the ham.

James brought in the milk and poured a cup for John and himself.

"Shouldn't take too long. The basic frame will be finished in a couple of days. Then the roof. That'll be the hardest part because of having to climb up and down so much. I thought I'd see if Will Thomas knows someone I could hire to help me for a couple of days." Tucker got a mug for his coffee and poured a cup for Daisy, too.

"When are we going to town?" James was always ready for an adventure.

"First thing after breakfast." Tucker took his seat at the table and extended a hand to John for the now-familiar blessing over their meal. It was John's turn to pray. Then they all served themselves.

"I didn't know you wanted to go to town today," Daisy said to Tucker.

"We need to get the horses. I need them for clearing the next section of land before Christmas. That only gives me a couple of months. I want it to be ready for next spring. There are a couple of other things that need to be taken care of." Tucker tore his bread and put a large bite in his mouth, cutting his ham while he chewed.

"You're planning on clearing more land? I thought we might talk about the finances and this year's harvest, and plan next year's planting before you actually started any work like that." She spread butter on her bread and waited for him to speak.

"The boys told me where the land lines are. I've ridden over everything and think clearing about ten more acres on the northernmost field would add nicely to the profit next season." He'd scoped out the land the morning after their wedding. Expanding the cultivated acreage every year was vital to his plan for the success and growth of the farm.

"I really think we need to talk before you make a lot of plans, Tucker. It's not like the ranch. Cultivating ten more acres is harder than adding ten acres of pasture for increasing the herd size. Planting season and harvesting for cotton is a lot more labor than herding a bunch of cows."

Tucker pushed his plate away and ran a finger around the rim of his mug. "Is it now?" It was becoming crystal clear to him that he and Daisy had a lot to learn about who the other had become over the past ten years. She was no longer the owner's little girl, and he wasn't just a ranch hand.

"I'm sorry. I didn't mean that the way it sounded," Daisy gushed like James would in the same situation. "You know what I meant."

"I thought we were going to get past all this apologizing, Daisy. You can say what you mean. I can take it. You're not sure I can handle cotton farming." She squirmed in her chair at his words. He stood and moved for the door. "Tell you what. Tonight after supper you can teach me all I need to know about cotton farming. And since tomorrow is Sunday, if you don't think I've learned it all tonight, you can teach me the rest after church in the morning." He took his hat from the peg and turned to the twins. "Want to help me hitch up the wagon?" Before Daisy could say anything they were all out the door, leaving her to do the dishes and prepare to go into town.

It felt awkward for Daisy to go into town with Tucker as her husband. Their trip on Monday had seemed almost surreal at the time. He'd been a friend from the past helping to preserve a future for her and her sons. Today they looked like any other family. She and Tucker knew it wasn't true, but others would see them and assume it was. In the hotel on their wedding day, Daisy didn't see anyone she knew well. Today they would encounter friends. Introductions would need to be made. Some people could ask questions. On the farm with just the family, they conducted themselves like the friends they were. In town, would people expect something else? And how many would judge them for marrying so quickly after Murdock's death? Feeling out of control again bothered Daisy.

"We need to go to the bank before we go to the livery," Daisy announced as they approached the edge of town. She chanced a glance at Tucker as he slowed the rig. He'd been quiet since breakfast, speaking only when necessary.

"The matter of the horses is settled, Daisy. I won't go into it again." The muscles in Tucker's jaw worked as he clenched his teeth together.

"But, Tucker, we have money to take care of the farm. The horses are part of the cost of running the farm." Daisy didn't understand why he couldn't see her point. She pulled her shawl closer around her shoulders against the chilly morning breeze.

"I gave my word, and I won't back down. The matter is closed." Tucker's voice was even, but allowed for no argument. Daisy wouldn't risk undermining him in front of James and John, who stood up to hang on the back of the bench seat as they entered Pine Haven.

"Can we have candy, Momma?" James hoped for a treat from the general store.

"Not today. We've had a lot of special things this week. We'll wait for another time." Daisy's tone was tight and controlled. James knew better than to persist.

"I still need to go to the bank." Daisy turned to Tucker as they stopped in front of the general store. The boys jumped off the back of the wagon and headed inside. "And the land office."

"Now just why is that, Daisy?" Tucker set the brake and shifted toward her. He dropped one hand to rest on his knee, elbow bent upward, and waited. "What do you need to do at the bank and the land office?" His expression was clear and open, which surprised her. She expected to see storm clouds in his eyes. She had mistaken his silence during their ride to town for controlled anger. Now she realized it was his refusal to argue when he considered the matter of the purchase of horses to be resolved.

"Well…" Daisy lowered her eyes and twisted the

drawstrings on her reticule between her fingers. She noticed how her new wedding ring caught in the sunlight. "I need to change my name on the accounts. And we need to add your name to the bank accounts and the deed for the farm."

"I see." Tucker was quiet for a moment and didn't take his eyes off of her. "So you're always planning and plotting in that mind of yours, aren't you?" He hopped to the ground and turned to help her from the wagon. "I'd be pleased to go with you to the bank and land office before we head back to the farm." He smiled up at Daisy and reached to take her by the hand.

Daisy stood and moved to the edge of the wagon without looking at Tucker. For the entire trip to town she'd considered how it would feel to acknowledge him publicly as her husband. Now she was taking the legal steps to prove his position in her life. Part of her felt disloyal to Murdock. Her mind knew that moving on was her only choice, but her heart wasn't ready to release the past. She was wrapped up in thought as she stepped from the wagon. Too late she looked up to put her hand in Tucker's. Her heel caught in the hem of her skirt, and she tumbled forward, missing his hand entirely. She let out a small squeal and felt her feet come out from under her.

Tucker's reflexes were quick. Strong hands encircled her waist to catch her in midair between the wagon and the ground. Daisy crushed against his chest with a thud, knocking the wind out of herself as he planted one leg backward to keep them both from falling.

"Got a lot on your mind, Daisy?" Tucker chuckled as he set her upright and released her.

"I just lost my balance," she harrumphed, stepping back to escape the fresh scent of his soap.

"Well, you nearly caused me to lose mine, too." Tucker teased and straightened his hat. "Are you okay?"

"Fine. Just fine." She turned to glare at him. How did he have the power to make her so uncomfortable? One minute he was her old friend laughing and teasing, and the next he was... The next minute she didn't know what he was. Daisy smoothed her skirt and pulled her shawl back into place before putting a hand to her hat and hair. Tucker stood blocking her path. Her gaze rose from the front of his broad shirt and climbed to his face. At his inquiring expression she added, "Thank you." Was everything about this man a question? She was much more comfortable in a world of absolutes. She'd easily read Murdock like the open book he was. She sensed Tucker held hidden layers she had no idea of, certain she held no experience to handle those many intricacies.

Making another attempt to peel away and discover something, Daisy asked. "Now exactly why are we at the general store? Aren't we buying horses today?" Taking a no-nonsense tone helped to restore her composure.

"More questions? Are you planning the morning in your mind?" Tucker teased her but only for a moment. She wondered what he'd think if he knew she was struggling internally to plan their entire relationship—not just the morning.

"There are some things I need to order. Will you help me choose?" Tucker took her by the elbow and escorted her into the store. The simple gesture sent a message of familiarity with a dash of possessiveness through Daisy. She was sure anyone seeing them would notice it, too. Once again she struggled to swallow the sense of betrayal she felt by allowing Tucker to hold her in ways only Murdock had.

A bell rang as Tucker pushed the door open, and the spring on the frame caused it to slam shut behind them. Daisy paused to allow her eyes to adjust to the dim interior. The smell of burlap and coffee beans assaulted her senses. Open barrels in the center of the floor boasted new merchandise. Worn wooden shelves against the walls held mundane, yet necessary, supplies. Bolts of fabric were stacked on two large tables under the front window. Tools hung on the back wall, and jars with brightly colored candy lined the counter by the cash register.

"Be right with you folks." Liza Croft called from behind the counter where she assisted a customer. Daisy saw James and John in the far corner looking through the small selection of toys. The swinging half doors, which separated the store from the storage room beyond, swung open and Liza's husband, Donald, came through.

"What can I do for you?" Donald Croft approached Tucker before he recognized Daisy. "Why, hello, Mrs. Mosley, how are you today?"

"I'm fine, thank you, Mr. Croft," Daisy answered and with one hand gestured toward Tucker. "I'd like you to meet Tucker Barlow." She took a slight breath as Mr. Croft reached to shake Tucker's extended hand. "My husband."

"Nice to meet you, Mr.—" Donald Croft stopped in midsentence still gripping Tucker's hand, and turned to look at Daisy. "Your husband?" He released his grip.

"Yes, Mr. Croft, Tucker and I got married on Monday." Daisy blushed slightly, quite uncomfortable with the explanation.

Tucker came to her rescue. "Tucker Barlow. It's nice to meet you, Mr. Croft."

"Call me Donald, Mr. Barlow. And congratulations on your nuptials." Donald turned to Daisy, "And you, too, Mrs. Mosley. I mean, Mrs. Barlow. Please forgive me. It might take me a time or two to adjust to your new name."

To Tucker he continued, "Welcome to Pine Haven. Now what can we do for you today?"

"We'd like to look at your furniture catalog. There are some things we need to order," Tucker explained.

"Right this way." Donald led them to the counter at the rear of the store. He lifted the hinged board at its side and stepped behind the large unit to retrieve the catalog. "What kind of furniture? I've got a couple of different companies. I can recommend what I know to be good quality if you'd like."

"That will be a great help. We need some bedroom furniture." Tucker answered because Daisy still had no idea what they were doing. She blushed again at the thought of discussing her bedroom with the store owner she knew only as a tradesman.

"I think this will be just what you need. The prices are marked, so I'll just leave you to browse until you see what you want. It takes about six weeks for most of these items to come, so bear that in mind when you're choosing. There are a couple of items the supplier keeps plenty of stock in, so those things come a mite sooner. The pages are marked. You can see the difference." Donald went to answer the clanging bell as yet another customer entered the store. He called, "Let me know when you decide," as he walked away.

Daisy stood close to Tucker and whispered, "Bedroom furniture?"

"Yes, bedroom furniture. Remember we talked about this." Tucker flipped the pages until he found something that suited his taste. "What do you think of this?" He pointed to a large bed with tall posts on each corner. The posts were carved with a curving scroll design. There was a matching dressing table with several drawers beneath a large mirror crowned with the same scroll design. Dark rich marble topped the drawers.

"It's lovely, Tucker, but I don't need anything fancy. We can just get a simple iron bed. I can use the chest I have now, and the mirror in the corner is more than adequate."

"I like it. This is what we'll get. Do you mind waiting the six weeks?" Tucker lifted his hand to signal Donald.

"Tucker, it's too much!" Daisy kept her voice low. "We can't afford it." Her eyes pleaded for him to understand before Mr. Croft came close enough to hear.

"It's part of the gift, Daisy." Tucker leaned close to her ear. His warm breath teased her neck and caused her flesh to tingle. "I never intended to build a room and not buy furniture. You said you'd accept the gift. This is part of it." Daisy was beginning to realize some battles with Tucker could not be won.

"If you insist," she finally acquiesced and stepped back, rubbing a gloved hand against the side of her neck to warm her skin.

"I insist." Tucker smiled down at her and leaned in close again. "Now that I know that works, I may have to insist on you not being so stubborn when I'm trying to be nice to you." He chuckled then, and Mr. Croft approached them, effectively cutting off any response from her.

Daisy watched Tucker place the order, wondering how he could afford such a purchase. The cost of the room and furniture was more than she could imagine, and he still insisted on paying for the horses. He was a mixture of what she needed and what she feared. She needed help with the farm and the twins, but she couldn't feel secure while he continued to spend so much money.

She prayed silently.

Lord, Tucker is a good and kind man. Help me. I'm so accustomed to handling everything in marriage the way Murdock and I did. I don't know how to deal with Tucker making decisions without discussing them with me. Give me patience. And give him wisdom. Please.

Chapter Eight

❧

"Daisy!" Peggy Dismuke's voice drew Daisy's attention to the opening door of the general store. Peggy embraced her, then pulled away to look into her face. "How are you, dear?" Peggy smiled at Daisy.

"And you, Mr. Barlow, how are you?" Peggy included Tucker in her boisterous greeting.

"Well, Mrs. Dismuke, and you?" Tucker nodded a greeting to the reverend's wife.

"You must tell me how you are, Daisy. I noticed your wagon and hoped you'd still be here when I arrived. I came to pick up my order." Peggy's excitement required no comment from Tucker. He excused himself and went to check on the twins.

Peggy turned and looped arms with Daisy. Closing the space between them, she whispered, "How are you? Really? Is he kind? Are you and the boys all right?"

Daisy laughed gently at her friend, "Yes, Peggy, we're all fine. Remember Tucker and I have been friends for years."

"I know, but it's been a long time since you've seen each other. And Murdock's passing was so recent. I just don't think I could do what you've done if I lost my dear David." Peggy squeezed Daisy's arm. "It's just unimaginable to me that you've got another man in your home so suddenly. I mean, I know the boys need a father figure, but what about your own feelings?"

Daisy extricated herself from Peggy's pull. "Peggy, as my friend I must ask you to stop and think about what you're saying." Pain filled Daisy's eyes, and tears threatened to fall from her lashes.

"Oh, Daisy! I'm so sorry." Peggy hugged Daisy close before tugging her through the front door and around to the side of the building for a small semblance of privacy. "I could kick myself. What was I thinking running on like that and you having to live through it? Please forgive me? I didn't mean to be insensitive."

"Don't worry about it. I'm just a little prickly these days. It's been a lot to absorb, and I'm not sure I'm handling it all well. I seem to keep saying things that upset Tucker. I don't mean to. It just happens." Daisy stared at the dust at her feet. "I didn't think it would be so hard since Tucker and I are friends." She looked up then. "I don't think I truly considered what it would mean to be his wife. I know my father wanted the best for me and the boys, but it's not easy to lose a husband. Murdock and I were together for over ten years." *Ten years.*

Daisy shook her head slowly back and forth. "My emotions are so confused right now." She clung to Peggy's hand like it was a lifeline. "Yet Tucker has been so kind. And generous. He's very good with the twins, too."

Peggy patted her hand and offered, "Daisy. I'm sorry. I know this is difficult for you. I should never have spoken to you as I did."

"You only said the things I've been afraid to think about. I feel like I'm being disloyal to Murdock if I don't mourn him properly, but I feel like I'm not being appreciative of all Tucker is doing if I hold back from building a relationship with him," Daisy lamented. "Pray for me."

"I will. I'm here for you if you need me and I promise to be a better friend from now on. I'll start by thinking before I speak." Peggy hugged Daisy again. "If you're okay, we'll go back into the store and see how your guys are getting along."

The two stepped around the corner and onto the wooden sidewalk. Daisy recognized Tucker's hat as he disappeared into the lumber mill office. She collected her sons and followed him, stopping briefly to post the promised letter to her father. Papa Warren would really be surprised the next time she wrote and told him all Tucker had been doing. She was having a difficult time absorbing it all herself.

Tucker had come onto the porch looking for Daisy. He was about to round the corner when he'd heard her talking to Peggy. His scowl had twisted into a look of tortured resolve as her words of pained confusion reached his ears. Soundlessly he turned and walked away from the corner, going in the direction of the lumber mill.

In his mind's eye he could see his mother wrestling with her feelings for the owner of the hotel where she worked when he was a boy. How often had he heard her crying when she thought he was asleep? Loyalty to her love for his deceased father had won. The owner's attempts to build a relationship with her were rebuffed, and she worked and mourned until the day she died.

Alone—except for Tucker. He knew Daisy was struggling with the same emotions. He also knew her love for Murdock would always be stronger than her friendship with him. It was a good thing he'd decided to keep his heart protected behind the barriers of his experience.

Tucker recalled the slicing anguish of separation he endured as a very young man when Alice Fields broke his heart. He'd surrendered it to her when he thought he'd won her love. How foolish he'd felt when she refused his proposal. She'd flitted away to her former sweetheart like a moth to a flame.

Pushing down the painful memories and focusing on the task at hand, Tucker entered the lumber mill looking for help to put the roof on the new addition.

Later, when Tucker exited the mill, Daisy and the twins were coming up the sidewalk.

"How did it go? Did you hire someone?" she asked.

"Two men for next Wednesday. We need to finish our business in town and get back to the farm so I can get to work. There's a lot to be done in a short time." Tucker tried to keep the gruffness out of his voice, but the echo of her conversation with Peggy still rang in his ears.

He wanted to get back to work on the cabin as soon as possible. Perhaps the exertion of swinging a hammer would relieve the tension building in the muscles between his shoulders.

Tucker set a brisk pace, and soon purchased two beautiful animals. He even asked James and John to give their opinions, assuring that each of them would be able to claim one of the horses for their own. They'd have to feed and care for the horse, but it would be theirs to ride. He stressed the primary purpose for needing the animals was to work the farm, so the boys would need to learn to work alongside him.

Not once at the livery did Tucker meet Daisy's gaze. He knew she'd think him upset that she tried to discourage him from buying the bedroom furniture. Why couldn't she back down from being worried about their finances? She'd been reluctant to let him give her the house addition, and now the furniture, as a wedding gift. He'd come here to make her life easier, but she seemed resistant to his efforts. Her grief was the most obvious reason for her to hold back her approval.

Actually he hadn't given her much choice. He insisted on paying for the horses. After all, it was their farm now. She had ten years invested in it, and she'd just told him she was going to sign it over to him. What was the price of a couple of animals compared to all she'd already given?

Tucker assured Jim Robbins, the livery owner, they'd be back within the hour to get the horses. Then he led his family onto the sidewalk and headed for the bank.

"Are you upset with me?" Daisy asked quietly. James and John were skipping ahead of them to join a young boy playing in front of the dress shop.

"Why would you ask me that, Daisy?" He kept his focus forward as he moved swiftly up the boarded sidewalk.

"Let's see. For one thing, you're not looking at me." Daisy stopped and stood still. Tucker took two long strides before halting.

"We've got a lot to do," he spoke over his shoulder. "I don't have time for one of your question and answer interviews right now. It'll have to wait till later." He immediately started walking again, leaving her no alternative but to try to catch him.

"Obviously something is bothering you. If it's about the furniture, I was surprised. I'm not accustomed to spending so much money." She increased her pace to keep up with him.

"You didn't spend any money today, Daisy." Without varying his speed or his tone, he corrected her.

"True." Daisy paused as if seeking the right words. "What I mean is I'm uncomfortable having that kind of money spent, especially on me."

"Your wedding present was money I spent on us." Tucker stopped abruptly and turned to face her, catching her off guard. If he wasn't so hurt by her words to Peggy earlier, he would have chuckled at her startled expression.

Tucker looked at her with deep intensity, daring her to misinterpret his next words. "I spent the money on our future, Daisy. On our marriage. I know you're mourning right now. I made it clear from the beginning I wouldn't rush you into anything. But I do see the bigger picture here. We are married. Once you've had time to grieve for Murdock, and absorb the fact that I'm your husband now, we'll need all the things I've been doing." He took off his hat and raked his fingers roughly through his red mane in frustration and rammed the hat back into place.

Taking a deep breath he continued. "Don't worry about the money I've spent or the decisions I've made. I'm a grown man, and I know what I'm doing." He heaved a low sigh and put a hand on her sleeve. "By God's grace, I'm a patient man. I can wait." He opened the door to the land office and ushered her inside, whistling for the boys to join them.

Daisy squared her shoulders and took yet another step toward making her marriage to Tucker official.

The land agent looked over his wire glasses at her. "May I help you, Mrs. Mosley?" he asked as he rose from his seat behind the massive mahogany desk. Its size lent an aura of power to the man whose stature was average at best.

"Good morning, Mr. Little. I'd like you to meet Mr. Tucker Barlow." Tucker moved to stand beside her, and the boys shared a chair by the front door. "My husband."

"Mr. Barlow, a pleasure to meet you. Please take a seat." Daisy and Tucker took the two seats facing Mr. Little's desk before he sank back into his chair. "What can I do for you today?"

Daisy spoke quickly. "Mr. Barlow and I married on Monday. I want to handle whatever paperwork needs to be done to make sure the deed to my farm is in proper order."

"I'm glad you came in. I was going to come see you myself next week. We usually give thirty days after the death of a husband before we call on the widow about the business of deeds." He took off his glasses and pulled a kerchief from his pocket to wipe the lenses. "Especially in a case like yours where there is no mortgage on the property. It gives more time for the business of death to be handled before a widow needs to move on with the business of life and the future," Mr. Little looped the temples of the glasses back over his ears. "My condolences on the loss of Mr. Mosley. He was a kind man. Must have been hard on you and the young ones—everything being so sudden and all."

"Thank you, sir." Daisy lowered her head to stare at the reticule in her lap, twisting the strings again. It was awkward to discuss her recently deceased husband with her new husband in the seat next to her. She'd have come alone to do this, but knew Tucker would have to sign the necessary papers. "We want to take care of the paperwork to transfer the deed, please."

Mr. Little reached for a dark accordion folder on the credenza behind his desk. He unwound the string and folded the large flap out of the way so he could retrieve two identical documents written on long thick parchment from inside. "I had this prepared for my visit to you next week, knowing you'd need to transfer the ownership of the farm after Mr. Mosley passed away." He turned the papers and pushed them across the desk for Tucker and Daisy to read.

"Transfer of Deed?" Daisy asked. "You were going to bring me a transfer of deed next week?" Her voice rose slightly, and she moved to the front edge of her chair. "Mr. Little, why would you have thought I would be transferring ownership of my farm? You did not know I was married."

"Mrs. Mosley," he began but started over when Tucker cleared his throat. "Mrs. Barlow, I meant no disrespect. It's my job to make sure the deeds in this region of Texas stay current. As a widow the property ownership of your farm came into question. That's not anything of my doing, but it's the way of land ownership since Texas became a state. I'm only doing my job." Mr. Little's words struck Daisy as a feeble attempt to prevent her from becoming upset.

"Mr. Little," Tucker said calmly, "I'm sure you must be aware of the law that passed just this year allowing women to own property in their name. A man in your position must surely keep up with such things."

Mr. Little put a finger inside his shirt collar and stretched it away from his neck. "I've read about that law, Mr. Barlow, but it hasn't been tested by the courts yet. Most land offices are not willing to take the risk of titling the property to women. The law is just too new. Men like me would be at risk of our jobs if something were to be handled wrongly." He swallowed deeply. "I'm sure you can understand my position."

"I understand the citizens of this community expect you to uphold the laws of the State of Texas, Mr. Little," Daisy interjected.

"Mrs. Mos— I mean, Mrs. Barlow, I am only one man. I do my best. Please, Mr. Barlow." Mr. Little sought support from Tucker but none came. Sitting up behind the desk and straightening the few stacks of paper he'd been working on, Mr. Little changed course. "It's no matter for concern now, anyway. Mr. Barlow here will go on the deed. There'll be no problems. So you see, there's a good solution for your family right here. It's good you chose to move forward so quickly Mrs. Barlow. Your life will be much easier than that of a widow who chooses to go it alone and loses everything. You made a wise decision indeed."

Daisy's eyes grew dark and dangerous. Tucker placed a hand on hers to keep her from coming out of her seat. "Mr. Little, if you will please make the deed to Mr. Tucker Barlow and Mrs. Daisy Barlow, I believe we'll both be satisfied." Tucker's request fulfilled his promise to ensure the land was safely hers.

"Mr. Barlow, we normally make the deed to the man only." Mr. Little showed his discomfort with the turn in circumstances. He obviously did not favor women owning land and was using his position in the official land office to resist the change in the law.

"I insist. Make the deed to Mr. Tucker Barlow and Mrs. Daisy Barlow." Tucker turned the heavy papers back toward Mr. Little. "I believe you have only to write our names on the top lines of both copies before we sign." With one finger he pushed the papers across the desk. Daisy was glad to see the land agent at the mercy of Tucker's insistence.

Mr. Little made a noise not unlike a snort and withdrew his pen from the ink well. "Don't come complaining to me if there's ever someone contesting this deed." He wrote their names as he spoke. "I tried to warn you. That law will never stand up in court. Women don't need to own property. Men are much more capable of handling business." He completed the wording and turned the papers for them to sign.

Tucker signed on the first signature line and turned the first copy to Daisy. She dipped the pen in the ink and blotted the tip. She took her time signing the paper. She took just as long to sign the second copy of the deed. Never had she imagined her name would be recorded in the government office on the deed to her very own land. She put the pen back in the stand, then held up the papers and blew the ink dry. A smile crept across her face as she turned to Tucker. She glowed with this new achievement.

Daisy passed the deeds back to Mr. Little so he could attach the land office seal, making the documents official. He retained one copy to keep on file at the land office, and Daisy carefully rolled her copy and tied it with a string he ungraciously offered. She and Tucker stood.

"Thank you, Mr. Little," Daisy offered, smiling.

"Mrs. Barlow," he grunted in reply.

"Mr. Little, I'm sure I'll be seeing you again. I trust the business relationship we have established today will stand us in good stead for any future dealings we may have." Tucker extended his hand and waited until Mr. Little shook it before turning to open the door. The twins exited first, followed by a very happy Daisy.

Tucker turned and said, "Good day, sir," before closing the door firmly behind him.

"Good day indeed." Daisy could hear Mr. Little grumbling, "Land owned by women! Humph!"

The business at the bank was expedited much more easily. Tucker was pleased to note how Daisy's mood was emboldened by the deed she held in her hand. Mr. Little's refusal to accept her as the legal owner of her farm reaffirmed Tucker's commitment to her. She needed him, even if she wasn't ready to accept him.

He raised one eyebrow slightly when he saw the amount of money Murdock had left for Daisy and the boys. Tucker could see Daisy's pride in being able to prove to him that she and Murdock had planned well. He also knew how quickly it could be gone without continued hard work and expansion of the crops.

If only Tucker's father hadn't been so sick before his death, he might have been able to make that kind of provision for Tucker and his mother. Maybe his mother would still be alive. Even if they hadn't been able to keep their land, maybe she wouldn't have died working in the hotel. There were a lot of things Tucker couldn't change, his past chief among them. But he was determined to pick up where Murdock left off and ensure Daisy and her boys had a hopeful future.

The twins were beginning to accept him. He hadn't sought to buy their approval with the purchase of the horses, but he was pleased to see them opening up to his efforts to teach them about responsibility.

Now, if only he could convince Daisy to trust him.

Would she be willing to work as well with him as she had with Murdock? He wanted her to come to the place where she could embrace his plans for their future. The joy of seeing her revel in the business achievements of the day was countered by the memory of her words when she confessed uncertainty about him to Peggy Dismuke. Daisy was a picture of contradictions. If he were honest, he'd see his contradictions, too. He was determined to avoid adding pain to her grief, but part of him grieved, too. Being so close to her and knowing she was out of his reach emotionally was wearing on him. He wanted them to build a family on their friendship. Would he have to let his guard down to do it?

Chapter Nine

Daisy eyed Tucker and the twins as they came in after working all afternoon on the addition. The new horses were safe in their stalls. She swatted at eager hands that reached for warm molasses cookies before supper.

"Those are for dessert. Go wash up, and we'll eat the soup. Then, and only then, you can have cookies." She smiled at Tucker who feigned a wounded look as he cradled his hand against his shirt.

"Watch out, boys! She wields a mean spatula!" he teased.

James and John hung their hats beneath his, and watched in disbelief as their mother refused Tucker even one cookie.

"The soup smells delicious!" John was first to the table.

"I like the smell of the bread best." James joined his brother.

Tucker took his seat and reached for John's hand. "It all smells wonderful, but I think we may have to fight for it." He chuckled and winked at Daisy before he bowed his head.

She didn't try to mask the mirth in her voice as she blessed the food and her family.

Passing the bread, Daisy spoke. "I see quite a bit of progress on the addition. You're all working very hard. I'm impressed."

James lifted his spoon and blew on the contents to cool it. "I think I might want to be a carpenter when I grow up." He put the soup in his mouth too soon and had to draw in a quick breath to cool his tongue.

"Slow down. Eat some bread while the soup cools." Daisy put a hand on his arm, causing him to lower his spoon. "You could save yourself a lot of pain if you'd learn to be patient."

Daisy realized as she spoke the words that she could benefit from their truth. If only she'd been patient with Tucker when the wagons of lumber had arrived at the cabin or when he was ordering the furniture. She could have saved herself the sadness of knowing she'd hurt him by resisting the things he offered her in kindness.

Tucker interrupted her thoughts. "We accomplished a lot today, but there's still more to be done." He looked to the tired boys. "Those horses of yours are going to need names. Any ideas?" He smiled at their reactions.

"We get to pick the names?" James was ecstatic. "Really? They don't have to keep the names they had at the livery?"

"How will they know to answer to their new name?" This came from John who was always thinking.

"They'll get used to it. You just have to remind them often. People do it all the time," Tucker explained.

"People don't change names," James insisted. "My name will always be James. James Rudolf Mosley." He stuck out his chest with pride at the sound of his full name. "I got the 'Rudolf' from Papa's papa. It's a family tradition."

"That's a fine tradition. I'm sure your papa was proud to have a son to name after his father." Tucker affirmed James. "But people do change names." He grinned as he challenged the twins. "Can you boys think of any time a person would change their name?" He put a spoon of soup in his mouth and savored it while they thought.

Daisy listened from her seat at the foot of the table, not sure she was comfortable with where this conversation could lead.

"What about when a man becomes a doctor?" Tucker offered. "People start calling him Dr. Smith, or Doc, instead of Mr. Smith. See what I mean? Now you try."

"Reverend Dismuke told us once at church that before he was a preacher he was a carpenter. I guess he had to get used to being called 'Reverend.'" John caught on to Tucker's line of thinking.

"That's good, John. What about you, James? Can you think of one?" Daisy asked.

James thought hard. "I know! When we got big enough to talk, we started calling you 'Momma.' No one called you that before. You were Daisy to everyone else." He smiled in triumph at contributing to Tucker's game.

"Good one, James," Tucker agreed. "I know another. I was a ranch hand before I came to live here with your momma and you boys. Now I'm a cotton farmer."

"Can you call yourself a cotton farmer before you farm any cotton?" James wanted to know.

Daisy laughed. "He's got a point. You are a cotton farmer in training."

"We'll see." Tucker laughed with her. "Just give me a chance to prove myself."

Quietly and without looking up, John said, "I heard Mr. Little call Momma 'Mrs. Barlow' today. Her name was Mosley like us before." Everyone was silent for a moment. Then Daisy spoke.

"Before that my name was Miss Daisy Marie Warren. That's the name my momma and papa gave me when I was born. That's what everyone called me until I married your papa. Then I became Mrs. Mosley."

"And now you're Mrs. Barlow, like the people in town were saying today." John's voice was soft and serious.

"That's true, John, but I'm the same person I was when they called me Miss Warren, or Mrs. Mosley, or Mrs. Barlow. I'm still me." Daisy tried her best to reassure John.

"But it's not the same, Momma. You were Mrs. Mosley when you were Papa's wife. Now Papa's gone, and your name's the same as Mr. Tucker's." His chin started to quiver. James began to breathe in deep slow breaths.

"I'll always be Momma to both of you." Daisy's voice was comforting.

"Boys, your momma is right. I've known her since she was a young girl. She's the same person she's always been. She's lived a lot of life since then. She had a good husband in your papa. She's got this farm. She has you boys. But she's still the same inside. Only her heart is bigger." Tucker explained in a way the boys would understand.

"How can you know that, Mr. Tucker?" John asked sincerely.

"John, I've known your momma a long time. I can

tell she's the same person when I look in her eyes. I can see right into that soul of hers and see all the love and kindness inside. She's still generous and good. That's how I know." Tucker looked straight into Daisy's eyes. She really felt he was seeing into the depths of her soul, searching for the young girl he'd known all those years ago. The slight tug at the corner of his mouth said he'd succeeded. She wondered what she'd see in his eyes if she searched deeply. The thought made her blush and look away. She wasn't ready to know the answer to that question—yet.

"Now, about those horses…" Tucker pulled his gaze from Daisy and focused on the twins.

"I wanna call mine Trojan. I hear that's a good name for a big horse." James immediately made up his mind.

John thought a moment longer and said, "I'll call mine Beauregard. It sounds important."

"Good names—both of them." Tucker dropped his spoon in his empty bowl. "Now if we can get some of those cookies from your momma without too much of a fight, we'll go out to the barn and make sure Trojan and Beauregard are settled for the night."

"I'll give you cookies, but we need to clarify one thing about names." Daisy brought the platter of cookies to the table.

"What's that, Momma?" James asked.

"Remember that a woman can be a doctor, too. I want my sons to grow up knowing women are important and should be respected."

"Your momma's right. There's another thing that happened today." Tucker snagged several cookies and took a big bite before finishing his thought. "Your momma is now a landowner. That's something that couldn't have happened before."

Daisy's face softened, and she looked at Tucker. "Thank you for your part in that, Tucker. I don't know what I'd have done if you hadn't been there today. Mr. Little made me so angry."

"That's what your papa was afraid would happen. Often new laws are resisted by the people who are supposed to implement them. I'm glad Mr. Little didn't have his way." He smiled at her and rose from the table.

"I mean it, Tucker. I appreciate the stand you took for me today. I won't forget it." Daisy blushed and reached for the empty soup bowls. "Now if you boys are going to see those horses again tonight, you better move. Mr. Tucker and I have some cotton farming lessons to do after you're in bed."

Chair legs scraped across the wooden floor, and small feet ran for the door. James had a cookie in his teeth, and John was trying to put one in his pocket.

"No cookies for the horses," Tucker called as he followed the boys onto the porch. He paused and turned to Daisy.

"You're welcome, Daisy. I only insisted you get what Murdock worked so hard for you to have. It wouldn't be right any other way." He tipped his hat at her and closed the door. She smiled, thinking about the deed safely locked in the box she kept hidden in the chest at the foot of her bed. She would forever be grateful to Tucker for helping to secure her ownership of the farm.

After Daisy washed the dishes, she pulled out the farm journal in preparation for Tucker's lessons on the cotton farm. It was difficult to look at the records and not think of the nights she'd spent recording the figures as Murdock taught her how to balance the many columns on the large yellow pages. She ran a hand across the heavy leather cover and remembered how happy Murdock had been when the crops started to pay off and their nest egg grew enough for them to put a bedroom on the house for the twins.

Daisy pictured him sitting by the fire, urging her to hurry and finish these same books so they could spend time together. She often sat at his feet in front of the fire, and he'd stroke her hair while they talked.

The love she felt for Murdock was so deep and long lasting that his absence created a void in her soul. They'd never talked about what they'd do if one of them passed away. They were so young they never considered the possibility. She should have known better because her own mother had died when she was a child. "Oh, Murdock, I miss you so." Daisy's voice was a soft moan. "If only we'd talked about this kind of thing, I'd know you'd be okay with the choices I'm making." Tears stung her eyes. She wiped them away with the back of her hand. She straightened her back and opened the journal to the numbers for the harvest they'd sold just weeks ago. "Know I'll do my best for our sons, Murdock. I promise."

With the boys in bed and a fresh pot of coffee on the stove, Tucker and Daisy settled at the table to go over the books.

"This is the journal for all our expenses and income." Daisy pointed to the page. "These are the figures for the harvest this year. We sold our cotton just before Murdock was killed." Her voice choked just a bit, and Tucker glanced up at her. He had chosen to sit on the bench the boys usually occupied so he'd be close enough to her to see the records as she explained everything. He reached and put a hand on hers.

"We don't have to do this tonight if you're not up to it," he offered.

"No. I'm fine." She slid her hand from beneath his and shifted a little farther from him in her chair. "It just brought back a lot of memories to bring this out."

"I understand, Daisy. You don't have to do this for me."

She shrugged one shoulder. "Really, I'm fine. This is important information you need to know. The sooner you start to learn the ins and outs of the farm, the better off we'll be come planting season. You've got to have all the facts about the finances. The profits, the time-tables and the costs."

Tucker pulled his hand off the page and reached for his coffee mug. "Teach away," he said, and the lesson began. Daisy showed him the detailed entries recorded in the pages of the journal since Murdock had bought the land. Tucker could see the wisdom they'd gained from their experience as each year progressed. Murdock had been a very diligent man when it came to his work.

An hour and a half later Daisy closed the journal and sat back from the table. "What do you think?" she asked. She seemed tired but not as emotionally spent as he'd first thought she would be. The mundane details in the journal must have helped her to detach from the sadness that threatened her composure earlier.

"Your records are excellent. I can see how you and Murdock managed to get the farm to this point." He stood and grabbed his coffee mug. "If you don't mind, I'd like to sit close to the fire while we talk. I've been folded up on that bench for about as long as a man my size can stand."

Daisy laughed. "It's a wonder you can walk at all." She put the journal away and joined him by the fire. He added another log and stirred the embers.

They sat in silence for a time.

"It's a lot to absorb in one sitting, but I think I have a good understanding." Tucker rocked slowly. "I did notice something, though."

"What?" Daisy sipped her coffee and stared into the flames.

"You didn't seem eager for me to clear that ten acres at the edge of the northern field."

"I just know how hard it was when we first got here. This next season will be a learning experience for both of us. I don't want us to take on extra work." Daisy finished her coffee and rocked gently.

"According to the journal, Murdock planned to clear that land this fall and have it ready for the next planting."

"That was before. I don't know if we can pick up where we left off last season. I'm not sure it's fair to you."

"So even though I instinctively picked the same ten acres Murdock chose, you don't think I'm up for the task?" Tucker stopped rocking and leaned toward her over the arm of his chair.

"That's not what I meant at all. Tucker, you keep misinterpreting my words." Daisy stilled her chair and leaned forward to meet his gaze. She shook her head as she spoke. "It's hard work. I didn't want to overload you as soon as you got here. Cotton farming is a lot different than ranching."

"I realize that, Daisy. I didn't just get off a train from a city back East. I've worked in Texas all of my adult life. Sure, I've spent most of my time on the ranch with your papa. But I've made a lot of friends over the years. Some of the closest ones own cotton farms. Your papa's ranch is almost surrounded by cotton these days. I've picked up a fair knowledge of the process. That's just one of the reasons your papa thought I'd be able to help you." Tucker turned to look into the fire. He couldn't tell her the main reason her father had given his approval of their marriage.

Tucker had been surprised all those years ago when Mr. Warren had approached him after Daisy had agreed to marry Murdock. *I know true love when I see it, Tucker. You might hide it from Daisy because she's so young, but I know how you feel about my daughter. Are you going to be able to let her marry Murdock without saying anything? I respect your feelings for Daisy. I'm guessing you didn't act on them because you're a little older than her, and the fact that you work for me—but most of all, because of her obvious love for Murdock. I don't want her to be hurt or confused right now.*

Tucker had thought no one knew his true feelings for Daisy. He'd done his best to conceal them. He had assured Mr. Warren he'd hold his peace and watched the woman of his heart pledge herself to the man of her destiny. He'd forced himself to bury his feelings for her all those years ago. And he succeeded. He was beginning to wonder if he'd buried them deep enough.

Daisy reached out and placed her hand on his sleeve, drawing him back from his thoughts. "Tucker, I'm so sorry. I had no idea. And here I was going on and on about the tiniest details. You should have stopped me."

"Don't apologize, Daisy. It's not your fault." He leaned back in the chair and closed his eyes, rocking again. "I'm not one to talk a lot about what I'm thinking. You should remember that, especially after all the times you and your sisters tried to quiz me about one thing or another." His slight grin gave a playful note to the words he spoke. He enjoyed teasing this woman who had a need to know the details of every situation.

She sputtered a small laugh. "Really? You mean you don't like to talk about your plans? Or what you're thinking? I would never have guessed you'd still be like that, Tucker. I'm so glad you reminded me." She laughed in earnest then.

When Daisy was a teenager, she and her older sister, Jasmine, had often asked him what he was doing or where he was going. She and Lily, the baby of the family, had been relentless in trying to learn his opinions on different people or situations. He never shared the slightest information, saying only that girls tended to want to know too much. They would tease him about being so quiet. She'd even told him once he'd wind up a lonely old man if he wasn't willing to talk to girls. His reply that girls would always be intrigued, as long as they thought he had a secret, had made them both laugh.

"Stop it, Daisy. Or I won't tell you another thing."

Her laughter deepened. Tucker enjoyed the ease of their banter. Many times over the years he'd reminisced about how she looked when she laughed, or how quickly she could become flustered. Even in her youth she'd been able to keep pace with anyone when it came to sharp conversation or a witty exchange. "I mean it. You'll be wondering what I'm thinking for a long time." Tucker teased her knowing it would be a good excuse for all the things he wasn't ready to say to her. "That's it." He rose from his chair. "I'm going to bed now. You'll just have to guess what time I'll be ready for church in the morning—" he grabbed his hat from the peg "—and don't even think about making me wait."

She was still laughing as he closed the door. He suddenly opened it again.

"Come bolt this door, Mrs. Barlow, so I can go to the barn." The door closed immediately. The firelight reflecting the laughter in Daisy's eyes had been more than Tucker could stand. He knew he shouldn't flirt with her the same night she'd been choked to the point of tears over her recent loss. Nor could he sit by the fire watching her laugh and not want to reach out and touch her soft face.

He stood on the porch, waiting to hear her light footsteps approach the closed door. When she slid the bolt into place, he backed down the steps with his hat spinning in his hands. He thought he'd seen a smile pull up at the corner of her lips when he called her Mrs. Barlow. Usually a humble man, a shiver of pride threatened to dance across his barricaded heart.

He turned and headed away from the cabin. Years before he had imagined proposing to her when she came of age. Instead, he'd watched her fall in love with Murdock. She was just as beautiful now as she'd been then. Her golden hair and tiny frame made her look fragile, but he knew her well enough not to be fooled. Daisy was a strong lady with her own mind. Her father may have asked him to come here, but if Daisy hadn't agreed, she would have sent him back to East River within an hour of his arrival. More than anything he had come here to take care of Daisy. His heart was frozen against the pain of rejection, but he couldn't sit idly by, working for her father, all the while knowing she was suffering as his mother had. The protective shell around his heart was in place to prevent others from hurting him. He was surprised that protecting Daisy and her sons was causing him to feel the tingling of new life inside. An unexpected thawing threatened his peace.

Tucker had loved Daisy long ago and never had the chance to show her. He had accepted her marriage to Murdock, squelched his feelings and contented himself to be alone. Now he had the chance to love her, but life had hardened him, and she was too hurt to receive his love. Even if he was able to resurrect it.

Chapter Ten

Freshly brushed hats on clean heads rode in the back of the wagon. Daisy sat next to Tucker as they left a full twenty minutes earlier than necessary. True to his word, Tucker had not told her what time he'd be leaving. She in turn had not told him what time the church service began. It was silly, but they both got a small pleasure from keeping the other guessing.

"Why did we have to leave so early?" James called from the back.

Daisy smiled and looked at Tucker. His eyebrows drew together, and he gave her a mock frown in admission of defeat.

"It's always good to be prepared." He answered James and then winked at Daisy, who knew he was covering for having teased her. "We're trying out these new horses today. I like to make sure I've got plenty of time when dealing with a new animal."

"Maybe you could open yourself up to the idea of sharing information now that you're married," Daisy chided in a lighthearted manner. "It could save you time and trouble in the future." She continued to smile, keeping her eyes on the road ahead of them. Tucker could play at holding back information from her if he wanted. He'd often won the mental games they'd played as friends before Murdock had come into her life. Winning was a refreshing change for her.

"Don't count on any great changes in the personality I've always had, Daisy." There was a sporting challenge in Tucker's tone. "You've known for years I'm not one for telling things just for the sake of telling. I like a good secret now and again."

Chatter from the back of the wagon interrupted them. "Mr. Tucker, I'm glad you let me and John help hitch the wagon. It's important for men like us to know all about our equipment." James was really getting into his role as a young man. Daisy wondered if perhaps Tucker was pushing them to grow up too quickly.

Tucker assured James, "You both did a great job."

John stood and put his hand on Daisy's shoulder. "Momma, did you know Mr. Tucker is gonna teach us how to shoot this afternoon?" His voice showed excitement about the adventure, but it also held a tremor of fear.

"Oh, Tucker, do you think they're ready for that?" Daisy turned in the seat to look at him, her lightheartedness gone in an instant. He held the reins loosely in his hands as he leaned forward with his elbows resting on his knees.

"These boys are ready to be young men, Momma. That means they've got a lot of learnin' to do. They'll need to know all about how to care for their horses and how to handle all the 'equipment' young James was talking about." He nodded in the affirmative. "And, yes, they'll be needin' to learn to shoot. It's important for a lot of reasons."

John sat down next to James, and the boys began their own conversation about all they would learn in the near future.

Daisy touched his arm. "Really, Tucker. I'm concerned about this. Guns are dangerous. Their father..." She remembered how horrified they had all been when she and the twins had come home from town and found Murdock dead in the corral, shot in the chest, blood everywhere. She squeezed her eyes shut in an effort to blot out the images in her mind.

Tucker covered her hand on his arm. "That's one of the reasons, Daisy." He spoke low so only she could hear. "They need to be able to protect themselves, and you, if necessary. They'd be scarred for life if something happened and they didn't know what to do."

He made sense, but the thought of her little boys handling guns troubled her. "What if they accidentally get hurt, or hurt one another?" Daisy's fear was unrelenting.

"I'll teach them about gun safety before I let them touch a gun. That's always first. Then they'll learn how to clean it. Then we'll move to the shooting phase. I promise to be careful and to teach them to be careful. But the last thing we need is for them to be caught unprepared in a dangerous situation." Tucker released her hand and focused on the road ahead. "Besides, they can help put more on the table than fish when they learn to shoot. I'm thinking about turkeys and other fresh meat."

Daisy still wasn't convinced. Her heart longed for the security of the life she'd known before Murdock's death.

Tucker reasoned, "It'll make them feel important.

They're old enough to learn. I'm sure Murdock would have taught them soon."

Her new fear of loss and vulnerability rose to the surface. "I know it makes logical sense, but I just couldn't bear it if something else bad happened to our family."

Tucker's heart squeezed tight when she called them a family. "That's where prayer and faith come into the picture. We'll both pray for their safety, and we'll do our part to prepare them for all they need to know in life. Then we'll trust God to protect them. It'll be fine." A family. He finally had a family to protect. All it lacked was the love he knew would never be his. He'd content himself with friendship. That's all Daisy had promised. It was all he could expect.

Daisy's smile was strained. "You're right. I'll just need to pray—now more than ever."

In an effort to lighten her spirits Tucker said, "I remember when you learned to shoot." His eyes were straight ahead, but there was humor in his voice. He knew she'd been successfully distracted from her worries when she cried out in her own defense.

"That's not fair! You know I wasn't trying to shoot you that day!" She blushed at the memory.

"I'm just saying the lesson I learned that day was to be careful when teaching young people to shoot." Tucker was trying not to laugh. "I still have a tiny scar where you got me with that buckshot." He could no longer contain his amusement. "I've never been so glad to be quick on my feet in my life!" Laughter burst from deep in his chest.

"Tucker, you know you walked right between me and the target!" Daisy again denied all responsibility for what she'd told him then was an unfortunate accident. "If you'd been paying attention, you never would have been hit. Besides all that, it was just a grazing sting. I didn't really shoot you!"

"If that's how you want to remember it, you go ahead. I was there. I know exactly what happened."

Daisy joined in his laughter now.

Tucker knew she was right. He had been distracted that afternoon. She didn't know *she* was the distraction. Tucker had tried to avoid her presence by retreating to the barn, not realizing her father intended to teach her to shoot. He'd come out of the barn thinking Mr. Warren and Daisy had gone back to the house, only to walk right in front of her target as she pulled the trigger for the first time. She'd rushed to check on him, after his dive in the dirt to avoid the full brunt of the blast. Daisy had been convinced she'd really hurt him, but only one pellet had grazed his left side. Horrified when she saw blood oozing through his shirt, she'd assumed he was seriously injured. He'd moaned and rolled in the dirt to torment her, until she found he was faking. Then the real trouble began as she pounced on him for scaring her nearly to death. Mr. Warren had to pull her off. Every hand on the ranch had teased both of them from that day on—him for walking around in a daze and her for bagging big game with her first shot. It was weeks before she forgave him. Smiling at the memory of the concern in her eyes that day lifted his spirits.

The smile faded. Daisy *had* been concerned for him that day. But she saw him as a friend then. And now. The precious love she had in her heart for a man—a partner for life—was for Murdock. Tucker knew the futility of loving someone who'd already given their love away.

Tucker's thoughts settled as they arrived at church, and he found a nice shady spot to leave the wagon. The boys jumped from the wagon and ran to wait for Mrs. Winters. Daisy had explained the woman would teach a Bible class for children fifteen minutes before the service began.

"Mind your manners," Daisy called as they disappeared around the corner of the church.

Tucker set the brake and jumped to the ground. He turned to offer Daisy his hand. She smiled down at him and said, "You know service doesn't start for another thirty minutes?"

"I gathered we might be a little early." He smiled at her before glancing around at the empty churchyard. "Are you going to stay up there until service starts, or are you going to come down here with me and remind me how important it is for me to talk to you about what I'm thinking?" he joked.

"Oh, I think I may just let you help me down and call a Sunday truce to the teasing." She giggled and moved the edge of the wagon seat. "I'm already tired. I was up an hour early not sure when you were going to try to leave."

"So what we have here, ma'am, is a tie."

Tucker lifted Daisy by the waist and set her on the ground. A lightness in her middle caught her breath. She tried to convince herself it was from the motion of being lifted and set to the ground, not from his nearness.

"Yes, I'd say we're about evenly matched," she agreed in a voice barely above a whisper. Looking into his face she was taken again with how masculine he was. Tall and strong, smelling fresh and clean. Her hands still rested on his broad shoulders where she'd balanced herself as he'd helped her from the wagon.

"Oh, you'd say that, would you?" His green eyes danced with merriment. "You think we're a good match?"

She meant as competitors; now he was being almost forward. She dropped her hands. Her eyes darted from side to side. Convinced by the warmth of her face, Daisy knew her cheeks flamed with color. Relief washed over her when Tucker spoke and eased her embarrassment.

"Definitely a day for a cease-fire," he agreed.

He offered his arm, and they walked toward the church. "Should we go inside and wait, or would you like to walk for a bit?"

"If you don't mind—" she turned to look at him "—I'd like to go in and spend a few minutes in prayer."

"That's fine with me." He opened the door. "Do you want me to join you, or would you like to be alone?" He waited for her answer.

Daisy looked in the doorway to the altar area. Her heart still raced a bit from having been so close to him. Had it really only been six days ago they'd come here and been married? So much had happened to her in the past month. She really needed a few minutes of solace with God.

"Would it be okay if I go in alone? I'd love to pray with you, but I feel like there are things I need to bring to the Lord alone today. Do you mind?"

Tucker lifted her hand from the crook of his arm and released her. "Not at all, Daisy." He looked into her face and smiled ever so slightly. "I do understand.

I'll join you for service." With a tip of his hat, he left her in the doorway.

Daisy knelt at the altar, hoping to find the comfort and strength she needed. She was flustered beyond distraction at how she'd reacted to Tucker just now. Could she grow to love him as her husband? She knew eventually they would have a more normal marital relationship, but would she really love him? The way she'd loved Murdock? He certainly was handsome, and kind, and committed. The list could go on.

He'd brought the kind of security the twins needed. But she wasn't sure she'd ever feel secure again. Not after losing Murdock and almost losing her farm. She hated feeling vulnerable. The men who'd killed her husband and stolen her horses had made her that way.

Would surrendering her heart to Tucker make her vulnerable to the same kind of loss again? For all his good points, she still couldn't handle the way he did things without even discussing them with her. Was she wrong to resist his decisive ways? A lot of women would see that as strength, but Daisy couldn't help feeling left out when she didn't know what was going on. He spent money—lots of money—without even asking what she thought. Her only hope was now that she'd shown him the bank balances and farm journal he'd understand more about their financial limits.

Daisy found it difficult to pray when she folded her hands under her chin as she knelt. The scent of him lingered on her gloves and drew her concentration away from her dilemmas. It weakened the sense of propriety she felt would require her to resist him for a reasonable time. What was a reasonable mourning period? Reverend Dismuke had said it was not too soon for her to marry. Many people in town hadn't been surprised by their sudden marriage. Peggy, on the other hand, had expressed disbelief that Daisy would even consider marrying again so soon. Maybe Daisy was trying to hold on to a past that was gone. Would that prevent her from considering all the possibilities a future with Tucker could bring?

I'm just not ready, Lord. Help me.

When the steeple bells began to ring announcing service would begin soon, Daisy took her place in the pew and waited for the twins and Tucker to take their seats with her. She sat staring at the cross behind the lectern, meditating on how good God had been to her. She'd seen some very hard things during the past few weeks, but God had provided for her at every step of the way. She missed Murdock terribly, but knew, according to the Bible she put her faith in, he was with God.

She thought about the verse in *Isaiah* that Tucker said he relied on to keep him from giving up. Over the past month she had definitely been walking with the Lord. Sometimes it felt as if she was so weak she could only crawl. Hopefully she would be able to run with God again—even mount up with wings as eagles and soar. She just had to wait on the Lord.

Tucker spent the time before service walking near the edge of the trees beyond the churchyard. He prayed, asking God to continue to give him patience and wisdom. Raising two sons would be hard for any man, but raising another man's sons in a way their momma could be proud of was difficult. His original concern for James and John was beginning to grow into a fatherly love. He could see their pain over their papa from time to time. At the oddest moments they would drift off in thought, and he knew they were thinking of Murdock. Daisy did the same thing. It was challenging to feel as though someone else was in the cabin with them sometimes. Murdock's memory was a powerful force.

Tucker had seen signs of God's healing love working in the hearts of Daisy and her boys. He thanked God for the moments when joy and laughter filled their home. As a lonely child, he'd craved the love of a true family. He had longed to receive the depth of love Daisy and the twins had for Murdock.

He asked God once again to help him walk when he couldn't run, and to build his strength and endurance. He no longer asked to fly like an eagle. He reminded the Lord of how long he'd been faithful knowing it had been God's will for Daisy to marry Murdock. He'd resigned himself to never having her in his life and had chosen to live alone, knowing there was no one else he would ever love. He needed to stay focused on his friendship with her and on building a relationship with the boys.

God had given him this chance to be with Daisy, and he was grateful. But he would keep his heart in check. He couldn't stand to be here day in and day out if he offered to love her and she refused. The only sure way for him to fulfill his commitment to protect her and the twins was to never open the door to the vulnerability of love. The risk of rejection was too great.

Alice Fields had taught him that lesson well. He'd tried to take the place of her former beau, only to be disappointed. Hope that he had found someone to spend his life with had turned to ashes when she returned to the young man who had earlier refused to commit to her.

It was a feeling he never wanted to experience again. More than once he'd learned the power that the love of a lifetime held over someone's heart.

Chapter Eleven

Reverend Dismuke preached of God's faithfulness, giving the example of God sending manna and water in the wilderness to the children of Israel. He stressed that God's provision didn't always come in ways we expected, but the Lord always provided for His children. The message comforted Daisy. She knew God would take care of her and the twins. He'd chosen Murdock to take care of her for the past ten years. She believed God had chosen Tucker to be her provider now. If only her heart would catch up to her new circumstances.

Daisy's shoulder brushed Tucker's sleeve as they stood together when the sermon ended. He smiled at her and offered to share his hymn book. He was so close, and so kind, yet so unsettling. He represented the comfort of familiarity and the apprehension of the unknown. Daisy was glad the hymn was familiar, so she didn't have to think as she sang the words. Her heart was stirring with the prayers she'd prayed earlier and the words the preacher had spoken. Healing was painful at best. Was the ache in her heart a little lighter today?

Had the divide in her soul begun to mend? How long would the process take?

The final amen was spoken and immediately Daisy and Tucker were surrounded by her friends and curious acquaintances. One by one, Daisy introduced Tucker to almost everyone in the small church.

Judy Thornton and her husband, Randall, were the last people to approach them. Daisy made the introductions, and Judy pulled her aside for all the details of her marriage. The friends hadn't spoken since Tucker had come to town. While Daisy was deep in conversation with Judy, she noticed Randall and Tucker walk outside. She hoped he'd make friends of his own now that he was living in Pine Haven.

Daisy smiled at the thought of her father's caution that it would be much easier to be married to Tucker than to have people make judgments if he were just staying at her farm. She could only imagine how differently this morning would have gone. As her husband, the people of Pine Haven were accepting of Tucker.

She turned her complete attention back to Judy and tried to catch her up on the happenings of the week. There was too much to tell in just a moment. The ladies agreed to have tea in the near future.

Daisy met Tucker at the wagon a few minutes later. The boys climbed into the back and complained of hunger.

Daisy accepted Tucker's hand. "There's a lunch of fried chicken and potatoes ready at the cabin. We'll be there before you know it. There are more cookies, too." She settled into her seat while he came around the wagon and climbed up to join her. "Since there's no need for more cotton farming lessons, we can make a picnic of it if you'd like. It's perfect weather today."

"Sounds good to me." Tucker released the brake and steered the wagon toward the street. Several people called greetings to them as they left the churchyard. "I like your friends, Daisy. They seem like nice folk."

"I'm glad. I know it's not easy to move to a new place and start over without knowing anyone." She folded her hands in her lap and held her back straight to keep from bumping into his shoulder as the wagon climbed onto the road.

Tucker cut his eyes to her. "I know you." He grinned. "And the boys."

"You know what I mean," Daisy countered playfully. "You left an entire life behind to come here. It's got to be difficult." Again she was surprised at the yearning she felt inside when they talked or spent time together. "Don't misunderstand me. I'm glad you're here, but I marvel that you were willing to come."

Tucker watched the road. "I had a lot of reasons." He paused, and she wondered if he was going to explain. "Life doesn't always turn out like we think, Daisy." She sat silent, and he continued. "Those boys needed a father. I know how that feels."

"But you'd never met the twins." What motivated a man to such a selfless act?

"Like I said, I know you." A slight smile pulled at one side of his mouth. She almost didn't see it in his profile. "I know you would want the best for them. If anyone could ever give it to them without help, it would be you."

Daisy looked at her hands as they twisted together

in her lap. "Thank you, Tucker. That's very kind of you to say."

"I mean it. You're a strong woman. But boys need a man." They approached the crossroads in the middle of town. He pulled at the reins and steered the horses onto the road that would take them to the farm. "And you needed a friend."

"It was still a big sacrifice for you," she insisted.

"I needed a friend, too." Tucker made a clicking noise inside his cheek to encourage Trojan and Beauregard to pick up the pace. "It was worth it."

Daisy pondered his words and matched his silence for the rest of the journey home.

Ants invaded the picnic, but it didn't keep the boys from enjoying their lunch by the pond. Daisy called them away from the edge of the water more times than she could count. Tucker stretched out on the grass, covered his face with his hat and dozed after eating his fill. She had laughed when he kept reaching into the basket of cookies saying, "Just one more." He'd pronounced her an excellent cook and promptly fallen asleep.

James and John played tag in the distance. Daisy was left to sit on the picnic quilt with her thoughts. She watched the twins frolic and missed their father. He had loved to come here on Sundays and play with them. She was glad the boys had those memories and hoped in time they would play with Tucker in much the same way. They were adjusting to working with him and had been pleased when he taught them about the horses. They respected him, but she wondered how long it would be before they accepted him as their parent.

Tucker moaned and she turned to study him, watching the even rise and fall of his chest as he slept. Tall and broad and strong was the impression he first made on her when she was a young girl. She'd watched him rope and brand cattle on her father's ranch. Daisy was always amazed at how gentle he would be with a colt and how strong he was in the saddle. More than once he'd held his temper when a lesser man would have lost his. She remembered his constant teasing, his sense of humor and most of all his friendship. Memories of their easy banter and the way he listened to her came to mind and made her smile. He really was a dear friend to her then. Never imagining he'd be her husband, she'd laughed with him and told him all her woes. She remembered the day she'd married Murdock, how Tucker had hugged her close and whispered against her hair to wish her happiness. He truly had been there for her in her youth. She understood why her father had sent him to her now. Papa knew their friendship was a good foundation for a successful marriage.

Daisy studied the ring he'd given her on their wedding day. It was uniquely beautiful.

"Do you like it?" Tucker's voice startled Daisy from her reverie.

She flattened her right hand across her chest to calm herself and caught her breath. "Yes, very much. It's beautiful. I never expected a ring." Daisy angled her hand for a better view of the intricate vines and leaves. "Tell me the story behind it."

Tucker propped up on one elbow and pulled a stalk of grass from the ground to twist in his fingers. He focused on the thin blade. "It was my mother's." He looked up at her then.

Her face softened. "Oh, Tucker, what a precious gift.

I'm honored to wear it." She fingered the tiny band with her other hand.

"Momma was small like you." He continued to twist the grass and look into her eyes. "She was determined like you, too. And spunky. She didn't like surprises too much, and she always wanted to know what was going on. A planner who didn't want to be caught unawares." He smiled at her. "Kinda like someone else I know," he said with a lift of his brow.

Daisy smiled at him and spoke softly. "I think I would have really liked her."

"I know she would have liked you. She was a survivor, too. I never felt like she'd give up on anything. She taught me to hang on to my dreams no matter what and never settle. Momma always said it would be better to do without than to settle for less than your heart's desire." His eyes grew distant, as if lost in the memory of her as he spoke.

"What was her name?"

"Grace." He spoke the name reverently. "She said her momma and papa must have known she'd need the grace of God to get through the hard life she had to face, so they spoke it over her every day when they called her name." He tossed the grass stalk away and sat up, resting his forearms on his knees as he watched James and John in the distance. "My momma was a good woman. She'd be proud for you to wear her ring."

"Thank you, Tucker." Daisy was humbled by his comparison of her to the mother he so obviously adored. "It's a truly wonderful gift."

A few minutes later they packed up and rode home. The boys were full of talk about who would be the best shooter. Tucker and Daisy went inside, while the twins headed to the barn to wait for Tucker to teach them about gun safety and maintenance. They balked in the beginning, thinking they should shoot first and then clean the guns, but Tucker held fast to his plan.

Tucker set the picnic basket on the table. "I'll be back to let you know before they actually start shooting," Tucker teased Daisy. "I wouldn't want anyone to get hurt accidentally." He smiled and closed the door as her dishrag sailed through the air. It splattered against the door and water ran down the wood in the exact spot his face had been. She could hear him laughing as he went down the porch steps.

Shooting lessons went off without a hitch. James was a good shot, but John was a natural shooter. Daisy had been allowed to watch as long as she promised not to interfere. The boys insisted shooting was a man's business, and they should learn from a man. They thrived under Tucker's watchful eye. She smiled at the bonds she witnessed forming in their relationship. James and John didn't even realize how much they were looking to Tucker for instruction. Once again, she offered a silent prayer of thanks for Tucker's presence in their lives.

After a supper of pancakes and sausage, the boys went to bed early. Daisy and Tucker sat in front of the fire, eating cookies.

"Do you still play dominoes?" Daisy asked.

"Do you still cheat?" Tucker laughed in response.

She planted both hands on her hips and lifted her head. "I don't have to anymore. I know how to win fair and square." The determination of her voice came across as the challenge she intended. She retrieved the box of dominoes from a shelf over the bed and moved to the table to set them out.

"Sounds to me like you're ready to prove something, Daisy." Tucker came to join her, bringing the plate of cookies, and set his glass of milk on the table. He reached for the dotted tiles. "I think we'll just have to see how much you know. Strategy was never your strong suit. You weren't patient enough to plot your opponent's defeat." He turned the tiles facedown. Daisy shuffled them around while Tucker adjusted the lamp so they could see the game.

"Oh, we'll see all right." Daisy perched on the bench and sat at his elbow so she could reach the game. "I'll even let you take the first move."

"No, ma'am, you won't. We'll do this fair and square as you say. Ladies first."

"Not and have you say you gave me an advantage. We'll draw tiles. High tile goes first." They both reached for the same tile, their hands touching for an instant. Daisy jumped back and then laughed to cover her reaction to his touch.

"You can have that one, I was using it as a decoy," she joked and reached across for a different tile. "Show yours first," she taunted.

"No. We'll show them together. On three. One, two, three." They turned the tiles over.

"I cannot believe it!" Daisy was indignant. "How did you get the double six tile?"

"You gave it to me." He smirked and stirred the tiles to mix them up again. "Thank you."

"Well, that's the only thing I'll give you in this game," Daisy insisted.

"We'll see."

Tucker started the domino train, but Daisy quickly proved her skill. After several minutes with Daisy leading the game, Tucker finally caught up to her score and passed her with one brilliant play. On his next turn, as he reached to play another tile, she grabbed his hand and contested.

"Oh, no, you don't! You can't play that there."

He laughed saying, "And just why not?" Tucker tried to tug his hand free, but she wouldn't release him.

"You must have moved something while I was getting more milk."

"Now that is just what I would expect you to do." He used his other hand to try to place the tile. Daisy promptly captured that hand, too.

"Stop trying to play that tile. We're in the middle of a contested move here." She laughed and held both his hands securely, her elbows on the table to leverage her hold on him.

"I moved nothing when you were getting your milk." He grinned and leaned close to her face to make his point. "Now about what I did or didn't do when you weren't paying attention—" he was laughing now, too "—I'll never tell."

"I knew it." Daisy narrowed her eyes and leaned closer still. "You were accusing me of cheating all those years ago, but it was you all along," she goaded him.

"I've seen you swap tiles when you thought no one was looking." He narrowed his eyes and matched her accusatory tone, their faces inches apart. "Don't try to deny it. You can't stand to lose."

Daisy shook her head playfully, "To that I must confess. I do love to win." A lock of hair fell across her forehead and in front of one eye. Tucker pulled a hand free and slowly pushed the stray tress behind her ear. Lamplight danced in his pupils as his gaze followed the motion. Her brown eyes widened. She drew in a small breath as she realized the intimacy of their posture. Backing away hesitantly and dropping her gaze, she released his other hand and pinned her hair back into place.

"I'll let it slide this time, but I've got my eye on you now." She picked up her glass and paused before taking a drink. "Don't let it happen again." Daisy sipped the fresh milk and set the glass on the table.

A cry from the bedroom brought Daisy to her feet. She was opening the door before Tucker was out of his chair.

John sat straight up in his bed screaming, "I'm sorry, Papa! I didn't mean it! I'm sorry!"

James awakened as Daisy pulled John into her arms and cradled the back of his head with her hand. "It's okay, baby. Momma's here. It's okay." She rocked him and made shushing sounds in his ear.

Tucker stood in the doorway.

"It was just a bad dream, baby," Daisy soothed.

"No, Momma! I shot Papa! In my dream I shot Papa! It's my fault Papa's dead. I should have been here to keep him safe the day the bad men came. It's my fault! I'm practicing to be a good shooter now, but I didn't even try to save Papa! I didn't protect him!" The small boy wailed and refused to be consoled.

"I miss Papa." James joined the crying of his brother, and Daisy reached with one hand to draw him into a circle of comfort with his brother.

Tucker came into the room. "What can I do?" he asked Daisy. She shook her head in response and gently rocked the boys in her arms. The sorrow in her soul slipped over her lashes to wet her cheeks.

"We all miss Papa. It's okay. We miss him because he loved us so much, and we loved him." Daisy tried to soothe them, but even a month after Murdock's death she didn't know how to explain this tragedy to her young sons. She didn't understand it herself. How could she make sense of it to them? The three of them sat on the bed, huddled together, rocking and crying.

Tucker quietly walked away, closing the bedroom door behind him. He put away the dominoes and stoked the fire. Taking his hat from the peg he had come to think of as his own, Tucker looked around the room. Signs of Murdock were everywhere. The peg, the rocking chair by the fire, the chair at the head of the table—all these things had belonged to Murdock. Even the scent of the sausage from supper came from a hog Murdock had provided for this family.

Tucker heard the muffled crying from the bedroom and walked outside. He closed the door and sat on the porch Murdock had built, in the rocker Murdock had made for Daisy, and waited over an hour until he heard her bolt the door with a bolt Murdock had installed.

Walking across to sleep in the barn Murdock had built, the vision of Daisy holding her sons and crying with them filled his mind. Their pain was thick and fresh.

How long would it take for them to heal? What would life be like when they did? What would his relationship with her be when the boys were grown? Would she grow weary of him and only tolerate him? He knew he'd never be who she truly wanted. He had endured his mother's sadness when his own father had died. It had stayed with her until her death. Daisy's father still held firm to a reverential love for her mother's memory. Such love stayed with a soul forever.

Tucker had tried and failed to be that kind of love. Suffering the bitterness of rejection from Alice as a young man had been painful. When the fresh-faced beauty he'd given his heart to in his youth pushed him aside and went back to her first love, his heart had fractured. Her love for another so strong, she hadn't even tried to keep from hurting him.

A man learned from that kind of experience that a woman's heart would always belong to the first man she gave it to. No matter how hard another man tried, he'd never capture the spirit of true love from her. Once spent, it was gone. Like fragrant perfume poured out, a lingering scent only on the one anointed. All others merely caught a hint of the essence of what once had been.

But the pain of losing Alice didn't match the anguish of seeing Daisy fall in love with Murdock and losing the chance to share his love with her. That's when he learned to withhold his heart. It was the only way he knew to protect himself from certain rejection. It would also protect Daisy by not making her feel she must love him. Because he knew she never could.

Again he prayed for the patience to walk when he wanted to run. Then he prayed what he was sure was a selfish prayer.

God, please heal this family of the pain they still suffer. Let us become a family.

Chapter Twelve

Morning dawned colder than the previous days. The sound of Tucker hammering could be heard before the twins finished their morning chores or Daisy had breakfast prepared. With only two days before the men came to build the roof, he had a lot to do.

"Breakfast!" Daisy called from the front door. James was carrying the morning milk when he followed John from the barn. Neither boy moved with their customary liveliness. Tucker watched them go up the steps and through the door before he approached the front of the house. He wondered what mood would meet him inside the cabin. Last night was probably not the first time Daisy had dealt with nightmares since Murdock had died. Were the episodes further apart now? Had he sparked some new pain by teaching the twins to shoot? Never one to avoid the inevitable, Tucker entered the cabin.

Silence greeted him. He hung his hat and poured his coffee. John watched with sad eyes as Tucker pulled the chair back to take his seat. Tucker felt like an interloper but knew it was best for the boys to accept his presence. He'd earned the right to be here by taking on the responsibility for this family.

"Good morning."

"Good morning, Tucker. I trust you slept well." Daisy set a basket of hot biscuits on the table and took her seat.

"Yes, thank you." He hesitated to ask after her night given the events of the previous evening. He reached for John's hand. Slowly John reached out without looking up. Tucker bowed his head and prayed.

"Lord, we thank You for this fine breakfast. May You bless it and the hands that prepared it. Guide us as we work today. Help us to look to You for comfort and healing. Amen."

"Amen" came from Daisy. Not a sound came from the boys.

"Eggs?" Daisy passed the bowl to James. "You're after it mighty early today, Tucker."

"The men I hired to help with the roof will be here on Wednesday. We've got to make sure we're ready before they arrive." He spooned a generous portion of eggs onto his plate. "Are you boys done with your chores? We could get started right after breakfast."

James pushed his eggs around on the plate with his fork. "I'm not feeling very well today. I think I need to stay inside." He never looked up from his food.

"Me, either. My stomach hurts." John didn't even pretend interest in his food.

Daisy reached out to touch James on the forehead. "No fever." She stood and did the same to John. "You're not warm, either." She sat back down. "What is it, boys? Why are you trying to convince me you don't feel well?" Daisy waited patiently. The twins looked at each other as if silently communicating what to tell their mother. It appeared James was to be the spokesperson.

"We don't want to help with the addition." He didn't look at Tucker but stared straight at Daisy.

"And why is that?" she asked with restraint.

John hung his head lower.

"We don't want anything to be different. Everything's changed too much. We want it back like it was—like Papa built it."

Tucker set his fork down and waited while Daisy processed this declaration.

"I see," she said. "Is this how you feel, too, John?" The voice was low, but tight with the effort to control her emotions.

"I don't know." John was not as certain as his brother.

"Tell me what you mean, John." Daisy pressed him.

"James and me talked after you fell asleep last night." John still didn't look up. "He thinks Papa wouldn't want us to change things—that Papa had it like it was supposed to be."

"Is that true, James?" Tucker admired Daisy's patience, but could wait no longer to get to the bottom of the situation. He knew the pain the boys were in and wanted to help, but he needed to hear from them what they were thinking.

James looked at him defiantly. "It is. Our papa built this house. And you just came here and started changing things. We don't want it different." A small chin jutted forward.

Daisy inhaled slowly. "James, apologize to Mr. Tucker."

"I won't do it. It'd be a lie. I don't like him changing things. I won't say I do."

"James!" Daisy began.

"James—" Tucker held up his hand to signal Daisy that he wanted to speak "—there are some things you need to understand."

"I don't want to understand," James interrupted.

"I want you to listen to me for a minute, son. I'll speak respectfully to you, and I'll expect the same from you," Tucker admonished.

"You're not my papa! You can't talk to me like you are!" James stormed from the table and ran out of the house, slamming the door behind him. Daisy's call for him to stop was ignored. She rose to follow, but Tucker stopped her.

"Let him go, Daisy."

He turned to John and calmly asked, "Is that how you feel, John?"

"Not really, sir." John looked up for the first time. He put a hand on the table and worried his fork between his fingers. "At first, I didn't know what to think about you being here." He looked at Tucker's face and held his gaze steady. "I miss Papa something terrible. I didn't want anyone to take his place. It was like if we left everything the same, maybe one day we'd wake up and Papa would be here—like it was all a bad dream."

Tucker patted John's hand on the table. "What about now?" he encouraged him to continue.

"Now I know you better. I know you liked my papa. And you're Momma's friend. I didn't want to like you at first, but now, I think it's kinda like you're trying to help us." The young head fell again. "And I know Papa's not coming back. It wasn't just a dream."

Daisy sat quietly. A lone tear slid down her cheek. Tucker imagined the intense clenching of her heart. One of her sons was tormented by the thought of letting go of his papa. The other was dealing with the emotions of actually doing it.

Tucker put a hand under John's chin and lifted his face. "Thank you, John, for being so honest. I think we'll be able to help your brother because of the way you've described all you've been feeling." Tucker pushed his chair away from the table. "Let's go find him and talk to him, man to man." He extended a hand to John.

John sniffed loudly and put his small hand in Tucker's much larger one. "Okay. But you may have to make him be quiet so we can tell him. James talks more than he listens." John spoke with the honesty of a child.

Tucker smiled. "We'll both talk to him. I'm sure he'll listen then."

He laid a hand on Daisy's shoulder as they walked by her on the way to the door. "Do you think you could put our breakfast back on the stove so it'll be warm when we finish our conversation? We're going to need a good breakfast because we've got a hard day's work ahead of us." She dabbed at her eyes with her apron and gave him a watery smile, nodding her head.

Tucker and John found James by the creek. He was skipping rocks but didn't turn around when Tucker was certain he'd heard their approach. Tucker picked up a few pebbles and encouraged John to do the same. They all stood on the bank for several minutes, skipping rocks in silence. Tucker threw his last rock and sat on a fallen tree trunk close to the water's edge.

"Seems like we've got some things we need to talk about, James." Tucker was the first to speak.

John came to sit by Tucker, but James continued to skip his stones.

"There's something you don't know about me, James." Still no response. "My papa died when I was five years old." James dropped his hands to his sides. The pebbles he held fell and rolled into the creek.

John looked up at Tucker in disbelief. "Really?"

"Yes."

"Then you know how we feel," John decided.

"I do," Tucker said.

"Did your momma marry some stranger then?" James asked but didn't turn around.

"No, she didn't. As a matter of fact, my momma never married again."

"Then you don't know how we feel, do you?" James was still defiant.

"I know how it feels for no one to care except my momma." Tucker kept his tone calm.

Silence permeated the air for several minutes. Tucker gave them time to absorb this new information.

"After my papa got sick and died, my momma took care of me all by herself. She had to work in a hotel, cooking, and washing dishes, and cleaning rooms. They paid her by giving us a room and food but almost no money. Sometimes, if a customer liked the food a lot, or wanted some extra work done, like washing their clothes, they'd give Momma extra money. That's how she bought our clothes and shoes."

"How'd you both live in just one room?" John was curious.

"At first I was little, and we'd sleep at the same time. Momma would make me a pallet on the floor next to her bed. She'd even give me her pillows so the pallet was extra soft. Then later Momma would sleep in the afternoon after her work was done, and I'd sleep at night while she prepared the meals for the next day. When I got older, I'd go to school in the morning. I think she took naps between cleaning the rooms and cooking the next meal."

"I never knowed anybody whose momma had to work a real job. Except Reilly Ledford. His momma sews dresses for ladies. But he don't have a papa." John relayed his only known comparison to Tucker's situation.

"What about your house before your papa died?" James finally asked.

"The laws were different then. The only way Momma could have kept our land was to marry again. Because Papa had been sick so long, he had to borrow money from the bank to pay the doctor. When he died the bank owned the land, and me and Momma had to move."

"That's not right!" James said. "Your papa probably wanted your momma to have that house."

"I'm sure he did," Tucker agreed, "but it wasn't possible without a husband to work and pay for the land. So we moved to town, and Momma got the only job she could find. I got a job helping at the hotel when I was twelve. I'd help clean tables in the restaurant or carry people's luggage to their rooms. It took all my money to help buy the things we needed. The last year we were there, I was able to get a small room for me so we'd both have a bed. Then we didn't have to take turns sleeping anymore."

"And she worked there for always and didn't want to get married to another man?" John wondered.

"Momma worked there for ten years. One day she got real sick. The doctor said she was so tired from all the work she just couldn't get well again." Tucker felt complete honesty was the only way James and John would see why sometimes adults made decisions that were difficult for children to understand. "And then she died. I got a job on a ranch outside of town and worked there for a couple of years. Then I met your Papa Warren at a cattle auction, and he hired me to work for him. I've been there ever since, until the day I came here and married your momma."

The twins thought about all he'd said for a few moments. "Is that why you married Momma? So she wouldn't have to go work at the hotel and make us sleep in a hotel room by ourselves at night? And so she wouldn't get tired and sick and…die?" John spoke again, his face full of worry.

"That's why I know what your momma was facing trying to raise the two of you without your papa. And how hard it would be for her to keep the farm your papa wanted you to have."

Tucker stood and went to put a hand on James's shoulder. "Easy or not, like it or not, life needs to be dealt with as it happens. That's how boys become men."

John walked to the creek bank and stood on Tucker's other side. All three stared over the rippling water.

"I won't try to take your papa's place. But I must take my place of responsibility. I came here to take care of your momma and both of you. That's what I'm going to do." Tucker asked, "Can you understand that?"

"Yes, sir," both boys replied. James's voice was quieter than John's, but just as sincere.

"Do you boys understand that your momma married me so you would be taken care of?" The twins nodded. "This is a difficult time for her, too. How about the three of us work together to help her through it?"

"I will," John agreed instantly.

Tucker had a hand on the shoulder of each boy now. He jostled them playfully. "What about you, James? Are you willing to give your best effort for us to become a family?" Tucker wanted to make sure James was on the same page with his brother.

"Okay. I will," he spoke softly, "but it still hurts."

"I know it does. I promise it will heal in time, but we've got to pull together and help one another now." Tucker turned and went down on one knee so he was eye level with the boys. He looked directly at James.

"One more thing. You can't disrespect your momma— or me. Do you understand?"

"Yes, sir," James answered. "I'm sorry."

Tucker wrapped the boy in a hug. "I forgive you. I know you were acting out of pain. I want you to know it's okay to feel the pain and work through it, but it's not okay to hurt others in the process. You'll need to apologize to your momma." He opened an arm to include John in the hug.

"I promise you both I'll do my best to take care of you and your momma." He released them and stood. "Now let's go eat a man's breakfast, so we can do a man's work. You ready?" They all walked up the hill together. Tucker hoped he'd been able to help the twins. And in turn help Daisy. He prayed as he walked toward the cabin.

Lord, please let these boys understand. Death is hard to deal with at any age. Please show mercy to these children. And I'm going to need more wisdom, too.

Daisy watched the boys work with Tucker that afternoon. They hauled scraps of lumber to the woodpile, held boards for him to saw and carried the nail bucket to wherever he was nailing. Tucker taught them a new tune to whistle while they worked. Daisy was sure she'd be hearing that song deep in the night in her sleep.

She took lemonade and cookies to them for an afternoon snack. They all laid aside their tools. The twins sat on the edge of the floor, feet dangling where the new back steps would be one day soon.

Tucker walked to the side of the house, and Daisy followed him. He drained his lemonade glass and wiped his mouth with his sleeve. She chuckled. "Try licking that off your face next time, so I don't have to wash it out of your shirt. Sugar is messy."

"Anything to oblige, ma'am." Tucker made a big show of trying to lick his lips clean of any lemonade residue.

"You are a silly one." Daisy laughed.

"How about you and I take a walk after supper tonight?" Tucker looked over the fields as he asked. "We haven't had much opportunity to talk without the boys nearby. I think it's time we did."

"Okay." She spoke tentatively. "Anything in particular you want to discuss?"

"No one particular thing." He turned and smiled at her, his green eyes alight with something she hadn't seen there before. "I'd just like the chance for us to spend some time alone." He handed her his glass. "Thank you very much. That was very refreshing." He touched the side of her face with the back of his hand and headed back to work.

She stared after him and said, "After supper, then." Her free hand moved to cover the side of her face, and a small smile tugged at her lips.

What could Tucker possibly want to talk about? Her impatient streak had wanted him to tell her immediately, but she knew his stubborn streak would hold out until after supper. Or could it be when he'd said there was no particular thing he meant it? Did he want to spend time with her—without the boys—like they would have if they'd had time for courting before they'd married? That would be an entirely different matter. One she couldn't get out of her mind for the rest of the afternoon.

Chapter Thirteen

❧

The boys sat on the floor in front of the fire, reading after supper. It was almost November. Daisy didn't want them behind in their work before they had to transition back to the town's school after Christmas. They asked her earlier in the afternoon what it would be like this year. She hoped that all of Tucker's spending wasn't giving them the idea they'd celebrate the birth of Christ by exchanging costly gifts. The homemade treasures in the chest at the foot of her bed were more valuable to her than anything from the general store.

Telling the boys they'd be in earshot if needed, Tucker and Daisy went out the front door for the promised walk.

The stars were amazing against the deep, bluish-black sky. Daisy threw her head back and spun in a circle, taking in the beauty of the night. Frogs croaked near the creek, and crickets chirped their night song.

"It's such a beautiful night. I don't remember the last time I was able to enjoy this time of night." She stopped spinning and stood looking overhead with her arms wrapped around her middle. "I've been so busy trying to be a momma and papa that I haven't taken time to relax."

"Shall we?" Tucker extended his arm, and she looped her hand in its protective circle. She appreciated the warmth of his nearness in the evening chill, but she was careful not to get too close. Her mind and heart sent each other mixed signals when she was in close contact with Tucker. They walked to the end of the lane in companionable silence.

"How are you, Daisy?" Tucker ventured as they strolled back toward the cabin.

She shrugged one shoulder. "Getting better I suppose."

"I'm glad to hear it." He pulled his elbow into his side and squeezed her hand against his torso, placing his other hand over hers. The warmth of his hand gave her a slight chill. He pulled her closer. Part of her wanted to pull away. Part of her didn't.

They walked on a little way before he spoke again. "You know, I'm a pretty good listener. It seems you and I have quite a history of you telling me your woes. I remember many talks about school, and your frustrations with your sweet sisters, and even boys." He stopped walking and stared down into her face. The full moon lit her golden hair like a beacon in the darkness. "I'm here if you need me. I didn't just come to work the land and help raise the boys. I'm here for you, too."

"Thank you, Tucker. That means more than you know." She started walking again. She would be more comfortable talking if she wasn't looking into his face. "I heard what you said to the twins this morning down by the creek."

"You did?" He paused for a moment. "I guess I'm

going to have to be watchful so you don't sneak up on me in the night," he chuckled.

She joined his laughter. "I promise to warn you first." Sobering, she added, "What you said to them was precious. I think it will help them to heal." It was her turn to stop and look at him. "I had no idea your childhood was so challenging. Your mother was a strong lady." Daisy lowered her gaze to the ring on her hand. "I hope I'm able to be as strong for my sons as she was for you." She ambled forward again, effectively pulling him along with her.

"You already are. She'd have loved the way you nearly shot me when I rode up on the property! No one could call you weak." They laughed again.

"You have no idea how scared I was. I could have shot you. Again." She smirked in the darkness. "I don't know what I'd have done if it hadn't been you, or if I'd missed, or if there had been more than one person."

"Thanks for not shooting me—again," he joked. "And thank you for letting me stay," he added, his voice tender.

"I know it was the good Lord looking after us the day you rode up the lane." She applied a reassuring pressure to his arm. "I needed a friend."

Tucker cleared his throat. "Tell me how you're doing. We saw last night and this morning how the boys have been struggling. How are you healing? Do you want to tell me what happened?" Tucker's voice was comforting in the darkness as they walked.

"It was terrible." Daisy's voice wavered, but she kept talking, hoping the telling would help her. "More terrible than anything I've ever seen or imagined. Murdock had taken the boys and me to town so I could visit with

Peggy Dismuke and Milly Ledford. You remember the dressmaker?" His hand still covered hers, and she was grateful for the comfort it brought.

"I remember."

"We were going to spend the day, and Murdock was going to come pick us up before supper. The boys were playing with Milly's son, while she and Peggy and I visited." Tears spilled over her lashes and trailed down her cheeks at the painful memories. "We had just sold the cotton, and Murdock thought we needed a day away from the farm. If only we hadn't gone."

"You can't torture yourself like that, Daisy. Murdock was giving you the gift of a day of leisure. He had no way of knowing what would happen."

"I know, but I can't help wishing." Daisy wiped her eyes. "When Murdock didn't come by suppertime, Reverend Dismuke and Peggy offered to bring us home." She gasped and sobbed at the same time. "It was almost dark when we pulled onto the property. Reverend Dismuke saw Murdock first. He tried to keep me away, but I had to see him, to hold him in my arms."

"What about the boys?"

"Reverend Dismuke and Peggy were able to get them into the cabin, but they knew their papa was gone. Then we realized the horses were missing. I don't know what I would have done without the Dismukes that day."

"I'm glad they were here for you and James and John." Tucker stroked her hand with his fingers.

"The next day Sheriff Collins came and tried to determine how it all happened. The thieves must have come up while Murdock was working in the barn. The sheriff thinks he surprised them when he stepped into the corral to get the horses so he could hitch up the wagon to come back to town. He didn't stand a chance against two of them. Not without a gun."

Tucker stopped walking and pulled her into his arms. Daisy buried her face in his shoulder and cried like she hadn't since the first week it happened. She had been determined to be strong for the boys. She didn't want them to hear her sobbing at night, so she'd held it all inside. Now she released the pent-up sadness and anger that threatened to drown her soul.

It was several minutes before she quieted. Finally Tucker spoke softly against the silkiness of her hair. "I'm so sorry for all you've suffered, Daisy. You and the boys." He still held her in the circle of his arms. Part of him never wanted to let her go.

Daisy pulled herself away from his chest and dabbed at the wetness of his shirt with her shawl. "Oh, I've gone and made a mess of you," she muttered.

Tucker caught her hands in his. "Don't worry about it. I'm just glad I was able to be here for you." He already missed the scent of her nestled beneath his chin.

"Thank you, Tucker." Daisy looked into his face and smiled a watery smile. "You really are a good friend. I haven't been able to talk to anyone about this since the funeral. I was trying to protect the boys. It all got bottled up inside."

"I'm here for you now. For anything you need." He released her hands, and they started to walk back toward the cabin.

Daisy spoke again. "I'm getting stronger every day. I won't lie and tell you it's easy. I've never known such pain, not since my momma passed. But this is a different pain. This was like losing my future. Murdock and I had so many plans." She walked slower with each passing word. "It's all gone now," she ended on a whisper.

"Not all of it, Daisy." He wanted to take away her pain. Tucker captured her hand again and gave it a reassuring squeeze. "Murdock lives on in his sons. You've been able to save the dreams he had for the boys. We can continue to cultivate the land. By the time the twins are grown we can have most of it growing cotton. There's plenty of room for each of them to build a house and raise a family. And there'll be enough harvest money to provide for three families and more." Tucker wanted to spark a vision in her for a future together.

"Are you sure, Tucker? Can we really do it?" Her voice was woeful and hopeful at the same time.

His thumb crossed her knuckles as he answered. "I'm sure, Daisy. Together we can make your dreams come true. I hope in time they can be our dreams."

They were back at the front steps now. He could hear James and John laughing inside.

"I enjoyed our walk—" Daisy turned to him "—and our talk." She stretched up on her tiptoes and touched her lips to his cheek, like she had as a young girl when he'd consoled her over the crisis of the moment. "Thank you."

Caught off guard by her kiss, Tucker released her hand. "I did, too." Tucker took a step backward and watched her in the moonlight. "Good night, Daisy."

"Don't you want to come in for coffee?"

"Not tonight." He wanted to go inside, but he wouldn't. He wanted to be there for her. His heart ached with the sorrow she'd shared. He'd done everything he knew to comfort her, but he needed to keep a safe distance tonight. Her tears had soaked through his shirt as if to trace the cold fissures of his heart. The release of her grief threatened to seep into his brokenness with healing strength and awaken long dead hope. No good could come from that. Only more pain for both of them.

"I stoked the fire and brought in more wood while you washed the dishes. You should be fine until morning." He stepped back from the steps, and she stood on the porch. "Bolt the door, and I'll be on my way." He lifted a hand slightly. "Good night."

"Good night." Daisy opened the door and slipped inside before turning back to him. "Sleep well."

Tucker heard the bolt slide into place and headed for the barn. Daisy shared her deepest pain with him tonight. Would there come a time when she could share her deepest joy? Was he willing to let her close enough to learn his deepest pain?

Mack whinnied at him in annoyance when he lit the lamp so he could read his Bible. His lamp burned late into the night.

Wednesday night after supper Daisy led the boys in their usual Bible study. Tucker joined them and even helped to answer some of the twins' questions about the verses they read.

That night she and Tucker sat on the porch and talked while drinking coffee. They slipped back into the comfortable friendship they'd shared for years. She would laugh and tell him her frustrations. He would listen and offer sound advice. If she caught him glancing at her hair or the curve of her neck, she pretended not to notice, though part of her was beginning to enjoy his attention. He was always a gentleman, and she grew more at ease in his presence with each passing day.

The men Tucker hired headed back to town just before dark on Thursday. The roof was on and covered with new shingles. She was surprised by the grand size of the room, but she still couldn't imagine how the new furniture would look in the space. She wouldn't allow herself to think about living in the room alone—or with Tucker.

After the boys went to bed that evening, Daisy and Tucker sat in front of the fire talking. Daisy asked, "Will you pray with me tonight?"

"Is something wrong?" Tucker was attentive at once.

"Oh, no. You had asked once before if I wanted you to pray with me. I needed to be alone that day, but I think it would be a good idea if we make it our practice to pray together," she explained.

"Okay. Is there a particular thing you want to pray about?"

"Our family." Daisy lowered her gaze to her lap. "I want us to pray together for God to help us be the family He wants us to be." She hesitated. "I realize you've never been married before." She paused again. "And I'm very grateful for all you're doing for us." This time she stopped entirely.

"Daisy, you don't have to say anything." He put a hand on the arm of her chair. "I'm in no rush. I'm enjoying our friendship." He lowered his head to peer into her eyes. "I hope you are, too?" The last part was a question.

She smiled a little and looked up at him. "I am." She picked her hands up and dropped them back into her lap dramatically. "I'm just so confused. I don't want to be, but I am," she lamented.

"Don't be, Daisy. I'd never want you to be upset on my account."

"That's just it, Tucker. One minute I'm missing Murdock, and I'm sad for the boys that he's gone. The next minute I'm so grateful you're here I could almost kiss you." Her face reddened as she admitted her conflicting thoughts.

Tucker reached into her lap and took her hand, the one with his ring on it, and looked deeply into her eyes. "I understand. You'll always love Murdock. I would expect nothing less from you. Your loyalty is admirable. I know you were his destiny. I saw it when you were courting." Tucker touched her face with his other hand. "The twins will miss him, too. That's part of the grieving process. It has to happen naturally. Daisy, I know what you're going through."

"How can you know? I don't even know how I feel right now."

"I've seen it more than once." His eyes were earnest, as if he willed her to believe him. "Your father loves his housekeeper. He has for years. But he's never advanced the relationship because he couldn't bring himself to replace your mother."

"Do you think that's why?" Daisy had seen the strength of her father's friendship with Beverly Norton, but she never even thought of him with any woman other than her mother.

"I do. And my mother loved the owner of the hotel where she worked, but would never let him court her. Her commitment to my father went beyond his death. She was unwilling to consider another husband."

"Maybe she didn't court him because he wasn't the

right man to be a father for you. Maybe he was good for her, but she was protecting you."

"It wasn't about me. She could never love anyone like that again. The same is true for your father. The same is true for you." Tucker's voice faded a little as he finished speaking.

"Oh, Tucker. Right now I'm still grieving for Murdock. I just need time."

"Time doesn't really heal all wounds, Daisy. You'll heal from the pain, but the love you shared with Murdock will forever overshadow any other relationship."

"Tucker…" She tried to interrupt, but he didn't stop.

"It's okay, Daisy. I knew that when I came."

"How can you be sure?"

"It's happened to me before."

"What?"

"When my mother passed, I went to work on a ranch. There was a girl there. Her name was Alice Fields."

Daisy searched her memory, but she couldn't recall him ever mentioning anyone named Alice. Tucker's voice was devoid of emotion as she listened to him now.

"She was the cook's daughter. Alice had her cap set for the foreman's right-hand man. They even got engaged. Then he got scared of the responsibility and called it off. She turned to me for comfort."

"What happened?" Daisy wasn't sure she wanted to know this story. She had a strange foreboding it would have a profound effect on her relationship with him.

"I was still hurting over the loss of my mother. It was nice to have someone who I thought understood my pain. We started courting. Her pa advised me to be cautious. She was young. Only sixteen. And vulnerable. Or so I thought." He stared into the fire now. Daisy sensed he was back on that ranch, seeing the events play out again in his mind's eye.

"You don't have to share this with me." Wouldn't it be better not to know? Did she want Tucker to give her some reason he could never love her? After she already married him?

He kept talking as if she hadn't spoken. "I fell hard. As hard as a young man of seventeen can. A few months later I proposed." Tucker leaned back in his chair. He didn't look at her. "She did everything but laugh in my face. Said she was courting me till the other man noticed. Said she could never love me. Her heart would always belong to her first love."

"She was young, Tucker. She didn't know any better." Daisy tried to soften the blows he endured so long ago.

"She knew what she was doing. She was young, but she knew her heart. And she was willing to do anything to satisfy it." He turned to look at her now. "That was right before the cattle auction where I met your father. He offered me a job, and I took it. I heard Alice got married the next month." He rubbed his hands down his thighs as though to relieve the tension of his soul.

"So you see, Daisy, I know you'll always love Murdock more. I came here for your friendship. If our friendship grows into a deeper marriage over time, that's well and good." He reached for her hands again as she wrung them in her lap. "If not, we'll be fine as friends."

Daisy pressed his hands with hers. He'd been such a help to her. She yearned to help him, but didn't know how.

"I came here with my eyes wide-open. I understand

your conflicting emotions." He brushed his thumb across the ring on her finger. "As for wanting to kiss me—" he paused and tilted his head to one side "—you can do that anytime you want to." He smiled slightly. "But not until you're ready. Okay?"

She nodded. Her head swam with his revelation. She never suspected his painful past all those years before. Perhaps youth had cast a hue of peace and love over her world. At the time, she assumed everyone was as happy as she was.

Tucker's voice cut into her thoughts. "I'd be honored to pray with you about our family."

Daisy was startled by his abrupt return to the reason for their conversation. She bowed her head after him and listened to him pray.

"Lord, You know the heavy hearts of this home. We're asking for Your healing touch on these broken spirits. We trust You to guide us as we grow together into the family You ordained for us to be. Help us follow Your leading at the pace You set. Don't let us get ahead of You or lag behind. We ask it all in the name of Jesus. Amen." Tucker squeezed her hands and released them.

He stood and moved to the door. Restraint tightened his voice. "Good night, Daisy."

She followed to latch the bolt. "Good night, Tucker. Thank you."

Daisy leaned against the bolted door with her face in her hands. It had truly been difficult to admit to Tucker that she was beginning to have feelings for him. Had she opened a door she couldn't close? If she'd known about Alice, she might never have told him. Grieving Murdock's death was emotional and difficult, but understandable because of the love they'd shared. Tucker had been in mourning for years for something he'd never had. How could he recover from the loss of hope?

The coming of November brought cooler nights and days that could be warm or cool. Tucker came into the house for breakfast wearing a jacket Daisy hadn't seen before. He warmed his hands by the fire before hanging it on the peg under his hat.

"A jacket? Either it's cold out this morning, or you don't plan on working up a sweat today," Daisy teased him as she set the table for breakfast.

"You're a funny girl," he jibed. "It's starting to get chillier at night. I'm feeling it a little deeper in my bones today." Tucker grabbed a mug and poured coffee.

"I didn't think about how chilly it was last night. I'm sorry." Daisy fretted at herself for not considering his comfort more. "You need to sleep in here tonight. I can make a pallet in the boys' room."

James and John came in from their chores and joined them at the table. "You're gonna sleep in our room, Momma?" James asked while climbing onto the bench beside his brother.

"No, James, your momma is going to sleep in her bed tonight—" Tucker looked pointedly at Daisy before continuing "—and every night until I have her room ready." He turned to the boys. "John, will you pray this morning?"

They joined hands, and John prayed before bowls filled with biscuits, ham and fried potatoes were passed around the table.

"This looks delicious," Tucker said as he heaped potatoes onto his plate.

"I hope it tastes as good as it looks." Daisy speared

a piece of pan-fried ham and dropped it onto her plate. "So what's the plan for today, gentlemen?"

"Mr. Tucker says we're gonna finish your room real soon. He said even though it's Saturday, we're not going to town. We're gonna work on the room. He says we gotta finish so we can start clearing more land for next year." James rattled off the information without stopping.

Daisy chuckled. "Is that so? Then you boys better eat up and get busy."

"I'm hoping to get the windows and back door in today after I finish the siding. You should be in by the middle of next week." Tucker reached for a second biscuit and pierced the side of it with his fork so he could pour it full of honey.

"That soon? I better get to work on some curtains then," Daisy said. "Do you mind if I go over to Judy's while you work today? I promised her I'd come visit soon."

"Can you wait until next week? I really can't leave today, but I'd like to go with you. I think an outing would be good for the boys, and when I met Randall on Sunday he was giving me some good information. I'd like to talk to him again." Tucker took another bite of his biscuit. "Maybe you and Judy could set up a time when we see them at church tomorrow. Something for Friday evening or next Saturday."

Daisy was surprised at how quickly he'd taken to Randall, but agreed to make the arrangements the next morning.

The boys finished eating before Tucker and went to the barn to gather their tools. Tucker stood and headed for the door.

"Thanks for breakfast, Daisy. It was definitely as good as it looked." He lifted his hat from the peg.

"Tucker, about last night…" She paused, as if unsure what to say, but wanting to say something.

"We both said a lot of things last night, Daisy." He turned his hat in his fingers.

"I appreciate everything you told me," she said. "You've always been the one who listened to me. I'm glad I could be a friend to you. Thank you for sharing your heart."

"Sorry to have burdened you so. It's been years since I thought about Alice. I wanted you to know I understand the way your pain anchors you to your past." He put his hat on. "You won't be pressured by me. For anything." He opened the door and looked out across the porch. "I do appreciate your friendship." The door closed, and he was gone.

Daisy stepped to the window and watched him walk to the barn. Before their conversation last night, she'd begun to think they could eventually build a true marriage. Now she knew he really meant it when he said he came to be her friend. She was grateful for his friendship, but what about James and John? How would they learn to love their future wives? Would time rob them of the memory of how Murdock had loved her?

The dishes were washed and the sounds of hammering and sawing filled the air when Daisy made her way to the barn to collect Tucker's dirty clothes. She hadn't been in the barn since he'd come to Pine Haven. He'd immediately taken charge of the animals and the boys' chores. Sunshine lit a shaft of dust across the middle of the building as she opened one heavy door. The smell of freshly spread hay assaulted her senses as she walked by the clean, empty stalls. Tucker let the horses roam free in the corral during the day.

She smiled at the order he'd restored to the stalls and tack room. It had been reduced to complete disarray during the weeks she'd tried to handle the farm on her own. Now feed sacks were piled neatly, and even the tools her sons used were stored in a perfect row. Glancing upward she noticed the loft had not escaped his attention, either.

Tucker's blanket was rolled and placed in a corner of the tack room where he slept. The few personal belongings he'd brought with him were stored neatly in the small space. Only his shaving brush and cup sat out where he'd left them to dry. Next to that, a towel hung on a nail under the small mirror he'd leaned against a post. A mental picture of him grooming intruded on her thoughts. His Bible was on a shelf near the only lamp in the room. The smell of his soap permeated the area. Daisy shook her head and stepped deeper into the room in search of his dirty clothes.

"Can I help you find something?" Daisy jumped in surprise as Tucker spoke just inches behind her.

She spun around, and he laughed at her guilt-ridden expression.

"You scared me!" Daisy stamped one foot.

"Did I now?" He still laughed. "I didn't expect to find you here. Is there something in particular you're looking for?" He stopped laughing and raised an eyebrow as if to taunt her. "Or did you just come out to see if I'm neat enough to move into the house next week?"

Daisy's heart was still racing as she took a backward step toward the corner of the small tack room. A room that seemed to shrink as he closed the space between them.

"Are you ready to tell me what you're looking for, Mrs. Barlow?" He was so close their breath mingled in the cool air.

She giggled. "Your dirty clothes, Mr. Barlow." Were her nerves betraying her excitement at his nearness? "If you'd like them washed today."

Without touching her, and without taking his eyes from hers, he reached around her and snagged a dark bag made of heavy fabric from the corner. He stood up straight, and she felt drawn to him, as if by a magnetic pull.

"Here you go, ma'am. Sorry I forgot to bring them to you this morning." He lifted the bag up beside them because there was no room between them.

"Oh, my." Daisy wrinkled her small freckled nose. "These smell strong. Must be the scent you get from being cantankerous." She grabbed the bag and dashed around him, fleeing to the safety of the open spaces outside the barn.

Daisy spilled the contents of the bag onto her workbench and set about scrubbing Tucker's clothes. She doused the first shirt into the hot water and pulled it up to rake across the washboard. By the time she got to the third shirt she knew she was in trouble. The rhythm of her heart kept pace with her hands as she repeatedly dragged the wet fabric across the board.

She reached to brush her hair back from her forehead as Tucker crossed the yard to return to his work on the cabin. Never looking her way, she wondered if he were avoiding her.

If the confinement of the tack room for such a short

time with him set her heart racing, how would she manage to control her growing feelings for him once he moved into the cabin? The only place she would be able to retreat would be the room he was building her. Could her mind escape him in a space he created for her? Would she want to escape him?

Thoughts of Alice, and Tucker's belief that Daisy could never love him, warned her that she might not need to keep her distance. He might avoid her.

Chapter Fourteen

A bright sun warmed the blustery day as they rode home from church on Sunday. Tucker was careful to keep some space between Daisy and himself on the wagon seat. He was finding it more and more difficult to concentrate on anything else when she was near.

During the service he'd been mesmerized by her closeness and the scent of her. He turned to admire her beauty as she folded a blanket across her lap and tucked it under her legs. The years had not been unkind to her. Her hair still shone with health, and she was as vibrant as ever. She'd maintained her tiny shape even after having twins. Many women didn't fare so well after ten years working the land.

Thinking back, he hoped he hadn't hurt Daisy by telling her about Alice. She needed to know he didn't expect to be loved. Not like she'd loved Murdock.

Yet something tugged at his cold heart. A tug of hope that maybe she wasn't like everyone else. Maybe she could love again. Was she still thinking about kissing him? What would he do if she did? Could he open up to her and put their friendship at risk?

Daisy shivered and rubbed her gloved hands together. "I saw you speaking to the sheriff after the service."

Tucker shifted his gaze to the road. "There's no new information on the thieves."

"Thank you for talking to him. I hope they've left the area."

"There's no way to know for certain. We'll keep alert and pray." Changing the subject, Tucker asked, "Did you speak to Judy Thornton?"

"Yes. We can go to their place Friday for a supper of venison stew."

John leaned over the wagon seat and tapped Tucker on the shoulder.

"Yes, John?"

"Mr. Tucker, you know what Reverend Dismuke preached today about showing your scars and helping other folks get better?"

"I did hear him say that. I think I have a pretty good understanding of what he meant. What did you think about that?" Tucker gave John time to form his answer.

"I think," John began and then hesitated. "Well, I think that's kinda what you did when you told me and James about you being a kid and your papa dying and all." John looked serious. "I think you showed us your pain, so our pain could heal. Is that what the preacher meant?"

Tucker nodded his head, but kept his eyes on the road. "That's one way to look at it, John. I sure hoped telling you and James my story would help you feel better." He flicked his wrists to urge Trojan and Beauregard to pick up the pace. "I don't want you boys to suffer like I did. That's why I came to live here and married your momma. I wanted to be a comfort to you all."

"That's what I thought." John clapped his small hand on the top of Tucker's broad shoulder. "I'm glad you did." Just as quickly as he'd interrupted, John sat down.

Tucker's heart compressed. John's words were evidence this family—his family—was growing in love. Deeply moved by John's words, he felt Daisy's gaze on him. But he couldn't look at her.

She spoke quietly so only he would hear. "Wow. Kids sure have a way of getting to your heart, don't they?"

"Yes. They do." His voice was lower than Daisy's, and those were his only words for the rest of the trip home.

Monday morning Tucker finished installing the windows. By lunch he was ready to start on the back steps.

"I'm glad the wind died down through the night. I plan to finish the steps and put in the windowsills this afternoon," Tucker told Daisy at the table.

"Really? You're working hard and fast. Don't hurt yourself." Daisy put a steaming bowl of soup in front of each of the boys.

"If it works like I hope, I'll be able to cut the door to the inside of the cabin in the morning. We can move your bed in there tomorrow evening. The new furniture won't be here, but you can have privacy." Tucker dipped his bread in the soup before taking a big bite. "This is delicious."

"Thank you." Daisy reached for the basket in the center of the table and took a slice of the still-warm bread. "I better get busy and finish the curtains today. I had no idea you'd be through so quickly." Daisy was making the curtains from fabric she'd bought on a whim. The soft green fabric had seemed to speak to her on the day she'd married Tucker. Mr. Croft had wrapped it in brown paper and tied it with string. She didn't even open it that night when they'd returned home, but had slipped it into the chest at the foot of her bed. The day Tucker told her he was building an addition she knew she'd use it for curtains.

"Can we go outside and play?" John asked. He dropped his spoon into his empty bowl.

"Yes, you may." Daisy excused both boys from the table.

"You've been working so hard, Tucker. I'm very grateful for your thoughtfulness in building this addition."

"Glad to do it. It's best for a lady to have space away from the main part of the house whenever possible. Those boys are going to be young men before we know it." He wiped the inside of his bowl with the last of his bread and popped it into his mouth.

"It will be good for you to come in out of the barn, too. It's getting awfully chilly at night now." Daisy stood and began clearing the dishes from the table. She was still uncomfortable with the thought of Tucker staying in the house—with her—but she knew it wouldn't be right for him to keep sleeping in the barn. "I've felt mighty guilty being so warm in here while you were out in the cold. It doesn't seem fair, as hard as you work every day." She had her back to him and was watching out the window as the boys chased each other.

Tucker rose and brought his bowl to the dishpan. He reached around her and placed it in the warm water. "No need," he said, resting a hand on her shoulder. "I've been fine. It's only one more night." He tapped the window to motion for the twins to join him for the afternoon's work. "Thanks for lunch." She missed the light pressure of his hand on her as soon as it was gone.

Daisy stood at the window, watching Tucker and the boys as they headed to the side of the house. Her heart had ached so much when Murdock had died and the boys lost their joy or will to play. It was refreshing to see them run and frolic again. Tucker plucked John's hat off his head and ruffled his hair before racing ahead of him. John soon caught up and retrieved his hat, laughing the whole time. James jumped to try to take Tucker's hat, only to be surprised as his hat was taken and launched high into the air with a flick of Tucker's wrist. Daisy smiled and prayed a prayer of thanks for the happiness she was seeing as the twins built a relationship with Tucker.

Lord, Tucker is so good with my sons. Help me to build the relationship I need with him. He deserves to be loved and appreciated. He's such a dear friend. I hope I can make him happy one day. She closed her eyes for a minute and dared to add, *Soon.*

Tuesday was busy. Tucker pushed Daisy's bed and chest away from the corner of the room and cut a hole in the wall. The door to her new room was mounted into place before lunch. Tucker swung it back and forth to ensure it was level before oiling the hinges.

Daisy was able to get the table clean enough for them to eat the ham left from breakfast on slices of bread. She handed out apples and glasses of milk to the hardworking men in her life.

"I may have to bake something special tomorrow as a way to thank you all for this wonderful room," she said as they crunched away on the juicy red fruit. "I'd do it today, but I'm afraid it might be full of sawdust."

"Yummy! Will you make cake or pie, Momma?" James got excited.

"Or more cookies?" John wanted to know.

"Why don't we let Mr. Tucker decide? After all, the room was his idea." Daisy looked to Tucker for his input.

"Do you still make buttermilk pie, Daisy?" He smiled at the memory of her pies.

"Oh, my goodness! I haven't made a buttermilk pie in ages." Daisy reached for a small box on the shelf above the kitchen cabinet. She opened it and started flipping through the small pieces of paper inside. Finally she stopped and pulled one from the rest. It was more worn than the others, discolored from time and previous handling. Holding it up for them to see, she said, "Here's the recipe." She perused it quickly. "I have everything I need to make this." She closed the box. "Buttermilk pie it is."

"What's buttermilk pie?" James sounded uncertain.

"Did we ever have that, Momma?" John asked.

"I don't think so, John. James, you'll just have to wait and see."

"I bet you'll like it, boys. Your momma made the best buttermilk pie in the county when she was a young girl. Even won a ribbon at the county fair when she was fifteen." Tucker smiled at Daisy. He remembered how young and beautiful she was that summer. How he'd had to outbid several young lads to win her pie. Even then, in his mind's eye he could see the lady she would become.

"You are going way back for that memory, Tucker."

Recollection dawned in her eyes. "Seems like you were the high bidder that year."

"I bought your momma's pie at the auction. She deserved that ribbon. It was the best pie I ever ate." Tucker made a show of rubbing his stomach in a satisfying motion while licking his lips. "Didn't know I'd ever get the chance to eat it again after she moved away from home." At the time he'd wished she was older so they could have shared the pie that night at the fair instead of him having to eat it alone.

"I haven't made it in years. Can't promise it will be that good now, but I'll do my best." She looked to James and said, "I'll need your help churning butter tomorrow morning, so I'll have fresh buttermilk for the pies."

"Yes, ma'am."

Tucker pushed his chair away from the table and stood. "Now you boys go take a few minutes to see your horses. I've got a couple of chores to handle. We'll start the cleanup after your momma puts away the food. Don't want to start stirring up the sawdust for a few more minutes. I'll need your help to move the furniture." James and John were out the door and halfway to the corral before Daisy could wrap the remaining bread in a towel.

"I can't believe you remembered that pie." Daisy stacked the plates from their lunch and moved them to the dishpan. "Murdock didn't care for it, so I quit making it."

Tucker drained the last of his milk from the cup and handed it to her. Their fingers brushed, and she almost dropped it.

"I have a lot of fond memories, Daisy." He gave her a

smile. "I'll confess I'm looking forward to the ones we'll make together and share." He stepped to the front door.

"As long as you don't try to shoot me again." Laughing, he went out relishing the sight of her—mouth agape, cheeks pink and speechless.

The cleanup went quickly with all of them working together. The twins helped Tucker move the bed and chest into the new space. Daisy was certain he could have managed more efficiently without them, but knew he was teaching them by letting them help.

"Can you help me hang the curtains?" Daisy asked Tucker when the boys went to do their afternoon chores.

"I can. Give me a minute. I'll need to get some things from the barn to hang them with."

Daisy laid the curtains across the quilt that covered her bed. She smiled to see the soft hue of the curtains pick up the green of the vines woven among pink roses. She ran a hand across the intricate stitches in the quilt her mother had made before marrying Daisy's father.

She stood lost in thought when Tucker stepped through the doorway. Late afternoon sunlight streamed through the window on the back wall. He cleared his throat. "Do you want me to come back later?"

"No," she answered. "I was just admiring how well the curtains match Momma's quilt." She straightened the corner of the quilt and picked up one of the curtains. "Papa had Jasmine send it after Murdock died. He thought I needed something of Momma's close to me for comfort."

She sat on the side of the bed, taking care not to wrinkle the freshly ironed curtain she held. "He was right. Those first nights when I would lie down, all I could think about was Murdock. Then the quilt arrived. It reminded me of how much Papa loved Momma. But it also made me remember how he got on with his life after she passed. It was like having known her somehow strengthened him to move forward. His love for her didn't die. It propelled him into the future and helped him take care of us. Now at night when I curl up under this quilt I think about how strong and wonderful love is. I think about how even when you're separated from the ones you love, that love can motivate you to keep living."

She looked up from the quilt and met his kind gaze. "It also makes me think about how I wouldn't even exist if it hadn't been for the love my papa and momma had for each other." She gave him a watery smile. "You know all of us are named after flowers because of Momma?" At his nod she continued. "Jasmine had such exotic beauty, like Momma, with pearly skin and black hair. Her eyes dark and deep like richly brewed coffee. She was long and graceful from the beginning. I'm more like my papa. The blond hair, brown eyes and freckles are like his momma. He told me once that Momma said I was so petite, and looked so fresh and light, that I reminded her of a daisy. My baby sister, Lily, is dainty and fragile, like a delicate flower, with vibrant blue eyes."

"I can see why they chose the names they did for each of you," Tucker said.

"I'm the most ordinary of the bunch, but Papa knew I needed to be reminded of Momma's love. That's why he sent the quilt."

Tucker came to stand near her. He touched her hair and looked into her eyes. "You may be fresh and fair, but you have never been ordinary. Far from it." Daisy saw a swirling of emotion in Tucker's eyes. Could it be longing?

Heat climbed into her face at his compliment. His nearness caused her heart to race.

"Thank you, Tucker." The quiver in her voice could be interpreted as sadness or anticipation. Tucker must have thought it was sorrow because he immediately dropped his hand and reached for the curtain she held.

"Tell me how you want this to look." He moved to the window and held the curtain up so she could choose the correct placement.

Now she was sad. Sad Tucker had misunderstood her emotions. She didn't want him to think she would move into the room he'd built for her and bring Murdock's memory along as a way to shut him out. As she'd sat on the bed and reminisced about Murdock, the memories hadn't tormented her. The love they'd shared was beginning to serve to move her forward into the happy life she knew Murdock would want for her. She wasn't even surprised to feel it happening. It had been a gradual moving from a place of constant pain, to loss and then toward hope. What she didn't know was how to communicate the changes in her heart to Tucker.

The curtains were hung and Daisy went to look out the window. She realized a couple of things immediately. Tucker had planned the layout so she wouldn't see the path to Murdock's grave from either window in this room. It had been barely visible from the window in the cabin before he'd built the addition. Now she'd have to make a special trip up the hill to see it. She was comforted by the thought of being separated from the constant reminder of her loss.

Then another thought hit her.

"Tucker!" He came back into the room when she called. She met him with an accusing stare. "You moved that outhouse so I wouldn't see it from this room." She put her hands on her hips and waited for him to reply.

"I did." He stood unflinchingly. "It took a little figuring, but I wanted it out of sight as much as possible. Just had to keep it on the side of the house away from the well."

"You worked off your anger that day by doing all kinds of manual labor, and the whole time you were planning this for me." Her toe tapped under the edge of her skirt.

"And you have a problem with that?" He smiled.

She shook her head and blew out a breath before walking across the room to stand in front of him. "Not one bit. I just can't believe how thoughtful it was. You are sweet." She reached up and put a kiss on his cheek. "Even when you're upset." Caught off guard by the day's growth of beard and the scent of his soap, Daisy drew her bottom lip in and bit it and tried to back away.

Tucker captured her waist with his hands and pulled her so close they were almost touching. The emotion she'd seen in his eyes an hour ago was still there, but there was more. "You definitely know how to upset me, Daisy Barlow. I'll give you that." He released her and turned for the door. "I'll be in the barn until supper. I've got to work on some tools."

Daisy stared at the doorway after Tucker went through it. Could he receive her love if she gave it?

Or would he think it was pity? An unwelcome notion fluttered through her mind. Pity might be what Tucker felt for her.

Chapter Fifteen

Supper was eaten and tired boys went to bed early. Tucker sat by the fire with Daisy. "So do you like the room?" he asked before drinking from his coffee mug.

"It's perfect. I can't believe how big it is. Or how much more room there is in this main area without the bed and chest." She turned in her chair and looked behind her at the empty space where she'd slept for most of the past ten years.

"Well," she asked, "now that you've finished this addition what will you do?" Daisy settled back into her chair.

Tucker thought for a minute. "That ten acres is going to need to be cleared. I'm thinking I'll head over in that direction tomorrow."

"Why don't you take a day to rest? You've worked nonstop since you got here." She had a distinct feeling she would miss not having him nearby every day.

"I'll rest on Sunday."

"What about your things for tonight?" she asked "You didn't bring anything in yet."

"I'm good in the barn for now." Tucker added a log to the fire.

Daisy stilled her chair and turned to him. "Tucker Barlow, you said that room would keep you from having to sleep in a cold barn. The room is ready. There is no reason for you to stay out there anymore." She tapped the toe of her shoe on the wooden floor and frowned up at him.

"I know why I built the room." He turned from the fireplace and pulled his hat from the peg on the wall. "And I know why I'm sleeping in the barn right now." He set the hat onto his head and adjusted it slightly forward. "I'll see you in the morning for breakfast." Tucker winked at her before he opened the door and left.

Daisy sat dumbfounded in her chair at his abrupt exit. She placed the fingertips of one hand over her lips and silently gasped at the possible meaning of his words. She was dragged from her thoughts by his knuckles rapping on the front door.

"The bolt, Daisy," he reminded her.

She vaulted from her chair and opened the door. He ambled backward, surprised. Daisy stepped onto the porch in front of him and looked straight into his face. The moonlight behind him kept his face in the shadows and lit the porch with a soft glow. She reached one hand up and laid it flat against his chest.

"Tucker, did you come here out of pity?"

"No, Daisy. You are not a woman to be pitied." His brows drew together. "Bolstered, perhaps. Protected, even. But never pitied." His tone was genuine. Just as she knew he was.

Daisy stretched up on her tiptoes and pressed her lips softly against his. The warmth and gentleness of his response held no pity. Her hands found their way to his shoulders as she lost herself in the sweetness of the moment.

She backed away from him and lowered her eyes, not willing to risk him seeing the hope in her gaze.

She retreated into the cabin.

"Good night, Tucker." She closed the door slowly and threw the bolt.

Without taking a breath, Daisy prayed. *Lord, I've done it now. I just took a big step down a slippery slope. I hope I'm ready.*

She opened her eyes and drew in a gulp of much-needed air.

Daisy checked the twins before picking up the lamp on the table and heading into her new room. She set the lamp on the floor beside the chest, knelt beside it and reached inside for her nightclothes. She was lowering the lid when she caught sight of the bag containing her wedding ring from Murdock.

Carefully raising the lid, she retrieved the small velvet pouch. She untied the drawstring and turned the bag upside down, allowing the gold band to slide into her palm. She closed her hand tightly around the ring and treasured the past it represented. Opening her hand again, she slid the ring back into the bag. This time she tied the drawstring into a bow and then knotted it. She tucked it deep in the corner of the chest where she kept her mementos. Tonight she knew she was truly tying up the past. Murdock had been good to her. He'd been a wonderful husband and father, but he was gone.

Daisy had no choice but to move on. She'd pledged herself to Tucker for the sake of her sons and her land. But she knew that pledge meant she must also honor

Tucker and become his true wife. Was she finally ready to move beyond her fear of loss?

She stood and stared around her at the room Tucker had built for her. And for him. Tucker had proven he was here so she and the boys could have a good future. Daisy realized that he, too, deserved the future he was working so hard to give her.

The chatter of twins covered the awkwardness Daisy felt the next morning when Tucker came in for breakfast. He brushed his arm against hers as he reached for the coffeepot. When her face flushed warm, he smiled and moved to sit at the table.

"Are you boys ready for schoolwork today?" Tucker wanted to know.

"Oh, do we have to?" they sang in unison.

Daisy and Tucker laughed. "Yes, you do," she answered while putting a platter of pancakes on the table.

James reached to spear one with his fork, but Daisy sent him a look that warned him to wait. She took her seat, and they prayed. "Now you may put food on your plate, James."

"What will you do today, Mr. Tucker?" John was pouring syrup liberally onto his plate.

"I'm going to start clearing the ten acres I told you about—at the edge of the northern field."

"Can't we help you?" James asked with his mouth full of pancakes. Daisy signaled for him to mind his manners.

"You can work with me in the afternoons if all your schoolwork and chores are done. And remember, James, you've got to help your mother make butter today so we can have buttermilk pie tonight." Tucker smiled at Daisy.

"I've done my morning chores," John asserted. "Can I go get the schoolbooks, Momma?" He was rising from his seat as he spoke.

"Sit down, son." Daisy motioned him back to his bench. "You've got to eat well if you're going to work hard. And the table will have to be cleared before the books can be brought in here." She pointed at his plate. "Finish your sausage and drink your milk."

To Tucker she added, "I wish they were this eager to do their lessons. I think they like your teaching better than mine."

"He teaches us fun stuff, Momma," James said. "Things men need to know about life and work—not book stuff. The lessons we do here and at school are boring." He crossed his arms and huffed.

"James, apologize to your mother." Tucker immediately squelched James's attitude.

James hung his head. "I'm sorry, Momma," he muttered under his breath.

"James," Tucker warned.

"I'm sorry, Momma," James repeated more sincerely. "I just want to learn how to be a man. I don't need all that other stuff."

Tucker leaned his elbows on the table. "A man has to be educated to take care of the business of life. You'll need to know how to read and understand contracts, like a deed when you buy land. And how to calculate sums to make a deal for a major purchase like seed for your crops. Farming and ranching require more than just hands-on training for working the land or the animals. You've got to be able to take care of the business side, as well."

"I hadn't thought of that," James admitted.

"Have you ever seen your momma working on the journal for the cotton?" Tucker asked.

"I remember Papa and Momma working together on the journal at night. Papa taught Momma how to do the figures and all." John's voice was restrained.

"She needs both of you to study so one day you can learn how to handle the journals. You'll need to be able to decipher the figures and keep the ledgers. There's more to life than a hard day's work. A man has to know business, too." Tucker rose and came to stand behind the boys. He put a hand on each head and leaned them backward until they were looking in his face while holding on to the bench to keep from toppling over.

"So are you boys going to work hard at your schoolwork today?" he asked.

"Yes, sir!" James was the loudest.

"I am," John agreed.

Tucker released them and said, "Good, because I'm sure I'll be needing some help after lunch." He turned to Daisy. "Thank you for breakfast. It was good."

Daisy followed Tucker onto the porch. "Here's a little something in case you get hungry before lunch." She offered him an apple and a chunk of bread wrapped in a towel.

He took the towel from her. "I want you to be careful while I'm away from the cabin. I won't rest easy until I know those thieves have been captured."

"We'll be fine. I think they must be long gone from this area. It's been over a month now." Daisy's tone wasn't as convincing as her words.

"Just be careful. For me." He touched the side of her face for a brief moment before stepping from the porch. He climbed on Mack and rode off to work.

That night, supper was eaten and so was most of an entire buttermilk pie. Tucker was glad to see Daisy had baked two.

After the boys were in bed, he asked Daisy if she'd go for a stroll with him so he could walk off some of the pie he'd eaten. They took the familiar trek to the road and back, walking slowly with Daisy's hand hooked over his arm, his other hand caressing her fingers. More than once he rubbed his thumb across the ring he'd given her at their wedding.

"Did you sleep well?" Tucker asked.

Daisy chuckled a little. "I did," she answered. "I did think about you in the barn, though." Her voice was very low. He had to lean in to hear her.

"You did?" He was almost teasing her, but not quite. He tilted his head to see her better in the moonlight.

"I did," she repeated the same words awkwardly.

Tucker laughed. "What else did you did?"

"Oh, stop." Daisy joined his laughter for a moment, but her voice was serious when she spoke again. "I've been doing a lot of thinking these last few weeks." Daisy looked down as she walked, casting her face in shadow even under the bright moonlight. He waited when she paused. "Last night when I went to get ready for bed I found the wedding ring Murdock gave me." Tucker tensed.

"Are you okay?" Once again a first love rose up to recapture a heart he thought might be warming toward him. He should have known better.

"Yes. I'm actually better than I thought I could be by now." She stopped and turned to face him. The light now covered her face, and he could see her clearly. "I know you came here for the boys to have a chance at a future on this land." She looked down and slid her small hands into his strong ones before looking back into his face. "I also know you came here to give me that chance." Tucker gave her hands a gentle squeeze. "I'm just beginning to realize how good that future can be." She smiled at him.

There was an invitation in that smile that had him leaning toward her and pulling her just a step closer.

Daisy continued, "I want you to know I put the ring away. I'm trying to move forward with my life now. I can't forget the past, but I know I can't live there, either."

"Oh, Daisy, I don't want you to forget it." Tucker brushed his hands slowly up and down her arms. "I only want to give you a good life, so you can be happy and fulfilled."

"Thank you, Tucker. I really want that, too." She took a deliberate breath. "I know we're married, but what I'm asking is that we go slowly."

"Oh." He backed away a step and paused for her to continue.

She stumbled over her next words. "We've been friends for a very long time. And I really enjoy your company." She rubbed her arms as if his touch had left her cold.

"Good. I like you, too." He was matter-of-fact. Her mixed signals were confusing him.

"I'm just asking that we go slowly to a deeper rela-

tionship as husband and wife," she finished, looking
up at his face.

Tucker recognized fear when he saw it. Daisy was
afraid to move forward even though she was beginning to want to. He knew her mind must be a jumble
of emotions. The only way to help her through it was
to be patient. In all likelihood she would never be able
to love him. No matter how much she tried.

Tucker pulled her into his embrace. With great effort he offered her comfort that demanded nothing from
her. He whispered into her hair, "You set the pace that
is comfortable for you. Our future is worth the invest-
ment of the time it takes to get it right." He kissed the
top of her head before turning toward the house and
offering her his hand. "Shall we?"

Daisy slid her hand in his. He walked her back to the
cabin and told her good-night.

The cool of the barn kept him awake. He stretched
out on the bedroll he had cushioned with hay. His mind
swirled with thoughts of Daisy. One minute he knew
she was thinking of Murdock. The next minute he found
himself hoping she was thinking of him.

*God, I'm still walking in faith here. It's been a long
time since I ran or flew like an eagle. I'm just not sure
where I'm going at the moment.*

Chapter Sixteen

The days passed and were spent in much the same manner. Chores and school were completed in record time by two boys wanting to clear land and work their new horses. Tucker taught them how to dig up stumps and move heavy boulders. Every night they tumbled into bed exhausted, and every morning they eagerly began again.

Some evenings Daisy and Tucker walked outside. Sometimes they sat by the fire drinking coffee or milk and talking. Their friendship was deepening.

Daisy enjoyed the casual way Tucker reached for her over the past couple of days. He might rest his hand on the small of her back while putting his mug in the dishpan, or place a hand on her shoulder when she sat at the breakfast table before he left for the fields. She drew comfort from his nearness, but wasn't threatened by it. They were growing closer. The pain of her grief still flared at odd moments, but she was adjusting to Murdock's death and accepting Tucker's presence. She no longer saw them as two people solving a problem.

Now she hoped they were two people who were growing into one.

On Friday they loaded into the wagon shortly after lunch for the trip to the Thorntons' ranch. Daisy brought two loaves of fresh bread and two buttermilk pies.

Randall and Judy Thornton's three children were a little older than James and John, but as close neighbors, they all played well together.

"How late will we get to stay, Momma?" James was always happy to see his friends.

"We probably won't stay long after an early supper. We'll need to get back before it's too dark." Daisy answered.

Tucker contradicted Daisy. "Randall and I talked about riding over the ranch. There are some things I'd like to see, and he agreed to show me. We may have supper a little later than usual. You'll have plenty of time to enjoy your visit." He smiled at Daisy. "We haven't had much free time. I think it'll be okay to spend some extra time relaxing and visiting tonight."

"Oh, boy!" James was excited.

"Are you sure, Tucker? It's getting cooler earlier in the evenings now. We can come again another day, too." Daisy was unsure. To think of being out after dark left her ill at ease. Hadn't he cautioned her just this week about the need to be careful?

"I'm sure," Tucker said as he reached for her hand. "We'll be fine. It's a clear day and promises to be a clear night. I stowed a couple of blankets in the back of the wagon. The boys can wrap up in one, and you can have the other to protect you from the night air. You can even ride in the back with them if you want." He gave her a sympathetic smile and squeezed her hand.

"Remember the Thorntons are moving away as soon as he sells the ranch." Tucker released her and took the reins in both hands again.

Some of the joy of anticipation Daisy was feeling ebbed away at the reminder. Judy had been a dear friend for years. Daisy would miss her.

The Thornton children raced up the lane to meet them as soon as they topped the last hill. James and John leaped over the side of the wagon and tore off across the fields, carefully avoiding anywhere the cattle had been. Daisy was amused when James tumbled and rolled as he hit the ground.

She laughed and said, "I declare that James goes so fast after everything in life, it's a wonder he doesn't get hurt. He's constantly on the go."

"John does seem to be more cautious," Tucker acknowledged.

"He is," Daisy agreed, "but James is determined not to be left out of anything. He'd rather be hurt in the attempt than bypass a possibility."

"You used to be that way when you were younger."

Daisy thought about his remark for a moment. "Sometimes the hurts of the past teach you caution."

"That can be true. I think John is wary of the consequences of moving full steam ahead." Tucker watched the boys run as he pulled the reins to lead the horses off the main road and drove toward the front gate. "I understand John because in some ways he's like me. He likes to think and plan before moving. Sadly, even at his young age, he knows there are times when things can't be like you planned. James wants to enjoy the process and is sometimes in the game before he knows all the rules."

Tucker set the brake and hopped to the ground before turning to Daisy. He reached for her waist and lifted her to the ground. She rested her hands on his shoulders to keep her balance. He set her on her feet, and one side of his mouth lifted as he released her. His eyes invited her to respond to him.

She wasn't ready to put their growing relationship on display for their friends. "Thank you, Tucker." Daisy shyly turned away as the front door of the house opened, and Judy came onto the porch.

The Thornton house was much larger than their cabin. White siding seemingly rose to the sky and large dormers lined up across the face of the second floor. There were stables behind the house, and a bunkhouse that slept as many as twenty men. A large barn stood beside the bunkhouse. Several men were moving around the numerous outbuildings, working the busy ranch. Every time Daisy came here it reminded her of home and Papa.

"Daisy!" Judy descended the steps and drew her friend into a hug. Backing away to look at her, Judy spoke quietly. "You look good, Daisy. I can see your heart is mending." She turned and greeted Tucker. "Welcome to our home, Mr. Barlow. At least it's ours for the time being."

"Thank you, Mrs. Thornton. From what I've seen so far, it's a real nice place. You and your husband must be very proud." Tucker returned her greeting and put a hand up to acknowledge Randall Thornton as he approached from the stables.

"Good to see you again." Randall extended his hand to Tucker.

"You, too, Randall," Tucker said as they shook hands.

"Are you ready to ride?" Randall wanted to know.

"Already?" Judy spoke with mock rebuke. "Well, you men go have your ride. Daisy and I are going to sit in the shade of the porch and catch up on lady talk."

Tucker retrieved the basket filled with pies and bread and left it on the porch with the ladies. His hand rested on Daisy's shoulder for the briefest moment as she sat in the rocker opposite her friend. "We'll be back in time for supper," he told her.

"Enjoy yourself," Daisy encouraged him. "It'll be nice for you to ride some open range after all the weeks you've been confined on the farm."

Daisy and Judy talked while the children played in the yard. Daisy saw Tucker and Randall ride off a few minutes later. Tucker's mount was a large black thoroughbred, but she preferred the way he looked on his pinto, Mack. Something about the uniqueness of his horse matched his spirit. He didn't fit into a mold, but rather, his value came from his individuality. Tucker was strong and dependable. He was more than one usually expected in a man who worked the land. His sacrificial heart and deep sense of caring, even his humor, set him apart from other men of equal strength. If only he didn't harbor such deep pain.

"So tell me about him." Judy's voice brought Daisy back from her thoughts. "I was so glad to hear you married. My relief in finding that Tucker has been a friend for so long was great. How horrible it would have been for you to lose your land and for those boys to never own what Murdock worked so hard to give them. But it would have been worse for you to marry someone you couldn't abide just to keep Murdock's dream alive."

Judy watched the men disappear over a hill. "It certainly doesn't hurt that he's such a fine-looking man."

"Judy!" Daisy's cheeks turned pink at Judy's last statement.

"Now, don't you try to pretend with me, Daisy Mosley—I mean Barlow." Judy grinned widely and narrowed her eyes. "We've been friends too long for you to think I can't see how you feel about this man."

"You're embarrassing me, Judy!" Daisy started to fan her face with both hands.

Judy reached to lay a hand on Daisy's arm. "I'm sorry," she said soberly. "I'm just so happy for you."

Uncomfortable talking about Tucker, Daisy redirected the conversation. "I've been praying for your parents. I'm trusting they'll be better just by having you there to care for them,"

"Thank you. That means so much. I hope having the kids around will inspire them, too. The Bible says a merry heart doeth good like a medicine. Maybe the joy of having us home will help them heal." She lifted a hand and gestured toward the cattle grazing in the distance. "I'm going to miss this place.

"I will truly miss you, too, Daisy." Judy smiled at her friend. "I'm glad to know your future is safe. God has been good to both of us. Even if our blessings have come on the heels of great sorrow."

"You're right. I will miss you, too." Daisy's tone was reflective.

The rest of the afternoon and evening seemed to hurry by. The large dining room table hosted lively conversation as the two families shared news of their lives and future plans. The children had been saddened to learn they would soon part, but were determined to enjoy every minute of the time they had left. A roaring game of tag ensued immediately following the heavy meal. The adults watched from chairs on the front porch.

"Your place is nice," Tucker directed his opinions to Randall. "Larger than it seems on first sight. Very impressive."

"Thank you. It's been a long labor of love, but we made it." Randall smiled at Judy. "It'll be difficult to part with, because it's become such a part of who we are."

"It will be nice to be with my family again," Judy added. "We haven't been able to spend time with them since we moved here. You know how demanding a ranch can be, don't you, Tucker?"

"I do. That experience also makes me appreciate the value of what's been accomplished here," Tucker responded.

"I love this place." Daisy sighed. "It reminds me of home."

"It really is like your father's ranch," Tucker agreed. "Of course, the house is newer, as are all the buildings, but the size of the ranch and staff are comparable."

The enthusiasm in his words reminded Daisy of the sacrifice he'd made to come to Pine Haven for her and her sons. "You're a farmer now, but you still sound like a rancher."

"I will admit this place speaks to the rancher in me." Tucker looked across the fields, and she wondered if he could ever be as happy on their farm as he had been as a rancher.

The evening wore on, and, too quickly, they said their goodbyes. The children promised to see each other on Sunday, and the adults agreed to at least one more meal together before the Thornton's moved away for good.

"Very nice family," Tucker observed as he and Daisy rode home under the moonlight.

"Yes, they are," she agreed. "I'll really miss them."

James and John slept soundly under the blanket he'd had provided. An afternoon of running and playing had caught up to the small bodies. Daisy was wrapped snuggly in the other blanket. As the wind started to pick up, he turned his collar up around his ears and set his hat lower on his head.

"Do you want to share the blanket with me?" Daisy offered.

Tucker smiled his thanks, but said, "No, I'm fine."

"Well, at least sit closer, so you'll be warmer." Daisy tried unsuccessfully to scoot closer to him on the wooden seat. She was hindered by the trappings of the heavy blanket.

"Be careful, or you'll roll off the wagon like a sack of potatoes," Tucker laughed. "I'll come to you." He slid nearer to her and, holding the reins in one hand, put an arm around her shoulders, pulling her head toward his shoulder. "I'm sorry about the wind. You were right. We should have left earlier."

Daisy burrowed into the warmth of his coat collar and shook her head. "The extra time with the Thorntons was worth it."

"I'm going as quickly as we can safely make it in the dark. We'll be home in about a half hour. Just stay close, and you'll be okay."

Daisy pulled the blanket around her head and shoulders and was unaware of the kiss he dropped on the top of her head as they rode in silence. She must have gotten warm enough to relax because, when they arrived at the cabin, Tucker had to gently shake her shoulders to wake her.

"We're home," he whispered near her ear.

Daisy sat up and yawned heavily, while stretching her neck and shoulders.

"Oh, Tucker, I'm sorry. I didn't mean to fall asleep."

"No apology necessary. You've had a busy few weeks and needed to rest." He set the brake and climbed down from the wagon. "I just hope you didn't get a crick in your neck."

She chuckled and slid to the edge of the seat before standing and reaching for him. "I'm good. Just a little stiff."

Tucker reached for her waist and hoisted her to the ground. He smiled at her disheveled appearance. With both hands, he pushed loose strands of hair behind her ears before cupping her face and leaning down to brush a soft kiss across her forehead. "You need to get these boys in bed so you can rest. I'll take care of the wagon." He put a hand on each shoulder and spun her around to face the front steps. "Go ahead. I'll bring the boys in. You turn down the blankets."

When he entered the room a moment later, Daisy had lit the lamp on the table and prepared the boys' bed. Effortlessly he laid James on the far side of the bed and returned to the wagon. She removed James's coat and shoes before Tucker came back with John. He took John's shoes off while Daisy pulled his limp body from his coat. She piled an extra quilt on top of the sleeping boys and followed Tucker into the main room.

"Let me make some coffee," Daisy said, lighting the stove.

"That's sounds like a good idea." Tucker lit the fire he'd laid before they left that afternoon. "I'll take care of the horses and be back in a few minutes."

When Tucker reentered the cabin, he found the coffee warm on the stove and Daisy sleeping in her chair by the fire. He quietly poured a mug of the rich brew and went to stand by the fire to warm himself. He stood with his back to the fireplace and wrapped his cold hands around the warm mug.

Sipping the dark liquid, he watched her sleep. Thick blond lashes cast shadows across her pale cheeks. The dotting of freckles across her nose had faded due to the cooler weather. He knew from years of loving observation that those freckles would resurface with new color at the beginning of spring and deepen in beauty through the hot summer months.

Ten years was a long time to be separated from her. In the beginning Tucker had often wondered why God put such a dire love for her in his soul and then refused to let him have her. Over time he'd realized sometimes in life people don't get what they want. It was a difficult lesson, but he'd learned it. He had accepted God's ways were best even when he couldn't understand the reasons.

Standing in the dimly lit cabin tonight, Tucker prayed a prayer of thankfulness that Daisy was his wife. Hope had faded to disappointment ten years ago. Now it threatened to spring to new life with each passing day. Every comforting touch she permitted, each smile of agreement, any time she laughed, the hope grew.

Daisy stirred in her chair, and a quiet moan escaped her. Tucker drank in the sight of her for one moment more. Then he put his mug in the dishpan, pulled the coffee off the burner and turned off the stove.

He squatted in front of her chair with a hand on each chair arm and spoke gently. "Daisy, it's time for bed." She muttered softly. "Daisy, it's time to go to bed," he said again.

"Murdock?" Daisy whimpered. "Murdock?" She sat straight up then, completely disoriented. He doubted she knew she'd spoken aloud.

"It's Tucker, Daisy." He gently shook her shoulders. "Daisy, wake up."

"Oh, Tucker." She put a hand to her forehead and rubbed her brow with her fingers. "I'm sorry. Did I fall asleep again?" She smiled at him through tired eyes.

Tucker pulled his closed lips inside his mouth to form a thin line before he spoke again. He gave her a small smile that didn't reach his eyes. "Yes, you did. It's time for you to go to bed." He took her hands and tugged her out of the chair. "Do you think you can bolt the door and make it to bed without falling asleep again?" he teased.

"I can try." She grinned sleepily.

He put on his hat and coat and stepped into the cold night. "Good night, Daisy," he whispered as he closed the door behind him. He waited to hear the bolt move and then turned toward the steps.

One minute she was reaching for him, and the next she was withdrawing to a place where she wasn't ready to let him be.

How could he move into the cabin with her, sit in the lamp-lit room every night, listen to her voice, and not lose his heart completely to her?

Even now Murdock was the man of her dreams.

Why had Tucker allowed himself to hope for more from Daisy than it was possible for her to give?

With each porch step he descended a little further away from the hope he'd been relishing moments before.

Chapter Seventeen

Saturday morning Daisy stood on the parsonage steps and waited for her friend to answer the door. Her mind struggled with Tucker's mood today. He'd been quiet on the way to town. After they left the boys to play with their friend Reilly, Tucker told her he had business to tend to and would be back in an hour.

Recent days had seen a new closeness in their friendship. What could be troubling him now? From the sidewalk in front of the general store, she'd watched him drive away. His blank expression offered no clues.

Peggy opened the door and welcomed Daisy. "Join me in the kitchen. I'm baking today." The rich aroma of cinnamon filled the air.

"It smells delicious," Daisy said as she hung her coat by the door and followed Peggy into the kitchen.

Peggy put a plate over the cake pan and, holding the pan and plate together, flipped it upside down. She pulled the pan free to reveal the golden cake.

"How about a nice cup of tea and a piece of warm cake?" Peggy went to the stove and picked up the kettle.

Daisy sat at the worn table in the middle of the room. "That sounds good."

"How are you, Daisy?" Peggy set a cup of tea in front of Daisy.

"I'm doing well." She stirred the tea with a spoon, watching the swirls as the milk she added mellowed the brew. "Better than I expected."

Peggy turned to look at Daisy, whose face glowed with a faint blush. "Are you falling in love?" The blush deepened. "You are! Oh, Daisy, how wonderful!"

"It is," Daisy agreed. "But it's not easy. I'm afraid of hurting Tucker. He's been so good to the twins and me."

"How could you hurt him, Daisy? Most men are content with a woman to cook and clean. A lot of men don't concern themselves with love. It's a bonus to Tucker for you to love him." Peggy passed a piece of cake to Daisy. A trail of cinnamon and brown sugar ran through the middle of the thick slice.

"Do you really think so? You weren't so keen for me to marry Tucker in the beginning," Daisy pointed out, lifting her fork.

"That was before David talked to me about how good Tucker would be for you."

"There is one problem," Daisy said softly.

"What?" Peggy asked. "I'm sure it's not anything that can't be fixed."

"I still dream about Murdock." Tears poured down Daisy's face. She hadn't been able to speak to anyone of her dreams. "Not so much now as before, but I don't know how I can move ahead until the dreams stop."

Peggy patted Daisy's hand where it lay on the table. "Tell me about your dreams."

Daisy sniffed and stared at the table, the cake forgotten. "They usually begin with me washing dishes and looking out the front window, or on the porch looking across the fields in front of the house. I see Murdock walking away in a haze of light. I call out to him, and he turns and looks at me, smiles and waves, and then turns back and disappears into the haze."

"What do you think about the dreams?"

"I think he's going away, and I'm trying to hold on to him." Daisy's tears stopped, but her composure was still vulnerable.

"Maybe in your heart you're trying to hold on to him," Peggy offered.

"I dreamed it again last night, but it was different." Daisy's voice quivered.

"Do you want to tell me about it?"

"It started the same. I was on the porch. Murdock was walking away. I called to him, like in every other dream. Only this time—" she sniffed again "—he didn't turn around. So I called again. He still didn't turn around. He just kept walking." Daisy was crying again now.

"How did the dream end?" Peggy asked.

"That's just it. This is why I'm concerned about hurting Tucker."

"I don't understand." A frown creased Peggy's brow.

"The dream didn't end. I had fallen asleep in the chair by the fire. After I called out to Murdock in the dream, Tucker woke me up. I was startled, but I didn't know what to say. I don't know if I cried aloud or only in my sleep."

"Have you told Tucker about the dreams?"

"No. Not even then." Daisy dried her eyes and took a deep breath. "He's been so kind. For the last several days we've been becoming more friendly, if you know what I mean."

Peggy smiled. "I think I may have an idea."

"Nothing serious, but we've been making a real effort to strengthen our friendship and build a good relationship. I don't want to endanger that now. It's too fragile." Daisy put her face in her hands and rested her elbows on the table.

"I have a feeling everything is going to be just fine." Peggy declared.

"Why do you think so?" Daisy lifted her head.

"Because you, my friend, are in love." Peggy smiled. "I think your last dream may have been the last one you'll have. In your heart you're letting go of the past. It's been a hard road, but I think you're ready to pursue your future."

"I did think that might be the case, but I feel guilty for letting go of Murdock," Daisy bemoaned.

"You won't ever let go of the essence of Murdock. Those boys will keep him in your life. But it's time to release him as your husband," Peggy assured her.

"Thank you, Peggy. You're right. I think I'm ready to release Murdock." She smiled. "And embrace Tucker."

She silently prayed. *Lord, help him to be willing, too.*

As Tucker and Daisy met back at the wagon later that afternoon, Mr. Croft came out of the general store.

"Mr. Barlow, Mrs. Barlow. How are you fine folks today?" Donald Croft walked to the edge of the wooden sidewalk and greeted them.

"Just fine, Mr. Croft. How are you?" Tucker helped Daisy into the wagon and answered for both of them.

"I'm fine myself, thanks for asking." To Daisy he

said, "I'm sorry I didn't get to speak to you earlier, Mrs. Barlow. I trust my Liza was able to get you everything you needed today."

"Yes, thank you. The twins loaded everything in the wagon earlier."

"That's good, that's good." He addressed Tucker again. "I wanted to let you know I ordered your furniture."

"Will you let me know as soon as it arrives?" Tucker climbed up to sit next to Daisy. James and John vaulted into the back of the wagon, carefully avoiding the day's purchases.

"Well, that's what I come out here to tell you." Mr. Croft nodded his head in the affirmative. "I heard back from the company. It seems they had that particular set on hand. They were set to ship it out last week. Should get here by Tuesday." He held up a hand. "Now I know that's a might earlier than we thought, so if you need me to hold it for a week or two, until you get the money, I can."

"That won't be necessary, Mr. Croft." Tucker released the brake. "I'll be able to pay you as soon as it comes. I'm not one to order something before I can pay."

"Oh, no, sir, that's not what I meant, Mr. Barlow. I was just trying to be helpful. I didn't mean to offend. I'm not the least worried about the money. Just wasn't expectin' it to come so soon."

"No offense taken." Tucker held the reins in hand.

"Oh, well. That's good." Mr. Croft stumbled over his words. "And don't you worry about a thing. As soon as it comes, I'll send a boy out there to let you know. I can even deliver it, if you want."

"Just send word. I'll pick it up." He lifted his hat in dismissal and set it back on his head.

"Thank you for your business, Mr. Barlow. Good day to you and the missus."

As they rode home, Daisy tried to think of a way to draw Tucker out of his silence. He had kept to himself all day, barely speaking a dozen or so words to her. He had even grabbed a biscuit and a slice of ham that morning and eaten it while he hitched the wagon instead of coming into the house.

She finally asked, "Did you get everything done in town that you wanted to?"

"I did." He kept his focus on the road ahead.

Daisy looked to make certain the boys wouldn't hear her next question. "Did you speak to the sheriff?" Daisy didn't want to ask, but she couldn't stand not knowing.

"Still haven't caught them," Tucker replied. "He did say he got word some more horses were stolen. Looks like they've made a big circle and have headed back this way."

"How can we know it's the same people?" Daisy was troubled at this turn of events.

"Can't. We'll have to be extra cautious and pray somebody catches them soon." He did look at her then. "I'm sorry, Daisy. I know you want this to be over." Turning back to the road he added, "No more than I do, I promise you that." He made no further attempt at conversation.

Tucker's continued withdrawal convinced her she must have cried out in her dream last night. Without wanting to, and really without being able to avoid or control the circumstances, she'd hurt him. The question in her mind was how to fix it. She turned slightly to study him as he drove the wagon.

His red hair was starting to curl in the back. It was time for a haircut. She'd ask if he wanted her to trim it after she cut the boys' hair tonight. Maybe he'd relax and talk to her then.

"Boys," Daisy called over her shoulder. "I want you to finish up your chores quickly when we get home. I need to cut your hair before supper. I don't want to be on the porch too late in the day. You might take a chill."

"Yes, ma'am." The boys were riding near the back of the wagon, away from the supplies she'd bought at the general store and the crates that contained Tucker's purchases.

"Would you like me to cut your hair, too, Tucker?"

He rubbed a hand across the back of his neck. "That'd probably be a good idea. Haven't had a cut since the day I left to come here."

Daisy's heart was warmed at the thought of him preparing so carefully before he came to offer to save her family. "Really?" She couldn't help but tease him. "And what else did you do the day you left to come here?" Daisy leaned in close to ask.

Tucker exhaled a short breath from his nostrils and smirked. "I told both my girlfriends goodbye and sold my interest in the saloon."

"Tucker!" Daisy jerked up straight in surprise. "That's terrible! What if the boys heard you say that." She was incredulous. First he wasn't talking at all, and now, in an instant, he was teasing her mercilessly.

He chuckled and smiled. "Then you'd have to explain to them why you're always asking me questions. Sometimes a man just doesn't want to talk." He gave her a smug look. "We sure don't want to tell our secrets when we're not sure how they'll be received." His voice had been so low she'd had to lean in to hear the last sentence.

"We can share secrets," Daisy offered, looking directly at him as she spoke. "If you want."

Tucker observed her open gaze and decided to test her intentions. "Okay. You go first."

"Okay," Daisy agreed, inhaling deeply. "What secret do you want me to share?" She was still turned toward him and leaning in close.

Tucker knew the boys couldn't hear so he asked, "You were calling for Murdock in your sleep last night." He kept his eyes forward. "Will you tell me how you're feeling? Are you still grieving terribly?" He cleared his throat in an attempt to cover how vulnerable he felt having to ask her this question.

"Is that what's been bothering you today?" Tucker slid her a sideways glance before turning back to the road. He'd known she would notice his cool manner but hadn't been able to relax and be himself. He couldn't erase the memory of hearing her call Murdock's name.

"I wondered if I spoke out loud." Daisy shifted away from him slightly, but remained close enough to keep the conversation private. "I had a dream about Murdock."

"Are you okay?" Tucker wanted to know how she was feeling about her late husband. It was only natural that a part of her would always love Murdock, but a part of him was beginning to hope he could help her heal and move on with her life. If she was still dreaming about her first husband, she might not be ready. He didn't want to confuse her heart by falling in love with her again. Not if she wasn't ready to receive his love.

He'd lost her before. He wouldn't rush ahead now and risk having her mistake his love for pity.

"This may seem crazy to you, but that dream helped me realize something." She appeared to be having a difficult time choosing her words. Tucker held the reins tighter, as if by doing so he could hold his thoughts in check. "Peggy told me I should consider telling you about this."

"So you've discussed this with Peggy?" Tucker longed for Daisy to confide in him. He'd come all this way to be here for her, and she still wasn't comfortable enough with him to share her most sensitive thoughts.

"I saw her today. She was very helpful." Daisy turned back toward Tucker. "Peggy helped me see that my dreaming about Murdock was a way my heart was trying to hold on to him."

Tucker wrestled his heart back into the bonds of patience he'd only recently begun to loosen. "I see." Echoes of rejection hammered in his ears before she spoke another word.

"No, Tucker. It's not what you're thinking." Daisy became more animated, but quickly lowered her voice. Leaning in again, she said, "I've had the same dream many times since Murdock was killed. Each time I called him back, and he turned to me." Tucker sat in silence, watching a sad smile crease her face. "Last night in the dream he kept walking. He didn't look back." She looked at him with pleading eyes. "Can't you see? I'm finally able to let him go. He's not coming back. I know that in my head, but now my heart has realized it. I'm letting go of him."

Tucker sent her a puzzled look full of uncertainty.

Daisy elaborated. "When I called him back, and he

didn't respond, it was my heart knowing I've released him."

He wasn't sure he understood her. Why would she still be calling for Murdock, if she'd really let him go?

"All day long today, I've noticed how distant you've been," Daisy said pointedly. "Today I didn't miss Murdock." Tucker looked down at her and waited. A glimmer of hope started to flicker in his soul. The fire of hope had been extinguished the night before when Daisy spoke Murdock's name. Was it possible for her to speak the same name again and reignite the flame?

Daisy looped her arm into his as he held the reins and lifted her eyes to meet his. "Today I missed you." She grinned mischievously. "I've grown accustomed to your easy friendship and fun manner. When you didn't want to tease with me today, I felt part of me slipping downward into the sadness I'd just begun to escape."

Tucker smiled at her now. "Is that so?" He pulled his elbow into his side, pressing her hand against him. Did he dare consider that Daisy could actually let go of her past? She was stronger than any woman he'd ever known. Stronger, even, than his mother. Maybe there was a chance for them. "Well, we can't have that, can we?"

Looking ahead so he could lead the horses onto the lane to their cabin, Tucker asked, "So you want to cut my hair, do you?"

Daisy reached up timidly and threaded her fingers through the red curls at the base of his neck. "I think it would be a good idea. If you can trust me with the scissors."

He reached up and captured her hand in his. "You must promise there'll be no bloodshed." He tugged on the hand he held. She laughed and he tugged again. "Promise or it's no deal."

"I promise to make every effort to prevent bloodshed." She giggled.

"Is that the best you've got?" He put her hand on his thigh and, and without releasing it, pressed his hand on top of hers.

"You can't guarantee something like that. Accidents happen." She still laughed. "I promise to do my best."

Tucker gave her hand a squeeze and released her. He was pleased when she let her hand continue to rest on his leg as they pulled up to the cabin. His pleasure came mostly from the hope that once again they were forging toward a deeper relationship. He prayed again for God to help him.

God, thank You for continuing to heal her pain. She's releasing her past. Will there be room in her heart for me?

Chapter Eighteen

Daisy arranged everything she needed to cut hair on the table between the porch rockers. She moved a straight back chair so she'd have good light to work.

"John, are you finished with your chores?" Daisy saw her youngest twin come out of the barn.

"Yes, ma'am." He started walking to the porch.

"Let's get your hair cut first, then." John hopped onto the chair, and Daisy draped a towel around his shoulders. He sat extremely still. She carefully worked around his face and ears, after she'd cut the top and back. She was shaking the hair from the towel, and he was going to get his brother within minutes.

James wasn't as eager. "You need a haircut. Hop up on the chair, and let's get it over with," Daisy admonished.

He obeyed, but not without complaint. "Why does my hair need to be short, if Mr. Tucker can have long hair?"

Tucker came out of the barn in time to hear Daisy tell James to get in the chair. By the time James started to try to convince her he didn't need a haircut, Tucker was on the porch steps. "James, don't argue with your momma. She said you're getting a haircut. That's the end of it."

Daisy was adjusting to Tucker's active role in the boys' discipline. She knew he had every right to correct them, and the boys had accepted this new authority quicker than she had. Their initial resentment had faded when he gave them, not just correction, but also his attention.

"Yes, sir." James pushed his bottom lip out and hung his head. Daisy took full advantage of his posture to trim the back of his hair.

James was too boisterous to be silent for long. While Daisy cut his hair, he told her all about his day in town playing with Reilly. He was still jabbering away when Daisy finished and removed the towel from his neck.

"You and your brother have a few more minutes before I'll need to wash your hair. Don't go far. I'm heating the water now. Baths for both of you tonight." James opened his mouth to protest, but she silenced him by holding up one hand.

"Don't even try, James. It's Saturday. You know the routine." Little feet dragged across the dirt as he headed to the barn to relay his mother's message to John.

Daisy turned to Tucker who leaned against the porch rail and gestured for him to take his seat.

"Remember your promise." Tucker lowered himself into the chair, but kept his eyes on her face.

"I remember. But don't make me nervous." She moved to stand behind him and laid the towel across his chest, overlapping the ends at the base of his neck. "That always makes me snip an ear."

Tucker instantly put a hand over each ear. "I do hope you're kidding." He pulled his shoulders up close to his ears for added protection.

"Stop that. You're making the towel fall." Daisy pulled his hands away from his ears. "You'll have loose hair down your collar and everywhere. Now be still."

Tucker straightened, and she repositioned the towel under his chin.

"How much do you want me to take off, sir?" Daisy asked in her best barber voice and made a show of wiping the comb on the towel across his shoulder. "You want a good cut, or do you prefer to keep a slightly scruffy look?"

Tucker smiled at her tone. "I'd like to keep my ears, please, sir. Just clean it up around the neck and sides for me. And cut this out of my eyes, too." He flicked the hair away from his forehead with one hand.

Daisy laughed. "Okay. I'll leave your ears this time, but there are no guarantees about future cuttings. I've been known to be distracted from time to time."

She reached up and ran her hands through his hair to get a feel for how long it was and where she'd need to trim. She wasn't prepared for her reaction to the simple act of touching his hair. Suddenly what was supposed to be an act of kindness for a friend became a very intimate moment. Until she caught her fingers in a knot above his ear, and he cried out in mock pain.

"Ouch!" He leaned his head to one side to lessen her hold on him and chuckled. "Are you going to cut it, or pull it out by the roots?"

Daisy jerked her hands away, glad he couldn't see her face. "You just be still. You're worse than the boys. I'd never have thought you'd be so tender-headed." She could feel the heat of his body. It warmed her, but also sent a tingle up her spine.

"I didn't know you were so strong," he countered, rubbing the spot her fingers had snagged.

Forcibly gathering her wits, she cut the red curls away from his neck, and they fell to the porch. She was able to cut the back and sides without being directly in his line of vision. Neither of them spoke. Daisy wondered if the nearness affected him as much as it did her. She stepped around the chair. His eyes closed as she combed his hair down in the front so she could cut it straight across. The sight of him with red hair almost covering his eyes as it curled on the ends made her laugh.

Tucker opened his eyes and sent her a teasing glare. "What is so funny, Mrs. Barlow?"

"Why, you are, Mr. Barlow, with your red curls hanging in your face."

In a swift motion, he reached out and encircled her waist with both arms and pulled her against his chest. With a quick breath, he blew his hair away from his face. He sat staring up at her with clear green eyes. She put her hands on his shoulders, the scissors open in one hand, bracing herself away from his face, and realized again how tall he was—the top of his head even with her shoulders.

"So you think I look funny, do you?" His brows rolled up and back down again inquiringly as he looked into her face.

"No, sir, Mr. Barlow, not at all." She giggled.

"Are you ticklish, Daisy?" he teased, and a dark gleam entered his eyes.

"Mr. Barlow, if you value your ear, you will release me at once," she warned with a grin. "I cannot be held responsible for these scissors if you try to discover the answer to that question." Tucker released her so quickly she stumbled backward, and he had to catch her.

"Easy there, ma'am." He set her upright and put his hands up in surrender. "We don't want anyone to be hurt here today." He winked at her then, and she laughed.

Daisy took a deep steadying breath and approached him again. "You be still, or we won't ever finish." She straightened the towel and combed his hair back in front of his eyes, causing him to close them.

"I'm in no hurry," he said with a grin.

"Well, I've got water on the stove to bathe those boys. I'm sure it's boiling by now," Daisy said as she finished cutting his hair. She was surprised by how relaxed and playful Tucker had become. Her prayers for God to open his long-shuttered heart must be working.

"You really are an easily distracted barber," Tucker said as she removed the towel and shook the loose hairs into the dirt in front of the porch. "I'll definitely be back to see you again." He stood and put the chair back in line with the others on the porch. Daisy began to gather her tools.

Tucker came up behind her, leaned close to her ear, and asked quietly, "Do you think I could get a shave next time? Or would that be too dangerous for me?"

She turned and snapped the towel in his direction as he bounded from the porch laughing.

"You come back in half an hour. I'll have the water ready for you then," she called at his quickly retreating back. "I don't want to be out on the porch all night while you boys take your baths."

"Yes, ma'am. I'll be there."

Sunday morning dawned unseasonably warm. Daisy's heart was lighter than it had been in months as she sat in church with Tucker and the twins. She spent the time before service in prayer thanking God for the healing balm that Tucker was to her.

She reflected on how God had impressed that into her spirit on the way into town the day she married Tucker in this very room, and a smile crossed her face. Tucker turned in time to see it, and he reached for her hand, holding it in his for the duration of the service.

Reverend Dismuke approached the lectern. "This week I studied *2 Corinthians* 5. Verse seventeen says, 'Therefore if any man be in Christ, he is a new creature: old things are passed away; behold, all things are become new.' It's exciting to me that we can experience new beginnings all through our lives."

"Many times we come to a hard place, or the end of something familiar, and we feel at a loss. This verse gives us hope, because even when the old is gone, God has something new for us."

Daisy didn't hear much of the rest of the sermon. She prayed for Judy and Randall Thornton and the new beginning they were about to encounter. Her sons had a new beginning when Tucker came and protected their future. He also filled the much needed place of a strong man in their lives to lead them into manhood. She sat, holding Tucker's hand and thanking God for new beginnings. She chanced a glance at him and caught him looking at her. Daisy squeezed his hand in silent thanks for who he was becoming to her.

Sunday night, after a supper of beans and cornbread, the twins spent time with their horses. Tucker and Daisy sat on the front porch enjoying the mild weather.

"Randall Thornton told me today the railroad is coming through this county," Tucker informed her.

"Really? We were told last year it was going to run to the south of us."

"That was the original plan, but the water supply south of here has dried up, so the land scouts chose Pine Haven as the best alternative." Tucker used one boot to rock his chair as he looked out over the fields. "It'll sure make getting the cotton to market easier for all the local farmers. The profit margin will go up considerably. Ranching is a lot easier when there's a railroad nearby, too."

"How long did Randall think it would be before they get here?" Daisy asked.

"Next year some time, probably in the fall," Tucker responded. "He said the scouts are already purchasing property in the area. He sold them the south edge of his property so they can lay track. Said they'll probably want to run across the south of our property, too. The scouts were on their way back to meet with the owners of the railroad when he saw them last week. They won't be back in Pine Haven until January, but if they approach us, I want to consider selling them an easement. They'd be able to run the track across the land, but we'd still own it and be able to plant on either side of the tracks. I think we'd both benefit from an arrangement like that. What do you think?"

"That sounds wise," Daisy agreed. "I'll be glad to see the railroad come here."

"It has the potential to completely change the lives of this community," Tucker observed.

"Do you think so? I hoped it would come so I could take the boys to see Papa. I miss him terribly."

"It will be easier to do that, but I remember how it changed East River. Your father's ranch is able to sell cattle and transport herds much easier, but people are constantly moving in and out of town. Something about transportation unsettles folks. They start hankering to move away in search of something they don't really know. The town isn't like it was when you left, Daisy."

She looked at Tucker so intently that he stopped the motion of his chair. "Tucker, I'm glad you were willing to make the move into the unknown." She didn't blink. "I don't know what the boys and I would have done without you."

"I didn't move to the unknown, Daisy. I came to you." Tucker pushed his boot against the boarded porch and smiled before looking back at the setting sun.

After a dessert of pumpkin pie, Daisy sent the boys to bed and went to hear their prayers. Tucker stepped outside to bring in more firewood. When he unloaded the logs onto the hearth he heard their voices from the other room.

He went to door and leaned against the jamb. His arrival went unnoticed by the boys. He watched Daisy's back as she talked with them.

"If we love Mr. Tucker, does it hurt Papa?" John asked as he climbed into bed.

"No, son." Daisy squeezed his small frame into a hug. "It means your papa taught you so much about love that you have room in your heart to love more than one person." Daisy cupped John's face in her hands and looked deep into his eyes. "Your papa would be so proud of your heart. I am, too." Daisy kissed his forehead and brushed his cheek with the back of her hand. "Now you lie down and go to sleep." She pulled the quilt up close under his chin.

"Momma?" his voice was just above a whisper.

"Yes, John."

"Do you have enough room in your heart to love Papa *and* Mr. Tucker?" Tucker held his breath. He hadn't meant to overhear, but now he needed to know her answer.

"Oh, John, I already do. I love your papa. He was an amazing man, and he gave me wonderful things. Like this farm. But most of all he gave me you and your brother." She took his chin between her thumb and forefinger and gave him a playful squeeze, then smiled at James who was listening closely from the other side of the bed. "And I love Mr. Tucker. He's been my friend for many years."

"But, Momma?" John persisted. "Do you love Mr. Tucker like you loved Papa? You know, like a papa and a momma kind of love, with all the kissing and stuff? I saw you smiling at Mr. Tucker today like you used to smile at Papa. Is that what it's like?" Tucker was amazed at John's young mind. He was trying to understand things Tucker was still struggling with in his heart. Could Daisy love him?

"Yes, John, my heart can do that. It just has to heal from the pain of losing your papa. Like your heart is healing." She patted the side of his face and stood. "Now you boys need to get to sleep."

Daisy headed for the bedroom door. "Momma?" This time it was James.

"Yes, James?"

"Isn't God love? That's what Mrs. Winters said in our class at church today. She said God is love, and that He heals us, too."

"That's true, James," Daisy answered. After hearing

John's insight, great curiosity filled Tucker. What would James, who was so like his mother, say?

The boy asked in a serious tone. "Then won't it help your heart to heal if you go ahead now and love Mr. Tucker? Is that how God makes it work?"

Daisy stood and Tucker quietly backed away from the touching scene. He heard a slight tremor in her voice when she responded. "Yes, James, I think you've got that exactly right. God uses love to heal our hearts.

"I'm so glad we had this talk tonight, boys. Sleep well." She closed the door quietly and leaned her forehead against it.

"Are you okay?" Tucker asked from his chair. He'd only just taken a seat; Daisy's Bible was in his lap. He didn't realize that in his haste to move away from the boys' bedroom door, he'd opened the Bible and now held it upside down.

Hope that she would completely embrace him as her husband was growing with each passing day. Overhearing the bedtime conversation let him know the twins expected the relationship between him and Daisy to move to a deeper level.

"I'm more than okay, thank you." Daisy wiped her eyes with the bottom of her apron and went to pour coffee for them. "It just touches my heart to learn the lessons of God from my sons. That's all." She sniffed and brought a mug to Tucker.

His fingers wrapped around the mug and captured hers. He looked into her eyes and smiled. "We can both learn a lot from those two."

At breakfast on Monday, Tucker told the boys he'd need their help in the fields for the morning. Their elation at foregoing schoolbooks for a day was enormous. A jovial meal was followed by the twins heading off to prepare their horses for the day of labor. Tucker lingered in the cabin with Daisy.

"Will you make us a few sandwiches? We may not make it back before supper. There are a couple of large stumps I need to get moved today."

"Sure. Do you have any requests?" Daisy asked.

"Some more of that pumpkin pie?" His eyes lit up.

"Okay. Only if you promise me you boys won't eat and then fall asleep up there instead of working. I don't want to hinder your progress in clearing that acreage."

Tucker went to help James and John. Daisy prepared their lunch and left the basket on the table. She went to make her bed, humming her way through the morning chores. With her back to the door, she fluffed the pillows.

The sound of Tucker clearing his throat drew her attention to him standing at the threshold of the room.

"I didn't hear you come in." She joined him at the doorway. "Be careful. I don't want either of you to be hurt trying to move those stumps. We can get a couple of men to help if you want."

Tucker looked into her face and cupped the side of her delicate throat with one hand. "We'll be fine." He rubbed the pad of his thumb across her cheek. "You have a good day. And you be careful, too. We still need to be cautious." He dropped his hand and stepped toward the front door. The warmth of his touch left a coolness behind. Daisy wondered if that's what had happened to her heart. Had she wanted the touch of healing love, only to resist it and leave her heart cold?

She followed him and put a hand on his arm as he

reached for the latch. "I'll be careful." She rose up on her toes and pressed her lips to his for a brief moment.

He raised his eyebrows and looked at her with a slight smile.

"You said I could do that whenever I wanted to," she reminded him. She clasped her hands behind her back and lowered her head.

Tucker put a hand beneath her chin and lifted her face. Her brown eyes met his green ones. "I'm pleased for you to take me up on that offer." He smiled and stepped outside, then whistled to get Mack's attention. Daisy stood on the porch, watching the three of them ride around the side of the cabin toward the fields. She put a hand to her throat and caressed the place Tucker had held in his hand. With a smile she turned and went back to her chores. The tune she hummed was a happy one.

Chapter Nineteen

By midafternoon Daisy had the wash on the line and was going inside to put bread in the oven. She stepped onto the porch and heard the sound of horses galloping over the top of the hill on the lane that led to the road. She knew Tucker and the twins were working in the opposite direction. Dropping her basket, she ran into the house and bolted the door. She snatched the shotgun from the rack over the fireplace and went to bolt the back door. She was at the front window within seconds with the gun ready to fire.

Two riders came steadily up the lane. She pushed the barrel of the shotgun through the front window. Her elbows rested on the cabinet by the dishpan. Her aim was hindered by the speed of the riders. She narrowed her sights on the man in front. He was of average height and wore a striped poncho. A felt sombrero rested on his head. The second rider was in her periphery. A fleeting glance told her he was probably a Texan.

Afraid there would be no time for Tucker to come to her aid, Daisy fired a shot high in the air. Dust flew into a cloud at the hooves of both horses as the riders pulled hard on the reins and jumped to the ground on the opposite side of their mounts. Each drew a gun and aimed for her window.

"Don't shoot!" the first rider called loudly.

"Drop your guns," Daisy ordered the strangers, "and step out where I can see you."

"How do we know you will not shoot at us again?" Concern laced the heavy Mexican accent of the lead rider. Neither man moved a muscle.

"Who are you? What's your business here?" Daisy was no-nonsense in her questioning.

"My name is Paco Morales," the first rider spoke again. "This is my amigo Lawrence Walker. We are here to see Señor Tucker Barlow." He adjusted his sombrero in an attempt to see her better. "We are at the right cabin, no?"

"What's your business?" Daisy hoped that was Tucker's horse she heard riding in the distance.

"We are here to join with him in the business of ranching," Paco answered. "Are you Señora Barlow? The daughter of Señor Warren? We come from his ranch in East River."

Daisy heard Tucker's voice from the side of the house. "Paco! Lawrence! What's going on here?" He came into Daisy's line of sight. "Daisy!" he admonished. "Did you try to shoot my friends?"

"It's so good to see you Señor Tucker. Your wife is a strong woman. If you did not come we would be in danger still, no?" Paco shook hands with Tucker and clapped him on the back.

Daisy lowered her gun, and lowered herself, trembling, onto a chair by the table. She could hear the men talking and knew she was not in danger. But she'd been frightened too many times lately to take chances.

Through the open window she heard Tucker welcome his other friend. "Lawrence, it's good to see you. Let me see if I can talk Daisy out of shooting anyone and maybe get us something to eat."

She caught sight of Tucker as he turned and whistled twice—long and even. Then he cupped his hands around his mouth and shouted, "Boys, take care of all these horses for me, and come inside for supper." He must have had the twins hang back at a safe distance when he'd come to investigate the gunfire.

Tucker opened the front door and spoke to Paco and Lawrence over his shoulder. "Give me a minute, please." He entered the cabin and closed the door. Daisy dropped her face into her hands and wept like a frightened child.

She crumpled into Tucker's arms when he went down on one knee beside her chair. She nestled into his shoulder, and he cradled her head with one hand. "It's okay, Daisy. You're safe."

She spoke against his shirt, scolding him in garbled words she knew he wouldn't understand. He pushed her away from his chest. She tried in vain to resist his effort to pull her hands away from her face. She hated being afraid. It went against her nature. Yet she couldn't mask the shadows of terror in her gaze.

"Oh, Daisy, I'm so sorry." He pulled her back into his arms. "You must have been frightened to see more strangers ride up here, but you're safe now."

She jerked away from him. "Why didn't you tell me someone was coming to see you?" She flung the words at him. "I could have killed them!"

"They weren't supposed to be here until next week. I don't know why they're early." He rubbed his hands up and down her arms in an attempt to calm her. "That was a great idea to fire off a shot so I'd come back to the cabin. No one can accuse you of cowardice." He leaned in to smile at her still-angry face. "If anything, we might need to post a sign at the road warning people about what a good protector you are."

Daisy made a kind of snorting sound, somewhere between crying and laughing. Tucker laughed with her. She stood and wiped her cheeks dry with both hands. "Maybe if men didn't just show up and startle women they wouldn't be in such danger." She knew the argument was feeble, but felt compelled to defend her actions.

"Wait a minute." Daisy's face clouded with the beginnings of a fierce rage.

"What is it?" Tucker's tone was clipped, reflecting his surprise at the sudden change in her expression.

"What business of ranching are these two men here to join in with you?" She leveled an accusing stare at him and crossed her arms.

The front door burst open, and James and John exploded into the room. "Are you okay, Momma?" The twins wrapped themselves around Daisy's middle.

"I'm fine." She put a hand on each boy's back to comfort them. "I fired the shot so Mr. Tucker would come quickly."

"He ran when he heard that shot, Momma!" James was full of drama. "He jumped on Mack and was riding away before we could move! He told us to follow him, but not come over the last hill unless he gave the signal." James took a deep breath for air. "Then he told us to go to Mr. Thornton's if we didn't hear the signal five minutes after he rode over the hill. It was exciting, Momma!"

"I'm glad you're okay." John didn't let go of her waist. He'd wrapped both arms around her and clung to her still.

"I'm fine now. The men who rode up are friends of Mr. Tucker."

James had gained a second wind. "We know. We saw 'em outside. They're holding our horses for us while we check on you. That's what men do. They help each other with their horses."

"You young men better go outside and help those men with their horses, then." Tucker stood by the door that had swung wide when they entered. "I'm proud of both of you for following my instructions so well. If there had been a true emergency, everything you did would have been a great help. Those will be our signals from now on. Gunshots when we need help and two long whistles when everything is safe. And don't forget to ride to the Thornton ranch if we ever need more help."

"Yes, sir." The twins marched outside like real men. They flourished under Tucker's instructions.

"Is it safe to come in?" Paco peered into the front door as the boys went down the steps. Lawrence came onto the porch after handing the boys the reins to all the horses.

Tucker looked over his shoulder. Daisy sent him a glare. She was not anywhere near being satisfied with their conversation. He gave a wink before mouthing, "Later," to her. Swinging the door open again, Tucker welcomed his friends to the cabin.

"Come in. I'd like you to meet my wife."

Paco and Lawrence removed their hats as they came through the door.

"I'm so sorry we frightened you, *Señora*. We did not

know you did not know we were coming today." Paco took the lead in the conversation again. He dipped his head in her direction.

"I'm Lawrence Walker. It's nice to meet you, Mrs. Barlow." The younger man nodded a greeting. "Please forgive us for catching you off guard."

Daisy listened to all of this and did her best to steady her breathing. "If you'll excuse me for a moment, gentlemen?" She turned on her heel and went into her room, quietly closing the door behind her.

Paco looked at Lawrence and then at Tucker. "You are in trouble, amigo." Paco chuckled. "I think this sister is more like Jasmine than Lily. This one is like a fireball. You better be careful with her." He laughed.

"I'll say," Lawrence added with a chuckle, "or she'll shoot you one day."

"She already has," Tucker admitted, and they all erupted in laughter.

Daisy opened the door to her room and came out. "Is something funny?" She moved to the table and uncovered the dough she had left to rise earlier. "I'd hate to miss a good laugh." She narrowed her eyes on Tucker. "Unless, of course, it's at my expense."

"Now, Daisy." Tucker came to stand beside her and put an arm around her shoulders. "You've got to admit there's some humor in the fact that you tend to want to shoot any man who comes in your vicinity."

She slipped from Tucker's embrace and retrieved a baking pan. Returning to the table she began to grease and flour the pan. Daisy stopped in midmotion and looked up at the men standing around the table in the small cabin. Lifting a floury finger she pointed at each one of them in turn.

"Consider yourselves warned." She jerked a thumb in Tucker's direction. "You can ask him if I know how to hit a target." They all laughed, and she joined them.

"Now if you'll all go make yourselves busy somewhere else, I've got to add some more vegetables to the soup if we're all going to eat supper tonight." She picked up the bread and dropped it into the pan.

The three men headed out the door. Tucker was the last to leave and turned to her. "I'll explain everything as soon as we get a moment alone."

"Yes, you will." Daisy pointed at the door. "Now go so I can get my thoughts together, or I'll grab that gun again."

"Amen." All the men echoed Daisy as she finished giving thanks for their supper. She passed the bread around the table and asked Paco, "You said you came from my father's ranch?"

Paco took a slice of the warm bread and passed the basket to Lawrence. Reaching for the butter, he answered her question with one of his own. "Did Señor Tucker not tell you I work for your papa?" Paco shook his head in Tucker's direction. "It is not good to keep secrets from your *señora*." To Daisy he said, "I work for your papa for many years now. Seven years. I meet him on a cattle drive before the railroad come to East River. He is a good man, your papa." He smiled at Daisy.

"I didn't know. I'm sorry. What did you do for Papa?" she asked. Paco's friendly manner made it impossible to be upset with him. Daisy was happy to meet someone who could bring her news of her family.

"I was a ranch hand for many years." Paco wiped the

corners of his mouth. "This soup is very good, *señora*. It is much like your sister Lily makes."

"How is Lily?" Daisy's face softened as she thought of her family. Lily had been only twelve years old when Daisy moved away.

"She is well. She is a lovely woman." Paco praised her sister.

It was hard for Daisy to imagine Lily as a young woman. She still remembered the braids of blond hair and the dainty features of a schoolgirl. It was bittersweet to hear her described so kindly.

"It's so nice to have you here, Paco. I look forward to hearing news of my family."

Tucker spoke up then. "Lawrence worked for your father, too. He's only been there a couple of years, but Paco saw a lot of potential in him and decided to bring him along."

"I had no idea you both worked for my father. I'm sorry for the reception I gave you this afternoon." Daisy lowered her stare to her bowl and stirred her soup absentmindedly. "I've had some difficult experiences lately. It's left me a bit jumpy at times.

Lawrence said, "We understand, ma'am. Mr. Tucker explained about you being nervous of strangers. No harm done." The young man couldn't be more than eighteen. His dark hair was too long, but it was clean. His clothes were neat, but his manner was clumsy, like a colt.

The rest of the meal passed quickly. Paco and Lawrence gave Daisy news of her sisters and father. Before leaving to take a walk after supper, Paco gave her letters from her family. He and Lawrence said they'd been in the saddle for several days and wanted to walk for a bit.

Daisy went to take the wash off the line, and the boys headed to the corral to see Paco's and Lawrence's horses again.

When she came back into the cabin with the basket of wash Tucker was alone in the front room.

Tucker began to explain the arrival of Paco and Lawrence. "I'm sorry I didn't know they were coming today. I would have warned you."

She wasn't interested in that detail. "Why are they here, Tucker? The when has already been established. What I want to know is what they meant when they said they were here to work a ranch with you." She set the basket on the bench and walked to the other side of the room so the table was between them. She put her hands on her hips and tapped the toe of her shoe, willing herself to remain calm.

"I'll get to that part. I just want you to know I intended to tell you all about this before they arrived."

"I wish you'd just tell me what's going on." Daisy's patience was almost completely gone. She never liked being in the dark in a situation. Today she felt completely blindsided by something Paco and Lawrence thought she was aware of. She placed her hands, palms down, on the table and took a slow breath, waiting for his answer.

"They are here to work a ranch," Tucker began again.

"We don't have a ranch. We have a farm," Daisy contradicted him. "And we don't need full-time help. We hire migrant workers during the planting and harvest. We do the rest of the work ourselves."

"I'm well aware this is not a ranch." Tucker began to show his impatience to her. "If you'll let me finish I can explain."

"I'm listening." Daisy's tone was curt.

"Please let me finish."

"Please do." Her toe tapped louder.

"Daisy, stop interrupting me for one minute, and I'll explain." She opened her lips again, but he held up a hand to silence her. "I bought the Thornton ranch. They're here to work it for me."

The blood left Daisy's face. She lost all her breath and opened her mouth only to close it again. She knotted her fists and released them at her sides. Again she made fists until she felt her nails digging into her palms. Just when she started to trust him, he overwhelmed her with a major surprise.

"You did what?" The quiet restraint of her voice was extremely menacing.

"You heard me." The frustration in Tucker's tone was electric. "I didn't want to tell you like this, but you won't listen."

All the progress they'd made in recent days disappeared. He still kept things from her. Important things. It was especially painful after her efforts to be so open with him about her grief and feelings for Murdock—and even about her feelings for him.

"I won't listen?" Daisy turned her back to him, only to immediately spin around again. Her voice rose a notch. "I won't listen? I don't seem to remember you trying to tell me anything lately." She pushed both palms against her forehead and thought.

"Oh, I do remember something." She lowered her hands and leveled her gaze at him, speaking slowly and calmly. "On Saturday you said you wanted us to share secrets." Her eyes grew wider with each sentence. "You wanted me to tell you my secrets. And I did." She stopped and nodded her head as the memory of their ride home from town flitted through her eyes. "But I don't remember you sharing any secrets with me."

"Daisy, be reasonable," Tucker implored. "We've been busy. There's more to this than I can explain in just a couple of minutes."

She launched into speech. "We can't afford a ranch! We make a decent living, but you've spent money like there's no tomorrow ever since you got here. How are we supposed to keep up? We don't have money for a mortgage payment." She listed every reason as soon as she thought of it. "How could you do this without talking to me?"

"There is no mortgage. I bought it." Tucker's tone was clipped and controlled. "The ranch will pay for itself. And I'm not accustomed to having to ask permission before I make a business decision." The intensity of his irritation caught fire. She saw it in his face as he retreated to a place she couldn't go. A solitary haven behind protective walls. She knew she was driving him there, but couldn't stop herself.

"How can you be sure it will pay for itself? A ranch is a huge undertaking." Daisy refused to listen to him. Her anger at not being included in the decision process thwarted all rational thought.

"It may come as a surprise to you, Daisy, but I've actually got some experience in this area." Tucker snatched his hat from the peg by the door. "Now if you'll excuse me, we have guests. I'm going to spend some time with them tonight."

The quiet shutting of the door sent a more powerful message than if he'd slammed it shut.

Chapter Twenty

James and John came in full of tales Paco had told them about life on a ranch. The stories were animated and colorful. It took Daisy almost an hour to get them in bed.

She stepped onto the porch for firewood and was surprised to see Tucker sitting there with Paco and Lawrence. All three men had a cup of coffee and were talking quietly. Tucker stood when she came outside.

"I just need some wood." Daisy spoke quietly and headed toward the woodpile. Tucker stopped her with a hand on her wrist.

"I'll bring it when I come in. You go on to bed. I'll be in after a while." Tucker held the door for her to go inside.

"Well, I'll just say good-night." Daisy included them all in her statement. Then she had no choice but to enter the cabin and prepare for bed. Paco and Lawrence wished her a good evening as the door closed. Did Tucker just announce he'd be sleeping in the house without discussing it with her first? He was definitely trying her patience.

Daisy hadn't cried herself to sleep in weeks. Tonight she wept quietly and prayed until exhaustion took her into a deep sleep.

Tucker was at the stove the next morning when he heard Daisy open the bedroom door.

"Good morning," he ventured.

Daisy just looked at him blankly, but didn't speak.

"Were you able to rest?" he asked.

"Yes." She pulled the cast iron skillet to the front burner and started slicing bread.

Tucker came to stand behind her and put his hands on her shoulders. Daisy tensed and stood completely still. He leaned in close to her ear and whispered, "I'm sorry."

Daisy let out a deep sigh and slumped her shoulders. "Me, too," she admitted. "I was rude and impatient."

He knew they had to get past this argument to heal their relationship, but he wasn't sure how to do that. Her next words surprised him.

"Please forgive me."

Tucker turned her to face him and looked into her eyes. "If you'll forgive me."

Daisy reached up a hand and covered his where it lay on her shoulder. Meeting his gaze, she said, "I do. I don't know where we go from here, but I know we have to be forgiving." She asked, "How did you sleep? Oh, wait. Where did you sleep?"

"In the chair by the fire." He nodded to his usual place in the cabin. "It's the warmest I've been in weeks," he added wryly.

"Oh, Tucker, that couldn't have been comfortable. You should have let me know when you came in. I'd have given you the bed."

"And risk Paco and Lawrence discovering we don't share a room?" He shook his head. "I don't think so. Our personal business will stay personal. I won't give anyone cause to discuss our relationship." He cupped the side of her face with his hand. "I'm sorry I didn't get a chance to ask about sleeping in the house before you came onto the porch last night. I was trying to protect you. I didn't want to risk them hearing you throw the bolt and make judgments about us. I moved my things into the far corner of your room while you were taking the wash off the line yesterday. I hope nothing was in your way."

"I didn't notice anything. I went straight to bed without turning on the lamp. Thank you for considering that Paco and Lawrence might have questions," Daisy said. "I didn't even think about it."

"As for the Thornton ranch, I should have told you about all of this earlier. I really had no idea they'd get here so soon."

Daisy huffed another small sigh. "You don't see the real problem here, do you, Tucker?"

"I didn't tell you about the ranch before Paco and Lawrence got here. That's why you're upset, right?"

"No, Tucker." Daisy shook her head. "I'm not upset because you didn't tell me about Paco and Lawrence coming to work the ranch. I'm upset you *bought* the ranch without discussing it with me first. I thought we agreed we'd discuss all business before we made the transactions."

"Daisy," Tucker began, only to be interrupted as James and John entered the room.

"Good morning, Momma. Morning, Mr. Tucker." James spoke immediately. "Can we get started on our chores early? I wanna go with you and Mr. Paco and Mr. Lawrence when you go to the Thornton ranch today. Mr.

Paco says there's a lot to learn about ranching, and I wanna get started right away." Sometimes he didn't know how the boy talked so fast, while never seeming to stop for air.

"Not today, James. Your momma let you off yesterday. Today you'll be studying before you go working at anything other than your chores."

"Yes, sir." James hung his head and went to the front door.

John was at the door before James and stopped as he reached to unlatch the bolt. He put his hand on the latch and turned to look at his mother. "Momma?"

Daisy turned to face John. "What is it, son?" There was a hint of uncertainty in his voice.

"The bolt is latched."

"I know son. We latch it every night. It's for our protection," Daisy confirmed his observation.

"But Mr. Tucker is inside." John eyes were searching her face.

"And…" Daisy prompted.

"And if Mr. Tucker is inside, and the bolt is latched, then does that mean Mr. Tucker stayed inside?" There was a childish innocence in his voice.

"Yes, Mr. Tucker stayed in the cabin last night." Daisy blushed. "Now go do your chores. Both of you." She turned back to the stove, but John didn't move.

"Momma?"

"Yes, John." Daisy kept slicing bread.

"Does that mean Mr. Tucker will stay inside every night now?"

Tucker looked at Daisy. He shrugged to indicate he didn't know the best way to answer the child. Her eyes clouded with indecision and then cleared. She turned her gaze back to the stove.

"Yes, John, Mr. Tucker will be staying in the cabin from now on. It's too cold for him to stay in the barn anymore. He built that fancy room on, so yes, Mr. Tucker will be staying inside. Now go do your chores, or you'll be late for breakfast."

The front door opened, and both boys tromped down the steps and ran toward the outhouse before beginning their chores.

Tucker stared at Daisy's back, startled by her announcement.

"I can feel you looking at me, Tucker Barlow."

"I'm trying to figure you out, Daisy Barlow. I don't know from one minute to the next what is going to come out of that pretty little mouth of yours." He couldn't keep the happiness out of his voice.

"It's important to me that we don't send mixed signals to the twins. They've been through enough. It wouldn't be good for them to see you inside one night and outside the next." She dropped the first pieces of bread in the pan to fry, and it sizzled as the smell of the melting butter filled the room.

"So you're saying you only told them I'd be staying inside to keep them from getting mixed signals?" Tucker asked carefully.

"That's part of it." She still refused to look at him.

He came to stand close behind her again. "I think it will be important, Daisy Marie, for you and I to get all our signals straight. And the sooner, the better."

The tingle on Daisy's neck remained long after she heard Tucker close the front door as he, too, went to handle his morning chores.

Lord, this man is so frustrating I don't know what

to do. One minute I want to leap into his arms, and the next he's gone and done something I completely disagree with. What am I going to do?

If Daisy were truly honest with herself, she'd admit that she didn't know if she should disagree with him about buying the Thornton ranch. It wasn't so much about the ranch to her, as it was about him not including her in the decision. And it was about the ranch because she didn't know how they would pay for it. How was it possible there was no mortgage? Then she remembered that he'd said her mouth was pretty. And she smiled. Daisy really needed to talk to Tucker, but not with so many people around.

As if to confirm her frustrations, the front door opened and both boys came in followed by Paco and Lawrence. Tucker came a few minutes later carrying a folder much like the one Mr. Little had used at the land office. She could only guess what it contained.

After breakfast the men rode off to the Thornton ranch. Daisy got James and John started on their reading and went onto the porch to read her letters from home. Her sister Jasmine wrote briefly in a strong, bold hand, talking of the ranch and her love of the land. Lily wrote of cooking and gardening. Graceful strokes of ink curved across the pages of her letter, which ended with an update on their father's health.

Daisy smiled at the differences in the two letters and tucked them into her pocket. Then she opened her papa's letter, carefully breaking the seal on the back of the envelope. She prayed there would be wisdom for her on the pages inside.

Dearest Daisy,

I trust this letter finds you in a better state than my previous note. I received your news that you have followed my advice and married Tucker. I pray for both of you every day. Knowing you as I do, I'm sure there have been many moments of frustration as the two of you adjust to one another. Even dear friends must adapt.

To marry when you are a woman is different than when a girl marries. A girl can survive on dreams, and hopes, and, dare I say, love. A woman knows she must deal with the realities of life. It is somewhat sad to me that this is true. For a woman should not be robbed of her dreams simply because she has grown beyond the age of innocence. I pray you will have new dreams, and that those dreams will come true.

Tucker contacted me by telegraph and letter about his plan to buy the neighboring ranch. He sought my advice and counsel, but not direction. I agree with his assessment of this property. He has my full endorsement in this decision. I have the utmost confidence Tucker's strong business sense will benefit your family for years to come.

If I had to guess, I'd say you have not yet come into agreement with Tucker on this business of ranching. Your sister Jasmine was always the one who had a love for ranching. Your love for farming drove you to the life you now have. Sometimes it's as though life, or God, throws things into our path solely for the sake of causing us to grow and stretch beyond who we currently are.

Please give my love to James and John. I hope above hope that the coming railroad will afford us the opportunity to see one another.

Be good to Tucker. I continue to pray for God to heal your heart and bless your new marriage.

All my love,
Papa

Once again, a letter from Papa brought hope to Daisy's troubled mind. She sat wondering if it was wrong for her to want to be included in the business decisions Tucker made for their family. She knew many women had no idea of their husband's financial holdings, but Murdock had always included her. She'd worked alongside him for everything they had. He'd taught her how to handle money and run the farm. She had no desire to sway anything in a negative direction, but she did want her abilities to be put to good use. She hoped Tucker would come to value the skills she brought into their marriage.

Daisy sat on the porch meditating and praying for almost an hour. She couldn't say she'd reached a resolution in her soul, but she was comforted and helped by her father's letter. Praying helped her most of all. Daisy knew Tucker was a good man. And she knew he had her family's best interest at heart. She just didn't want there to be any secrets between them. She had opened up to Tucker; she needed him to be open with her.

When Daisy stood to go inside and help the boys finish their lessons, a rider came up the lane. Thankfully she recognized him immediately because of the distinctiveness of his white mount. She really wasn't up to shooting anyone today.

Jay Winters, the postmaster's son, rode up to the porch.

"Hello, Jay. What brings you out our way?" Daisy greeted the lad.

"Mr. Croft wanted me to ride out here straightaway and let Mr. Barlow know the furniture he ordered has arrived. It came this morning." Jay pulled the reins to keep his horse from getting too close to Daisy. She reached out from the porch and rubbed the mare between her dark eyes.

"Mr. Barlow is out right now, but I'll let him know as soon as he gets back. Please tell Mr. Croft thank you for the message." Daisy patted the mare a final time.

"Do you think Mr. Barlow wants it delivered? Mr. Croft told me to be sure and ask."

"No, I don't think so. If he does, we'll send word." She took a step back on the porch. "Thanks for coming, Jay."

"You're welcome, Mrs. Barlow. Have a good day." With a tip of his hat, Jay sent his horse up the lane at a fast trot.

Daisy watched Jay leave and turned to enter the cabin. Out of the corner of her eye, she caught just a glimpse of something red in the trees near the end of the lane. She turned to see what it could be, and it was gone. "Hmm. Must have been a bird," she mumbled to herself and went into the cabin.

"Are you boys about ready for your spelling words?" Daisy moved to the table where James and John studied.

"I am." James was eager to finish. She knew he'd

rather be with his horse or with Tucker and their visitors over at the Thornton ranch.

"What about you, John? Are you ready?" Daisy picked up the spelling primer.

"Who's that, Momma?" John pointed out the window over the kitchen cabinet.

Daisy moved toward the window saying, "It's probably just Jay Winters coming ba..." Her feet tangled in her skirt, and she fell to the floor with a thud. Pain shot through her right ankle when she stood. James and John jumped up to help her.

"Are you hurt, Momma?" James asked as he reached for a chair to help her sit.

"I'll be fine." She refused the chair. "How silly to stumble over my own feet." She tried to laugh. Daisy shuffled over to lean on the kitchen cabinet so she could see out the window. Panic filled her mind as a flash of red became visible close to the spot she'd noticed before coming inside.

"Boys! Go out the back door as quickly and quietly as you can. Run straight for the tree line behind the smokehouse. Stay as low as you can so you won't be noticed. Then run for all your worth to the Thornton ranch and get Mr. Tucker." Daisy limped to the front door and slid the bolt. Grabbing the shotgun from over the fireplace she stumbled back to the front window and watched two men on horseback weave their way around the front edge of the property toward the barn. They kept just beyond the line of the trees in an effort to move unnoticed.

"We can't leave you, Momma!" John was trying not to cry. "I can stay here and help you shoot. Who are those men?" His bottom lip was quivering now.

"John, you have to be a big man for Momma today. I'm not planning to shoot anyone. I need you and James to go get Mr. Tucker. I can't run, or I'd go with you." The twins had come close to her when they'd heard the panic in her voice. She looked directly at them. "It's important to stay calm and to not be seen. Can you do it?"

"We can." James spoke for both of them. "And Mr. Tucker will come and protect you, Momma. That's why he came to live here." He hugged her and headed for the back door. "Come on, John. Let's go!"

John hugged Daisy for a brief instant. "Can I take the pistol and fire it so Mr. Tucker will come? That's the signal."

"John, that's a great idea. Get a chair and get it off the mantel." John pulled a chair to the fireplace. "Be careful," she warned.

"I will, Momma. Mr. Tucker showed me how." John seemed older than his eight years as he took the loaded pistol in his hand and climbed off the chair.

"Don't fire it until you top the last hill past the cotton field. You'll be close enough to Mr. Tucker then that he'll be sure to hear the shot. I don't want whoever is out there coming after you." Daisy looked at her boys at the back door. "Go now. And be careful. I love you."

"Come bolt the door, Momma," James insisted. "Mr. Tucker wouldn't want us to leave you without the door being bolted.

"Okay. Be quick." She shooed them out the door and slid the bolt. She hobbled back to her vantage point at the front window, looking for any sign that the intruders noticed her sons. She must have forgotten to breathe because she had to gasp for air when the two men came into full view near the end of the lane. The one leading the way wore a red bandana tucked into the front of his shirt. That was the red she'd mistaken for a bird earlier. They must have waited in the woods for Jay Winters to ride away before making their move toward the barn. The second man wore a dingy brown hat and spit over his shoulder as he surveyed the horizon.

Daisy didn't recognize either man, but she did recognize Murdock's horse. The one with the red bandana rode Murdock's bay, Dutch. The three white socks and star on his face ensured that Daisy would recognize the horse anywhere. His beauty was probably why the murderous thief had kept him.

Daisy watched from the shadows as the men crossed the lane. They showed no signs of interest in the cabin as they neared the barn. She would lose sight of them if they went into the corral. Which is exactly what they did. She moved to the boys' room hoping to keep them in sight through their window. Just as she lowered herself onto the edge of the bed and rested the barrel of the shotgun on the windowsill, she heard a shot in the distance.

The two riders had entered the corral and were trying to lasso Trojan and Beauregard. The sound of the shot caused all the horses to start. The man in the brown hat sat straight in his saddle, looking in the direction Daisy had sent the boys. Then a second shot rang out.

The thieves appeared to argue. Their heated exchange lasted for a couple of minutes, and they went back to work trying to lasso the horses. Trojan and Beauregard must have sensed danger because they refused to cooperate. After several attempts, the man on Murdock's horse snared Trojan around the neck. Beauregard was only able to hold out for a short time before he, too, was captured.

When the men led the horses through the barn, Daisy came back to the front window so she could see them when they came out. She opened the window slightly before they exited the front of the barn, in full view of the cabin. Daisy lowered the shotgun into position. She almost jumped out of her skin when the butt of the gun knocked a tin cup off of the cabinet, causing it to bounce on the wooden floor.

The bouncing cup echoed in the cabin sending the sound into the yard. In an instant the thieves were both focused on the cabin, pistols drawn.

Daisy knew she had no choice. If only she hadn't knocked over the cup, they would have left without knowing she'd seen them. She drew in a deep breath and prayed.

Dear Lord, protect the horses. And me.

As the thief with the red bandana took aim at the window, Daisy closed her eyes and pulled both triggers. She heard the window shatter and a bullet flew by her head. Daisy opened her eyes as cries of pain erupted in the yard. Both men had fallen from their horses. Trojan and Beauregard ran for the field behind the cabin. Dutch was dancing all around the thief in the red bandana as he rolled in the dirt writhing in pain. The man in the brown hat had one foot hung in a stirrup and was clutching his belly. Blood stained his shirt.

Thundering hooves sounded over the hill behind the cabin. Tucker came into view first, followed by Paco and Lawrence. All three had their guns drawn and were ready for battle. As they reined in their mounts Daisy was surprised to hear laughter. Guffaws! It was the last sound she heard as blackness overtook her.

Chapter Twenty-One

"**D**aisy. Honey. It's me, Tucker. Daisy." Strong hands patted her cheeks firmly. "Daisy." Then the cold water came. Splashing her into consciousness. She sputtered and spewed, shaking her head from side to side. When she opened her eyes she was cradled in Tucker's arms. He knelt on the floor beside her, holding her firmly against the broad expanse of his chest. A chest that was covered with a very wet shirt.

"I am so sorry, Señora Barlow. I did not know how else to wake you up." Paco stood above them with an empty pitcher. The smile on his face offered sympathy and humor.

"Were you trying to wake her or drown her?" Tucker shook his head and drops of water rained on Daisy.

"Are you okay, Daisy?" Tucker's voice gentled, and he looked into her eyes.

"The thieves? Are they…?" Daisy muttered.

"Tied up outside under Lawrence's watchful eye. Paco and Randall Thornton will go with Lawrence to take them to the sheriff. And the doctor. They told us they came back here figuring you'd have new horses and maybe no husband around." Tucker's gaze searched hers. "Did they hurt you?" His voice grew very serious. "In any way?"

Daisy smiled a weak smile and patted his chest. "No, dear. I'm fine."

"You're sure?" he asked her.

"I'm sure. They never saw me until just before I pulled the trigger."

"That's my girl." Tucker pulled her closer and pressed his face into her hair. "I couldn't live with myself if they'd harmed you," he whispered low so only she could hear.

"The twins?" Daisy worried aloud.

"They're great." Tucker sat back so she could see his face. "They did exactly what you asked. Thank God, we were on our way back here when John fired the warning shot. Randall was coming with us to get the folder with the paperwork I left on the table. I forgot to take it to him this morning. He picked up the boys and let Paco, Lawrence and I come ahead to protect you." Tucker chuckled.

Paco laughed out loud. "Señora Barlow does not need your help to shoot people, Señor Tucker. She does pretty good all by herself. Those muchachos outside are lucky she is not a better shot. She is shooting two at a time now. And not one injury to a horse."

Color returned to Daisy's face, and she attempted to sit up. "You fellows better stop teasing me and help me up. I can't just lie on the floor all day." Tucker helped her sit up and then stood to pull her to her feet. She flinched when she tried to put weight on her throbbing ankle and fell against him.

"Sorry. I fell earlier." She smiled up at him.

Tucker picked her up to carry her to her room. She wrapped her arms around his neck. "Thanks for coming to my rescue." As they crossed the threshold into the new room, Daisy slid her fingers into Tucker's hair and pulled his face to hers. He stopped and stood still while she kissed his lips. When she pulled back he looked into her face and a groan escaped him. This time he leaned in and kissed her.

Tucker lifted his head. "Thank God you're not hurt."

Daisy saw the protective look in his eyes. No longer a look that protected him from a relationship with her. Now the look promised to draw her in and keep her safe.

He lowered her onto the quilt. "Boys, come see your momma." The twins were in the room in an instant. "Stay with her while I make sure those thieves are dealt with."

To Daisy he said, "Don't go anywhere. I'll be right back to see about your ankle." He adjusted his hat and took one more look at her before he left the room.

"Momma, are you okay?" John spoke with calm concern.

"Yes, son." The boys stood by the bed. She reached a hand to both of them. They eagerly latched on to her. "You were both very brave."

James launched into speech. "We ran so fast nobody could catch us! Then Mr. Thornton let us both ride on his horse with him."

Tucker entered the room. "You boys did exactly what needed to be done. I'm proud of both of you. Why don't you head out to the well and get some cool water for your momma? I'm gonna see about her ankle."

With a quick, "Yes, sir," they were gone.

Tucker propped her up by pushing another pillow behind her shoulders. Then he sat on the edge of the bed to inspect her ankle.

Daisy blushed at his touch. He was very gentle.

"How bad is the pain?" Tucker didn't meet her eyes.

"Right now, I'm still so upset about all that happened, I don't know. It's tender to walk on."

"I'll wrap it tight to keep the swelling down."

He found what he needed in his roll that still sat in the corner of the room. By the time it was wrapped, the boys could be heard in the kitchen.

Tucker checked his work. "Better?"

"Yes. Thank you."

He stood. "I want you to rest for a while."

"That's not necessary." Daisy started to sit up in the bed.

"I insist."

Her nerves had started to settle some while he worked on her ankle. The pain had begun to ease. She leaned back against the pillows. "I could use some rest."

He moved to the door and looked back.

"You called me honey." She smiled at him.

"You called me dear," he countered with a grin. He closed the door as she closed her eyes.

Paco and Lawrence rode up as they set lunch on the table. Randall Thornton had headed to the ranch after helping deliver the thieves to Sheriff Collins with the news that one of their horses had been recovered. James and John were in the barn with their horses. They were so happy Dutch was home.

"Señora Barlow? Can we come in?" Paco called. Tucker opened the door and laughed. "Please don't shoot me," Paco continued to hail Daisy from the porch.

"Keep it up, Paco. Ask Tucker how patient I am," Daisy chided. "I wouldn't think there was a man in fifty miles of here that isn't scared of me now," she teased him with a laugh.

"I promise to be good, *señora*." Paco laughed, too.

Lawrence came in with Paco. James and John had heard their horses arrive and came to join the men in the cabin.

"Lunch is ready." Tucker motioned for the men to sit at the table. "Daisy's ankle prevented us from having a hot meal. I'm not much of a cook, but we do have pumpkin pie."

"Go wash up," Daisy reminded her sons. She set glasses on the table and reached for the tea pitcher. Tucker took it from her and asked her to sit while he filled the glasses. The boys climbed onto their bench.

Tucker took his place at the head of the table and reached for John's hand. He bowed his head and prayed. "Lord, we thank You for this bountiful meal. Give us wisdom and guide us in all we do. And we especially thank You for protecting our home and family from danger today. Amen."

"Amen," echoed around the table.

Daisy was looking at Tucker when he lifted his head. His green eyes reflected her mood. Her expression was confused, but hopeful.

The food was passed around the table. Then silence reigned while hungry men satisfied themselves with good food.

"*Señora,* this pie is delicious. I wonder if you use molasses to make it so sweet, no?" Paco seemed to know a lot about cooking.

"Actually, yes, I do." Daisy asked, "How do you know so much about food, Paco?"

"I spend a lot of time in the kitchen at your papa's ranch. I help your sister Lily. She is a good cook, too. Remember I told you?"

"I didn't realize you spent time in the kitchen. I thought you said you were a ranch hand," Daisy responded as she sliced pie for James and John.

"*Sí,* I was a ranch hand, but I also help in the kitchen. I need to learn from her so I can cook for the hands in the bunkhouse. The cook sometimes cannot come when we need him." Paco waved his fork in the air as he spoke. "So I spend extra time in the kitchen with Miss Lily. Now I am a good cook, too." Paco toasted them all with the fork and then took a big bite of pie.

"Mr. Paco, can you cook chili?" James wanted to know. "I love chili!"

"I make very good chili. I use lots of peppers—so maybe you need to drink lots of water or tea when you eat my chili." Paco smiled.

Tucker reached for a piece of pie. "Daisy, this is delicious."

"Thank you, Tucker." Daisy rose to refill everyone's tea glass. Tucker offered to do it, but she insisted. The wrapping of her ankle had helped the sprain, which wasn't as bad as she'd first thought.

"Oh, by the way," Daisy said, "Jay Winters came by this morning before all the commotion. Mr. Croft sent him to let you know the furniture arrived this morning." She lifted Tucker's glass and filled it. "He asked if you wanted it delivered, and I told him not unless we sent word for them to bring it."

"That's good. We can go to town this afternoon and

pick it up." He lowered his fork and cut his eyes at Daisy. "Will you be okay here, Daisy? I need to go so I can pay Mr. Croft."

"I'll be fine," Daisy assured him. "Especially now. I won't have to worry about those murderous thieves ever again." The relief was evident on her face. It eclipsed any signs of the stress of having faced down her husband's killers. She was grateful the entire episode had lasted only a few brief minutes. Certainly the shock of it could hit her later, but right now relief overrode all other emotions.

"If you're sure?" Tucker waited until Daisy nodded in the affirmative before addressing Paco and Lawrence. "Can I get you gentlemen to help me today? Paco, I'll feel better if someone is here with Daisy. Will you stay here while Lawrence and I go pick up the furniture?" Tucker cut another bite of pie with his fork.

"I would be glad to stay, Señor Tucker."

So Paco stayed at the farm to keep Daisy from being alone. He spent his time in the barn and the yard, telling her he didn't want to intrude on her privacy. James and John rode to town with Tucker and Lawrence. And Daisy prepared her room for the arrival of the new furniture. She stripped the bed of the sheets and quilt. Then she made a big pot of chili, with extra peppers for Paco, and left it simmering on the stove.

Daisy couldn't resist one more trip into her room. She stood at the foot of the iron bed—the bed she'd shared with Murdock. She caressed the curves of the metal and remembered the day they'd bought it shortly after they'd finished the cabin. When they'd set it up, she'd been so proud. They had slept in the covered wagon for weeks while they'd raised the cabin. It had seemed like ages since they'd been in a real bed. This was the first, and only, bed they'd owned as husband and wife.

Daisy smiled as she remembered having her babies in this bed—and nursing them in the middle of the night. She remembered the times the twins had climbed in bed with them because they'd been frightened by a storm or a bad dream. She laughed when she recalled how Murdock would tickle them until they begged for mercy. Then she thought about the love they'd shared and how she'd treasure it forever in her heart. She was able to say a prayer of thanks for all the good Murdock had brought into her life.

And now she stood at the foot of this bed and realized she was ready to move on with her life. The capture of the men who murdered Murdock brought that chapter of her life to an end.

The sound of the wagon coming up the lane reached her ears. She was glad the bed would be in the boys' room now. It was time.

In what seemed like a flurry of activity, and really was no time at all, the men had moved the old bed into the boys' room. There was enough room to keep their original bed, so now both boys could have their own space to sleep. Tucker told Daisy he thought they would appreciate that as they grew. She agreed.

The new furniture was arranged to please Daisy. She only had the men move the dressing table twice. The bed and chest were perfect from the time they set them up in the room.

Tucker had another surprise for Daisy. When the last of the furniture was taken off the wagon, and the twins had gone with Paco and Lawrence to the barn, she noticed a large crate in the corner of the bedroom. They must have put it there while she was out of the room.

"What's that?" Daisy asked Tucker.

"Are you sure you want to know?" he answered her with a question.

"Stop doing that."

"What?" He knew exactly what she meant, but he wanted to hear her say it again.

"Stop answering my questions with a question."

"What question?" He tormented her.

"Tucker Barlow, what is in that crate? I have no more patience in me today." Her skirt moved back and forth as she patted one foot on the floor.

"Would you like to do the honors?" Tucker offered her the iron bar he held.

"No, thank you. I just want to see what's inside. You open it."

"Your father was right when he reminded me how impatient you are." He smiled and pried the first corner of the crate loose. She tried to peek, and he shooed her away.

"My father told you I'm impatient?" She couldn't imagine her father talking to Tucker about what she knew Papa considered to be her character flaws.

"Yes, he warned me about that, and how you like to have your way." Tucker pried another corner loose.

"Everyone likes to have their way. Anyone who says they don't isn't being honest." She moved closer to watch him pry another section of the lid loose. "How many nails did they put in that box?"

"See, Daisy, you've got to learn to wait." Tucker methodically worked his way around the top of the crate, loosening one nail at a time. Finally he reached the last one, but he didn't lift the lid.

"Are you sure you want to see?" he asked again.

"Yes." She was tapping her toe.

"You're not going to be upset with me because I didn't talk to you about this first, are you?"

"Oh, Tucker, I can't stand it another minute. You have to let me see." Daisy pushed him aside and knelt down to slide the lid back so she could peer into the corner of the crate. She pulled at the straw that had been used for packing and threw it onto the floor. She gasped and reached into the box and touched the fine copper of the fancy bathtub. She fell backward onto her heels.

With one hand to her chest and her mouth hanging open, Daisy turned to stare at Tucker. "I can't believe it! It's beautiful!" She stood as quickly as her ankle would allow and threw her arms around his neck. "I love it! Thank you! How ever did you know?" She went on and on without stopping to breathe. "Why did you buy this?"

"So you like it?" He smiled.

Daisy laughed out loud. "You're doing it again. Well, I'll answer your question now, because I'm so pleased with you at the moment. I love it! It's the most beautiful bathtub I've ever seen. And judging from the size of this crate, it's huge!"

Tucker laughed at her exuberance. "This was a combination gift. I bought it for you because it's beautiful, and I bought it for me because I'm too tall for that wash tub you've been filling with water for me to bathe in on Saturday nights. I'd do better with a bowl and a cloth."

Daisy grabbed her side and bent double laughing at him as he tried to demonstrate how he had to fold up to get into the small wash tub she used for herself and the twins.

"Stop laughing at me, and go finish supper. I'll get Paco and Lawrence to help me get this out of the crate."

At the table, Tucker informed Daisy that Paco and Lawrence would be moving to the bunkhouse at the Thornton ranch after supper. They'd made the arrangements with Randall that morning.

"It's best for them to get right to work. Randall has agreed to show them the entire operation before their family leaves at the end of next week." At Daisy's downcast look, he added, "And I made arrangements for all of us to spend the afternoon with their family tomorrow. I know it's our normal Bible study night, but Randall and I thought it would be a good way to part. We'll meet together for Bible study, and the kids can play for the evening."

"That's a good idea. Thank you for arranging all of that." Daisy appreciated Tucker's thoughtfulness.

"We get to ride our horses over there after supper and spend the night tonight," James spoke up. "This sure is good chili, Momma. Did you get the idea to cook it because I asked Mr. Paco if he knows how to cook chili? Because I really like chili."

"I'm glad you like it, son. Yes, the idea came from you. It was a good one." Daisy looked at Tucker. "What's this about spending the night?"

"The boys can ride over with Paco and Lawrence after we eat. They'll be safe with them. They can come back with us tomorrow night," Tucker explained. "There's little time left for visiting. For the time being, there won't be any kids at the ranch after the Thorntons leave."

* * *

The boys made bedrolls with clothes for the following day and rode over the fields with Paco and Lawrence to the Thornton ranch. The experience would make the twins feel like real ranch hands.

Daisy stood alone on the porch, watching them leave. She knew they were safe. They were all safe now.

She also knew the twins would appreciate the time with their friends. What she didn't know was how to straighten out her conflicts with her husband. Glad of the opportunity to talk with him alone, Daisy went in search of Tucker.

He wasn't in the front of the cabin. She went out the front door and crossed to the barn. He wasn't there, either. When she came out of the barn and looked toward the house, he came out of the front door.

"I want to show you something. Can you come in for a minute?" Tucker called to her.

"Where have you been? I've been looking everywhere for you."

"Are you answering my question with a question?" he teased her.

Daisy limped across the yard, her brows drawn together.

"We've got a lot to talk about. I'm hoping we can get some things figured out while we won't be interrupted." Daisy walked past him into the cabin. He followed her inside.

"Me, too. I want you to see something first." He crossed the room and opened the door to her bedroom. He gestured for her to come and look. When she stood in the doorway he asked, "Do you like it?"

Daisy was speechless. In front of the tub, he'd placed

a hand-carved, accordion-style wooden screen. Each panel was a series of intricately carved squares. Some were carved in the design of her father's seal of vines woven into a heart shape. Others were filled with daisies. Every imaginable configuration of a daisy was represented on the beautiful screen.

She frowned and said, "It's gorgeous, Tucker." She walked close and ran her fingers over the raised patterns. "Did you carve this yourself?"

"I worked on it at night. I got the idea when I decided to leave the corner in the front of the cabin set up for the boys and I to use. I thought you might enjoy some privacy when you change clothes or bathe." He touched the panel and smiled at her. "I'm glad you like it."

Daisy shook her head. "It's all too much, Tucker." She shook her head again, and her frown grew.

"What's too much?" He seemed confused by her response.

"It's all too much." Gesturing toward each item with her hands, Daisy continued, "The room, your mother's wedding ring, the furniture, the bathtub, the horses, the ranch next door, a ranch hand from Mexico, a young man who worked for my father, not to mention someone shooting at me today! And me shooting not one— but two—men!" She paused for a moment and fingered the carving again. "And now this beautiful carving…" Her voice became so quiet he could hardly hear her. She continued to shake her head. "It's just all too much."

Daisy turned to look at Tucker. "Where does it end? When will it stop? What's next?"

Tucker put his hands on her shoulders and looked into her sad brown eyes. "I did it all for you, Daisy. I want you to be happy."

"I don't need all this to be happy, Tucker." She kept shaking her head. "What I need to be happy is to know you value my opinions. To know we don't have secrets. I need to not be surprised by some grand gift that's so expensive I can't imagine where the money will come from to pay for it. I need to know you want me involved in your life. I want to know what's going on and not be overwhelmed by surprise when I'm blindsided by your next mystery project. That's what I need to be happy, Tucker. Not all this."

She gestured with her hands again and turned away from him, causing him to drop his hands from her shoulders. "I need a plan to follow. I need to know the plan is going to work. That's what I need Tucker."

With each sentence raw emotion ripped from her soul. Daisy felt as if she were literally unraveling before his eyes. She abruptly stopped and turned toward him, just inches from his face.

"I love you, Tucker." Daisy looked him straight in the eye. "Even when I'm so frustrated I don't know what to do, I love you. I don't need all this to be happy with you. I just need you to be happy with me." Daisy's lip trembled.

Tucker returned her stare. "You've wanted everything to go according to your plans and at your pace…" He paused and drew in a slow steady breath. "Well, Daisy, I have plans, too. I'm a man who's always followed his own pace. I've been patient with you because I loved you, but enough is enough."

"You said for me to set the pace. When we got married, you promised not to rush me." Daisy jumped on the first thing that came to mind. "What plans are you talking about?" She kept talking in a feverish rush to keep from thinking. "We never once talked about you buying the Thornton ranch. Unless you count that first week when you teased me about buying it without talking to me first."

Tucker put a finger across her lips to hush her. He looked deeply into her eyes.

She talked around his finger. "You're the one who came here when Papa asked you to."

"Daisy, I'm warning you." Tucker's voice was calm and steady. His eyes never left hers.

"What do you mean, enough is enough?"

Tucker wrapped his large hands around the tops of her arms and pulled her to him as she continued to rant. He silenced her with his lips. She sputtered and jerked her head back to look at him, her eyes wide with wonder.

"You loved me?" she said, her voice a hoarse whisper. "What do you mean 'loved'?"

"Years ago, I loved you." Tucker titled his head to one side and shrugged one shoulder.

She still couldn't grasp all he was saying. "But I was married to Murdock." The statement was a question. She frowned.

"Not then." He stroked her cheek with the back of one hand while wrapping his other arm around her waist. "Before."

"Before? Oh, Tucker, I'm so confused."

"I know," he said, "but I can explain." He kissed her again, taking his time about it.

"Stop doing that," she protested when he released her. "I don't know what to think!"

"You think too much." He kissed her again, and she melted against his chest without resistance.

"Really," she whispered, "you've got to stop doing that. I can't think straight."

Tucker set her back a step away from him and looked straight into her eyes. "Listen, Daisy."

She opened her mouth to speak, and he held up a hand to stop her. "I mean it, Daisy. I want you to listen, because I'm only going to say this one time." He waited for her to agree. She closed her lips, and at her nod he continued.

"I fell in love with you years ago. I can't even actually say when it happened." His eyes reflected the memories of all the years they'd known each other. "You were barely more than a child when we met, and then we became friends. You'd come to me for advice or comfort. I was good with that—in the beginning. Then I started liking that you needed me. You were so beautiful, and clever, and so much fun. Impetuous, but at the same time, delightful."

"Tucker…"

With a raised finger, he signaled for her to stay quiet. "And then Murdock came along." His brows drew together and downward. "At first I was jealous. Then I saw you together." His brow relaxed. "Any fool could see how in love you both were. I really believe God put the two of you together. I can't say I was happy about it, but I knew it was the right thing. So I locked my feelings for you deep in the recesses of my broken heart and resigned myself to working on your father's ranch and being alone. I actually got used to it and was content. When I thought of you it was a pleasant memory, without jealousy or envy."

Daisy tried again to speak, but he put his hand to her

lips. "Please let me finish. That's the only way you'll understand." She nodded again.

"I was happy for you when you got your farmland and had the boys. I wanted God to bless you and give you a happy life." She smiled slightly, and he continued. "And my heart ached for you when I found out Murdock had been killed." Tears slid from her eyes and spilled over her lashes at his words.

"I knew you'd be heartbroken, because I knew the depth of the love you had for him." He drew in a deep breath. "It was not unlike the depth of love I had for you all those years before." He smiled then. "That's why I came when your father asked me to help you."

Daisy saw a hint of sadness in him.

"And now I've grown to love you again. I thought that part of me was dead." Tucker continued, "I know you'll never be able to love me like you loved Murdock. But your friendship caused my heart to crack open so the sun could shine into my soul and that long-buried seed of love began to grow and flourish." He leaned in close to her face now and whispered, "I can be happy loving you to whatever degree or depth you'll let me."

"Oh, Tucker." Her voice was barely more than a whisper. "I had no idea." She stepped closer and snuggled into his embrace without looking away from his tender eyes.

"It wasn't our time then, Daisy. That was Murdock's time. I know he was your destiny." He nodded his head in the direction of James and John's bedroom. "Those fine young men wouldn't be here if it hadn't been for the love the two of you shared."

Daisy squeezed him with gratitude. "Thank you for saying that."

"I mean it."

"God has taught me so much in such a short time." Daisy's sober voice held his attention. "Murdock is gone. I can't go back to him."

"The twins are Murdock. You see him every day." Tucker's words were a clear attempt to comfort her.

"Do you think I love John more than James?"

"Of course not."

"I love them both." Her eyes never left his face. "But they are unique individuals. They each complete me as a mother in a different way." Her eyes softened, and she willed him to believe her.

"Like Murdock, you are my husband." A flash of pain crossed his gaze. "I loved Murdock. I will always treasure his memory and the sons he gave me." She lowered her voice. "I love you—in a completely different way. He was my first love. The love of my youth. He's gone." A smile pulled her lips upward. "Now you are the love of my life."

She tightened her hold around his waist, willing him to receive the truth of her words. "You fill a different part of my life. Murdock was my past. You are my future."

"Oh, Daisy, I love you now more than ever before." Tucker put a soft kiss on her temple. "Do you remember I told you God had taught me that when I couldn't fly, He wanted me to run, and He wanted me to walk when I couldn't run?"

"Yes," she said, nodding.

"For you that verse was about not having the energy to run or fly because of the suffering you were going through. For me, it was an instruction in patience to wait until it was the time for me to run or fly."

Understanding of his meaning dawned in her eyes, and he continued. "I'd given up hope that I'd ever fly again." He paused. "Well, I'm ready to fly now. I've been walking in patience long enough. When our friendship began to grow, slowly at first, but deeper, I started to run. I'm letting you know now, my heart is about to burst with love for you, and I've got to soar like the eagle I am." He gave her a squeeze. "Do you think you can keep up with me?"

"Yes! Oh, yes!" Daisy stretched up to the tips of her toes to meet his kiss with her heart wide-open.

Daisy snatched her head back. "Wait!" She blurted out. "What about the money? Where did it come from?"

Tucker's eyes danced with mischief, and he started to laugh. "So you have to know now?"

"You've kept me in the dark long enough, Mr. Barlow. For this marriage to work, you're gonna have to fess up. No more secrets."

"I'll tell you. If you promise not to interrupt," he teased.

"But—"

"No *buts*. Promise?"

She exhaled. "I promise." Her smiled teased him back.

"It happened over a period of time. First, I learned that it pays to pay attention. All those years growing up in the hotel, listening to businessmen talk while I cleared away their dishes or carried their luggage, I heard a lot of good information. Especially about how important it is to save your money. And being a ranch hand, with no family or expenses for so long, gave me plenty of time to do that. Then your father gave me the opportunity to hone my business skills. He took me under his wing like the father I didn't have. I'll always be grateful to him."

"What kind of opportunity did Papa give you?" She grew more curious by the second.

"Everyone thought I was a simple ranch hand. No one knew that several years ago he partnered with me for an interest in his ranch. He taught me how to make business deals and land deals. Those lessons stood me in good stead. That's what took me so long to get here in the beginning. I was selling off some properties. Your father bought out my share in his ranch. I've actually built quite a nest egg."

"You're rich?" Daisy was befuddled.

"No. I'm not rich. *We,* however, are financially secure."

Tucker tilted his head to one side. "Are you satisfied? Is there anything else you want to ask me?"

"I think, dear Tucker, you have left me speechless."

"Finally." He smiled and claimed her lips. All other thoughts left her mind.

Epilogue

December 1880

"We better hurry, or we won't be there when the train comes." James jumped into the back of the wagon. "John, come on."

"There's plenty of time, son." Tucker set the empty Moses basket under the seat of the wagon. "Your momma is putting on her hat."

John climbed up beside his brother. "My stomach feels funny. I can't believe today is the day." His hat was freshly brushed, and he took extra care to keep his clothes neat.

"Are you ready, dear?" Tucker called to Daisy.

She came to the door of the cabin and answered. "Another question, Tucker? Really?" Her smile belied the tartness of her words. Daisy pulled the door of the cabin closed and descended the steps. She asked John to hop out of the wagon to help her.

"Here, John, hold your sister for me, please." Daisy carefully handed the small girl to her proud brother. Tucker offered his hand to Daisy, and she climbed into the wagon. Tucker took his new daughter from his son, kissed her soft cheek and handed her to her mother.

"Are you sure you want to make the trip to town, Daisy? We could just as easily meet the train and come back here. I'm sure you'll be able to hear the whistle from inside our cabin." Tucker waited for her answer while John climbed back into the wagon.

"I want to go. It's the first train to come to Pine Haven. I don't want to miss it."

Thirty minutes later, they were at the station. The new building had more windows than any other building in town. There was a giant clock on the platform. A huge water tank stood beyond the depot where the train would pull forward and take on water before leaving town. Everywhere they looked, they saw someone they knew. Many stopped to peek inside the blanket at the newest member of the Barlow family.

Daisy stood on the platform, her nerves in a tight bundle. Then they heard it. A distant whistle. It grew closer and louder. The earth began to vibrate with the power of the approaching train. Tucker put his arm around Daisy's shoulders.

"I'm glad we sold them the easement to the southern tip of our farm," he said.

"I am, too." She stole a glance at him. "I just wish I'd known then what a savvy businessman you were. I wouldn't have been worried about anything."

Tucker squeezed her shoulders. "I wanted you to love me for me, not for my money. I had to move carefully so you wouldn't find me out." He grinned and looked over her shoulder at the beautiful child she held.

"I still can't believe how quickly you got the Thornton place to the level it's at today, or how successful our cotton was this past season. You really do have the Midas touch." She looked around. "Speaking of the ranch, where are Paco and Lawrence?"

"They decided to skip the festivities. They're working on the new bunkhouse. It's got to be finished before the new ranch hands get here next week," he answered.

"How do you keep it all straight?" She smiled at him, expecting no answer.

James and John stood in front of her, watching as the train came into view. James hopped from one foot to the other, while John stood quietly and stepped closer to Tucker.

Tears formed in Daisy's eyes, and she blinked them away. She refused to cry on this happy day. She was even wearing her happy dress—the one she wore last year when she married Tucker.

The train roared into the station with great power.

"Papa Tucker?" John looked up expectantly.

"Yes, John?" Tucker was still moved by the name the twins had decided to bestow on him.

"Do I look okay?" John tugged on his hat and straightened his coat.

"You look fine, young sir," Tucker assured him.

The train stopped with a long blast of the whistle and a burst of steam as the brakes locked down. Almost before it stopped, people streamed from the line of cars. Daisy searched every face. And then she saw him. With a wave of her hand, she had his attention, and within seconds they were embracing.

"Papa!" she whispered against his wet cheek. "I've missed you so."

Daisy stepped back to look in his face and smiled at the man responsible for the happiness she enjoyed today.

If it hadn't been for Papa's letter, Daisy wouldn't have understood the wisdom of marrying Tucker that day.

Satisfied his health really had improved, she drew his attention to the bundle in her arms and pulled the blanket back. She placed the tiny babe in his arms and spoke to her daughter.

"Rose, meet your papa Warren."

James and John met Papa Warren for the first time, as he held his first granddaughter, named for his beloved wife, in his arms. True to their character, James had been excited, and John had been nervous about meeting their momma's papa. Both boys were soon reveling in the attention and joy of visiting with their grandfather. James led the way to the wagon, as the two generations shared excited stories and began to make new memories. This Christmas season would be a wondrous time for all of them.

Tucker pulled Daisy close to him and whispered against her ear, "Life really isn't fair."

"You're right." Daisy smiled her agreement. "Sometimes you get more than your share of good."

* * * * *

**WE HOPE YOU ENJOYED
THIS BOOK FROM**

LOVE INSPIRED
INSPIRATIONAL ROMANCE

Uplifting stories of faith, forgiveness and hope.

Fall in love with stories where faith helps
guide you through life's challenges, and discover
the promise of a new beginning.

6 NEW BOOKS AVAILABLE EVERY MONTH!

LIHALO2020

"Get back!"

Definitely a female voice, from the other side of the barn. He walked around the barn. If someone had asked him to guess what he might find there, he wouldn't in a hundred years have guessed correctly.

A young Amish woman—Plain dress, apron, *kapp*—was holding a feed bucket in one hand and a rake in the other, attempting to fend off a rooster. At the moment, the bird was trying to peck the woman's feet.

"What did you do to him?" Daniel asked.

Her eyes widened. The rooster made a swipe at her left foot. The woman once again thrust the feed bucket toward the rooster. "Don't just stand there. This beast won't let me pass."

Daniel knew better than to laugh. He'd been raised with four sisters and a strong-willed mother. So he snatched the rooster up from behind, pinning its wings down with his right arm.

"Where do you want him?"

"His name is Carl, and I want him in the oven if you must know the truth." She dropped the feed bucket and swiped at the golden-blond hair that was spilling out of her *kapp*. "Over there. In the pen."

Daniel dropped the rooster inside and turned to face the woman. She was probably five and a half feet tall, and looked to be around twenty years old. Blue eyes the color of forget-me-nots assessed him.

She was also beautiful in the way of Plain women, without adornment. The sight of her reminded him of yet another reason why he'd left Pennsylvania. Why couldn't his neighbors have been an old couple in their nineties?

"You must be the new neighbor. I'm Becca Schwartz—not Rebecca, just Becca, because my *mamm* decided to do things alphabetically. We thought you might introduce yourself, but I guess you've been busy. Mamm would want me to invite you to dinner, but I warn you, I have seven younger siblings, so it's usually a somewhat chaotic affair."

Becca not Rebecca stepped closer.

"Didn't catch your name."

"Daniel…Daniel Glick."

"We didn't even know the place had sold until last week. Most people are leery of farms where the fields are covered with rocks and the house is falling down. I see you haven't done anything to remedy either of those situations."

"I only moved in yesterday."

"Had time to get a horse, though. Get it from Old Tim?"

Before he could answer, a dinner bell rang. "Sounds like dinner's ready. Care to meet the folks?"

"Another time. I have some…um…unpacking to do."

Becca shrugged her shoulders. "Guess I'll be seeing you, then."

"Yeah, I guess."

He'd hoped for peace and solitude.

Instead, he had half a barn, a cantankerous rooster and a pretty neighbor who was a little nosy.

He'd come to Indiana to forget women and to lose himself in making something good from something that was broken.

He'd moved to Indiana because he wanted to be left alone.

Don't miss
The Amish Christmas Secret *by Vannetta Chapman,*
available October 2020 wherever
Love Inspired books and ebooks are sold.

LoveInspired.com

LIEXP0920

*Before he testifies in an important case, businessman
Michael "Mikey" Fiore hides out in Jacobsville, Texas,
and crosses paths with softly beautiful Bernadette, who
seems burdened with her own secrets. Their bond grows
into passion...until shocking truths surface.*

Read on for a sneak peek at
Texas Proud,
the latest book in
#1 New York Times *bestselling author Diana Palmer's
Long, Tall Texans series!*

Mikey's fingers contracted. "Suppose I told you that the
hotel I own is actually a casino," he said slowly, "and it's
in Las Vegas?"

Bernie's eyes widened. "You own a casino in Las
Vegas?" she exclaimed. "Wow!"

He laughed, surprised at her easy acceptance. "I run it
legit, too," he added. "No fixes, no hidden switches, no
cheating. Drives the feds nuts, because they can't find
anything to pin on me there."

"The feds?" she asked.

He drew in a breath. "I told you, I'm a bad man." He
felt guilty about it, dirty. His fingers caressed hers as they

neared Graylings, the huge mansion where his cousin lived with the heir to the Grayling racehorse stables.

Her fingers curled trustingly around his. "And I told you that the past doesn't matter," she said stubbornly. Her heart was running wild. "Not at all. I don't care how bad you've been."

His own heart stopped and then ran away. His teeth clenched. "I don't even think you're real, Bernie," he whispered. "I think I dreamed you."

She flushed and smiled. "Thanks."

He glanced in the rearview mirror. "What I'd give for just five minutes alone with you right now," he said tautly. "Fat chance," he added as he noticed the sedan tailing casually behind them.

She felt all aglow inside. She wanted that, too. Maybe they could find a quiet place to be alone, even for just a few minutes. She wanted to kiss him until her mouth hurt.

Don't miss
Texas Proud *by Diana Palmer,*
available October 2020 wherever
Harlequin Special Edition books and ebooks are sold.

Harlequin.com